Lethal Seasons

Alice Sabo

Trade paperback edition August 2014

Lethal Seasons

Published by Alice Sabo

ISBN: 978-1500526627

Interior design by Alice Sabo
Cover painting and design by Alex Storer
www.thelightdream.net

Lethal Seasons

For the Princesses, past and future

Acknowledgements

I want to thank everyone who has helped me with the editing, reading and general support. Matthew Fitzgerald for the statistics on the black plague and his encouragement on my initial idea. Marianne Pryor, Pat Bauman and Jim Weikart reading and feedback. Rose Sabo for editing and brainstorming (and cooking my dinner). Alex Storer for his beautiful cover painting and all his encouragement and help.

And the Princesses for my yearly reconnection and rejuvenation.

National Train Authority Ultra-Fast Lines

Chapter 1

"In what we would come to call Year Zero, a deadly virus was released in early fall by a madman. The records for that year are suspect, but the number of dead appears consistent with my own observations. Approximately 40% of the population died worldwide. We were not equipped to handle such a broad scale calamity. Nor were we prepared when it returned the following summer."

History of a Changed World, Angus T. Moss

Gale force winds rammed into Nick forcing him back into the train station. Rain slashed at him raking his skin like cold claws. Drenched in a second, half blind against the wind, he staggered into the building. The door slammed behind him, rattling under the assault of dangerous weather.

"Told ya." Frank shook his head in exaggerated dismay. "Shoulda listened." He stood far enough from the door to remain dry. The only note of untidiness about him was a stray curl of hair standing up from the wind Nick had let in. His blue National Train Authority uniform was spotless.

"Should have known you to be right," Nick agreed. He dropped his pack and bedroll to wipe his face. "Looks like I'm stuck here for the night."

Frank gave him a condescending nod. "The forecast was for category three winds 'til past midnight. What's got you in such a hurry to get back?"

Nick shrugged his uneasiness away. This trip had been different for a couple of reasons, but nothing he wanted to share with Frank. "Just want to sleep in my own bed," he said honestly.

"Can't blame you for that. Good trip?"

"Making progress."

"Good to hear." Frank's response was professionally cheerful. He didn't ask intrusive questions and was always satisfied with vague answers. "Got to check on the 8:27. I think it's coming late." He bobbed his head in a slight bow, turned on his heel and strode off to the control booth.

Nick grabbed his gear and headed for the shelter cubbies. High Meadow was one of the older style stations, built just as the world was coming to grips with climate change. It was barely far enough underground to remain in operation. Despite the thick walls and storm proofing, Nick could hear the howl of the wind and the pounding of the rain. But no thunder. He breathed a sigh of relief. Probably no tornados tonight. He considered using one of the ether booths to send a message to Angus, but was too tired to retrace his steps. Angus probably wouldn't see the message until tomorrow anyway, and Nick would be there by then.

An older woman, thin as a rail, in an NTA uniform came up toward him on the stairs to the lower level. The tailored blue jacket and slacks hung on her bones, a size too big. Another symptom of the changed world.

The downsizing of the population left a lot of resources behind, but not enough people to run the factories that would make new ones. So the people left had to make do with what was at hand. Nick didn't recognize her. He knew most of the people that manned High Meadow. She moved with a slight hitch to her walk, climbing the stairs slowly, arthritis maybe.

"Evening," he said politely.

She cast a measuring glance over him. Her eyes lingered a moment on the bedroll, then took in his two-day old scruff and wet clothes. It took a minute for her to complete her scrutiny. She startled at his green eyes, her gaze going directly to his neck to check for a tattoo.

"Evening." She climbed past him a bit quicker.

He got that reaction sometimes. People wondering if he was human. Green eyes and dark brown hair wasn't that odd of a combination. He'd stopped saying that his mother had had green eyes. Maybe if he'd had her red hair, it wouldn't look out of place. The woman's fear that he might be a biobot made him wonder if she'd seen any. It made him want to tell her that they could look normal, too. Before Zero Year, all the biobots he'd seen could have passed as human. That's why they started tattooing them in the first place. But in all his travels over the past ten years, he'd never encountered one. They might have been wiped out by the virus after all.

The shelter level was well lit. A long corridor of shiny white walls and glossy black enamel doors with black and white tiled floors stretched out before him. Each cubby was self-contained, lights, potable water, toilet, sleeping space. Although originally designed to be used in a disaster, Nick had seen several stations that had permanent residents. Knowing the rooms by the stairs were the ones used most often, he went halfway down the long corridor and chose one with a picture of an acorn on the door. Pictures now, not numbers, marked the cubbies, which probably meant the illiteracy level was rising.

The cell-sized room was immaculate and smelled of antiseptic. The NTA people were very thorough. Proud to have jobs in a world that had no industries left. He tossed his bedroll on the shiny metal shelf that passed for a bed, hoping the waterproofing held. It was a relief to be still for a minute. He'd been travelling for six days and the ultra-fast trains took a toll. He peeled off his wet clothing and dried off with the towel he carried in his pack. The clothes probably wouldn't dry tonight, but he draped them on the row of coat hooks that lined one wall anyway.

He sat on the shelf with a groan. He'd been gone longer than planned. There'd been some unexpected complications. Things that he wasn't sure he wanted to talk to Angus about. Nick had been gathering information for Angus's history book for the past three years. It gave him a purpose. A reason to go out into the world and talk to people. He was a man that needed those things—purpose, reason, order. Without them he was too easily lost in regrets and sorrow for all the people he'd lost. Whenever the ghosts and darkness came calling, he got out his pack and bedroll and went searching for new communities. The world had shattered, and Angus was trying to knit it back together with cobwebs and good intentions. It was a cause he could easily support.

He'd found a couple new communities to add to Angus's list. New lists of people and commodities. He searched abandoned towns for tools, books on self-sufficiency and any preserved foodstuffs still good after ten years on the shelf. This trip he'd found things that were all too unsettling.

Wind whined down the corridor outside the cubby and fingered the doors. Nick shivered, pulling on dry clothes quickly. He made a dinner of the packaged food stocked in every station. Boring but nutritious, the food only came in two kinds nicknamed Crunch and Stew-goo. He had one of each. Crunch was slightly sweet and would pass for dessert. He was eager to get home to the med center where he'd get a meal of real food, a hot shower and a bed with clean sheets. It made him a little uneasy sometimes that he called a re-purposed high school home. The world had changed that much.

He took out the waterproof sack to make sure his new discoveries were still in good shape. He'd found four boxes of table salt and one of sugar. Those were always welcome. A few good knives, three skeins of red wool and some odd notebooks wrapped in a frayed silk scarf. He'd glanced through the notebooks once. He wouldn't do so again. His own journal held the information Angus wanted—how many souls in a community, how many born or died each year, where were they from, how well were they surviving. Sometimes when he asked those questions people would get choked up. Stunned that anyone still wanted to know.

The first year that he started collecting he had often been the sole occupant in the train cars. Initially, it was a mystery to him as to why what was left of a struggling government would spend the time and effort to keep the train system running. But as he traveled, he figured it out. Partly, it kept the system in good repair. Partly it was needed to distribute the yearly vaccines. But the biggest reason was emotional. Despite the storms and drought and sickness, trains were arriving on time. It was one tiny foothold of normalcy in a world that didn't know itself any more.

He woke the next morning to the sound of the air scrubbers. He wandered upstairs to check the weather. Sunbeams slanted down through the skylights striping the concourse with light and dark. It was safe to go.

The location of the med center had been chosen

with the proximity of the High Meadow station in mind. It was a fairly new school complex with a recessed profile and surrounding storm baffles, finished the year before the world changed. Before the virus downsized the human population. According to the records left behind, it had been used for two years, but the curfews put an end to schools. It was abandoned and went unused for four years. In Year Five, Angus found it and claimed it. Then he began inviting like-minded people to move in.

The walk from the station had become so familiar that Nick didn't notice the abandoned homes any more. Block after block of empty houses slowly falling apart behind yards gone to seed. A few older homes had been torn apart by the weather. Pieces of them were scattered across yards and driveways. The council had talked about reclaiming some of them. The newer ones designed to withstand the superstorms would be useful for new families, but the med center hadn't reached capacity yet. People felt safer in groups. So the idea was scrapped. Nick took a new look at the houses as he walked down the fissured asphalt road. He should put together a team to search all of them for anything useful. Every year their needs changed. What they hadn't wanted before, they might need now.

Nick topped the rise of the small hill above the med center. He could see most of the campus from here. People were out working in the cool of the morning. The sky was a hard deep blue, sure to be brutally hot by the afternoon. The rising sun glinted off the lightning collection grids on the massive bulk of the storm baffles. As he started down the hill, the solar panels rose and turned their faces towards the sun. The Growers Committee bickered as they took the storm sheeting off the growing fields, which had once been the storm-proofed athletic fields. One of the main reasons Angus had chosen this place was the possibility of using those areas to grow food. Superstorms made short work of crops grown in unprotected fields. The football field was carved up into tidy vegetable plots. The soccer and track fields had been combined for a checkerboard of grains—wheat, amaranth, corn and millet. Old man Larson and his grandson herded their small flock of chickens to forage in the new orchard area. Nick felt proud of what they'd accomplished in the five years they'd been here.

He waved to the pair of men on Watch at the edge of the campus. They'd had little trouble since settling here. Nick worried that they'd grown complacent. He wanted to talk to Martin, the head of the Watch, to make sure they had some contingency plans in place. This trip had made him edgy. The med center looked ill prepared for any kind of confrontation.

The minute he entered the glass doors to the big foyer, he could smell breakfast cooking. His stomach growled as he made a beeline for the cafeteria. The enormous space, designed to serve a minimum of five hundred students, had been chopped up into smaller rooms with dividers pilfered from one of the auditoriums. There was a general eating area by the kitchen, a small area for meetings and a lounge that had recently received the upgrade of a firepit. In the climate-controlled buildings, they didn't need fire for warmth, but Angus had been wanting one for some time. There was something soothing about watching a fire, a primal penchant in the human spirit that made people want to gather around.

Nick waved to the few folks lingering over their meals. He was almost too late, breakfast had been served and eaten. He hurried over to check the steam tables. To accommodate their hundred or so residents, they had significantly downsized the original cafeteria line. The extra refrigeration cases, counters and steam tables were carefully packed away in storage to use as replacements. Angus didn't waste anything. Nick was glad to see that there was plenty of food left. He grabbed a tray and started loading it up.

* * *

Tilly considered herself Lady of the Manor and accepted all the responsibilities implied in that office. She and her husband, Angus, had taken on the duty of running a med center with eyes wide open. The registration people had frowned over their ages. It was true she and Angus were way past retirement age, but did that even apply anymore? They had the inclination and skills to make it work. From the beginning, she had tried to take on as much of the daily operations as possible so Angus could be free to do what he did best. She got people placed, fed and clothed. He kept the facilities working, the clinic up to date and posted storm warnings. If he was the beating heart of this center, she was the busy hands.

Tilly looked over the food inventory with a sinking feeling. She and the head cook, Susan, were working out how best to use today's odd combination of produce with the dwindling supplies of oil, salt and vinegar. They had green peppers and tomatoes by the bushel full, very little left of the new potatoes and no onions. Last night's storm must have spooked the hens because there were only a few eggs this morning. Susan used up most of the previous day's eggs with the breakfast omelet before they'd heard. They needed to have another planning session with the Growers Committee. She looked around the industrial kitchen, appliances for every conceivable chore and so little raw materials to work with.

A deep voice called her attention out to the eating area. Nick was back. Finally. Another day and she'd have been concerned. Tilly liked Nick, and not just because of the way he treated Angus. He was polite and smart. Two things that she felt spoke to a man's character. He kept his dark hair short and his face clean-shaven. Another statement. Just because the world had turned upside down didn't mean people had to start looking like barbarians. There was still hot water and soap available. Although sometimes you had to forage for the soap. Nick had a competent look to him. You just knew he could turn those long-fingered hands to anything from a chainsaw to a needle and thread. It didn't hurt that he had rugged good looks and the nicest green eyes she'd ever seen. But not nicer than Angus's sparkling blue eyes, which could still put a silly grin on her face.

"I think Nick's back," Tilly said. Susan was on her feet and moving toward the pass-through to check. Tilly saw Susan's face light up when she caught sight of him.

"He'll need to speak with Angus first thing," Tilly said.

"Of course." Susan smoothed her apron as she watched Nick load up a plate with eggs from the steam table. "Got a treat," she called to him. Her eyes crinkled in a smile. She tucked a stray curl back into the braid of light brown hair that ran down her back to her waist.

"I can smell it," he answered with a grin. "Been too long. Nothing like a good cup of joe!"

Susan leaned on the counter, head sticking out of the pass-through. "Any new contacts?"

"A few. But they've just gotten started. Won't have anything for trade for a while."

"Oh, well. Eat up while it's still hot."

Tilly watched the interchange approvingly. Susan and Nick would be an excellent couple. She'd been encouraging it for some time. Nick needed an anchor. Susan needed to produce a few children sooner, rather than later. Every woman needed to. If Tilly wasn't past her bearing years, she'd be considering it herself. It didn't matter how many they lost. She let her mind skip over that thought. No one here was unscarred. Every single person living had lost family and friends to the virus. And they lost more every year. So it was down to simple math. They needed to keep adding to the population.

Susan returned to the table where they did their planning. "Do we have any cucumbers? I could do gazpacho again."

Tilly groaned. "I think we've all had enough gazpacho." Between the uneven supply of crops and unskilled labor, it was difficult to produce good meals consistently. But five years into their residence, they were nearly self-sufficient. They only had to rely on train food occasionally. Like maybe tonight.

* * *

Nick loaded a little of everything on to his tray—omelet, salsa, roasted potatoes and a gloppy mix of amaranth and cornmeal. No bread today. He was disappointed. The spring wheat was supposed to be harvested while he was gone. He checked the tables. Angus waved to him from a seat by the window. The storm shutters were fully retracted allowing sunlight to shine off every surface including Angus's unruly white hair. It gave him a bright halo. As usual, Angus's table was covered with notebooks and pads, his knobby, veined hands working over paper and keyboards.

Nick nudged a pile aside and put his tray down. Angus brought his attention up from his studies and focused his bright blue eyes on Nick.

"I'm glad you didn't try to brave the storm," Angus said. He reached over and patted Nick's hand. "Good to have you back."

"It was too much even for me."

"Even for you," Angus chuckled. "You are late. I hoped that wasn't an indication of trouble."

Nick pulled a thick stack of folders out of his pack to hand over to Angus. "I think you'll be very pleased." He dug into his breakfast.

Angus laid the stack on the table and gave it a pat. "Anything out of the ordinary?"

Nick nodded with a mouth full. "Couple of dead ends..." He took a sip of coffee. "And a murder."

"Murder. Well, that sort of thing was quite common pre-virus. Though it pains me to find that as a species we are too stupid not to stop killing each other when we are facing extinction. Although from what you tell me, the virus has left us plenty of fools. What about this caught your attention?"

"It was an odd situation. Young girl. On her own, I think."

"A young girl murdered? Are you sure? Was it a rumor?"

"I saw the body. She was shot."

"Oh dear. I'm sorry you saw that, Nicky. How sad. And you're sure it was murder?"

Nick halted a laden fork to speak. "From the look of the scene, she shot back."

"I think that is the lawman in you speaking." Angus sat back folding his hands over one another on his stomach in his customary thinking position. "You believe there is more to it."

Nick gave him a dip of the head in agreement.

"Where did this happen?"

"Clarkeston."

"You've been there before without trouble. What's it like?"

"Not much different than here." He said with a gesture toward the windows. "Built around a med center. They specialize in wool, so everybody's got sheep. Might want to remember them when we're getting ready to barter some of the grain."

"When did this murder occur?"

"From the looks of it, a few days ago. Shot through the heart."

"Good heavens, what fool did this? Don't they know we can't afford that now? There are cities that have been completely depopulated. We cannot allow ourselves the luxury of crime! We need every human being left on this planet!"

Nick sipped the last drops of his coffee. "I know that," he said in what he hoped was a calming voice. He didn't think Angus needed to know about the other body, yet. Until he had all the facts, Nick didn't want to worry him.

"Kill a young girl." Angus threw up a hand in disgust. "She was of childbearing age?"

"She seemed young, but the body was a few days old." He finished the last bites quickly.

Angus slumped with a sigh. "How can people be so short sighted? What could a young woman have done to deserve being shot?"

Nick pushed his tray to one side. "The virus didn't change the fact that some people are flat out crazy," he said gently. He and Angus were old enough to remember the time before, when cities had police forces fighting violence of all kinds. When gangs killed indiscriminately and there were recreational poisons that people chose to put in their bodies. "I checked around. No one saw the murder. No one missed the girl."

"We would have missed her," Angus snapped back indignantly.

Nick nodded. Angus's settlement was a utopia compared to some of the places he'd seen. They had a Council and a Watch. People took care of one another. It was all because of the tone Angus set, thoughtful, gentle, caring man that he was. Nick had seen settlements that were little more than refugee camps, a few that were run with cold, military precision and others that were run by self-appointed tyrants. It was a new system, and the bugs hadn't been worked out, yet. A touch of anarchy that worried Nick. Why wasn't there anyone supervising the creation of settlements and med centers?

"She wouldn't have been shot here," Nick assured him. "Clarkeston is big. Spread out. They don't have a watch, and their council is shoddy. She lived at the edge of the population zone. It was down the street from an address I tracked down. The front door was off its hinges on an otherwise nice house. I went in to check and saw the body. When I went to report it to Clarkeston's council, they said they already knew. A family tried to move into the house and only went close enough to smell it. They reported the death, but that settlement doesn't have anyone to look into stuff like that."

"Why would a young girl be alone?" Angus was persistent in his questioning.

"Why are any of us alone, Angus?" Nick couldn't keep the sadness out of his voice. All the deaths behind him, all the lost loved ones he carried in his heart weighed heavily on him at times like this.

"We're not, Nicky." Angus grabbed his arm and squeezed gently. "We have each other. We have all these others," he said gesturing outward. "Good people that care about us."

"Yes. Sorry. Seeing some of these other places gets me down."

"It's hard." Angus patted him. "Hard to see how stupid and petty we still are when our very existence depends on cooperation."

Nick pulled a small bundle out of his pack. "I think this is hers. I found it in a bedroom." He unwrapped a silk scarf to show several small notebooks.

"Where is the poor girl now?"

"I buried her."

"Thank you, Nicky. Always a gentleman. Poor child." Angus took the top notebook and flipped through it. "Do we even know her name?"

"I haven't had time to look through them." He didn't say that just holding those books had brought on such deep depression that he'd wasted the afternoon staring into space and mourning the loss of a sweet young girl who liked to scribble in notebooks. Nor the cold fear he'd felt when he'd looked through the one that was dog-eared and grubby. Nick left Angus paging through the notebooks and took his tray to the kitchen.

"How is it out there?" Martin Asbury leaned against the wall by the dish station. Dark haired and dark eyed, he radiated strength. The head of the Watch asked the same question every time Nick returned. In a time when last names were cast off or reinvented, Martin had taken on the fashion of using a dead city as his last name. Asbury Park, like much of the coast was under water and had been for decades. It was a way to remember what nature had taken away. Nick doubted there were many people still alive that remembered the Jersey shore, white sand beaches and lazy days sunbathing. His mother had told him about it. Lying in the sun sounded like a quick death of hyperthermia and sun poisoning to him.

Nick debated what to tell Martin. At any rate, what he needed to say shouldn't be discussed here. "It's quiet. People are waiting for the sick season to start."

"It hasn't?"

"Not where I was. Have we had any reports on what to expect this year?"

Martin shook his head. "I hate it when they wait like this. It makes me worry that the information is so dire, they don't want anyone to know."

"They weren't this late on the Hoofed Flu. That was

a bad one for the food supply. Maybe it's good news, and they want to make sure before they say anything."

Martin gave him a shrug and a snort. "I don't hope for good news anymore."

Nick sorted his silverware and rinsed off his plate, stacking them in the racks for the dishwasher. "I need a word."

"My office?" Martin asked as he turned to go.

"Right behind you." Nick didn't especially like Martin, but he had to admit the man was more than competent. He projected an easy-going, relaxed manner that kept people calm, when underneath he had a sharper edge.

Chapter 2

"The subsequent year's virus was dubbed the flu by the government in an attempt, I assume, to have the populous believe it was more benign, more manageable. This was a mistake that would backfire egregiously. When the death rate stayed high, people lost faith. We knew it wasn't simply a flu."

History of a Changed World, Angus T. Moss

Nick grabbed his gear and followed Martin down to the Watch's office. He would give Martin a more in depth report and update the map they kept. As he entered the office, Martin dropped the map file into the smartwall at the back of the room.

"Bad news?" Martin asked in a quiet voice.

"Maybe just weird." Nick put his pack on the big worktable in the middle of the room. Martin might call it an office, but it felt more like a ready room. He pulled his paper map out of its waterproof case. It was creased and smudged and covered with notes in his tiny, tight writing. They kept track of trouble spots and new settlements which they might like to trade with.

"Weird how?" Martin asked, all his attention on Nick now.

"Saw a crime scene with way too many bullets, a dead girl and a dead guy in body armor."

Martin's brown eyes went a shade colder. "Could you tell what kind of armor? I've seen a lot of that stuff bartered. Stolen from police mostly."

"It was brand new. Gun, too. I thought about bringing it back, but it was big. Bringing it on the train would have been . . ."

"Obvious?"

"Yeah. And I'm betting we couldn't get ammunition for it." Nick pulled a sketch of the gun out of his journal and put it on the table. "You seen anything like this?"

Martin frowned at the paper. "Not exactly. And not since I left . . . the service."

Nick noted the hesitation. Martin didn't discuss his past. He never said what branch of the service he'd been in. Nick always let it slide, but today he was a little more curious. That gun was something special, not the usual army supply. Which might put Martin in some sort of special ops. Nick filed away that information. Might be something he could use later.

He tucked the drawing back into his journal. Ever since his last camera had broken, losing over two hundred images of files he'd unearthed for Angus, he'd stuck to pencil and paper. "Not a good situation. New gear like that on a guy that gunned down a young girl."

"Any idea why?"

Nick shivered. "Not sure." He busied himself with putting the journal back in his pack. He could feel Martin watching him. "Might be jumping at shadows. It's in Angus's hands right now."

"You told Angus about the merc?"

Nick wasn't surprised that Martin had judged the killer to be a mercenary. He'd already made that assumption himself. "No."

"Good."

Released from Martin's scrutiny, Nick walked over to the smartwall. Over the next half hour, they discussed the changes he had documented. There was a new dark station. It had been taken over by a gang of toughs and the train didn't stop there anymore. That gave him a faint hope that someone, somewhere might still be in charge. They saw these things and reacted. It wasn't in his experience to think that the country didn't have a guiding hand. Food and medicine were still distributed like clockwork. The trains ran on time. That had to mean something.

"The people in Clarkeston are keeping sheep now," Nick said adding the notation to the map. "It's a pretty orderly settlement. They hope to have meat to barter next spring. North of High Bluffs, about a half-day's walk, there's a settlement in a factory, but no med center. I think they decided on Riverbank as a name. They just got started, but said they'll probably have dried fish to barter by the winter. And they haven't had anyone down with a flu in three years."

"Because they're isolated." Martin said dismissively. "Once they start trading, they'll be seeing the flus again."

"They're new. Broke away from a walled compound. Want to make their own rules. Didn't know about the barter network 'til I showed up. They didn't know the ether was back up. Hadn't even tried."

"How many places like that are out there?" Martin asked. His eyes looked sad to Nick. "Folks that hid from the virus and haven't looked back?"

"Without train food?" The corner of Nick's mouth crooked up as he thought about the odds of the average settlement surviving without outside support. "If you had some unlooted grocery stores and a couple of neighborhoods to rifle through for hard goods, you could stay vanished for a couple years. Problem is, people like that don't think to work on self-sufficiency."

"Hunters and gatherers."

"That only works if you've got the skills. Look at our people. We've got over a hundred here—"

"One hundred twenty four," Martin interjected.

"How many of those people could live off the land?" Nick felt a sudden anger for the thoughtlessness of his species. "Without destroying it."

Martin rubbed his mouth. He looked sorry that he'd brought up the subject. "You, me..." He shrugged in agreement. "That's probably it."

"Two hunters for a community isn't enough. Ask Angus. He'll give you a lecture on the support structure of a real hunter-gatherer tribe. We don't have the skills. Worse, we don't know what half of them were. Do you know how to make rope or tan leather?"

Martin looked at him for a long minute. "Rough trip?"

Nick sagged back in the chair. "Yeah." He smoothed the wrinkles in his map. "Sorry." He turned his attention back to updating their database. "There's a new settlement at an old resort site on the southern lateral. They got the light rail cars back on line from the resort to the train station."

"That's impressive. I wonder if they've got some engineers. What are they trading?"

"Nothing yet. They've got some fields planted, chickens and I think they had goats. Didn't want me poking around too much."

"Paranoid or cautious?"

"Unfortunately, I was getting the paranoid vibe. They had an awful lot of armed guards. And when I asked about barter, they weren't interested at all. Said they needed everything for their own settlement, but I didn't see more than thirty, forty people in all." Nick didn't like the feeling he'd gotten from that place. "I don't think I'll go back there for a while." He'd had a close call or two over the years. People didn't always welcome a stranger asking questions. He didn't blame them for caution. A settlement had every right to its privacy. It was the strict religious societies, cults and militia compounds that he was wary of. Now he thoroughly scouted a new community before approaching it. Any hint of rigid regimen or an excess of firearms, and he gave it a wide berth.

Martin updated the map and posted a edited version to the ether. They only shared problems and closed settlements. The High Meadow Council had agreed that if a settlement wanted to be advertised on the ether, they should do so themselves. Most didn't. High Meadow itself was simply listed as a med center. Despite Angus's altruistic view of human nature, there were still plenty of thugs and bullies in the world.

Nick went to his room to drop his things and take that long-awaited hot shower. He wanted to give Angus plenty of time to look through the notebooks. If that's what had gotten the girl killed, they had to be very important. And yet, the rest of the house hadn't shown signs of a search. They'd been tucked under a bedroll. Not the most secure hiding place. The girl had been living there with other people. Nick had seen three bedrolls. Things had been tidy, other than the dead bodies: one young girl and one heavily armed and armored man. He couldn't shake the feeling that there was a whole lot more to this than he was seeing. If they hadn't wanted the notebooks, why had they killed the girl?

Showered, shaved and in clean clothes, Nick went to Angus's office to see if he had any questions. The wide, clean hallways were cool despite the sunshine flooding in through the skylights. With most of the building underground, the few places that let in natural sunlight were vital to maintain. Angus insisted the storm shutters be retracted as often as safety allowed. Nick had seen settlements where everything was bartered: food, water, sunlight. Something inside him clenched tight while he was out in the world, and it didn't release until he got back to High Meadow and saw that Angus's dream continued.

Chairs, benches and overstuffed oddities lined the sun drenched halls, clustered into intimate groupings. Most were empty this early in the day, as it was the best time for work outside before the blast furnace heat of the day arrived. A few elders sat together doing whatever their skills and health allowed. As Nick passed them, he realized they were making a baby quilt.

A chill hit him at the same time his throat tightened. There were three pregnant women in the settlement. He couldn't imagine how they could face bringing a baby into a world as screwed as this one. But every child was needed. Every normal-looking child, every mutated one, gave them clues to their future. And three out of five wouldn't live past their first flu season. Angus tracked them all—the blonde, blue-eyed and the mottled-hair, orange-eyed. Nick forced a smile for the three old women bent over their sewing. Their smiles in response looked equally sad. No matter the pain, they must all put on a brave face for the young.

Nick burst into Angus's office with a little more force than he'd meant, but Angus was absorbed in his research and gave no notice. The office had been a small classroom. The walls were covered with the med center's family trees. Angus kept track of all the births and deaths, changes and surprises, illnesses and vaccinations. But he hadn't discovered any pattern to who survived. And going backward into peoples' family ties hadn't provided any useful information. Too many of the branches dead ended. Nick's ended with him. He was the only one in all the siblings, parents, aunts, uncles and cousins that had survived through all the mutations of the virus. Most of his family had died the first year the virus was released. Dead and buried before people found out it wasn't supposed to kill normal humans, just the biobots.

Again he had that strange longing that tightened his guts and raised hair on his arms. Wasn't someone, some large government department, doing this? Tracking the immune and searching for a cure? But Angus hadn't found any type of information available on that sort of thing. He'd searched the ether, sending out inquiries to a slew of dead ends. Not everything was on the ether. Nick asked wherever he went if anyone had heard of research labs or government installations. There might be secret labs out there. But Nick worried about why they needed to be secret.

"Nicky," Angus beckoned him over. He had the small notebooks spread out across his desk. "I'm sure some of these aren't the girl's. Different handwriting and some rather sophisticated formulas here." He tapped a blue notebook that sat away from the others. "This one though, was probably hers. I believe she had siblings." He squinted at a page before flipping back through it. "William and Lily."

"There were three bedrolls at the house. I asked around, but no one knew she was there, so they wouldn't have noticed if there were other kids around."

"We need to find them."

Nick nodded. He wanted this. He needed to unravel this mystery. Although he had hoped for a few more nights in his own bed and a few more of Susan's excellent meals before hitting the road again. Tracking down the children would be difficult. There wouldn't be any records of who they were or where they came from. He'd have to go back and canvass the area looking for anyone who might have encountered them. Unfortunately word-of-mouth was the only information available.

There were no national databases to consult, no official registration of births and deaths. Old records were useless. The population had scattered as it was being decimated. When the dead began to outnumber the living, people fled. There was an animal instinct in human beings to flee when an unseen killer was stalking the neighborhood. Although the drive might be universal, the response was anything but. Frightened people had headed for the mountains or the desert or the coast, or a relation with medical knowledge, or a commune promising safety, depending on their own logic. There was no mechanism by which to determine when they had reached their destination. Or if. No government agency to track the movement of the survivors. That lack had at first been simply an oddity to Nick. Now that he'd seen a good portion of the country with its deserted cities and abandoned towns, that lack frightened him.

He reasoned that there were too few hands to keep the country's skeleton of infrastructure going to spend any precious time on simple data input. Or perhaps that information wasn't available to the average citizen. The vaccine centers knew how many doses were required for each med center, so they must have an idea of what the population numbers were. But it seemed as though not enough questions were asked. When Angus ordered vaccines, he wasn't required to list names or ages of people living in the settlement. The why of that worried Nick the most.

"Nicky?" Angus called him out of his musings.

"Huh?" He shook aside his concerns and focused on Angus.

"Weighty thoughts," Angus commented with a knowing smile. "You have an inkling of what these notebooks might be."

"I read a few of the entries in the older one. Could be the ramblings of an idiot." He folded his arms tight against his body, unwilling to speak his fears aloud.

"But you felt they were important enough to bring to me."

"Something got that girl killed."

"These notations are beyond me. I can't tell if they are true or as you said mere ramblings. But these are all related. The girl," Angus gestured to the newest journal, "says that these are her father's."

A chill shivered down Nick's back. "Is it him?"

Angus's eyes were dark with sorrow. "If these calculations pertain to the original virus, and if they are over a decade old and if the author of this journal turns out to be an insane racist . . . then yes. We could be looking at the source of the illness that killed millions."

For a raw moment those words hung in the air between them. Angus stacked the books up and pushed them to one side. He rubbed his face then ran hands through his hair making it stand up in unruly tufts. "But...there are many ifs in that sentence."

"Yes." Nick chewed on his lip, knowing in his gut that this would bring trouble.

"Will you try to find William and Lily? The fact that their sister was murdered worries me."

Nick swallowed his first response. He didn't need to add to Angus's burdens. "I'll leave tomorrow."

Chapter 3

"The origin of the virus is unknown. Many rumors circulated as to who or what might have released such a deadly agent into our world. Foreign governments and terrorists were at the top of the list. As the virus circled the globe, killing indiscriminately, for a while we stopped caring where it came from."

History of a Changed World, Angus T. Moss

Wisp could sense the person waiting for him. It was a girl, and she was frightened. Her fear tasted sharp and too long held. She was worn down with the burden of it. He paused in the darkened corridor of his home and pushed his senses out into the surrounding woods. There was no one else in the vicinity of the old factory where he had lived for the past three years. The aging site had been a derelict long before the virus hunted his kind. Thick brick walls and steel beams still stood against the ravages of the weather. But it was the cellars and sub-cellars that he called home.

He continued upstairs to ground level. Twilight softened the harsh angles of debris in the yard. Old pallets and piles of stone, a tumble of bricks where a retaining wall had given way, cans and broken glass and the skeletons of weeds made a labyrinth of unsteady steps to his door. The girl waited where she was told, in the potholed remains of a parking lot. Hulking stacks of crumbling sidewalks took up much of the cracked asphalt. It held a certain symbolism for him. Someone had ripped up the sidewalks and piled them here, perhaps to be recycled. But to him it said that pedestrian traffic was no longer possible in this area. He held it as a totem, hoping it would ensure his solitude.

She was small. Not more than ten or twelve years old. A mental shiver wracked her as she stood alone in the fading light waiting for a meeting with a monster. Wisp regretted the charade, but fear was often his only weapon.

"I am here," he said stepping into her line of sight.

She jumped. A gasp, cut off, shuddered into a whimper. "Are you the finder?"

"I am."

"Can you find my brother?"

"What do you offer?"

Her fear was suddenly drowned with loss, with desperation and hopelessness. He could taste the ashes of her grief, the spiky pain of regret. "I have nothing."

She was a refugee, a fugitive. Her pain was something he understood. This close he could smell her unwashed body. A child, hungry and alone and knowing there was no solace. She trembled with exhaustion. He knew he couldn't refuse her.

"I will help."

She cried then, the relief so great. It pushed back on her burden of grief, and eased his own pain. She swallowed the tears away, stronger than her years.

"What should I do?"

Wisp looked up at the clouds scudding in from the west. A storm was approaching. He smelled rain on the rising wind. The child needed food and rest. They couldn't start out until the morning. "Come." He reached out a hand to her. "We will prepare."

Her steps were heavy, the fear rising up. In the half-light, he wondered how much she could see. What startled her the most? His thick white hair falling loose below his shoulders, eyes so pale a blue they were almost white, or was it the tattoo down his neck that marked him as not human? As she touched his hand, he had his answer: just a man. She registered his calloused hands and muscled arms. He was a big, strong stranger, and she feared all the things that could come from that.

"I won't hurt you, child."

"Lily. I'm Lily," she spoke in a bruised whisper heavy with tears.

"They call me Wisp."

She looked up at him in the growing shadows. "Is that your name?"

He bit off his response. *My kind have no names*. She was too young to know that story. "It will do," he said gently. "Come. I have food and water."

He felt her wariness lose ground beneath her hunger. She was too young to be out in the world alone. Too sweet, too innocent. He'd find her brother and send them somewhere safe. Then perhaps it was time for him to move on.

Chapter 4

"Children born in Year One showed signs of DNA manipulation. The virus had changed them. Eye color was the first change documented. The most common was an orange-brown, close enough to normal that most people didn't notice it."

History of a Changed World, Angus T. Moss

"Tell me about your brother," Wisp said as he led her into the old brick building.

"William," she said.

He saw the boy in her memory, brawny and angry, dark hair and eyes. There was another girl, almost woman. And hunters. Through her eyes he saw gigantic men in black with screaming weapons that sprayed bullets. William took her hand, and they ran. Through streets and alleys and backyards. They ran until they had to stop. William did not let go of her hand. He hid her and promised to return.

"The rule is," she said, watching as Wisp lit a small

candle lantern, "wait a day, then walk north for a day."

"Whose rule?" Wisp led them down a level in the musty darkness. Lily's anxiety level rose as they descended.

"Iris. She said if we get separated. Wait a day, go north a day. That way we always know which direction to look." He saw the young woman again in her mind, but wavering. A curtain went down. Lily would not ask about Iris. There was a question she didn't want the answer to. Pain forced the curtain in place, solid and aching.

"Logical. And did you wait a day?"

"Of course. I waited all night and 'til the sun came up. William didn't come back. So I walked north all day." Her confidence crumbled into sniffles. "It's been three days."

They arrived at his den. The bright light scattered her uneasiness. He'd rigged the solar generator for only this room. No one would see the lights from two floors below the surface.

"You have train food." Lily skipped over to stand before his larder. The white packets of Crunch and soft pouches of Stew-goo were stacked on some shelving he'd appropriated. He could feel her ache to snatch, but she looked back to him for permission. Good. She'd learned some lessons in the world. Food was money, power, survival.

"I have fresh food, too." He opened the cold locker and showed her the forest's bounty: strawberries, asparagus and cress. The look on her face said she had no experience of food that wasn't packaged. She had been too young when the world changed. She knew nothing else. Looking at her, Wisp realized that she was part of the change, too. Her eyes were the color of ripe cherries.

He let her eat what was familiar. A small comfort in a trying time. Her eyes wandered the room, took in his books and blankets and stockpile of food. "This is a safe place," she announced.

"For the moment." Even two levels down, he heard the storm when it arrived. A crack of thunder penetrated the brick and steel.

Lily looked up. "Still safe?"

"It's not the weather that would make this place unsafe."

The shadows in her eyes said she understood. Wisp felt sadness for her. It was a lesson he'd learned in his first year of existence. But human children shouldn't have to know that danger so soon.

"How will we find William?"

"Do you have anything of his?"

She pulled a compass out of her pocket. Held it up to show him. He put out his hand. Lily froze. He saw the suspicion in her eyes. She wanted to trust, but doubted strongly. He felt her need, and the ache for resolution but the compass was precious. Too dear to share, unbearable to lose. And he was an adult, unreliable and dangerous in her estimation.

Wisp spoke softly to soothe her. "I can sense him through things he has carried. Did he carry this all the time?"

She nodded, eyes wide and glistening with tears. She believed him without question. A child of the new world where the unlikely could be normal.

"I won't keep it. I just need to hold it for a minute."

Her eyes lingered on the scars on his hands that criss-crossed his palms and ran up his arms. Did she understand the source of them, or just see a difficult path walked? Her fingers brushed his palm as she carefully placed the compass in his hand. She saw his trials with a child's mind: rough and tumble sparring or investigating in abandoned places—skinned knees, splinters and bruised shins. She knew nothing of torture, and he was glad for her.

He let the cold metal of the compass warm in his hand. He got a stronger sense of William. A half-grown man with responsibilities beyond his years. An anchor for a small girl, an ally for the older one. He was a tumble of anger, resentment and devotion to his sisters. William had carried the compass every day because it was a gift from his father. The only thing left to secure a fragile memory of brown hair and a hearty laugh. Wisp followed the thread out into the world searching until he felt the tug to the boy's spirit. "William is alive."

Lily laughed. She clapped her hands together and squeezed them tight. "I knew it." But Wisp knew she lied as that dreadful knot inside her frayed away.

"He's not far. We might be able to reach him tomorrow."

"Good." Her response was simple, practical and made Wisp smile.

He gave her the compass back. She pushed it deep into her pocket, clutching it tight. He piled some blankets into a nest for her and dimmed the lights. She sank into slumber immediately. He started packing. This was not a simple finding. There was a great deal more going on here than the child understood. Her innocence might be tarnished with doubt and distrust, but William's was gone now. Wisp had established a link to William. Her brother was learning about pain.

Chapter 5

"Violence was widespread. Looting in the cities became so bad that the army was deployed. Some government officials tried to block the use of the army based on existing laws, but there was too great a need. Police, fire and emergency services were overwhelmed. The dead lay in the streets outside hospitals and clinics. At the very least, the army was needed to dig mass graves."

History of a Changed World, Angus T. Moss

Nick visited the armory before he went back out on the road. It was a locked display case for the school's trophies that Martin had moved into his ready room. They had collected some shotguns and hand weapons over the years. Nick knew that a few of the residents had kept their guns rather than share them with the community. Once new people settled in, sometimes they changed their minds. Every now and then the inventory would turn up something extra. Martin would make a new page in the notebook, no questions asked.

He stared at the weapons, trying to make his decisions before Martin showed up with the keys. Long guns were out of the question, too obvious. He'd like the power of one of the automatics, but not the bulk. This was the first trip in a while where he felt he needed more than stealth and wit to stay safe. It would be foolish to track armed men without a weapon of his own, but he would be outgunned regardless of his choice. High Meadow didn't have that kind of firepower.

"Window shopping?" Martin asked.

Nick chuckled. They were both old enough to remember what that meant. To remember money and spending it on things you didn't need. "Yes. I'd like to see something small and powerful, please."

Martin grinned at him. "Yes, sir. I'll see what I can find in your size." He unlocked the cabinet and took out the inventory notebook. A long, heavy minute passed as Martin stared at the first page, unseeing. "Think we'll ever get back to that?" he asked. His voice was low and thick with emotion.

"We can hope," Nick said. But he knew his words were hollow. Whatever the future held, it wouldn't look like the past they pined for. And as he thought about it, the past probably wasn't the way they remembered it either.

Martin gave him a compact pistol that would fit in his pocket, a pair of spare clips and a long, notched knife. With these weapons, he was as heavily armed as he'd ever been on his travels, but he still felt vulnerable.

"You good with hand-to-hand?"

Nick nodded. "I think I remember a thing or two."

"You should come to our sparring practices."

"I suppose," he admitted. He tucked the weapons away, patting them down to get used to their placement. He and Martin tended to rub rough edges against each other. Aside from reporting to him about his travels, he tried to steer clear of the man. Nick thought maybe they were just too much alike. He might not like the man, but he did respect him.

"You were a cop right?" Martin asked.

Nick hefted his pack. "FBI." He gave Martin a sloppy salute, which put a smile back on the man's face.

"Be careful," Martin said, returning the salute.

"Always am." Nick walked away with that feeling again. Like Martin had told him to tie his shoes and button his shirt. It wasn't said to annoy him, but it always did.

* * *

Nick spent the hour's walk to the train station formulating a plan. He would go back to Clarkeston with questions about anything but the murder. If the armed men were hunting the missing siblings, asking would only draw attention. He would chat with anyone willing to listen, somewhere along the way he'd find the lead he needed. Angus told him that the children were younger than the dead girl, he estimated that Lily should be about twelve and William about fourteen. That was old enough to know how to run and hide. Which left Nick wondering how he was going to find two kids that did not want to be found.

He picked up a few packets of food at the stock-up on the train platform. Even though he carried enough food from the med center for a few days on the road, he liked to be prepared. He noticed that the shelves had been refilled. That always gave him a good feeling. As long as things kept arriving in an orderly fashion, he could pretend that the government was operating normally.

He always checked through the stock-up room. Sometimes there were things other than food available.

Once he'd found stacks of clothing, simple pants and t-shirts. Another time it was first aid kits. Today there were just the usual packets of Crunch and Stew-goo. They were always available, so that no one could use them as currency, although in the early days several people had tried. There was a fine layer of dust on a stack of food packets. He ran his finger through it and a fine red powder stained his skin. He'd seen dust like that before. It took a minute for him to remember where. Missawaug. It sat at the edge of the new badlands, miles of drought-starved red earth. The raging winds that scoured that land dry coated everything in red dust.

Nick went out to the lobby to check the system map. Taking up an entire wall, a large board showed the railway superimposed over a map of the United States. Over the years the train lines had shrunken away from areas that were no longer livable. Open stations were indicated with a green light. The ones along the coast were all dark, endangered by rising sea levels. Some places had been claimed by storms years ago. A couple of lines that ran through the plains were dark also. Decades of drought, windstorms and wildfires made that part of the country too dangerous to live in. When Nick traced out the northern branch he saw that Missawaug was dark. It could mean bandits or a closed settlement. Disease and weather were the main reasons that settlements were closed. He hadn't heard anything, and made a note to check when he got home.

Seeing the food from Missawaug had him wondering where it was produced. There was a factory somewhere churning out these meals. And farmers delivering produce to them. And truckers packing it all up to cart away. But it wasn't anywhere nearby. And no one he'd spoken to knew where those factories might be. Or didn't care to share that information. Another secret that the government was keeping.

A bright metal box, sticking out from the wall caught his attention, shaking him out of his morbid musings. It was new. He went over to inspect it. Blue letters stenciled across the shiny surface read *US Mail.* His throat tightened when he read the words. Hanging below it was a water-proof sack marked *High Meadow Med Center*. He looked inside. There was a letter for Angus and the first piece of junk mail he'd seen in a decade. It was a hand-lettered sheet for cheese orders coming from a settlement on the southern branch track. He laughed out loud. "We're making progress," he said to the empty station.

He left the bag hanging there, planning to pick it up on his return. It buoyed his spirits to see things like that. Another sliver of normalcy. Not just mail, but the possibility of cheese. The Hoofed Flu in Year Four decimated the cattle industry. Anybody with milk kept it for themselves. It became a precious commodity. Goat, sheep and other sources for milks were just as badly hit. Cheese went scarce; a common household staple gone from the marketplace. He wrote the location in his journal. If he came home empty-handed, he might run by that settlement. Sometimes people would barter for labor. It'd be worth a day of mucking out stalls to bring a wheel of cheese home to High Meadow.

Nick went down to the platform. Frank waved from the observation window of the control tower high over the tracks. Nick acknowledged him with a nod. Not every station was manned. From what Frank had told him, Nick knew the trains could run pretty much on their own. A human being was mostly a safety officer. And the eyes and ears of the train company.

The train shushed into the station, right on time. Sleek and silver. The doors opened to empty cars. Nick entered and took a seat. A clock over the door counted down minutes to departure. He took out the breakfast

Susan had packed for him. The first of the spring wheat was finally in, and she'd made bread. She'd met him at the kitchen door with food that she'd packed up early this morning, giving him a sweet smile that had him wishing he wasn't back on the road so soon. He bit into a thick egg sandwich, relishing the taste of the bread. They were still sorting out the garden to table ratio. The first year the crop of wheat barely lasted a few days, but the amaranth had lasted for months. Not the best flour for bread, but it could also be eaten as hot cereal. The chime sounded a warning and the doors slid closed. He wondered if they could trade some amaranth to the cheese folks. That would have made this sandwich just about perfect.

The train came up to speed and the windows darkened. Looking out at cruising speed would cause vertigo. It was only minutes before they decelerated for the first stop. Nick hoped to be at Clarkeston by lunch.

He went over his plan. Now that he knew about the mail and the flyer for cheese, he could use that. Ask people about it. Distract them from his actual goal. Ask if anyone had traded with them. People were always happy to give their opinions. He took out his journal and made a few notes about things to discuss with Angus and Susan. The train slowed, rising toward the Clarkeston station. There was a river to cross, one of the few bridges on this old line. The train would go above ground here and proceed at speeds under 100mph. Nick liked the view out over the water.

The train burst out of the tunnel into murky sunlight. The windows cleared showing roiling gray clouds. Nick lurched forward to see more clearly, something was terribly wrong. Then the scene came clear. The train didn't stop. Clarkeston was burning.

Chapter 6

"Subsequent years of the virus were named by the animals that died. Year One was rats. Their populations had swollen the previous year due to an increase in food and lack of exterminators. When they died off in mass numbers, many people were thankful. We didn't yet know that they were the harbingers of a new outbreak."

History of a Changed World, Angus T. Moss

Wisp was ready to leave the minute Lily woke. He'd packed some food and medical supplies. William would need help. He wondered what the children could know that would have soldiers torturing a boy for it. And how to speak of it to the girl? She would need to know what they would find at the end of their quest. He hoped William would last that long. This morning the link to him felt weak, faded, yet jagged with pain.

Lily's waking was like a small explosion in his head. She was bubbling over with eagerness and questions. He let her choose a breakfast of train food.

She ate while he cataloged his possessions. There was always a possibility that he couldn't come back to this place. And with mercenaries in the neighborhood, perhaps it was time to move on. He collected a few items that were hard to find: a good knife, his favorite canteen and some clothes that were fairly new.

“You did a good job with your braid,” Lily said.

“Thank you.” Wisp knotted a bandanna around his neck. Today might have fighting in it. Loose hair was a liability.

“Can you do mine, too?”

He sat her on a stool to comb the tangles out of her long, brown hair. When he touched her, he saw Iris for a moment and another woman, older, with the same red-brown color of hair, perhaps her mother. Both memories were pushed down hard as soon as they rose. Avoidance was sometimes survival. “Today will be difficult,” he warned.

“Because we have to walk far away?”

“Because we go to a dangerous place.” He tied off her braid with a bit of string.

Lily turned and gave him a serious look. “Will the men with guns be there?”

“Yes.” He collected his pack. “Come.”

She followed him up through the darkness and out to the cluttered yard. The morning was cool and moist from the night's storm. Tendrils of fog rose from damp corners like smoke. Wisp led her to the road on the back side of the factory. A narrow strip of asphalt, crowded with saplings and crumbling from seasons without repair, followed along the bank of a broad river. Trees leaned over the road shading them from the first rays of morning sun.

“Oh, what's that?” Lily ran to edge of the road where it came near the river.

“Dragonfly.”

“It's pretty.”

"We need to hurry," he said, not pausing in his stride. She caught up with him and skipped a few steps ahead. He spread out his senses. There was no one about. The child was safe to stray.

"Will we find William today?"

"Yes." He didn't say that the boy might not see tomorrow if they didn't. The girl didn't need to know that pain yet.

"By lunch time?"

He thought about the right words to use to make her understand without frightening her too much. "Lily, I need to talk to you about the men with guns."

A tremor of anxiety shook her. "Okay." Her voice was small and shy.

"I will find a safe place for you to wait. Then I will go and look at where the men with guns are. Then I will come back to the safe place and tell you what we will do next. So I need you to stay where I tell you to stay. Can you do that?"

"Yes."

Her hand stole into his, small and frightened. He let her set the pace. Her short legs were muscular. She had fled before. What she lost in stride, she made up for in speed.

The sun rose above the trees heating even the shade to a level of discomfort. Wisp called a stop, and they ate the train food he'd packed for lunch.

"Is it much further?"

He opened himself to William, feeling his pain and confusion. The boy was close. Reaching out, he felt the men guarding the boy. Four, maybe more, if some were sleeping. He didn't like the feel of the men.

"Are you talking to William?" Lily asked.

"No."

"But you know where he is?"

Wisp pointed in the direction they were headed. "I can feel him there. Lily, he is hurt."

Her lip trembled before she bit it. “Did they shoot him?”

“I don't think so.”

“Shooting is bad. If they didn’t shoot him, he’ll be okay.”

Wisp considered her oblivious optimism. She hadn’t yet experienced all the ways a body could be damaged. Sometimes the worse injuries were internal. But she didn’t need to know those things yet. “Maybe,” he said, all the warning he could give.

Lily hopped up. “We better go.”

* * *

When he decided they were close enough, Wisp led Lily down to the river. They walked the damp verge until he found an undercut high above the water. The roots of a lumpy old sycamore splayed across the bank like ancient steps. The lowest were exposed as the river washed more soil away every flood season. At the top of the bank, a root as thick as his waist ran horizontal creating a small cave beneath it. It was dry and sandy and large enough for Lily to hide in. “Here is the safe place for you to stay.”

Lily grabbed his hand. “What if you don't come back?” At her touch, her panic hit him hard, racing up his arm like an electric shock. She'd been covering it very well for someone so young.

“This time is just to look.” He knelt down to be closer to her. “I will come back and tell you what will happen next.”

She nodded, eyes wide, lips tight, not quite able to trust his word. Her small fingers squeezed his hand nervously before letting go.

“I will be back before you can count to one thousand.” He tossed his pack into the undercut.

“One thousand is a lot! I don't know one

thousand!" Her fear of abandonment was shoved aside by a sudden spike of resentment.

"What do you know?" he asked, dismayed at her lack. The children born since the virus weren't being educated. It was a failing that he found inexcusable.

"A hundred. I know how to count to a hundred." She glared at him, hands on slim hips.

Wisp smoothed a place in the damp earth. He took a stick and wrote the numbers one through ten. "One thousand is ten hundreds. So count to one hundred ten times. Each time you get to one hundred, cross out one number." He handed her the stick.

"Okay." She frowned at the numbers in the sand. He worried that she couldn't read either. "That's not really a two. You didn't do it right." She said poking the stick into the dirt.

He glanced at what he'd scratched out. They looked like normal numbers. "Cross off one symbol each time you count to one hundred."

She seemed more assured when she gave him a wide-eyed nod. He double-checked the area for strangers. No one was closer than the men who had taken her brother. "Start counting."

Her voice was swallowed up by the sound of the river in the time he'd taken three steps.

* * *

Wisp slipped through the undergrowth stealthily. Here at the edge of the water, thickets of bramble and saplings made the woods quite dense. He kept his senses open, making sure that the only human minds in the area were William and his captors. And yet, at the very edge of his awareness, he could feel another person. Someone from the settlement downriver perhaps. The person was far enough away not to be an immediate threat, and felt clean, a mind bright with healthy curiosity. Maybe just a fisherman looking for a good spot. There was a greasy darkness to the men holding William. A heavy shadow of wrongness that Wisp had felt once before in mercenaries that had tracked him for the reward. He doubted that the bright mind was working with the darker ones. Although if it wandered closer, Wisp might need to intercept or divert it.

The mercenaries were holed-up in a derelict factory. There were dozens of similar sites along the river. When he'd first come to the area, Wisp had looked at this one, but it had no basement. It was older than the one he'd finally chosen. The forest was taking it over. Trees and weeds and vines had thrust up through floors and scrambled out windows. From the look of it, a storm could bring down the remaining walls any time now. Wisp wondered if they were foolish or had access to weather forecasting. He would never have made a camp in there.

Breathing in the rhythm of the woods, Wisp moved through the undergrowth like one who belonged. Hard to see in the dappled light, and protected by a broadcast suggestion that he was just another shrub swaying in the wind, he advanced confidently. The trees petered out into saplings and weeds working hard to reclaim the parking lot. He settled in a patch of long grass and concentrated on pinpointing every mind in his surroundings.

There were two men out in the woods. Possibly walking patrol, but they were arguing, their attention on each other, not their environs. Sloppy. One was angry, distracted, the other smug. Neither was doing his job.

In the building, he could sense three men with the boy. Listening, tasting, sensing them, he realized they were not guarding. They were bored and frustrated, but there was no remorse for the damaged inflicted on

William. They wanted better food, beer, to be more comfortable, for the job to be over. Like the men in the woods, they were careless, not expecting any inconvenience beyond the recalcitrance of the boy.

When he had located every mind in the vicinity, and knew he was out of any sightlines, Wisp crossed the parking lot to peer inside the building. Streamers of sunlight filtered in through the broken brickwork and crisscrossed the dark interior. A damp smell of leaf mold and woodrot pervaded the space. He checked first for the weapons, body armor and whatever supplies they had. The camp, aside from being badly placed, was badly organized. Equipment, clothing and discarded food lay scattered across the leaf-strewn floor. Although the equipment was new and well designed, the soldiers were slovenly. Their uniforms were wrinkled, stained with mud and sweat. The three men inside were busy with their own pursuits, one eating, one dozing and the third trying to start a fire in a small ring he'd made of broken bricks.

With Lily's countdown running in the back of his mind, Wisp memorized the placement of supplies, weapons and exits, then he looked into the shadows beyond the men. William was tied to one of the remaining support columns. He hung slack in his restraints. There was blood on the floor. And when he saw it, he was aware of the smell. The boy was unconscious, but Wisp was close enough to feel the pulse of life within him. He was alive, but not for much longer. William couldn't take much more punishment.

The two walking patrol were returning. Wisp could hear their voices, raised and angry. Satisfied that he had collected all the information he needed, Wisp returned to Lily.

Chapter 7

"As a way to stop the looting, the government began distributing food in the mistaken belief that hunger fueled the unrest. It wasn't hunger. When society breaks down, so too do the social niceties such as obeying rules. The authorities were too busy trying to bury the dead and relocate the living, they didn't have time to chase criminals."

History of a Changed World, Angus T. Moss

The sun was high overhead making Nick sweat as he trudged up the river road. It hadn't taken him very long to get a lead. The minute he had stepped off the train in White Bluffs, he'd been mobbed by people demanding news of Clarkeston. They could see the smoke. A call for assistance had gone out over the ether. Clarkeston had firefighting equipment, they just needed more hands. Nick had been leaning toward joining the crew of volunteers when the whispers reached him. Most of the settlement believed that mercenaries had started the fire. Nick had to believe that there couldn't be two groups of mercenaries in the area right now. He followed the whispers.

There was no consensus, only rumors of troop movements, wildly inconsistent. Or maybe it was only one heavily armed man. Or a fleet of black trucks packed with men armed to the teeth. Everyone he spoke to had seen at least one man in black military gear and more than one sleek black vehicle. But they weren't regular soldiers. No one had seen the country's soldiers since the riots during the first days of the virus. Back when there were cops and national guard and a formal army. Regular soldiers would be welcome. Mercenaries were not. They made people nervous. Nick heard the same questions repeated whenever the topic came around to the armed men: who were they? What did they want? They were strangers. They must be responsible for the catastrophe in Clarkeston.

The only thing they all agreed on was that the men went north along the river road. Nick had walked that way on his last visit to High Bluffs. Up that way were old factories, one after the other in ranks along the water's edge. It was all the clue Nick needed to hear. The description of automatic weapons and body armor matched the kind of gear he'd seen on the dead man in the murdered girl's house. Too much of a coincidence for them not to be the same group. He drifted away from the gossiping crowds that had gathered by the train station. In the confusion of the volunteer fire fighters organizing a convoy, no one noticed him go. He took a roundabout route to the edge of town watching for anyone following. Once he was sure that no one was dogging him, he headed north up the river road.

It was a long walk to the first factory, but he made good time. The sky stayed clear, not a cloud in sight. There would be no storms today, when Clarkeston could use a pounding downpour to help with the fires.

The hot dry days of summer were coming in. Another few weeks and a fire like that could rage unstoppable across the bone-dry countryside. He set a quick pace, keeping to the shaded side of the road.

Nick was sweaty and hungry by the time the first rusting water tower came into sight. He moved off the road and into the cover of the woods. A quick look told him this one was unoccupied. By the twisted roots of a toppled tree, he hunkered down for a brief rest. During a quick meal, he thought about the situation. He could be walking into an armed compound, alone. If the mercenaries had the children, it was going to be an extremely difficult extraction. But he had no doubt that the children needed to be rescued. Their murdered sister was all the proof he required to know the mercenaries had ill intent. He only hoped that he'd get there in time. Without a motive for the murder, he had no clue as to why the children were targets.

After stowing his trash and taking a long slug of water, he resumed his trek. What he wanted most of all, at this point, was information. Being on his own meant he had to be smart. He'd take a good look at the compound, locate the children and hope for a plan. Back on the road, he marched past a line of rusted train cars before approaching the next factory. Fallen trees had taken down the fencing, but the driveway was still obvious. Nick slipped back into the trees.

Placing each foot carefully into the forest litter, testing every step for solidity and sound, Nick moved toward the factory. The birds were noisy this deep into the trees. Swallows swooped by on their way to the river. The forest felt alive with sound. Enough, he hoped, to cover his approach.

The sky glinting through the canopy still held light, but the floor of the forest was filling with shadows as he crept up on the derelict building. Someone was there. He could smell food cooking. Still at a safe distance, he stashed his pack under a bramble patch and loosened his weapons. Then he slowly worked his way forward until he heard voices. Crouching in the weeds, at the edge of a pot-holed parking lot, he waited, listening and watching.

Very few minutes passed before an armed man came around the side of the dilapidated building. Over his shoulder, hanging loose on its strap, was an automatic weapon. Nick concentrated on breathing as quietly as possible, but his heart speeded up. The man was wearing black body armor like the dead man at the murder scene. He'd found his quarry. The fact that he was out-gunned and out-numbered was frustrating. He'd need to get closer to see if they had the children. Bright light speared out of cracks and crannies from within the building. Luckily, with all the doors and windows missing, that would make it much easier to see inside.

As he was assessing the cover closer in, his eyes were drawn to a flicker in the undergrowth to the left of the man. A heartbeat later, inexplicably, the guy was gone. He blinked hard, staring at the sun-bleached grasses in the long shadows of twilight. A soft rustle in the weeds, and he saw a pair of boots dragged away. A shiver pricked its way down Nick's spine. Someone was hunting the hunters. That was an unforeseen complication.

Another mercenary stepped through a collapsed doorway with a mug in his hand. He looked both ways. "Allen?"

Nick held his breath.

There was a soft groan from the weeds.

"Allen?" The man dropped the mug and drew a sidearm. The movement was fluid, practiced. Nick had no doubt this was a professional unit. From the body armor to the weapons, it was obvious they had the kind of resources that didn't seem to exist anymore. He looked closer at the gun. It was a small, powerful looking thing that Nick coveted immediately.

"Allen, are you okay?"

There was no answer. The mercenary moved cautiously toward the weeds. Dried stalks and new growth combined to make a seemingly impenetrable mat. He looked behind, to the sides, one step closer. Nick felt sweat running down his neck. He hesitated to warn him. If these were the men that he was looking for, they had gunned down a young woman for no apparent reason. Or was there a war he was unaware of? Was this a retaliation from the other side? Should he remain silent and let some other, unknown party take action? Nick saw the flicker again and the man went down. Not quite as soundless. A grunt and a muffled thud of impact. The hair stood up on Nick's arms. His hesitation may have cost a life, and he had no way to judge the consequence. He wasn't even sure if they were dead or unconscious.

Someone ran in a crouch from the weeds to the factory wall. Nick got his first look at the assailant. He was thin, but muscular, long white braid down his back, bright against tanned skin. Only a faded green tee shirt and jeans. Not a soldier. Not a mercenary. Then he turned and looked right at Nick, putting a finger to his lips for silence. Nick locked eyes on him. The man pointed to the wall and raised three fingers.

Nick was stunned. How had he seen him? How did he know that Nick might be an ally? Before he could think of any answers, the man ghosted into the building. Nick ran over and took his place at the wall. Two against three were better odds, although he still wasn't sure what the sides stood for. At the very least, he'd be able to see if the children were here. If not, he'd get back under cover in the woods double-time.

The mercenaries had made a haphazard camp in the far corner of the building. Lamps flooded the area with light. Nick reassessed his assumptions about the soldiers. The setup didn't look as organized as it could be. Three men sat at ease, one reading, one eating and the third poking at a cook fire. To one side a teenage boy was tied to a pillar. He'd been badly beaten. Nick felt sick looking at the kid. He concentrated hard until he saw the boy's chest rise. At least he was still alive. Who were these bastards that they would torture a boy? That eliminated any remorse he felt about the bodies in the weeds outside. But then another element of the scene hit him. One of the floodlights was trained on the boy, showing him clearly in the dark interior of the building. In Nick's experience, that meant he was bait. Since he didn't see a little girl, Nick assumed that she was the one they were hoping to draw in with bloody and battered William as the lure. Not a solid proposition for attracting a twelve year old girl.

That lead him to believe that these men probably didn't know that Iris was dead. It made more sense that the hostage was to get the older girl's cooperation. When Nick found her body back in the house in Clarkeston, the dead mercenary was still there. He must have been alone when he attacked her. Nick didn't think these men would be so sloppy as to leave behind one of their own to be identified. Which would explain why no one had searched the house for the notebooks.

He looked through the shadows to find the white-haired guy, but couldn't locate him. The mercenaries were still oblivious of the intruder. Nick was impressed with the guy's skills, moving through broken glass and tumbled bricks without a sound. There were a million places to hide in the slumped walls and piles of debris inside the building. Nick would never have set up in a place like this. These guys were over confident. But Nick didn't think three to one were good enough odds that he would have infiltrated on his own. He wondered what the white-haired guy's plan was, and if he was working alone. The next move surprised him.

The white-haired guy sauntered into camp. Apparently he'd been too quiet, so he scuffed a toe across a loose pile of stone. That caught their attention. There was an explosion of reaction, of anger and swearing. The mercenaries were on their feet, grabbing for weapons in a hot minute. The intruder was too fast to watch, white braid flying, tanned arms a blur. The first man went down with a roundhouse kick to the jaw. The second man shot at him as soon as his colleague hit the dirt. The intruder came in close with a rapid sequence of martial arts moves that made Nick think of the old Chinese movies. The gun flew across the factory, kicked out of his hand, and the second man went down. The guy at the cook fire charged with a burning branch. By the time Nick climbed through the broken window, that guy was down, too. He grinned. Who needed a plan when you had mad skills like that?

"Come. The boy is injured." The white-haired man stood examining the boy, clearly illuminated by the floodlight. Nick tripped over a brick, his question frozen in his throat. Pale eyes, super strength, and in the light he saw the numbers tattooed down his neck. The guy was a biobot. What did he want the child for? Nick raised his gun.

"You did it!" A child's voice, high pitched and gleeful cut into Nick's deliberation. Out of the rubble a young girl ran over and hugged the biobot. "Oh, Wisp, you were right. The bad men hurt him. Can you fix him?"

Nick was flummoxed. These two children must be William and Lily. There had not been any mention of a biobot. He was sure Angus would have definitely told him about something like that. "Are you Lily?"

She slid a step behind the biobot, taking his hand. "Who are you?"

The biobot spoke to her softly. “He will not hurt you Lily. He is a good man. He will help us with William.”

Nick stared. How did he know?

Chapter 8

"At this point, with one crisis after another, the authorities stopped hunting any escaped biobots. Those with keepers were assumed to be under control. Those on the loose were expected to succumb in similar numbers to the virus. Records concerning them are difficult to find."

History of a Changed World, Angus T. Moss

"I will cut the ropes, please hold the boy. He is unconscious."

Nick hesitated. It was a reasonable request, but he didn't like taking orders from a biobot. Helping the children was the reason he was here. But it seemed he might not be alone in that. Lily looked totally at ease with the biobot, but considering her age, she couldn't know what he was. To Nick, that was the biggest problem: what had the biobot been designed for? They ran the gamut from nursery maids to assassins, and considering what he just witnessed, this one hadn't been built to care for babies. Nick needed to find out what their relationship was. She had obediently left when the biobot asked her to retrieve his pack.

The biobot turned to look at him, his face gave nothing away as he waited. Nick twitched a nod of assent and moved closer to the boy. He flinched when the biobot flicked open a knife, but the blade only cut rope. Nick got a careful grip on the boy, William. He smelled awful, vomit and blood and urine. The bindings fell away, and he gently lowered William to the floor. The boy needed medical care. “We'll need to make a stretcher. I think White Bluffs has a doctor.”

“No. Too close to the train station,” the biobot said.

Nick frowned, not sure why that was a problem. Lily climbed in the window, dragging a heavy pack behind her. It thumped down the brick pile scattering broken bits and rusty red fragments. The biobot took it from her, lifting it easily. He knew they didn’t really have super-strength, but this one looked especially strong.

“The stations are monitored. Until we know why the children are hunted, and by whom, we must remain out of sight.” The biobot pulled out a bottle of water and a scrap of toweling.

“You don't know who these guys are?” Nick asked. He was starting to worry about which side he had inadvertently joined. But surely the one *not* torturing children was the right one.

“No.” He wet the cloth and started wiping away the blood on William’s face.

“Why are you here?”

The biobot stopped. He turned his full attention to Nick for the first time. Nick felt his hackles rise as those pale blue eyes drilled into him. Then they turned away, and he felt sweat run down his back.

“Lily, can you go get the guns I took from the men?”

Nick watched the child skip off on her errand. He

shivered. *Collect the weapons from the dead men, little girl.* This was all kinds of wrong. When he looked back, the pale eyes were measuring him again.

"I am a finder. Lily hired me to find her brother."

"*Hired* you?" Nick shook his head. That wasn't at all what he'd expected. Then the words sank in and a hot anger rushed through him. "What was your fee?" The biobot didn't react to the accusation, just looked him over before turning back to caring for William.

"How could I take anything from a child who had lost all? She was alone." He nodded at William. "This is her only family. I work for whom I choose."

Lily skipped back in to drop an armful of guns at the biobot's side. He picked up the one Nick had admired and handed it to him.

Nick's head spun. Too many oddities to put together, but the injured boy had to be the first priority. "I'm Nick." The pale eyes flicked over to him. "You got a plan?"

"Can you drive?"

"You have a car?"

The biobot gestured to the bodies. "Theirs."

Despite the circumstance, Nick found himself grinning. A car. He hadn't even see a car in months, much less driven one. That thought followed the usual track and dumped him into gloomy reality. Did anyone still make cars? Were there enough hands left to run the assembly plants? And that made him turn back and look at the dead men lying in the dirt. Five less humans in the world.

"Would you want their kind to procreate?"

The hair stood up on Nick's neck. "Are you really reading my mind?" A flicker of those pale eyes again. He thought he detected just a hint of amusement in them.

"You think loudly."

Nick ignored the possible implications there and

turned his attention to William. The biobot had washed away enough dirt to see the damage more clearly. It made him sick to see this kind of injuries on someone so young. Although in the world as it was these days, adolescent might now be an adult. At a glance, it looked like no bones were broken, but the bruises were dark with blood. His mouth was cut in a couple places. His cheekbone and one eyebrow had split open under what looked like repeated blows. Both eyes were swollen shut. The bruises across his stomach could indicate internal injuries. Even with a stretcher, carrying him miles down the road to the train was a good way to make things worse. The car was the best choice. Nick could bring William and Lily back to High Meadow. Although not as quickly as the train. It would be a long drive. They wouldn't get there until nearly this time tomorrow.

"The car is over here."

Nick trailed the biobot out a wide doorway to what had probably been a loading dock. The wind was picking up, dead leaves scudded across the parking lot in the dim light of early evening. A big black van, shiny and sleek, sat on the cracked pavement. It matched the descriptions he'd gotten in High Bluffs, but most people had agreed on multiple vehicles. That worried Nick. The others might be on the way back.

The biobot had opened a couple of lockers exposing more weapons, food and a large tool box with a caduceus on it by the time Nick stuck his head in. Then he stepped away, as if offering Nick all the booty.

"Wow." Nick couldn't contain his amazement at the treasure trove—guns, ammo, bottles of water, packages of food that weren't Crunch or Stew-goo, medical supplies that were hard to find. The vehicle looked like it could hold ten adults and their gear easily. The seats were designed to easily reconfigure. He looked over to see if the biobot was as surprised.

Nick saw a different look on his face, the white-haired man was assessing him.

"What is your interest in the children?"

Nick shrugged. "What's yours?"

"I told you. Lily hired me."

"And you chose to work for free." Nick could hear Lily's voice, back in the building, but not the words. She was using a soothing tone as if to a restless baby. A child of the new world. She'd hired a biobot without a second thought. But he was from the old world, and he had lots of second thoughts. "I don't know you. Why would I trust you?" Nick said in a tone he hoped wasn't offensive. It was simply the truth.

Pale eyes met his, but suddenly lurched away. "We need to go."

"Why?"

"Something bad is happening."

"To the boy?"

"No." The biobot turned in a slow circle, head cocked as if listening for a faint sound. "Trouble at the settlement." He gestured north. "We need to hurry."

"Why?" Nick was nervous about the situation. He didn't know this man, or his reasons for helping the children. The last thing he felt like doing was getting in the van with him and heading to a strange settlement.

"They may need help." Pale eyes met Nick's. "You know them. Riverbank."

"The folks drying fish?" Nick nodded. He had just visited that settlement. They were good honest people trying to establish a settlement away from a med center. "What's the problem?"

"Unknown."

The statement sounded like a report to Nick, reassuring and unnerving at the same time. It would be good to work with a trained operative for once, but Nick wondered again what the biobot had been created for. And what had happened to his keeper. "Then how do you know there's a problem?"

"Panic. Fear." As he spoke he closed up the lockers, collapsed a row of seats and lowered a panel that turned into a bed. "If I can feel it from here, it is a powerful emotion. Many people." He stepped out of the van and faced Nick. "You do not need to come. If you wish to remain with the children, I can investigate on my own. But I will need the vehicle."

Nick didn't like that option any better.

* * *

They loaded William into the back. Nick ran to collect his pack as the biobot made a quick survey of the camp collecting things from the bodies. He wasn't sure if he wanted to know what he was taking. Looting the dead wasn't something Nick was comfortable with. By the time they were both back to the car, Lily had stationed herself at her brother's side. He looked at the sky, clouds were moving fast. A storm might be coming in after all.

Nick got into the driver's seat as the biobot took shotgun. "What's your name?" He wasn't about to start addressing him by the number on his tattoo.

"My kind don't have names."

"Call him Wisp," Lily piped from the back seat.

Nick looked at the solidly muscled man sitting next to him. "Wisp, huh?"

Wisp didn't look up as he opened a variety of controls on the dashboard. "We should go." He pointed forward.

Nick checked the gauges. The batteries were only at half-charge. That didn't surprise him, having seen the slap-dash camp they'd set up. He started the engine, and it purred quietly. The headlights illuminated the fractured asphalt of the old driveway. He pulled out of the parking lot and onto the river road headed further away from White Bluffs.

"I have disabled the trackers."

Nick blinked, a shiver of unease ran through him. The biobot knew more about this vehicle than he did. "Good thinking."

Chapter 9

"The virus of the third year was called the Pig Flu. It devastated pig farms and had a great impact on the food supply. The government began distributing vaccine that year, but not in time to stop another season of death."

History of a changed World, Angus T. Moss

Tilly stood momentarily in the doorway of Angus's office to watch her husband work. He was muttering under his breath, scribbling away as he referred to a small notebook. She loved watching him when he was unaware of her. This new life suited him so well. He was the happiest he'd been in years with too many things on his plate and a tribe to guide, which made it rare for either of them to have a quiet moment alone, or together. She tapped on the doorjamb to announce herself. "Interesting stuff?"

The look Angus gave her stopped her in her tracks. "What?" she asked, her heart racing.

He leaned back in the chair and rubbed his face.

"These notebooks were in the possession of the murdered girl."

She knew his every expression and mood. There was something very wrong here. She nodded without speaking, giving him the silence he needed to form his thoughts.

"I think..." He frowned at the notebook, shook his head and leaned forward to give it a firm tap. "Tilly, I think it's the virus."

"*The* virus."

His eyes had a far-away look, but he gave her a slight nod.

"You said *girl*. She wouldn't be old enough to have cooked it up." Tilly tried to remember every scrap of information that was known about the virus. At first, people thought it was simply an especially virulent form of the flu. That year's vaccination was useless against it. Hospitals filled up and overflowed. People panicked. Schools were shut down. Curfews, embargoes, the world came to a standstill as the virus circled the globe. The government announced it was researching it and released sheaves of reports on what they didn't know. Then the rumor started that it had mutated in a biobot. Riots erupted killing innocent people. The next rumor was that someone had released it to kill the biobots. That didn't stop the riots. Within a matter of weeks, the world had changed. Mass graves, empty cities, people looting and fleeing and fighting and hiding. Doing anything to survive, until winter brought an end to the flu season. Spring brought hope. People came together to plan, rebuild, restructure. Summer brought the disease back, and the world descended into despair and chaos.

"Angus, does that tell you how it started?"

His blue eyes were troubled when he looked at her. "It's a bit above my understanding. I think that the person who wrote these journals was..." He looked at a loss for words. Tilly waited for him to sort through his thoughts, but the silence stretched too long.

"You're scaring me."

"Reading this is like a fairy tale. This person was not living in the real world."

"Insane?"

"Too generic a classification, I think. Paranoid, definitely. Delusional, most probably. And sadly, absolutely brilliant."

"You think that person cooked up the virus?"

"I don't have the expertise to say. And I don't know who I could trust to look at this. The formulas...they might have an important clue, and they might be useless. They're at least ten years old. But there might be something in here that is worth murder."

"Someone knows about them and wants them." Tilly was surprised by how calm her voice sounded. Her hands had gone ice cold, and her stomach was in knots. "If they murdered the girl for them, why didn't they take them?" A tiny voice in her head was screaming, *And how soon will they be on our doorstep?*

"That might be a question for Nick when he gets back. He was there. He could tell us where he found them. Perhaps the others didn't look in the right places."

"Do you think he's found the children?"

Tilly saw his eyes widen as a thought hit him. "What?" she snapped. Her heart was pounding so hard she could feel it shake her whole body.

Angus grabbed the notebook and held it up. "Children!"

"You think they're infected? A vector?"

Angus tapped a finger against his mouth. "Perhaps inheritors."

"What does that mean?"

"I'm not sure, my dear. I am afraid there are currents in the world we are not prepared for. And I've sent Nick out into them without adequate warning."

Chapter 10

"Population numbers were no longer available after the third year. Cities emptied out into the suburbs, suburbs emptied into the countryside. People were on the move, and there was no way to track them."

History of a Changed World, Angus T. Moss

Nick drove up the river road toward the settlement of Riverbank. It was a relief to put some distance between them and the dead men. He hoped whatever Wisp was sensing wasn't too serious. That thought made him shake his head. He was trusting a biobot, believing that he had some kind of extrasensory skill. There was a sincerity about Wisp that made Nick want to trust him. Unless that was another weird skill, and it was all manipulation. He didn't even know if biobots could do things like that. There had been some blood-curdling rumors of supernatural powers that Nick had put down to idle minds. But now that he'd experienced it himself, he had to wonder how much of those rumors was true.

The other side of it was the possibility that a human settlement was in trouble. If there was a chance that he could help out, he couldn't pass on it. And if it meant fighting the bastards who had hurt the boy, he wouldn't mind leaving a few bruises of his own.

Nick looked over at his passenger. Wisp had his eyes closed, a frown creasing his forehead. "Anything more?" he asked, feeling doubtful and hopeful at the same time.

"Pain. Fear. Anger." Wisp shook his head like a dog shedding water. "I can decipher no more. Perhaps death."

"That doesn't sound good. How close are we?"

"Very." Wisp glanced back to the children. He leaned toward Nick and lowered his voice. "Riverbank knows me. I believe they sent Lily to me. If the hunters would do that to a child." He pointed to the back seat. "What would they do the adults in that settlement?"

Nick had no doubts on that account. He wanted to find out what was driving this. Why were these men hunting the kids? "How are you with a gun?" Nick asked, but was pretty sure he knew the answer.

"Accurate." Wisp went into the back and opened the weapons locker.

Giving a weapon to a biobot was breaking a slew of laws. Laws that no one was around to enforce anymore. Just being without a keeper would have earned Wisp a death sentence before Zero Year. For a second, Nick thought about calling Wisp back. Refusing to arm him. Something told him that Wisp would acquiesce. But that would leave Nick walking blind into a dangerous situation, without adequate backup. They needed to be prepared for the worst. That meant arming the biobot, but Nick didn't feel happy about it.

He wanted more information. Trouble at the settlement didn't automatically mean that the mercenaries were involved. They could be having some sort of internal struggle. He didn't want to get caught up in a settler's coup d'état. Part of him knew he was spinning tales because his nerves were on edge. The quicker he got into it, the better he'd feel. Lights in the distance showed him that the settlement was right on the road. The bloody bodies in the road showed him that Wisp was absolutely right. He stopped the van and turned the headlights full on the two men bleeding in the dirt. Multiple gunshot wounds on each of them and no weapons in their hands.

"They are dead," Wisp said

"You're sure?"

"I cannot feel anything from them. But I can feel great pain from the settlement. Someone is being tortured."

"Can you tell how many mercenaries are here?"

"No. There is too much emotion. It blurs the..." Wisp grunted, his shoulders hunching. "Someone has died. Go up the driveway."

Nick drove off the road, carefully avoiding the bodies. Once past them, he pulled into the narrow strip of asphalt that led back to a manufacturing plant that looked to be ten to fifteen years old. The profile was lower. No storm baffles, but there was a protected solar array in use. That explained why the place was lit up like a train station. They passed another unarmed body in the weeds by the side of the road, and Nick lost all compunction about arming Wisp. He gritted his teeth against the angry words rising in him. When he pulled in front of the building, he saw an identical black van and two more dead on the front steps. One was a woman. Nick could feel his neck muscles knot as his anger increased. There was no possible reason for the deaths of all these unarmed civilians.

"I would not kill indiscriminately," Wisp said, as if in answer to Nick's emotion. "That vehicle is empty," he added, answering Nick's next question. Wisp opened the roof hatch and flipped a lever that raised a step beneath it. He was holding a long gun. Some kind of rifle.

Nick turned back to watch the building. "You got a plan?"

"Is it the bad men?" Lily asked, her voice thin and fearful.

"Stay with your brother," Wisp said calmly. "Nick and I will take care of this."

Nick looked back in time to see Lily's face as she nodded to the biobot. There was so much trust there, it tightened his throat. She believed that they would keep her safe. He had to make sure not to fail.

"Someone approaches," Wisp warned.

Nick shifted his attention to the building. The door opened and a man in body armor, with an automatic weapon hanging from his shoulder, came out. Nick reached for the gun Wisp had given him. He checked the ammunition, his hands moving over the weapon automatically. Some habits became ingrained.

The man frowned at the van. "What're you doing..." He raised the weapon as he squinted into the headlights.

Nick flinched at the report above his head. The mercenary was down with a bullet hole in his forehead. A calm part of his mind noted that Wisp was an excellent shot. A less calm part was screaming that a biobot with weapons training was taking headshots at humans. It was like a headline from the supermarket scandal sheets in the years after biobots hit the market. They were *More Than Human* and *Taking Over the World*.

The building's front exploded out, as two men shot their way out of the building. Glass flew from doors and windows. The violent roar of automatic weapons tore through the night. Bullets pinged off the windshield, even as Nick ducked. Bullet proof, apparently.

One man went down. The other ran at the car, gun blazing. Nick opened the door, and used it as cover to returned fire. A hot line of pain seared his scalp. He aimed low, below the armor. The man stumbled, but the gun kept roaring. Nick ducked back behind the door. He braced himself for another attempt. He was panting and his heart was pounding. It had been a hell of a long time since he'd been in a fire fight. He took a deep breath, but before he could move, the night went quiet.

He checked. The man was down. Inside the van, he heard Wisp say something to Lily. The side panel opened and Wisp stepped out. Blood dripped from a wound on his right arm. He held his bandana out to Nick.

"How bad?" Nick asked as he tied the bandana tightly around Wisp's arm.

"It went through. It will heal."

Nick stared at him, shaken by the unreal calm. "Don't you feel pain?"

"Very much so. But we don't have time for it right now." Wisp walked past Nick, and collected the weapons from the dead mercenaries.

Nick hurried to catch up with Wisp, so they entered the building together. The lobby looked like it had once been a reception area. Now it was full of drying racks that held fish. The smell was overpowering. Five more civilians lay dead on the floor. Racks had been thrown down, fish scattered across the floor and lying in puddles of blood. Nick checked every body. All died of multiple gunshot wounds. All were unarmed. He stood over a woman, her arms thrown wide, eyes open, mouth agape. She looked astonished that she was dead. He had talked to her about fishing when he'd been here, only days ago. A fist clenched tightly around his heart, but this wasn't the time to mourn.

"This way." Wisp went through an archway into a carpeted corridor that led to offices.

Rooms with glass-paneled fronts and solid wooden doors lined the hallway. Halfway down the corridor a doorway was open, the glass wall shattered into pellets across the floor. Tied to the doorjamb was a young man, bloodied and limp.

"Dead," Wisp said as Nick stopped. He checked for a pulse anyway. It was just like what the others had done to William.

The next room held hostages. Nick saw Wisp recoil from the doorway. "Too much fear," he said backing up. He turned to Nick. "The only ones left."

Wide eyes above gagged mouths, the stench of sweat and urine, muffled keening, the sounds and smells hit Nick hard. He wondered what another layer of emotion on top of it all would feel like. "Check the rest of the place anyway," he told Wisp.

Nick took a quick survey. Two women, two kids and a bloodied man who looked unconscious. He chose the woman whose brown eyes looked more angry than scared. "I'm here to help," he said. He cut her loose and put the knife in her hands. "Hurry."

He bent over the man. Alive, but badly beaten. He'd need Wisp's help to carry him to the car.

"You're the guy from High Meadow."

Nick turned to see the angry woman holding his knife out, but not to return it. "I'm Nick."

The other woman and children, now free of their bonds, huddled behind her. The hand holding the knife was shaking but Nick didn't doubt her intent. He quickly thought through a couple things that might calm her down. "Lily's safe. Wisp found William."

"Thank God!" She lowered the knife. "I'm Jean."

"There's a car out front, Jean. Can you get these people into it? Wisp and I will carry him."

"Bruno," she said with a hitch in her voice. "He's our leader." She pointed to the hallway. "His son..."

Nick shook his head. "I'm sorry. There's no one else alive."

Her eyes brimmed with tears, and it looked like she might give in to the grief. She scrubbed her face, then gathered the others. Wisp entered the room before Nick could call him. They carried Bruno out to the car, following the women and children. Jean shepherded them past the blood and violence, their grief redoubling at every body they passed. A brisk wind rattled the fallen racks and sent leaves flying. They stepped over the broken glass of the front doors, the bodies on the steps were the last straw for the other woman. She collapsed, sobbing.

The wind shook the trees and plucked at their clothing. Grit flew up into Nick's face making him squint. He paused next to her, shifting his grip on Bruno. "We need to get the kids out of here," he said firmly. That seemed to galvanize her. She staggered to her feet. Lily opened the side door as they approached. No one spoke as they climbed into the van. They lay Bruno on the floor next to William. He looked to be in as bad shape from an equally brutal beating. Jean helped herself to the medical supplies that Wisp had previously laid out for William.

As Nick got in the front, Wisp stepped back out to investigate the other vehicle. He returned with an armload of supplies which he dumped on the floor. The second trip over was for weapons. The third time to disable it. Nick wished he could have taken that van, too. It was a waste of a perfectly good vehicle.

Wisp secured all the doors and took his seat. In a moment he had mapping options open on the dashboard screen. "Where is your settlement?"

Nick shot him a startled look. "Why?"

"Is that not where you wish to bring the women

and children?"

Nick mulled that over. He wasn't sure that he wanted to bring a biobot back to High Meadow. Angus would be delighted. There couldn't be very many of them left. And Angus loved a good surprise. But Nick didn't know what had happened here. He didn't know who these mercenaries were or why they wanted the children. High Meadow had little more in the way of defenses than Riverbank. He didn't want to endanger his home.

Wisp leaned forward and spoke very softly. "I do not feel any more of those men in the area. If we leave now, they should not be able to track us."

That reminded Nick that they needed to put some distance between them and the latest set of dead bodies. Nick started the van. He turned around in the parking lot and headed back down the driveway. Where could he take frightened women, children and two wounded? Ordinarily he'd head for a train station, but Wisp said they were watched. Something he used to consider a good thing. Now he wondered who was watching them.

He stopped at the bottom of the driveway. Angus would take these people in without any hesitation. And if Wisp could be trusted, and there were no other mercenaries left in the area, there was a good chance they could get away clean.

"Nick?" Lily came into the front pulling food out of a wrapper. "Look it's weird. Not Crunch. But it tastes good." She broke it in half showing him brown chunks in a red sauce.

He stared at the pocket of dough she gave him. Could it be a calzone? Things kept going sideways. None of the new rules seemed to apply. Here was food he hadn't seen in a decade. Armored men with shiny new vehicles. Blatant killings. His familiar world turned upside down, and he felt a sudden deep need to talk to Angus.

Wisp touched his arm pulling him out of his swirling thoughts. He pointed to the map he'd brought up. "We are here. Where do you want to take them?"

Nick had a sudden crushing sense of responsibility for the fragile freight he carried. Since the death of his family, he hadn't been responsible for anyone else. That's why he liked being on the road, looking out for just himself. Now he had women and children and two badly injured people to protect. It frightened him in a way that a gunfight never would.

Feeling more out of his depth than he had since his first days in the FBI, he made a choice. "High Meadow."

Chapter 11

> "After rumors and accusations of cults and gangs restraining people to inflate numbers, the government declared that settlements must go through an approval process in order to receive food and medicine allotments. That drove fringe groups further away."
>
> *History of a Changed World*, Angus T. Moss

Fighting the surges of raw emotion from the back of the van, Wisp tried to turn his attention to finding a safe route to High Meadow. His head pounded with the waves of grief pouring over him. For a moment, he floundered, awash in the raging anger and sorrow. His vision blurred and his heart raced until he could shore up his mental defenses. Turning into himself, he strengthened the imaginary walls he had built to trigger the mental exercises he had perfected. As each granite block came clearer in his mind, the turmoil around him faded. When he was done, the world felt grayed out, at distance, everything a shade less real without his ability to know what lay under the surface. He hid his unease as he uploaded the destination into the mapping program. The system responded by superimposing a route over a map of the area. "The most reliable roads," he told Nick.

"Thanks."

He didn't need his talent to see the doubt and confusion in Nick. Like many adults, he felt he should trust the feelings of children. That Lily trusted Wisp, made Nick want to trust also. Unlike many adults, Nick seemed to be more discerning. He had a strong skepticism that kept him from blindly following such inclinations. Wisp approved of that sentiment. Very few people were trustworthy. And Lily was too naive. Nick was a survivor. Wisp approved of that, too.

But Nick would also care for those who could not protect themselves. That could be a liability. If they encountered these soldiers in greater numbers, Nick might be willing to sacrifice himself for the safety of the others. Wisp did a threat-survival assessment of Nick and himself against various configurations of attackers with the women and children as noncombatants. The results left him hoping that none of those scenarios would occur. It might be best for him to leave at this point. Considering all the factors, the possibility of more deadly encounters was high and Nick's skills were unknown.

Adding to that, he had already broken every law on the books for biobots. Not that anyone was still enforcing those laws. But the fact that he had a van full of witnesses made him nervous. He had been running from the authorities all of his short life. The instinct to stay out of sight was deeply ingrained. Whenever he stayed too long in one place, or tried to trust someone, people came looking for him as a finder. Once that happened, inevitably someone tried to kill him for simply being a biobot. It always came down to the base fact that he wasn't considered human.

Lily brought him a selection of packaged food. "Look Wisp," she said, confusion clear in her voice. "All differed kinds of train food. Do different stations have different stuff? " She shuffled them and handed him one with an orange wrapper. "Try this one."

"All stations stock Crunch and Stew-goo," he said as he ripped open the package. "These are for the soldiers." Inside was another type of dough pocket. This time filled with white cheese and ground meat. He broke off a piece for Lily. She glared at the food skeptically before consenting to accept it.

She chewed with a frown scrunching up her forehead. "It's different, but I think it's okay."

He offered her the rest of it. "No, you should eat," she offered wisely. He had to agree. His head ached almost as much as the bullet wound in his arm, and it was sure to be a long night ahead.

Thinking of Lily, Wisp decided he would stay with them for a while, if only to be sure that she and William were taken care of. And the Riverbank people had been good to him over the years. He would miss those that had been killed. Some of the grief tried to rise again, but he pushed back at it. There was no time for that now. Later, when the children were safe, he could think about how many people Riverbank had lost. Nearly the whole settlement gunned down to find a little girl. If he had known what was happening, he would have returned sooner. For all the kindnesses over the years, he owed it to Bruno to make sure that his few remaining people were safe. Then he could leave. Should leave.

As Nick drove, Wisp went into the back to help them settle in. He gave out blankets and water. Lily had already distributed food. Only the children, Tom and Lucy, were eating. Margaret, their mother, and Jean were trying not to cry in front of them. Their pale faces and swollen eyes told Wisp enough. Grief would steal their appetites, close their throats and knot their stomachs. Maybe in the morning he would try to make them eat, but now it was pointless. He took the packages from limp fingers and put them back in the food locker. Jean gave him a teary nod. Margaret sat staring into space.

Wisp sorted the supplies he'd taken from the other van and stowed them. He checked on the medical supplies, then gave the injured a look. Bruno was still unconscious. He knew it was an unkind thought, but Wisp was glad for one less spill of emotions. William felt just on the edge of consciousness.

Jean knelt down next to him. "What can I do to help?" This close, he couldn't avoid her emotions. She was angry and scared, but the top note was sorrow.

Wisp handed her antiseptic and gauze. "Can you bind the wounds?"

Her fear eased back with a task in hand. "Will he be okay?"

"Bruno is strong," Wisp said, avoiding the obvious. The man probably had broken bones and internal injuries. Like William, Bruno's outcome depended on the kind of medical treatment they could find at High Meadow. If they survived the journey.

Tom's fear dropped out as he fell asleep. Lucy and Lily followed almost immediately. After food, warmth and safety had been supplied, they collapsed into sleep. Margaret's grief flowed out in silent tears, edging her toward sleep also. With the level of raw emotion sinking, Wisp went back up front to think. Margaret's mind went quiet with sleep. He allowed his granite walls to soften and the internal workings of Jean and Nick solidified.

"Can you tell if we're being followed?" Nick asked.

Wisp rubbed his eyes. "That's not something I can do."

Nick's distrust flickered up and down, a sign of

internal debate. As Wisp waited it out, he engaged the controls and did a locational radar search, originally designed to track traffic. He reported the results to Nick. “According to this, no one is following us, or ahead of us for a good ten miles. There aren’t any usable roads that run parallel of us along this stretch. I haven’t seen aircraft in...two years.”

That got a spike of surprise from Nick. “You saw a plane two years ago?”

“It was a helicopter.”

“Huh.” Nick’s uneasiness leaned toward curiosity. “Where?”

“Big military base in Texas.”

The curiosity soared for a moment before twisting into caution. “Was it American military?”

Wisp approved of his wariness. “Is there another?”

Nick made a point of looking around the van. “Seems like it.”

“These men were well armed, but not well trained. I don’t think they are connected to the base I saw. Different uniforms. Private security perhaps.”

Nick’s distrust became more focused. “I agree with you about the training. But just because they’re sloppy, doesn’t mean there aren’t a lot of them.”

“Harder to control larger numbers of men without better discipline. We may have eliminated the major part of the group.”

“Or just a patrol,” Nick said sourly. He leaned forward, peering through the windshield. “Is that fog?”

Wisp caught the scent at almost the same time. “Smoke.” He pointed. “Look at the sky.” Ahead of them an orange glow painted low clouds bright against the night sky.

Nick slowed the van. “The fire in Clarkeston must have jumped.” As they crept forward, the smoke got worse. “We can’t go this way.”

“We can’t go back.”

Chapter 12

"The government conscripted a number of labs and set them to working on a vaccine. It wasn't until the fourth year that they were able to distribute them widely. The clinics with the vaccine were swamped. People traveled miles in dangerous conditions to get treated. The few remaining hospitals were overrun. The next year, new rules were laid out establishing the med centers."

History of a Changed World, Angus T. Moss

Tilly made sure that Susan had dinner underway before she started looking for Martin. She didn't have to go far. He sat at his usual table in the corner of the cafeteria, papers and notebook in front of him, sipping a cup of something. She frowned. Probably coffee. He was probably drinking more than his fair share. Again.

"Martin?"

He looked up guiltily, and she knew she'd been right about the coffee. "Tilly. Problem?" He gave her a sheepish look, his big brown eyes twinkling with warmth.

Despite wanting to give him another lecture on sneaking coffee, she knew that was the least of their troubles right now. She sat down across from him, so she could keep her voice low. "What did Nick tell you about the murder?"

"That there was one?" He answered lightly, but a muscled jumped in his jaw.

"I have reason to believe he might be in trouble."

"He's armed."

Tilly felt a bit better hearing that. And Nick was trained in law enforcement, so he should be able to take care of himself, but something about this situation had her nerves on edge. "I don't want to overreact," she said carefully.

Martin's eyes widened. He could read her almost as well as her husband. "Have we got a problem?" His voice remained carefree despite the scrutiny he gave her.

"Nick brought home some notebooks. Angus thinks they are very important." Martin's face changed, the warmth dropping out. Tilly saw the cold, efficient soldier underneath. Martin had become so playful lately that she forgot how rigid he'd been when he arrived. He was one of the first people Angus had recruited. Tilly never asked why Angus chose the people he did. Most of the time, they were a perfect match. Very few had failed, and those that had usually left of their own accord. Martin had been a quandary for her. He was obviously a soldier, probably the only remaining member of his platoon or troop or whatever they were called. The shadows in his eyes made her heart ache for him. He'd surely seen more than his share of horrors. But Angus had chosen right. Martin loved this community, and Tilly knew he would protect it with his life.

"Important enough to get the girl killed?" he asked.

She nodded. "I'm worried about Nick, but..."

"But what if he was followed?" Martin finished her thought.

"We should prepare—"

"If he was followed, they'd already be here, Tilly." Martin cut her off with a shake of his head. "They would have been right behind him."

She shivered at the thought. "Not if they went back for reinforcements."

Martin gave her an indulgent nod. "If it been me, I'd've hit him before he got back here. If they scouted us out, they'd know our strengths and to be perfectly honest, Tilly, they wouldn't need reinforcements."

"But if they came..."

Martin looked around the room, but from the look in his eyes, Tilly knew his thoughts were on manpower and placement. "We have some options."

She took a shaky breath. She didn't want to be right. "If we closed the storm shutters..."

"They aren't bomb-proof, but they could act as a last defense."

Tilly didn't like hearing those words–last defense. The knot in her stomach tightened. "Should we bring in the animals?"

Martin rubbed forefinger and thumb together in small circles, eyes on the table as he thought. "We need to drop the security gates in the tunnels and maybe barricade them. We can bring the chickens and horse into the small garage. That has a good solid door on it. Any idea what kind of people we're expecting?"

Tilly shook her head. "I'm not even sure if anyone is coming. It just seems prudent to prepare."

"I'll see how long it'll take to set it all up. When we put up the shutters, we'll lose the sunlight. It'll scare people."

Tilly looked up as a group of children arrived with

a giggling clatter to check the menu board. She knew all their names. The littlest had been the first child born here. Up until now, the center had only had to deal with a handful of bandits that the Watch had easily run off just by showing up armed and determined. Her people were in danger, and this time she didn't know how best to protect them. She stiffened her spine and tried to think as the Lady she pretended to be. Her castle was in danger of...attack? What would make the most sense? The answer came to her—prepare for a siege.

"Let's get the animals moved and the tunnels barricaded first. Do we need to worry about water and power?" Martin gave her an approving look that made her cheeks flush.

"Access to the power plant and water system is under this building. As long as we are secure, so are they. If we aren't, don't think we'll have time to worry."

"What about the children?"

"There's the big storm shelter three floors down. I'll take a look, but I think it has a couple of access points. If we shut down all but one, it would be easily defensible. We can evacuate the kids and elderly there if there's a breach."

"Let's make that a plan. I will announce it at dinner. We can run a drill tomorrow." Tilly nodded, checklists piling up in her head. "I'll have the gardeners bring in everything that's close to ready. We should send someone for a cartload of train food, just in case."

"Will do." Martin scooped up all his papers. "I'll increase patrols. Excuse me, I need to talk to the Watch." He tucked everything under his arm, gave her a slight bow and left.

Tilly blew out a sigh of relief. Talking to Martin had been the right choice. He hadn't questioned her, or accused her of panic. He'd just taken it all in and responded with action. Now that preparations were in the works, she felt better. They had a plan. She could only hope that they would have enough time to get ready.

Chapter 13

"There was a period of time when the government spent most of its resources herding people. After the riots, they ushered people into smaller units. After the cities failed, they tried to corral people into settlements. Finally, by establishing the med centers as hubs, they forced people to settle nearby or do without."

History of a Changed World, Angus T. Moss

Nick felt too exposed, stopped in the middle of the highway. Smoke sailed across the road in gauzy streamers, and the glow ahead seemed to be getting brighter. "Think the fire's hit the highway?"

In answer to his question, Wisp pulled up the navigation again. "This program only updates once a week."

Nick wondered how he knew that. He seemed too well informed about things that Nick didn't even know existed. "So it won't have the fire," he acknowledged. He watched Wisp's hands run over the controls pulling up different programs. He wasn't just looking at maps. There was an air filtration system that he turned on, and the ground radar was up again. "What are our options?"

"I may be able to stitch together some side roads."

Nick took a deep breath trying to ease the tension in his shoulders. The back of his neck prickled. He felt like there were eyes on him. "We need to get off this road."

"Turn around."

Nick followed Wisp's instructions to a smaller road that felt like it was going in the wrong direction. The pavement was broken into an uneven mosaic. Despite the excellent shock absorbers, the ride was more lurch than wobble. He had to drive slower, worrying about the effects on his injured passengers. In a few minutes, Wisp directed him on to a dirt road, which was often safer because there was no asphalt to disintegrate. This road was smoother, but narrow and largely untended. He had to maintain a slow speed, sometimes tearing through sections overgrown with vines and weeds, other times barely able to locate the road from the fields on either side of it. The van was well enough equipped for the off-road portion of this trip. They drove in silence for nearly an hour. His hands were locked on the wheel, and his eyes gritty from staring at the meandering lane in the jouncing headlights.

"Do you want me to drive for a while?" Wisp asked.

Nick didn't take his eyes off the road as he considered it. Did he trust this person enough? This biobot? Had they gotten that far already by sharing a firefight? Did he trust him with the fragile passengers? His head ached from it all. He didn't know where they were in relation to High Meadow. Roads changed every year, some washed out, got buried by landslides or a forest of trees tossed by a tornado. Landmarks melted under the onslaught, and the land he knew as a kid changed too quickly. Without a compass or GPS, it would be hard to make his way back. He was still mulling over his answer when Wisp touched his arm.

"Trouble ahead."

"Now what?" Nick grumbled. He increased the beam illumination and the headlights showed a barricade of broken furniture blocking the road ahead. A handful of men with long guns stood at the edges.

Wisp made a sound like a growl. "This is a bad place."

A bullet pinged off the windshield. Nick flinched automatically. "Son of a bitch. They're trying to kill us."

"Not bandits. Worse." Wisp said. "They will kill the men and take the women."

Nick didn't slow. "Think we can plow through that crap?" He was worried. They didn't have a lot of choices here.

"This is a very sturdy vehicle. Escape is our best option."

Another bullet pinged off the windshield.

"Better tell them to hold on," Nick said. Wisp went into the back to warn the others.

Nick headed straight for the barricade. As he got closer, he saw that it was more than just furniture. There were logs and tires. He probably wasn't the first person to try ramming it. But he was pretty sure he was the first to try in an armored vehicle. He gunned it.

The impact wasn't as spectacular as he had envisioned. The van crashed through wood, climbed over tires, hit a brief free area before ramming into a pair of old pickup trucks and pushing them yards down the road. As soon as the van's tires were solidly back on dirt, Nick threw it into reverse to get around the trucks. The bandits were firing, bullets pounding the vehicle. The sound got louder, and Nick realized Wisp had opened the roof to return fire. He almost told him not to, but if a tire was hit, they'd be sitting ducks.

Nick swerved around one of the trucks and found the road again. When he saw the next barricade in the headlights, he hit the brakes so hard it knocked Wisp off his feet. Across the road, bound into place along a chain, were captives. In the glare of the headlights, they looked like children. A high cackle broke through the sound of the gunfire, followed by catcalls and hoots. Nick felt a gut-deep loathing for the man who had thought this up. Someone scrambled forward from the back of the van.

"My God!" Jean leaned against his seat. "We have to help those kids!"

Nick was thinking the same thing. But his mind wasn't working fast enough. Men were lining up in front of the van. Dirty men with greasy hair and clean rifles. They wore animal pelts at their belts and strands of odd shaped beads around their necks. There was a feral-ness to them that raised Nick's hackles and made his muscles twitch in anticipation of violence. As long as Nick kept the doors locked, they were safe in the van. But the longer they sat, the bolder the attackers would become. He needed a plan right now.

"Get out of that thing!" A slightly larger, somewhat cleaner man with a bald head banged on the hood of the van. He grinned, showing a mouth full of rotting teeth.

"Wisp, can you tell how many there are?"

"Many."

Nick heard Wisp moving in the back, but he kept his eyes on the men.

The bald man threw his head back and cackled again. The sound had the sharp edge of insanity to it. Then he spun and shot one of the children.

"No!" Jean screamed as the slender figure dangled limp from the chain. The remaining children huddled in on themselves.

Nick lurched to his feet as automatic fire sounded

above him. Wisp was firing on their attackers from the roof hatch. The men in front of the van crumpled to the ground in bloody heaps. Jean shoved a gun into Nick's hands. "Lock this," he snapped at her as he charged out the door.

He started firing before he had his bearings. Jean had given him an automatic weapon and the kick tossed him back a step. He blasted the woods around the car as he headed for the children. He could hear Wisp firing single shots from the top of the van. The area was pitch black but for the headlights. He couldn't imagine how Wisp was finding targets.

He didn't look at the kids. He knew if he did it would make him so angry he'd stop thinking. He went straight to the the chain and tracked it to a huge metal ring anchored to a massive old tree. He'd need a grenade to get that loose. A bullet whined by him and thudded into the tree showering him with chips of bark. He spun scanning for the enemy. A skinny boy of about fifteen was hiding by the side of van. He raised a gun and aimed. Nick ducked behind the tree as another bullet slammed into it. When he looked out, low and slow, the boy was down. Nick looked for Wisp, but couldn't see him above the headlights.

"Look for a key," Wisp called to him.

Six men down and Nick didn't have the slightest doubt they needed killing. He located the bald-headed man among the bodies in the road as that one seemed to have been the leader. Close up the bandit was even more disgusting. His teeth weren't just rotten, they'd been filed to points. A new level of repulsion welled up in Nick as he realized the pelts were human scalps. The odd beads were small bones, probably also human, he didn't want to look too closely. The man stunk of old sweat and rancid fat. His clothes were filthy. Nick felt contaminated as he searched the pockets in the stained jeans, but was rewarded with a ring of keys. Now he had to face the prisoners.

With occasional gunshots sounding behind him, Nick worked at releasing the prisoners. Taking a better look at them, he realized they weren't children. They were men and women, starved and broken. The taut chain across the road held them on their knees, some straining up or down to remain at the imposed height. None of them looked at him as he unlocked the steel collars around their necks. One man bolted as soon as he was free, scrambling away on all fours. There were six women and three men, not counting the one that ran. One man was wheezing badly. Once released from his collar, he collapsed on the road, gasping for breath.

The captive who'd been shot was starvation thin. Nick unlocked the collar and lowered the body to the ground. He barely weighed anything. Signs of abuse were all over his body. Nick kicked the chain away. He needed to bury this man, to put him to rest with a shred of dignity. He dragged the body out of the road and lay him on a strip of grass. He looked back at the rest of the prisoners. They remained where they had slumped, eyes down, unmoving, festering sores from the collars weeping pus onto their stained clothing. They needed food, water and medical supplies. He was momentarily caught between wanting to give aid and cautious at using their dwindling supplies. With William and Bruno using up the bulk of medical supplies, and all of them needing food and water for at least another day, he wasn't sure how much they could afford to give away.

As if she'd read his mind, Jean made the decision for him. She brought water and train food to the captives, but they didn't respond to her. Eyes lowered, most of them shied from her where they crouched on the road. She left a bottle of water and packet of Stew-goo, both opened, in front of each one. Then she came to where Nick was coiling the heavy chain at the side of the road. "What should we do?" she asked.

Nick didn't want to bring these people to High Meadow. They were damaged, physically and mentally. Angus wouldn't turn them away. But they would probably need care for the rest of their lives. It was a cold thought, but they were a liability. If they had any other trouble on the road, this lot would be of no help. He regretted letting Wisp talk him out of riding the train. A clean, well-lit station would be a god-send right now.

"You got em fed and watered. It's warm enough to sleep out tonight. See if any of them will let you check their wounds."

Jean winced, a look of revulsion crimping her brows.

"Sorry," Nick said. "I can do that in a bit." He turned to look for Wisp.

The biobot was standing by the front of the van watching the woods. Nick went over to him. "We need to do something about these folks."

"Grand View is just north of here. They have a med center."

Nick felt a fast flash of anger. He didn't want to go further north. He wanted to get to High Meadow.

Wisp flicked a pale-eyed glance at him before returning his scrutiny to the woods. "We can leave them here, but I am not sure that we were able to eradicate the entire cult."

Nick shot a frown at him. "Cult? You know who these nuts are?"

Wisp walked a few steps away, standing over one of the bodies. "Without a closer look, I didn't realized who they were. The bone necklaces and scalps gave them away. They call themselves Maneaters." He gave Nick an eye roll. "Not the most imaginative bunch. They are cannibals. There are a few groups of them around. They believe the only way to survive is to eat those that appear immune."

Nick felt sick, defeated. Cannibals. What had happened to these people that made them believe that was a viable course? He stared out into the surrounding woods. Small towns scattered across the country had become entirely isolated over the years. Many agricultural communities had carried on in their own tradition without much fuss. Other towns had devolved into petty oligarchies or church-based cohorts. Then there were pockets of pure evil, like this one. He felt a strong longing for High Meadow and its high ideals.

Despite how sick this made him, he felt responsible for the captives. The best course was to take them to the closest source of medical help. "How far to Grand View?"

"I will look for a road."

As Wisp went back in the van, Nick walked around the vehicle to check it. A few scratches and dings. The tires were all in good shape. He came to the boy that had shot at him. Close up, he could see he was wrong again. Not a boy at all, just a skinny, runt of a man with filed teeth and three scalps on his belt. He felt no regrets. This was a death deserved for a vile predator.

"Wha' abou' da chirren?"

Nick spun, startled. One of the captives stood near him. She stared at the dirt. Nick's gut twisted. Her bones had been broken and healed at odd angles. She looked badly put together, all angles and lumps. "What?"

She shot him a quick look, one eye socket was sunken. She gestured with a stick-thin arm. "Da chirren." Her words were garbled from a lack of teeth and a mangled tongue.

Nick followed her gesture, peering into the darkness. Wisp exited the van and joined him.

"You understand her?"

"She's fearful and hopeful and yearning for

something over here." Wisp walked confidently into the night.

Nick wondered if his pale eyes let him see in the dark. He had to shuffle along, snagging his feet on vines and weeds. A wobbly finger of light came from behind him. Jean joined them, flashlight in hand.

"What are you doing?" she asked.

"Not sure yet."

Jean stayed a half-step behind him as they followed Wisp. In the thin beam from the flashlight, Nick saw the jumbled remains of a collapsed house. High piles of splintered lumber and crumbling bricks lined a well-trod path through the debris. When they caught up to him, Wisp was standing at an old-fashioned wooden cellar door, the paint peeled and deteriorated. A well-kept chain and padlock ran through the handle.

Wisp tugged on the padlock. "Do you still have the keys?"

Nick patted his pockets, surprised to find he did still have them. A shiver ran down his back. Standing in the pitch dark with just Jean's flashlight made him feel too vulnerable. He handed the keys over to Wisp, but he wasn't sure he wanted to know what was in that basement.

Wisp sorted through the keys, trying each one. The lock fell loose, and he pulled the door open without hesitation. Nick figured he must know that whatever was on the opposite side wasn't going to come out fighting. Prudently, he took a step back, bumping into Jean. The flashlight wavered for a moment, then she pointed it at the black hole of the cellar.

"Come out," Wisp said softly. He knelt at the lip of the stairs.

A young boy, not more than five, climbed out. In the weak light, he was pale and shaking. Two girls around Lily's age followed, then another boy slightly older. They were dirty, shy and well-fed. They huddled together darting nervous looks at the strangers. The older boy frowned at them and then deliberately turned his attention off to his right. Jean moved the flashlight to see what he was looking at. A few steps away a squat table made out of thick wooden beams sat in the middle of a clearing. It was splotched with dark stains, knives and cleavers were racked to one side, chains hung in loops off the other. With a jolt, like a kick in the stomach, Nick realized it was a makeshift butcher block. He had to take a couple deep breaths to settle the emotion squeezing his chest and tightening his throat.

Beside him, Jean burst into tears. "No! No that's, oh God..." She dropped the flashlight to cover her face, sobbing. Nick put an arm around her. He needed the comfort, too. He did not want to connect the dots between the kids in the cellar, and what he was looking at now. She pushed away from him and retrieved the flashlight.

When she swept the light over the area, he realized the children were gone.

Chapter 14

"It started from tragedy, a man so distraught at the loss of his child that he did the impossible. He loaded her cells into a bio-printer and re-built her. His attempt failed, but from that single desperate act, the biobots were devised. When they were finally perfected, they were touted as the solution to all man's ills. From manual labor to complex calculations, one could order a Biological Robot built to almost any specification."

History of a Changed World, Angus T. Moss

Who am I? Mm, mmm, me. Not right, but close.

The day always started the same way, trying to remember who she was. The walls were white. Lights came on and went off without her asking, or wanting. Food arrived when the lights came on. There was a name for it. A word that meant just that thing. Food in the morning was...breakfast. Yes, that's right, breakfast. That was the word for the first meal of the day.

She sat up slowly, feeling like she'd been wrapped

in cotton. Sounds were muffled. Everything felt like flannel or rubber, even her body. Sometimes she wondered if she was made out of skin and bones, because they didn't feel right. And that would make her wonder why she thought that. How was it supposed to feel? Had there been a time before the white walls and cotton? It was too hard to remember.

The small door in the wall opened with a snap. The sharpest sound in her world. A tray of food slid onto the narrow shelf across from the bed. A scratchy sound that made her stomach growl. The air in the room changed from a soapy smell to something else...toast? Coffee? Any change was special and must be appreciated. She let the smell float around awhile. If she ate the food, the smell would go away. But if she waited too long, the tray would be removed, and she would be hungry.

She put bare feet on a cold, tiled floor. The floor was not white. The floor was gray. She squinted at the edges where the white stopped and the gray began. The gray was important to her because it was not white. Her pants were white. Her shirt was the palest shade of blue. Sometimes her shirt was another color. Once it was pink. That had been a big surprise. It made her think of things that she couldn't bring to mind today. It made her want something. Her shirts were never pink anymore.

She shuffled over to the lavatory on rubber legs. Toilet, shower, sink, toothbrush. She named each thing carefully before using them, proud to remember their names. Walls, ceiling, bed, tray. She rattled off all the items allowed in her world.

Who allowed?

That was another thought that she wasn't sure she knew the answer to. Her parents? Parents. What were parents?

She sat on the chair in front of the shelf and put

food into her mouth. She was pretty sure she had parents. Two of them. A man and a woman. They were important. Not like gray was important, or saying the names of things. But she couldn't remember why they were important. There were a lot of things she couldn't remember. Sometimes things floated up in her mind, and she had no idea where they came from.

Little triangles of yellow on her plate were sweet. She liked sweet. Not every tray had sweet. They were tart. She looked for the name along the gray of the floor. Apple? No, pineapple. The smell was a memory. She closed her eyes. Blue sky and yellow sand. A pounding sound that came from water...no, ocean. It was the ocean. And her skin was hot and smelled of coconut. An old ache of longing rose in her. But she didn't know what to pine for. Was it the ocean? Did she ache to see that blue sky and blue water? But it didn't make sense. She had always been here inside the white walls with the gray floor. Across the sand, a voice called, like the birds that swooped above her. Birds, gulls, seagulls. The voice said her name, and she remembered it. Melissa.

Chapter 15

"Biobots soon became a political nightmare. Unions were against them for replacing workers. The Human Rights organizations were apoplectic over the insinuations that these creatures were not human. Definitions varied wildly. The industry insisted that since a biobot was not grown in the womb and birthed from a woman, it was not a person."

History of a Changed World, Angus T. Moss

Wisp heard a motor kick over and felt Nick's lurch of alarm.

"The van!" Nick spun back to the path.

Wisp grabbed his arm. "The van isn't over there. It's a different vehicle. The prisoners are leaving."

"We need to stop them." Jean shone the flashlight across the debris piles. She was searching for a way toward the sound of the engine. Her fear and disgust were so high, Wisp wondered how she could form a lucid thought.

"Why?" Wisp touched her shoulder to stop her. "The prisoners don't trust us. They're fearful and angry. They have taken their children and left."

"*Their* children?" Nick demanded. "You're sure?"

"The children went willingly. The adults think only of the children's safety." Wisp could feel the confusion in Jean. She so badly wanted to fix something. "They are better off seeking their own kind. The woods here have many small communities. They will be with people who want to care for them."

"What's that supposed to mean?" Nick barked. He was angry at the situation and relieved not to be responsible for these people and oddly, angry at his relief. His emotions flickered so fast, Wisp worried that he was becoming unstable. Guilt steamed off him like a vapor. It was illogical for him to feel such pain for circumstances he'd stumbled across, but he was definitely not a logical man.

Wisp chose his words carefully. He used a calm voice and tried pushing a little on their overwrought emotions. It was not a time for Jean and Nick to go haring off after people who did not want their help. "We have our own responsibilities. Bruno, William, Lily. They deserve our undivided attention. The prisoners would require a lot of care and attention and still they would be questioning our intentions every step of the way. They would be fractious and defensive. Possibly violent. They are much happier making their own choices."

"But the kids?" Jean asked. She was teetering toward accepting his point of view.

Wisp felt her fragility. She was battered from the attack and the deaths. She didn't want to be wrong about something she might be able to fix. "The children felt safe with the people who took them. I wouldn't have let them go if I felt fear. But they got much calmer when the people that had been chained came to them."

He waited for that to sink in. Then he added bare facts, nudging her towards acceptance. “They share a trauma. They will heal best together.”

Jean hesitated, too tired to decide. Nick’s emotions consolidated, the fear and anger dropped away leaving duty as the top note. He gave Wisp a curt nod. “Let’s get out of here.”

Chapter 16

"The term *keeper* was coined as the person responsible for the well-being of a biobot. That didn't prevent abuse by that keeper. Ownership soon came to include any inventions or discoveries made by the biobot. A lucrative side business evolved from that which had the markets spinning to produce brilliant minds to order. No one gave a thought to how these brilliant minds would react to this legally permitted slavery. Later, it was declared that the keeper would also be responsible for any crimes committed by their charges."

History of a Changed World, Angus T. Moss

The morning sun was peeking through the trees when the low-battery alarm chimed. Wisp engaged the receivers on the roof to catch any light making it through the canopy. He and Nick had taken turns driving all night. Everyone wanted to put that place behind them as swiftly as possible. After continuing along the dirt road out of the Maneaters' village, they connected up with the highway again. Wisp had kept a close watch on the roads and the areas they traveled through. With everyone but Nick asleep, he could stretch out his senses, tasting for trouble. Once back on the highway, they made good time.

His head ached with the recent stresses of so many people's high emotion. The rest of the journey would be uncomfortable. For the moment, Bruno and William were either unconscious or sleeping. Lily and the other children slept. Jean was waking. Wisp felt the stab of grief when she became aware of her surroundings. Margaret was dozing, dreaming of the attack and whimpering softly. Sharp images flashed from her, each a mental blow, the mercenaries looking larger than life, their weapons massive, her own helplessness making everything hurt all the more. Nick slept in the seat next to Wisp, but his rest wasn't easy either. Luckily, he didn't broadcast as easily as Margaret.

The truth was no one would rest well until they reached the settlement and the safety of its guarded walls. He might take advantage of that safety to rest for a bit. Once he was sure that Lily and William were safe, he could find a place to sleep and eat. It shouldn't take more than a day or two to assess the settlement. To be sure that was the best place for the children, then he would be on his way.

The road wound downhill in sweeping loops through healthy bands of deciduous forest. Trees leaned over the road reaching hands across the slim passage, almost touching. Saplings marched along shoulders, crowding the edges of the asphalt. In another few years, without maintenance, the forest would reclaim the land. The road curved back toward the east. Long fingers of sunlight reached through the canopy dappling the road. Wisp eyed the forest, worrying that the battery wouldn't charge in time.

A sudden change to full sunlight showed a swath of fallen trees that marked the path of a tornado. Trunks lay stacked like matchsticks with roots and branches intertwined. A thin trail of sawdust from the road to a small clearing indicated the wood was being harvested. Wisp reached out to check for watchers. Whoever was working the timber, wasn't present at the moment. He stopped the van. The gauges on the collectors reported an upswing in solar collection. Wisp slipped into the back helping himself to food and water. He stretched the kinks out of his spine before returning to the front.

"Why are we stopping?" Nick mumbled.

"Battery," Wisp said, handing him a bottle of water.

Nick took a long drink. Suspicion and uncertainty wavered until he became aware of his surroundings. "Oh. We're at the Big Blowdown. We're almost there." Wisp felt his own muscles loosen as Nick relaxed.

"I'll take over," Nick said.

Wisp swapped seats with him, glad for the break. He offered Nick a packet of food. "This says *Biscuit Sandwich*."

Nick ripped the package open and stared at the contents. "Where are they getting this stuff? Have you seen train food like this?"

"No."

"It really is a biscuit," Nick said sounding perplexed. He bit into it. "Well, I've had worse."

"It is adequate."

A flare of pride colored Nick's response. "High Meadow has real food."

* * *

Wisp could see the bulk of the storm baffles long before the settlement came into view. A buzz of curiosity and alarm alerted him to sentinels hiding in the trees. They came around the next curve to find armed men blocking the road. A pair of saw horses made a polite barrier. Wisp knew they could blow through them easily in the powerful vehicle. One man raised his arm, requesting they stop. The men were clean, decently dressed in tidy clothes and looked well fed. There was a wholesome solidarity to them that bandits rarely had. Nick felt strong approval at seeing them.

"You know them?"

"Yup. Not sure why they're up here, though." As they coasted up to the barrier, Nick leaned out the window and called to them. "Just me!"

The men waved, apprehension sliding off them, replaced with curiosity and pleasure. Nick was well liked. Wisp felt the welcoming in them. When Nick walked up to them, they gathered around him with honest smiles.

"Where did you get that thing? Martin's gonna have a fit!"

The men gossiped. He waited for them to settle a bit before opening his door. Every eye riveted on him. They stopped speaking. Trickles of curiosity, apprehension and confusion lapped through the men.

"He's with me," Nick said with a forced casual air.

"But he's a..."

"Yup."

Nick signaled for him to get back in the van. They radioed ahead to arrange for a medical team to meet them. There was an efficiency to the men that Wisp hadn't seen in many settlements. Perhaps this place would be as safe as he had hoped it would be. Once Lily and William were settled, he could go.

As they approached, Wisp got the usual ache at feeling too many minds in one place, but the general flavor was unsullied. No predominant fear or resentment. He could feel the whole range of human emotions— anger, joy, regret, contentment. That spoke of freedom. He could almost make his assessment from just that.

Nick drove up a wide driveway to the main entrance. People burst out of the building with two gurneys, followed by more men, with more weapons. There was suspicion in the air. Wisp got out of the van and stood by the front of it. Away from the doors where they retrieved William and Bruno. Away from the women that scooped up Lily and the other children, cooing over them. There was a welcome for Jean and Margaret. And people dressed in white, like a real medical staff, calling for procedures and medicine as they wheeled the injured away. William would survive. Lily would thrive here. Wisp could feel the bright minds of curious children poking around the edges of the worried adults. The feels and smells and sounds all said that this was a good place. The people he'd brought here would be safe. As soon as he was rested, he could leave.

In the surrounding woods he could feel the occasional flicker of busy minds. There were a few outliers. People living nearby but not of the settlement. That was fairly unusual. Most of the settlements he'd seen were like little forts. They didn't trust those that would not throw in their lot with the rest. But there was no anger or suspicion that he could sense.

Closer in were the fields and people diligently working them. A sore back here and a worried mind there, but those people felt an ownership of the crops. They weren't slaves. The smell of green growing things and healthy soil was rich in his nostrils. The crops looked healthy, well protected. Someone planned well. Lily would learn here what fresh food looked like. She would do well here. He was not needed.

The curve of the hills combined with the storm

baffles would protect the area against the most powerful storm. This was a good place. Well designed for the modern climate. The shade of the woods called to him. A den up there might be pleasant. There was a train station not too far away for emergency food. Or he could try bartering with the people here. They seemed like they might accept a day in the fields as payment.

"Wisp?"

He startled. His mind had been so far away in possibilities that he hadn't felt Nick return.

"Angus would like to talk to you."

"He is your leader?"

"Sort of."

The tension of earlier had been replaced with worry. Nick seemed weighed down by thoughts that spiral up into alarm and back down to concern.

Wisp followed Nick into the building. There were a lot of people here. Not so many that they weighed too heavily on his mental barriers, but enough that living in this building would be uncomfortable. Nick led the way through wide hallways, brightly lit and ornamented with children's drawings. Classrooms had been converted into residences and offices. The use of the space seemed well managed. A few people glanced at him in passing. Wisp was surprised at the lack of reaction. "No one seems disturbed by my presence."

"That's because they know that I wouldn't bring any danger into this place." Nick's tone inferred that he'd make sure that was true.

Nick took a sharp left into an office. A man in rumpled clothing stood at a desk, staring at papers laid out before him. He had unruly white hair and a slight hunch to his shoulders.

"Angus."

The man looked up, bright blue eyes refocusing from puzzlement to joy. "Ah! Our biobot!" A rush of excitement and wonder swirled around him. "Please."

He gestured to a sitting area, several mismatched armchairs arranged around a battered coffee table.

Wisp sat in a leather armchair that felt strongly of Nick. There was a tray on the table with mugs of coffee and plates of pie, a wonderfully convivial setting. Wisp hesitated, expecting the worst, but the undiluted joy that Angus exuded was hard to dismiss.

"Coffee, yes!" Angus said with a happy grin. "And Susan has graced us with a pie from the last of the strawberries. I'm sorry to say no milk or sugar. We don't have a cow and our stock of the sweet stuff is perilously low."

"I haven't had coffee in years," Wisp said as he sniffed the aromatic steam. "I didn't think anyone was eating fresh food anymore."

"So Nicky tells me." Angus was handing around the mugs and pie when a fourth man joined them. "This is Martin. He is the head of our Watch and bursting with questions."

Wisp nodded to the man. He wondered if Angus was a bit gifted because he was absolutely right about Martin. The man barely hid his anger and distrust. But he did contain it, purely out of respect for Angus. Wisp felt the strong connections to Angus in both Nick and Martin. They both held deep affection and respect for the older man. As Angus was in charge, this would be a discussion, not an interrogation. Wisp relaxed a little and let himself enjoy the food. The coffee was lovely. The pie, excellent. But the tension in the room was rising.

"What do you wish to know?" Wisp asked.

"Everything!" Angus said with a laugh. "But I will have to restrict myself to the here and now, eh?"

Angus felt decent, honorable. There was almost a sparkle to the feel of him, light, giddy, and yet underneath the strength of bedrock. Wisp believed that he strived to know everything. The man had an insatiable curiosity constrained only by an equally boundless respect for the world. Wisp felt that as long as Angus retained power as head of this settlement, Wisp would be safe. He gave Angus a nod of acknowledgment.

Martin opened his mouth, but Angus waved to cut him off. "Let me get all the awkward questions out of the way." He looked to Wisp as if for permission.

"Ask."

"What were you made for?"

"I was not designed for a specific purpose." Wisp felt a swirl of uneasiness pass through Nick. Distrust ratcheted up in Martin.

"Excellent. How old are you?"

"Fifteen."

"What? How long do they live?" Martin asked. Astonishment colored his distrust.

Angus tsked at him with an amused smile. "They may have been built, not born, but I assure you that they are entirely human. Something certain factions tried very hard to play down." He shook his head, his mouth twisting with distaste. "Built. Never liked that term. Makes it sound like you were put together from spare parts."

"Cooked?" Martin offered. His shoulder twitched as his unease cranked up. He blinked, looking away as a flashback burst out. It was powerful enough that the images lingered, bleeding into the room. Wisp had a harsh flash of rows of burned out tanks, half formed bodies rotting on the floor. Martin had been to one of the raided labs. The disgust and anger was hard to decipher. Wisp wasn't sure if it was the process or the destruction that disturbed the man so deeply.

"God, that makes us sound like cannibals." Angus poked his mug in Wisp's direction. "What do you call it?"

"Printed."

"Hmph. Can't say I like that term much better. Makes you sound like a book."

"You're sure there isn't something else added?" Martin asked Angus. Wisp sensed that he doubted the facts but not the man.

"Absolutely. There was some tinkering done with DNA, but it was all human to begin with. Tell me, Wisp, I'm so curious, have you grown at all?"

"I have. But only a few inches."

"I knew it!" Angus was extremely pleased with himself. "They said you were all full grown, but the body has its own imperatives, doesn't it? No one gave it enough time. No one *waited* to see how you would mature. I would love to have more data on this. I knew that the human body would grow and age regardless of the claims put forth."

Wisp felt them sizing him up. Angus's words had layered a new worry into the mix. Neither Martin nor Nick was sure of the implications of the information they were getting. Wisp wanted them to calm down. He gave them a minute to come to their own conclusions. Whether he grew another inch in a few years wasn't going to endanger the settlement. He sat quietly, passive, accepting.

"So." Angus broke the silence. "You are one of the older ones. What lab?"

"Hendricks."

There was a heavy silence after that. Wisp could feel the distrust and a thread of anger welling up in Martin. Nick was thinking hard, perhaps trying to remember the rumors and reputation the Hendricks Labs accrued.

"Not Cyrillic?" There was a touch of alarm in Angus.

"Greek."

"Ah! Excellent. And your designation?" The alarm melted away, thawed by the onslaught of curiosity.

"Tau."

"Well, that's a relief. Hendricks did have some rather unstable creations." Angus was pleased, but Martin and Nick remained unsure. "He created in batches if I remember correctly. I never understood how they were able to design a person to order."

"It was not an exact science," Wisp offered. Angus leaned forward eager for information. "He designed for increased intelligence, but the specific skill came after awakening. He could design a dozen geniuses, but they might all be mathematicians or neurosurgeons. There wasn't any way of telling until we began acquiring knowledge and communication skills."

"Born as an adult," Angus said with a touch of awe in his voice. "I can't imagine how that shapes the psyche." He shook his head and leaned back into his chair. "So tell me about your generation, the Greeks."

"Not many of my brothers were retained. The ones that were kept were already reserved by their keepers."

"Brothers?" Angus's curiosity piqued. If that was possible. Wisp almost smiled. The man was bubbling with eagerness. "Please, tell me about them."

"Khi went to the army. He is a biologist. Epsilon went to a private institute. His specialty is patterns. Lambda is a neurosurgeon. He went to the Navy. Theta went to a hospital, but his gift is linguistics."

"That's four and you make five. The Greek alphabet contains 24 letters. What of the others?"

"Some did not achieve life. Some didn't thrive. Some were not as expected, and they were terminated." The word came out harsher that he'd intended. His audience went still. Startled. There was the brief taste of emptiness, minds stunned beyond feeling for a fleeting second.

"What does that mean?" Angus's bubbling joy guttered with disbelief.

"Executed." Wisp said softly. He was surprised at

the emotion that rose with his explanation. A gunshot and the smell of blood. An aching loss and fury. The potency of the flashback unsettled him.

"Awful," Angus barked. He threw up a hand in disgust. "Reprehensible! The man was insane. It's no wonder his own creations killed him off."

Wisp held back a smile. It wasn't his generation that ended the man, but it was satisfying all the same. "Ocho."

"Yes." Angus pointed at him. "It was the Spaniards. His last generation."

"You don't look Greek," Martin's voice was as heavy with suspicion as his mind.

"I'm not. It is simply the counting system for our generation."

"And what is your gift?" Angus asked. His mind swelling again with that ineffable buoyancy.

Wisp hesitated. Not many people called them gifts. "I'm a double E."

"Fabulous!" Angus jumped to his feet. "Fascinating. I will have a million more questions for you."

Wisp thought that maybe Angus's questions would be fun. But the other men in the room were not as happy.

"What does that mean?" Martin asked. Nick was jittery with suspicion, but Martin was on the verge of anger again.

"Extrasensory Enhancement!" Angus crowed. "Oh, this is going to be wonderful!" He started away only to jerk back. He shook a finger at Wisp, his eyes alive with mischief. "But Hendricks didn't believe in that. He never tried for double Es."

Wisp measured the feelings and the facts. He couldn't wait too long, or they would think he was plotting. Did it matter anymore? With his strength and training, he could easily disable Martin and Nick and be in the hills before others were alerted. But that was unlikely to happen here. Angus would not want that to happen here. He chose to answer Angus honestly. “No. I was an error. That's why I was slated for termination.”

Chapter 17

"Hospitals were the first to suffer from the devolving of distribution networks. Great gaps had developed in industry from the sudden demise of so many people. All the way up the line from delivery men to truck drivers and packers, back to the manufacturers themselves. There weren't enough hands to do the jobs and food, medicines and materials stopped moving across the country."

History of a Changed World, Angus T. Moss

Who am I? Mm, mmm, me. Not right, but close. Another morning of cotton-headed numbness. She opened her eyes to absolute darkness. Even through the numbness, she felt a slight thrill of fear. This was out of the ordinary.

The lights came on flashing bright against the white walls. That was right. But she still felt off. Her arm ached. A tiny spot of blood on the sleeve of her pale green shirt brought a bad feeling on. Something she didn't like. Something wrong. But she couldn't remember what it meant.

She put her feet on the floor. Cold. The bed was warm. The floor was cold. She wanted to get back under the blanket and sleep. But when the lights were on, she should be awake. That was a rule, but she didn't know whose.

"Tile." Sometimes saying the words out loud were the only sounds she heard. Her voice was dry and scratchy. As she stood, a wave of dizziness hit. The white walls blurred, sliding past her eyes. She sat down breathing hard. Again that bad feeling rose up. Something wrong. Something she didn't like. *Make them stop!*

Them?

Stop what? Those thoughts were too slippery to hold on to. They darted into her head and away before she could fully grasp their meaning.

"Them." Saying the word out loud didn't help. She couldn't remember who *them* was or why she wanted them to stop. Or what they did that she did want them to not do. Thinking about it made her feel queasy.

She stood more carefully this time and shuffled over to the lavatory. The faucet squeaked. Water splashed into the sink. Normal morning noises calmed her trepidations, but a shiver of wrong still wobbled in her brain. She had woken in the dark. That hadn't happened before. The lights were always on when she opened her eyes in the morning. Listening and looking found nothing out of the ordinary in her small white room with the gray floor. Over the sink was more white wall. Today that didn't seem right. She touched the smooth white surface. Just wall. There had always just been wall. Why did she think there would be something else?

She was already seated and waiting when the food door opened. She wasn't usually waiting when the food arrived. Or was she? Waiting didn't feel right, but she couldn't imagine what else she would be doing. Sleeping, eating and trying to remember who she was took up all of her time. The tray made its scratchy noise as it slid over the shelf. That sounded familiar, but something had changed. It wasn't right. A bottle of water and a white package was all that sat on the tray. She stared at the items unsure of them. There were no good smells from the tray. That was wrong, too.

Her arm ached when she reached for the bottle. A large bruise in the crook of her elbow showed when she pushed up her sleeve. Dark colors that clashed against the paleness of her skin. That was wrong. The bad feeling came back a little stronger. Something had been taken from her. Something very important. But thinking made her head ache. And the white package caught her attention again.

She drank water and ate the crunchy bars that were in the package. They were sweet. Chewing them was noisy. It almost made her laugh, how loud the sound of her food was. The tray sat in front of the little door for a long time. Usually the tray went away after she ate. Or so she thought. After food...breakfast, the tray went away and clean clothes came through the little door. She waited, but no clothes came. She tapped on the door, but nothing happened.

Waiting became tedious. Time stretched long and weary before her. The room felt smaller suddenly. And she noticed new things. Her bed was a mattress on a steel shelf. Something about that seemed very familiar, but out of context. The door was flush to the wall and she couldn't say whether it might open in or out. She couldn't remember ever seeing the door open. But that couldn't be right. She wasn't born in this room.

Born.

The word opened up a chain of memories. Misfitting images of people and places dashed in and out of her head tantalizing and confusing. Faces that looked so sweet it brought tears to her eyes. Rooms that she was sure she must have seen once. She tried to pin them down, to find names and feelings to go with the shattered images. It only made her head hurt more.

She paced the room wondering how much time had passed since breakfast. She counted her footsteps, laying one bare foot exactly in front of the other on the cold tile floor. Walking slowly to the wall until her nose touched the cool surface. Turning, she put her back against the wall and started back. She got the same number every time, but counted again, just in case it might somehow change.

Chapter 18

"In some parts of the country money became obsolete overnight. It no longer stood for anything. People's needs had changed. They wanted safety above all else. And with the drastic drop in population, goods were easily acquired without money. Stores and homes were empty, unattended. Once could walk in and take whatever was needed."

History of a Changed World, Angus T. Moss

"But you ran away," Angus said with full certainty.

"Yes." It was close enough to the truth. Wisp didn't want to go into the details of how that had been arranged.

"Because you knew it was coming!" Angus added cheerfully. His supposition about Wisp's skills set off a ripple of reaction in the other two men.

"Are you reading our minds now?" Martin demanded. Anger steamed off him with a dark thread of outrage twisting through it.

Wisp kept his voice level and calm. “No. I deduced it, and one of my brothers overhead the preparations. I'm more empath than telepath. And I can't feel anything at a distance.”

“We were about a mile from Riverbank when he warned me that there was trouble,” Nick added. A glimmer of pride flavored his statement. Wisp wasn’t sure what to think about that.

“A mile!” Angus was wide eyed.

“There were many people, very frightened.” Wisp chose his words carefully. “That...large of a...an exertion of energy is easily located.”

“But he couldn't tell me how many people,” Nick added.

“No. The fear blanketed the underlying emotions. If they had been calmer, I might have sensed the people that didn't fit.”

“Yes. A tragedy. A whole settlement wiped out. Just these few left, Nicky? No one else?” Angus took his seat again. His joy had cooled to concern.

“They left a trail of bodies. It wasn't a very big group to start with.”

“We left no one living behind,” Wisp assured them.

“Please, start at the beginning,” Angus asked.

Nick began with the fire in Clarkeston.

“We sent a crew,” Martin interjected. “You think these mercenaries set the fire?”

Nick gave him a hesitant nod. “Maybe to burn down the house where they killed Iris?”

“That's cold.” Martin's anger had banked down to resentment. “Set fire to a house in a settlement? This time of year with the winds so unpredictable? Reckless.”

“They killed off a settlement and tortured a child,” Nick snapped back. “They're monsters.”

“Why?” Angus asked. “What did they want?” He was suddenly bereft. The loss of so many lives weighing heavily on him.

"The notebooks, I assume," Nick said.

Wisp felt all the attention turn to him. "I can only feel intent. The men had a mission. They were concerned with achieving their goals. I cannot tell you what those goals were."

Angus walked over to his desk and picked up a small notebook. "Then I will have to agree with Nick. It was because of this. I've been through these, and I think they were written by the person who released the virus."

Martin didn't react. It was obvious Angus had already spoken to him. Nick shook his head, skepticism growing. "How could that hold any importance now?" Nick asked.

"I don't know, Nicky." Angus's words carried a weight of emotion—frustration, concern, grief. He pointed across the room to a family tree worked out on one of the whiteboards that lined the walls. "Lily and William may be all that is left of this family. But I don't understand why anyone would want to kill them."

Martin's anger ratcheted up. He gave Nick an angry glance. "Were the mercenaries human?"

"What?" Nick asked, momentarily baffled.

Martin shot a smoldering glance at Wisp.

"Ah, Martin, you have insufficient facts. The virus kills us all because we are all human." Angus said in a soothing voice. "There might be animosity, or even a thirst for revenge among our newest brethren, but *think*, how could they field a small army like this? There aren't enough of them left. There's barely enough of us. That's why this just doesn't make any sense to me."

Nick turned to Wisp, an honest question in him. "What do you think?"

He didn't want to say. He'd been giving it thought since he'd felt William through the compass. Despite turning the problem over in his mind dozens of times, he only had supposition. “They hunted children. I have no doubt they wanted to kill them. They tortured and killed without compunction to find Lily. A little girl. Easily captured, easily held. But to kill, not hold? The way they hurt William says they didn’t care if he survived. You say she and William may have some connection to the person who released the virus. That information would only be of interest to someone who is working in that field.”

A spike of unease shot through Martin. “Have we gotten this year's vaccine, yet?”

Angus let out a breath as though he'd been punched. “No.”

Chapter 19

"As the population had dispersed, it eventually began to drift back together. Human beings are hardwired to form families, tribes and clans. Before the med centers were established, people came together around a central unit such as a train station or church. Small groups eventually coalesced into communities. Without a national oversight and no way to track people, the possibilities for inbreeding becomes worrisome."

History of a Changed World, Angus T. Moss

Wisp could tell that the men wished to confer without him present, and yet didn't want him wandering around on his own. "Is there a place where I could dress this wound?" he asked.

Angus's curiosity snapped into annoyance. "Nicky, why didn't you say he'd been injured? And look at you. Is that blood in your hair? You must go down to the infirmary at once."

"Doctors don't treat my kind," Wisp said. He felt

the need to offer them a way out. An option to turn him away.

"Nonsense." Angus waved it away. "We treat horses and chickens and people."

"You have chickens?" Wisp asked.

"I will give you a tour once you're patched up." Angus eyed his bloody bandana. "That doesn't look very sanitary. Off you go."

Nick led him down the hall. Wisp looked up at the sunlight pouring in through the skylights. Nearby a group of elders sitting together, with busy hands, felt content. Somewhere children were playing. A scent of food cooking wafted by on the cooled air of the hallway."This is a good settlement."

"Thanks. Angus started it. He's the beating heart of it."

"A very kind man."

Nick stopped, head down, arms folded. Questions boiled around him. He hesitated to ask and yearned so badly to know. "Ask," Wisp said.

"*Can* you read minds?"

"Sometimes in the proper circumstances. But I am a trained observer. Sometimes I can intuit a want or a question. That isn't telepathy. It's a study of body language and micro expressions."

"Who trained you?"

Wisp hesitated for a second. He felt he should trust Nick. "Ten years of hiding."

Nick gave him a quick nod, the corner of his mouth curling in chagrin. He stared at Wisp, not ready to let go of his abiding concerns. "What are the proper circumstances?"

"I spend most of my time trying to keep people *out* of my head." He paused, waiting for the words to register with Nick. "Imagine a crowded room with everyone talking at the same time. You can't hear the words, but you can feel the sentiment. This one's angry, that one's happy, or hungry or in pain. That's the way it feels when I am around a group of people." Wisp wasn't sure if that helped Nick. His curiosity hadn't dimmed a bit. "Even up close, singled out, with time and quiet, I can't hear more than a person is willing to share."

"Really." Nick didn't sound like he believed him.

"When we were speaking of terms—built, cooked, printed—Martin had a memory. It was charged with high emotion. He'd been at a lab, probably not long after the riots. I saw what he saw and felt his disgust. The conversation triggered a powerful image. He relived that moment and sort of broadcasted it. But I don't know how, or why he was there. I don't know if he destroyed the lab or fought to defend it. He could have been a bomber or search and rescue. I have a single image out of context, wrapped in reaction. It tells me nothing. Like walking past a man on the street and hearing a piece of a conversation."

"Huh." Nick continued down the hall with a gesture for Wisp to follow. Wisp could tell Nick wasn't fully satisfied, but his distrust was simmering down into a gradual acceptance.

Wisp saw a doctor, who didn't seem the least bit upset at working on a biobot. He was competent, quickly cleaning and closing the wound. Then Nick showed him the guest quarters, the showers and the cafeteria. Wisp's pack had been left on the bed in one of the small rooms. It appeared to be another lecture hall broken into smaller spaces. It was sparingly furnished with a bed, desk and armchair."You have a lot of guests?"

"A few traders. And we put newcomers here until we decide if they belong," Nick said. He leaned against the doorway as Wisp looked through his pack to see what they'd taken.

"And if you decide against them?"

"Haven't had to cross that bridge yet."

Wisp found everything was still in his pack. That meant they were fairly honest and not overly paranoid. "Am I required to stay here?"

Nick blinked at him in surprise. "No. But why not?"

Wisp tapped his temple. "Too many people. Although I would gladly take advantage of your showers and cafeteria, I can't stay in this building. I am too used to the quiet of isolation."

"We've got a field house. Just some chickens and the horse down there. It's safe."

"I would like to see it."

Nick glanced at an ornate clock hanging above the desk. "I want a shower, too. And clean clothes. I'll meet you back here in about an hour?"

Wisp nodded. He wanted to trust Nick. He'd like to stay and answer questions for Angus. The settlement seemed like a very pleasant place to live, but they had no defenses. A couple of armed men on the road seemed woefully inadequate. If the mercenaries figured out who had taken the children, they'd come here. Wisp listened to the river of emotion in the settlement. There was a sweet top note of contentment. He thought back to the keening despair that had bludgeoned him at Riverbank. He didn't want that to happen here.

Chapter 20

"The economy failed, and not many people noticed. Jobs, salaries, working for a living made an about face. When your day is filled with disposing of the dead, priorities change."

History of a Changed World, Angus T. Moss

Nick stood under the pounding hot water for an indecent amount of time. There was more than just dirt to wash away. He wanted to eradicate the dead bodies, the blood, the gunfire. It wasn't going to vanish under the water the way mud could be sluiced down the drain. He shut the taps with an angry twist. Things had been just about perfect. High Meadow had food and water and storm shutters. The people here were as normal as could be now a days. He enjoyed going off looking for clues for Angus. It had been a quiet idle. Now he had to think about rogue armies and sick bastards who hurt children.

He pulled on a clean shirt and since he was home, some shorts. "Just a couple days," he mumbled.

"For what?" Jean stood in the doorway, a curious smile on her face. She was also freshly showered and dressed in the ubiquitous cotton slacks and tee shirts that the train stations stocked from time to time.

He frowned at her, wondering how long she'd been watching him dress. Clean and rested, she looked like a different person from the one he'd seen bound and gagged at Riverbank. It struck him that she was young, mid-twenties, and rather attractive. Her hair was a curly, black cap and her brown eyes were almond-shaped giving her an exotic look. Nick tried to place her looks—Asian and something, or Polynesian, maybe some Indian. She raised an eyebrow, and he realized his scrutiny had become obvious. "A couple of day to rest," he said with a sigh. "Without guns or guys in black or anybody getting killed."

Her eyes went hollow. "Only a couple?" She licked her lips and swallowed. "You think they'll come here?"

"I don't know how they'd know who took the children. We should be safe, but it would be sheer stupidity not to prepare."

"I'm sorry."

"It's not your fault."

"Wisp will know. He'll tell us. He did it before. Twice, in fact. He rounded up the fishermen and some kids in the woods when some bandits came by. He felt them coming and warned us."

"And you believed him?"

Jean gave him a confused frown. "He was right. He's always helped us."

"How long have you known him?" Something wasn't adding up. "You guys haven't been there that long."

"Oh," a relieved smile softened her face. "Bruno's known him for awhile. Met him while he was looking for a new place. Our old settlement got kind of...weird. Wisp showed him the factory." She dropped her eyes to the floor. “He's really a finder. That's why Bruno said it was okay to send those bastards to him.”

“What?” Nick was shocked. “You told them about Lily?”

“We knew they'd never find him.”

“How could you know that?”

“Because he's Wisp. How do you think he got that name? I've seen him disappear in the middle of the road in broad daylight. Bruno said it. More than a whisper but less than a ghost. Like a wisp of fog when the sun comes up. We knew he'd protect the child. And we knew he'd escape.”

“Then why did they torture Bruno and his son?”

“Because Wisp was too good at disappearing.” Jean sagged against the doorway. “They were so angry when they came back and said his place was empty. They thought we were hiding him. I was glad they didn't get the little girl. I think we all hoped that somehow Wisp would know we were in trouble and come back to help us.” Tears slid down her face. “And he did.”

Nick didn't want to tell her it was a coincidence. That if they'd taken another route, Wisp wouldn't have felt the trouble. “I'm sorry we didn't get there sooner.”

She forced a smile. “I know there's a story there. He never had a car before. Or guns like that. And I know now that they aren't yours, either.”

“Yeah, there's a story. Let's go sit—”

“Bruno asked for you,” she cut him off.

“Sure.” Nick gestured for her to lead the way. They returned to the infirmary in silence. He didn't need to wonder where her thoughts wandered. She wiped tears away as they walked.

Chapter 21

"The government spent a lot of energy on trying to relocate people. Perhaps they used up their assets in the endeavor. When things were most grim, the government went silent."

History of a Changed World, Angus T. Moss

By the time they got to the infirmary, Bruno was asleep. The nurse said they had him on pain meds. Jean looked lost. Nick felt bad for her. Margaret and her offspring had been absorbed into the tribe of other mothers at the settlement. They had a place with people who understood them. Lily and William had been easily pulled under their wings. Jean was neither mother nor wounded. It put her in the awkward position of unexpected houseguest.

"Are you and Bruno..." Nick made a vague gesture, unsure of where he was going with the question.

"No." Jean shook her head. "It wasn't like that. I'm actually kind of new to the group. But he was good to me. Took me in and let me stay." She stared at the floor as a long minute unfurled between them.

"I promised to take Wisp down to the field house, would you like to come along?"

"Yes."

Nick gave her an encouraging smile and led her out of the infirmary.

Wisp was standing in the hallway outside his room when they approached. Nick waved him over. Wisp nodded to Jean. She sighed and tried to speak, then tightened her lips.

"I'm sorry." Wisp said in a gentle voice. Nick noticed that he didn't touch her. In fact, he moved a little away from her, too much emotion too close for comfort, maybe.

"Me, too," she said in a shaky voice.

Nick took them out into the heat of the day. He pointed out the grain fields and the vegetable plots. "We're still trying to figure out the right percentages. We got a potato harvest that lasted a couple weeks, but the beets lasted months. And we never seem to have enough wheat."

"But you're growing real food," Jean said, a note of wonder in her voice.

"Yeah. We were lucky. There's a hardware store in town that had racks of seeds. Most of them were too old, but we got some. And I was able to barter for some, too. Now we have to save our own. It hasn't been easy. We don't have a farmer among us."

"I'll help," she said.

"All help is welcome. What kind of skills have you got?" Nick asked. He led them along the sidewalk toward the back of the fields.

"Oh." Jean's shoulders slumped. "Nothing really. I mean, at Riverbank they needed everything, you know? I did whatever needed doing. But I don't have any sort of skills."

"What did you do before Zero Year?" Nick asked.

He didn't usually pry, but thought maybe she wanted to talk.

"I worked for a..." she paused to breathe, swallow more tears, "...one of those companies that don't exist anymore. Data entry. Just punching numbers for a paycheck."

"Jean is a hard worker," Wisp said. "She is strong and diligent."

"Great." Nick squeezed her shoulder. "Look around. Take your time. Try different things. You'll find something that you like."

"Thanks."

Nick led them down to an area that was newly fenced with stakes and rope. A horse stood in the shade of a building, head hanging. Through a rough coat, his ribs showed.

"Is he sick?" Jean asked.

"Don't know. We haven't got a vet. Martin said he wandered in after the last storm. But if he lasted through the Hoofed Flu, I'd say it's something else. Maybe shock from being out in the weather."

Wisp ducked under the rope and approached the horse. He put gentle hands on him. "He's pining."

Nick tried to hide his surprise. "For what?"

Wisp looked out over the meadow toward a line of trees. "His herd."

"There's more?" Jean asked, excitement in her voice.

"More what?" Martin arrived with two men of the Watch in tow. Nick thought it was more than coincidence. "Where's he going?" They watched Wisp trot across the meadow toward a buffer of trees. "That area's not safe."

"Why not?" Jean asked.

"There's a brook on the other side of those trees. Floods with every storm. It's undermining the roots. A stiff breeze could bring those trees down. We don't let any of the kids in there."

Nick headed out after Wisp. "Better tell him." His movement acted like a magnet, bringing all the others trailing behind him. They walked across the meadow and into the slightly cooler shade of the trees. Nick saw a flicker of movement and worked his way through the undergrowth in that direction.

Wisp stood on a fallen tree, with his back to them, looking down the bank to the water. Nick called to him and a horse's neigh answered. Nick led the scramble to the edge of the bank. Below them a good ten feet, fallen trees and a minor mudslide had trapped three horses. They were muddy and dull eyed. And it broke his heart to see their weak struggles. "They'll die in there."

Martin sent one of the men back for power tools and more people. "We'll need to build a path, maybe some kind of ramp."

Wisp was gathering weeds and grasses and dumping them over the edge to the starving animals. Jean joined him, pulling handfuls of greenery. Nick watched the horses. They were so badly stressed and the presence of strangers wasn't helping. "They're terrified."

Wisp shook his head. "No. They're uneasy, but they are used to people. Not wild animals. Their hunger is topmost. They can put up with unreasonable restraint if there is food."

Nick went over to Martin, who was climbing around the site. "What do you think?"

Martin pointed to the trees that had fallen like pickup sticks. "We'll need to cut through a couple of these. Maybe we can build up the dirt here, cut down into the bank there..."

Nick saw a whole day of work with no profit. The horses were basically large pets. They didn't produce food or energy or security. They would require food the settlement didn't have and care no one knew how to give.

"You're wrong," Wisp said quietly. "You can use them for security. A mounted guard moves faster than a man running in rough terrain. And the manure would be good for the crops."

"You read my mind," Nick grumbled.

"You feel disapproving."

"One more thing to take on. Another thing we don't know how to do."

"They came from somewhere." Wisp moved past Nick, negotiating slippery steps down to the edge of the water. "Upstream, probably. There must be a farm. Maybe there are people who know how to care for them."

Nick looked back to the horses. A group of people came through the trees. They carried tools and rope and some had armloads of freshly cut grass. The lone horse in the meadow called high and longing. The trapped horses called back weakly.

"Martin," Nick shouted to him. "We're going to take a look." He pointed a thumb over his shoulder.

Martin looked puzzled. "Be careful!"

Wisp was already down in the creek bed when Nick turned back. He slid down the muddy, mossy bank into the water. In another couple weeks, this would go totally dry.

Wisp turned to him, a slight smile on his face. "He doesn't doubt your abilities."

Nick snorted. "Yes, he does."

"You're reading it wrong. Martin considers you irreplaceable. He has a high aversion for your job. He doesn't want to have to take it on himself."

"Huh. Good to know," Nick grumbled. But he felt a secret glee at knowing Martin didn't think he could do Nick's job.

They hiked through ankle high water or from boulder to boulder. Every now and then, Wisp would stop, close his eyes and get very still. When he did that, Nick tried to empty his mind, hoping that would take him off Wisp's radar.

Twenty minutes later, they found the carcass of a dead horse. It was halfway down the bank, crushed under a massive tree. Nick and Wisp had to climb through the branches to continue up the river. Once on the other side, Wisp headed up the opposite bank. Many of the trees had come down, making a steep climb almost impenetrable. By the time they got to the top, Nick was muddy to the waist and dripping sweat. They came out in a horse pasture. The fencing had all been knocked down. More trees had fallen here. In the distance, he could see the wreckage of a couple buildings. Nick followed Wisp across the pasture to the rubble.

"Someone is here."

"Is that good or bad?"

"I feel no ill intent."

Wisp led him around the pile of wood that might have been a barn to the remains of an old house. The upper floor was missing. An ancient stone foundation stood with a make shift lean-to built within.

"Hello?" Nick called out.

An old man made his way slowly up the uneven steps, a shotgun loose in his hands. "What do you want? Nothing here for you."

"We've come to ask your help," Wisp said. Nick looked at him in surprise. The old man was scrawny and dirty. He was limping, obviously in pain. And equally obviously the one that needed help. But he followed Wisp's lead.

"I can't help anyone."

"We found some horses," Nick said.

"My boys? You found my boys? And Molly?"

"They're trapped in the river. We're working on getting them out now. But the settlement doesn't know about horses. We need someone to tell us what to do."

"They're mine!"

"Of course. But they're half starved and hurt from being washed down the river. Once we get them out, shouldn't they rest a little before they come back here?"

Nick didn't need Wisp's skills to see the old man's sadness. His shoulders slumped and the gun slid down. This place was destroyed, no longer safe for man nor beast. Nick moved forward slowly. "I'm Nick."

"Harley," the old man said holding out a hand in his general direction. Nick took it, noting that Harley was probably blind.

"Can you come back to the settlement with us?" Nick asked.

"Settlement? I don't know about that. Don't much care for those places."

"It's a good one," Wisp offered. "I've seen a lot. This is better than most."

"For Molly and the boys?" Nick asked.

"Well, just for them." Harley limped a few more steps. "Gonna need the tractor. I ain't getting very far with this leg." He pointed to a recessed garage that held a tractor and a workshop. It spoke to the man's character that his equipment had better housing than he did.

Under Harley's shouted instruction, Nick managed to hook up a wagon to the tractor. Wisp loaded the wagon with hay and all the horse medicines in the shed. Nick got it started and brought it around to the front. He helped Harley into the wagon while Wisp took a look through the lean-to. He came out with empty hands. Nick drove the tractor out to the road, heading for the settlement.

Chapter 22

"For the first few years, each time the virus retreated, people believed that might be the end of it. Then each summer, as the virus resurfaced, a collective depression fell upon the country."

History of a Changed World, Angus T. Moss

"It's good to get to know one of our neighbors," Nick said. The tractor bumped along at a sedate pace. At this rate it might take over an hour to ride back around.

"I pretty much keep to myself," Harley grumbled.

Nick looked him over. The old man was too thin. His clothes were worn and dirty. He needed help. "Well, maybe you can stay with us till the horses are fit to travel."

"I'd be fine bedding down with them. I been worried sick about them."

"There was one that didn't make it," Wisp said.

"Was he a gray?"

"Yes."

“That's old Chester. He don't move very fast.” Harley sighed. His lips tightened, and he blew out a shaky breath.

“A tree came down on him. I'm sure he was killed instantly,” Nick offered.

“Good to hear he didn't suffer.” Harley wiped at his eyes. “I figured if they were okay they'd find their way home. As soon as my leg got a little better, I was going to go looking for them.”

Nick looked at the bloody bandage that showed below the cuff of Harley's pants. “How bad's that leg?”

“It's fine. Where are we going?”

“The high school.”

“Huh. That's where you folks got your settlement? I heard there was somebody setting up nearby.”

“It's a good space,” Nick said. “We've got power and water, storm shutters, and it's not too far from the train station.”

“And you're all eating that train station food aren't ya?” Harley asked with a tone of disgust.

“Actually we're trying to grow our own.”

“Are ya now?”

“But you know we're a bunch of city folk. Maybe we can barter with you for some help,” Nick suggested.

“Don't know what you got that I might want,” Harley said cagily.

Nick glanced at Wisp, hoping for a hint.

“Clean sheets, fresh baked bread, hot coffee,” Wisp said.

“You got coffee?” Harley asked eagerly.

“Sometimes,” Nick admitted. “We trade with a settlement that specializes in tea and coffee.”

“Don't suppose you folks got any whiskey?”

Nick chuckled. “Haven't found a source for that yet, but we do have some beer.”

“Oh, what I wouldn't give for a good cold beer some nights! You boys got yourselves a deal.”

* * *

By the time the tractor bumped across the campus to the meadow, the horses had been brought up from the river. They stood clumped together, facing a group of people with buckets and rags. As the tractor approached, all four horses raised their heads to look. Then they called out in high pitched whinnies.

"That's my boys!" Harley said. "I'm coming!"

Nick helped him down.

Martin came over. "They won't let us near them. The one in the middle is hurt."

Harley ignored him and headed right over to his horses. He patted necks and shoulders, clucking and murmuring to them. Once he got them settled, he accepted the help of a couple of people to wash off the mud and treat the injuries. With him close by, the horses were more amenable to strangers approaching them.

Nick saw Angus on the edge of the crowd. He and Wisp walked over.

"Amazing creatures, aren't they?" Angus asked with a pleased smile. "I'm so glad we were able to help."

"Harley's house has been destroyed," Nick said as Martin joined them. "I get the feeling he might not want to stay here with us. But he's willing to barter some farming expertise for beer."

Angus laughed. "Excellent! We will have to tell our brewers to work harder!"

"He can't go back if it's not safe," Martin said.

"What of the neighborhood?" Wisp asked. "Are there no habitable houses in the area?"

Angus looked out over the school grounds. "When I started this place, most of the people were fleeing. Running away, running to, God knows where. The school still has plenty of room for people. We haven't needed to look into alternative housing."

"What of the other neighbors?" Wisp asked. "Up in the woods."

Martin spun to look at him. "Who?"

Wisp shrugged. He pointed toward the line of trees on the far side of the fields. "I felt them as we came down into the valley.

Martin frowned. "I wasn't aware there was anyone up there."

"Well perhaps they don't want to meet us," Angus said.

"Harley might know of them," Nick said. "He said he'd heard of us. Must talk with someone."

"Everyone should be warned of the mercenaries," Wisp said.

Nick looked at Martin. "He's right. We should make the rounds and tell anybody we find that they can take shelter with us."

"Take shelter?" Martin barked. "You want to bring half the countryside in? We'll have enough trouble taking care of our own."

Wisp raised a hand to interject. "If they are content to remain in their homes despite a comfortable med center in their midst, there is every reason to believe that they will wish to remain in their homes regardless of the situation. However, if you warn them of the armed men, offer assistance, or food in exchange for warning, you may make new allies."

"Well said!" Angus said. "We need to do that, Martin. Let's put together a nice friendly group, some women, a couple of youngsters. We will not look too formidable that way. Wisp can tell you where these people are. We can make contact, introduce ourselves. We see plenty of strangers at vaccine time. It never occurred to me that some of them might live around here. "

Martin looked nonplussed. "Angus I don't think—"

“We have to,” Angus said firmly. “If what Nicky has told us is true, these men are brutes. I can't even call them animals,” Angus gestured to the horses. “Because I would be insulting these noble creatures. We cannot beat them by force, so we must be smarter.”

Wisp whirled around to look back at the horses.

“What?” Nick asked.

“Fear.”

One of the helpers ran to Angus. His clothes were wet and muddy. “It's Jean,” he burst out. “She's sick.”

Chapter 23

"Prejudices changed. Race and religion and all the other points of contention were no longer at issue. It came down to whether you appeared healthy or not."

History of a Changed World, Angus T. Moss

Wisp felt the fear spread like fire in dry grass. There was a helplessness behind it. He understood that. Despite the vaccines, a portion of the population succumbed every year. He had doubts that any of the medicines worked. It might just be a placebo to calm a terrified country.

Jean was taken to the infirmary with Angus clucking at their heels like a mother hen. He soothed the panic and sent people back to work. The distraction of Harley and his horses had been a welcomed one. Wisp felt people fall back into the ruts of their most recent concerns. This group worried about food, that one about illness, and the one around Martin worried most about attack.

That was something he could help with. Wisp slipped into the woods. For the rest of the day, he walked the far perimeter of the school. It felt good to be out on his own again. There were few people in the area beyond the school. He avoided contact and just made note of who was where. They all seemed to belong. None of the people he observed had the feel of a scout. A hunter here, a hermit there and luckily for Harley, a possible moonshiner. Solitary people, but none with ill intent.

It was full dark when he made his way back to the school. He ghosted past Martin's guards. That needed a little work. As he approached the front of the school, he saw Nick sitting on the steps.

“Where did you go?” There was concern in his question, but no accusation.

“To check the neighborhood. I didn't find anything alarming.”

“Good. Hungry?”

Wisp nodded. “I've got something for the kitchen,” he said holding up a sack.

“Susan will be excited.” Despite his words, Nick seemed unsure.

The cafeteria had just a few people lingering over coffee. It was later than he’d thought. Nick brought Wisp back into the small office off the kitchen. “Susan, have you met Wisp, yet?”

Susan's smile froze when she saw his tattoo. “Um.” She was startled. Her eyes darted to Nick for a clue.

“He's got a contribution for you,” Nick's tone was light and encouraging.

“Oh? What is it?” She eyed the sack uneasily.

Wisp stepped over to a counter and dumped out the contents. He'd foraged as he moved through the woods. It was second nature. This time he took more than he would have for just himself. “Mushrooms, cress, Lamb's Quarters, wild garlic.” He identified each item as he sorted it out of the sack. “There's a house not far from here that had a large vegetable garden. It's all gone to seed. There are some small plants struggling. I think you could dig them up.”

“Wonderful,” Susan poked through the bounty. Her alarm had been dissolved with the gift of food. “This will be a nice change. We've had tomatoes and peppers up to here. Seems to be the only thing we're doing right.”

“I'll go take a look at that garden tomorrow,” Nick offered. “We can harvest anything that's ready and try to gather some seeds.”

“That would be great. Thanks so much. Take Lottie with you. She's the closest we've got to a farmer.” She raised her eyes a little hesitantly to Wisp. “Thank you, too.”

“Got any dinner left?” Nick asked quickly cutting off her uneasiness. “He hasn't eaten.”

“I'm sure we've got something.” She jumped into action happy to be in her usual role of kitchen goddess. She filled a plate for Wisp and joined them when they settled at a table.

“Any word on Jean?”

“Angus says it must be a new strain.”

“From the horses?”

“They aren't sick,” Wisp said between mouthfuls. The food was well prepared. They even had salt.

“Then she brought it with her?”

Nick glanced at Wisp. He was uneasy. “The mercenaries?”

Mouth full, Wisp shook his head before swallowing. “I did not sense illness in any of them, but it is possible that they could have been carriers. Or the children. Or any of the people from Riverbank. That was an open settlement. I know that they were bartering freely with people from High Bluffs and Cold Water.”

Susan sighed. “So it could have come from anywhere.”

“Even me,” Nick admitted. “I'd been to High Bluffs and Clarkeston. The fire there could have been scared people burning out some sick folks. It's happened before. I figured it was the mercenaries.” He shrugged.

Angus joined them. He was deeply saddened and underneath a thread of fear. “I sent a message to the vaccine center.”

“Looks like bad news,” Nick said.

“They haven't responded yet.”

“That's unusual.”

“Very.”

“How's Jean?” Susan asked.

“She's doing well. Low fever and some dizziness. I think she must have some immunity to this one. Otherwise we could be looking at a very mild virus this year.”

“Is that too much to ask for?” Susan said sharply. “Every year we wait in terror wondering when it's going to wipe us all out. We deserve a break!”

“I'm so sorry to say that nature doesn't much care about us, Susan. Someone was messing around with natural systems. Now those systems are only trying to get back to what was normal. We don't get a lot of say in that.”

“It isn't fair.” Her voice was soft, but there was a burden of sadness below it. Tears stood in her eyes. “Excuse me, I need to plan something nice for Wisp's gift.”

“Gift?”

“I was foraging.”

“Excellent.” Some of Angus' spark returned. “You walk through the woods, and you see things you can use. That's marvelous. Did you visit with any of our neighbors?”

“No. I just observed on this trip.”

"Well done." Angus patted the table. "Although I think that we will wait before we contact any of them. With several flu cases—"

"Several?" Nick asked.

"Seems that some of the children were running mild fevers that no one noticed until Jean got sick. We have six people in the infirmary now."

"Six. And no response from the vaccine center."

Angus shook his head. Sadness settled around him again. "A cup of tea, I think," he said as he wandered off.

"Not good," Nick said.

"He's very worried," Wisp said in an undertone.

"He's not the only one."

Chapter 24

"The virus pared down the population in unexpected ways. The acutely ill were the first to go, as expected. It was when the chronically ill succumbed that statistics started to skew. In a matter of years, the remaining population was healthier than at any point in time—no diabetes, heart disease, asthma or other long term conditions."

History of a Changed World, Angus T. Moss

Nick could feel the tension in the air and wondered what it felt like for Wisp. Angus had called for a Council meeting in the cafeteria at breakfast. Between the new flu cases and word of the mercenaries, everyone was on edge. Meetings for the entire settlement were usually held in the small amphitheatre. The fact that he'd called it elsewhere just added to the worry. Nick looked around for Wisp, but wasn't surprised not to see him. He could probably feel this much tension from the other side of the fields.

Angus walked to the front of the room with a cup of tea in hand. He looked weary to Nick. “If I might have everyone's attention, please?”

Silence hit the room like a held breath.

“I wanted everyone to know that the new symptoms are posted on the newsboards in the hallways. Please come to the infirmary if you're feeling even a little off. This might be a very mild version this year, but we need to keep an eye on it anyway. That may be why we haven't received any vaccine as of yet. We'll stay on top of that.

“Also, Martin is looking for a few more volunteers for the Watch. Please let him know if you have some time to contribute.”

He paused to smile around the room. “We have a few guests in house. Harley,” Angus gestured to the man. Nick was glad to see that Harley was cleaned up and had a stack of empty dishes in front of him.

“Lily, and her brother William who is recuperating in the infirmary.”

Nick located the little girl in a group of children. Her hair was clean and braided, and she wore clean clothes. She smiled when she heard her name.

“And Wisp who does not seem to be with us at the moment.” Angus looked over to Nick.

“He's shy.” Nick said for lack of a better explanation. “And maybe a little claustrophobic.”

“Ah.” Angus gave him an understanding smile. “Well, let's try to make them all welcome. That's all for today” Angus bowed with a flourish and headed for Nick's table.

Nick sipped the last of his coffee. Angus sat with a grunt. “Ah Nicky, we need to talk.”

“Here?”

Angus looked into his teacup. “Probably not.”

Nick waited. He didn't have an office, so it would have to be in Angus's. The fact that he hadn't already said that was odd.

"Do you know where Wisp is?"

"I'm guessing out in the field house. With everybody so keyed up," Nick shrugged, "Probably giving him a headache."

"What a shame. He didn't get any of this lovely breakfast?"

"I don't know." Nick could feel something off in Angus.

"Well, let's bring him some."

Nick followed Angus as he collected a plate of food and a mug of coffee. Then they went out into the heat.

"What's the storm report for today?" Nick asked as he eyed the fluffy white clouds on the horizon.

"Oh, well, I haven't looked at that."

Nick shot a surprised look at Angus, but the man had walked away. Angus always checked the storm reports. It was one of the things that made this settlement safe.

As they approached the field house, Wisp stepped out the door.

"You knew we were looking for you," Angus said in greeting.

Wisp dipped his head in acknowledgement.

"Let's go back inside out of this heat."

Angus lead them down into the building that once held equipment storage, locker rooms and offices. He took them to a small office that had a desk and several chairs. He put Wisp's breakfast on the desk. "For you, Wisp. I didn't know if you'd eaten yet."

"Thank you. No, I haven't."

Nick noticed that Wisp smelled of a soap he didn't recognize. It was a small thing, but everyone in the settlement used the same soaps and shampoos, whatever they could barter for. Wisp smelled different.

"Thank you for your patience, Nicky. I know you have questions." Angus sat with a groan again.

Nick wondered if he was ill. That was a very worrisome thought. It wasn't until he questioned it that he realized how Angus' personality touched every aspect of the settlement. If he were to fall ill or worse, things might change radically. There wasn't anything set up to deal with that possibility. Nick felt a rush of annoyance followed by dread. They were fools playing at grander things than they understood. If the settlement lost Angus, would they be able to keep the dream going? That sobered Nick as he took a seat next to Angus. “No problem. I knew you'd get to it eventually.”

Angus folded his hands and stared at them. Nick looked to Wisp.

“Angus,” Wisp said in a soft voice, “speak the bad news, so we can help you make a plan.”

“I don't know if I can.”

Nick's heart started beating hard. “It's that bad?”

“The vaccine center is no longer on the ether.”

Not what he was expecting, but perhaps equally as dire. “Maybe it's just a glitch in the ether.”

“That's what I hoped yesterday when it disappeared.”

“What do you think it means?” Nick asked.

“In the short run, it means we may not get any vaccine this year. But if the flu is this mild, we might not need one. In the long run...” He shook his head looking lost. “I just don't know. Is it gone? Closed? We have a good stock of medicines for now, but if the ether dock is gone, how will we order more?”

A shiver ran up Nick's spine. The settlement seemed fairly self-sufficient. They had independent power and water as long as the current mechanisms didn't break. But they were still somewhat reliant on the train food, and totally reliant on the medicines from the vaccine center. Everything from antibiotics to bandages came from them. It was one of the givens in the new normal. Like the fact that anyone with chronic disease like diabetes or emphysema didn't survive the flus. The remaining population was the healthiest it had been in recorded history, which also might be coming to an end. Was anybody keeping those kinds of records anymore?

He thought of the dusty packs of food at the High Meadow station and the unlit lights on the rail lines. The food was good indefinitely. It made sense to redistribute it to an active station. But a worm of fear gnawed at him. He didn't know where that food was manufactured or by whom. What happened when there were too few hands do that work?

"You want us to find out what happened," Wisp said. Nick looked over. His plate was empty. He wondered how long the room had been silent.

"I don't know how." Angus knotted his fingers together. "I don't know what to do."

"You don't know where the vaccine center is?"

Angus slumped in the chair with a deep sigh. "I contact them on the ether. Post an order, and it shows up at the train station. I haven't had any contact with a person there in years."

"I know where my brother's lab is," Wisp said. "He is a biologist. He may be able to give us the information."

Angus perked up. "You know that his lab is still active?"

"I know that he is alive."

"How does that help?" Nick asked.

"Khi is owned by the army. If he is alive, he is being used for his abilities. Therefore, I assume he is working in a lab."

"The army?" Angus' blue eyes had their shine back. "That's excellent. Yes. If we could get in touch with him. Does he have an ether-dock?"

"Biobots aren't allowed to use the ether."

Angus huffed out angrily. “Honestly! Humanity as a bunch can be absolutely ridiculous.”

“Where's his lab?” Nick asked.

“Southwest of here near a town named Laurel.”

“I know of it. That'll take a couple days there and back.” Nick turned to Angus. “Wisp and I will head out to Laurel right away. We'll check in with his brother and find out what's going on. Maybe they're just changing systems or something.”

Angus reached over and squeezed Nick's arm. “You're too good to an old man! Nicky you have saved the day again. I have hope.” He stood up with a good deal more energy than Nick had seen all morning.

After he left, Nick looked at Wisp. “You up for this?”

Wisp nodded. “He is a good man.”

“He is.”

“Will the loss of the vaccines be so hard to bear?” Wisp asked.

“Many of us think that it is all that keeps us alive these days.”

“That is not true.”

“How can you know that?” Nick asked.

“How can you think that the vaccines are distributed equally across the country? There are settlements that never see them. And yet they survive.”

Nick stared at him. Obviously Wisp had seen more of the country that he had. “You've traveled?”

“The whole country. It is easier to avoid being found if you don't stay put.”

“What about Riverbank? They said you'd been around for awhile.”

“No one in that settlement hunts biobots.”

That simple statement chilled Nick. It put him back in the early days when the riots tore apart cities, and mobs killed anyone who looked a little odd. With the indiscriminant felling of people across the land, biobots had gotten loose. Some, like Wisp, went to ground. Others took revenge on the people who had held them as slaves. Or so it was reported. Horrible atrocities were chalked up as biobots out of control. In retrospect, Nick wondered if any of the crimes had been committed by them. News, like statistics, became more and more unreliable in those days.

Wisp looked away with a frown. “Trouble.”

Nick didn't even have time to respond before the storm siren went off. He ran to the door, debating whether he should stay here or go over to the main building. Harley passed him in the hallway leading in the horses. They were being stabled in a locker room for the time being.

“You guys have got this stuff pretty well under control, don't ya?” Harley asked Nick in passing.

“We've got people to keep an eye on the weather,” Nick said.

“It's a good thing.” Harley said with a wave. The horses snorted nervously. Their hooves clattering loudly against the tiled floor.

By the time Nick looked back outside, his decision was moot. Hail pounded the sidewalk in front of the doors.

“You are relieved that it is hailing?” Wisp asked.

Nick jumped. He hadn't heard him arrive. “Better than tornados.”

“This will delay our departure.”

Nick nodded absently, his mind already packing and prepping for the trip. “We'll need to change trains twice. The south branch doesn't go all the way to the southern line anymore.”

“You know the trains very well.”

“It's what I do. I travel a lot. How did you get across the country?”

“Walked.”

“That must have taken a long time.”

"Years."

Nick was shocked. He'd spent weeks wandering before he found Angus's settlement. That had seemed like a lifetime to him. But Wisp had spent years walking across the land avoiding people. It seemed very lonely.

The hail stopped as abruptly as it had started. Chunks of ice covered the grass and the sidewalks glistened in the sun. Nick went outside. Steam started rising from the grass as the hail melted in the fierce heat. He headed back to the main building to pack. An old van pulled in front of the building, battered by the hail. It had a broken windshield and several new dents. Two more vehicles pulled in behind it.

Martin met them on the steps. The crew that had gone to Clarkeston to fight fires had returned. Seeing strangers in the crowd, Nick wondered if they were visitors or new residents.

That would keep Martin busy while he got ready to travel.

Chapter 25

"The lack of information went unnoticed by most people as they were concerned with the simple necessities like food, water and shelter. No one wanted to stay where bodies remained, so every year when the flu hit, the population was on the move."

History of a Changed World, Angus T. Moss

Wisp hadn't unpacked, so it was simply a matter of retrieving his pack. He waited under the trees at the edge of the road to the train station. One of the parking lots had been stripped down to the soil to plant saplings. From the lines of them, Wisp assumed they were for food, fruit, maybe nuts. There were people here with forethought. That was reassuring. It was possible that there might be a place here for him. But that decision had to wait until this task was finished.

Nick arrived with his pack and a frown.

"You are worried."

"I don't know what this means. We don't get

enough information. We should be connected on the ether." Nick's frustration tumbled over into anger.

"To what purpose?"

"To know that we're not dying off!" Nick barked. The feather of fear in him grew heavier.

"The human race is very adaptable. It will change to survive."

"It is changing. You saw Lily's eyes. Nobody ever had eyes like that when I was growing up. Now I see kids with eye color that doesn't look human. It's scary."

"For most it is an indication that the viruses have infiltrated the body with new DNA."

Nick stopped walking. There was a trembling moment of anger and fear and confusion tumbling in him. "Could it be the vaccines? We don't know what's in them. They send them around each year, and we pump them into people, and we don't know what's in them."

"Lily is at least 10 years old. She may have been born before the virus was released."

Nick's fear was flattened with a wave of surprise. "She's been engineered?"

"That is not my area of expertise."

"What does that mean? She was changed somehow the year it was released?"

"Perhaps that wasn't the only virus. Or something more benign was released earlier that affected Lily's mother while she was pregnant. As I said, that is not my area of expertise."

"And you don't care?"

"Is Lily a threat?"

Nick frowned at him. "She's a little kid."

"She appears typical for her age and circumstance. I don't believe she is a threat. Therefore the possibility of changes in her DNA are not areas of concern for me."

"But it means someone was tinkering as Angus likes to say."

"I was printed fifteen years ago. Many people were *tinkering* at that point." Wisp started walking again.

Nick remained on the road behind him, thinking for another minute before he jogged up to Wisp. "But the vaccines and the train food, we just accept them as safe..."

"It does not make sense that a centralized organization of human beings that creates medicine and food to be distributed across the country would do so to the detriment of the population."

"No. I guess not. But they could be changing us." Nick's concern had a tinge of aversion to it.

"If it's to help you survive, isn't that a good thing?"

"Without asking?" Now indignation was the top note.

"If the only other option is death, do they need to ask?"

"Yes!" Nick said loudly, but there wasn't any anger behind the words. He was filled with a sadness and longing that Wisp understood intimately. But there was nowhere to go back to.

* * *

Wisp stretched out his senses as they approached the station. It was a convergence point and was most likely watched by someone. There were a few people around. Two in cubbies, settled, they might live at the station. Closer by, someone was hiding from them. It was a young person, male. He hid by the side of the road, fearful. Wisp stopped Nick with a hand on his arm. Nick scanned the area automatically. Good. He understood.

"There is a settlement an hour's walk that way." Wisp pointed down the road. "It is a safe place. Open to all. You can get shelter and food there. Medical help. They will not make you stay."

"Who is it?" Nick whispered.

"A child."

The sound of leaves crunching gave him away. A flicker of movement in the undergrowth and then silence.

"You think he'll go?"

"He is ill or injured. He needs help but fears it. I think he will find it in Angus."

"Wish we had a way to communicate. I could call Martin to pick him up."

"That wouldn't work. He must decide on his own that the settlement is safe."

Nick shrugged. He was worried about the boy now. It drowned out the melancholy, which was a relief to Wisp.

When they went into the station, Nick felt very curious. He checked the store room. It was well stocked. Then he went to the map. Wisp noted the dark stations. He knew the ones in the desert areas had closed because of a lack of people. Every time he crossed the country, he traveled north nearly to Canada to avoid the waterless wastes of the sun-blasted plains. There were more closed on the east coast than he remembered. Storms were still pounding the beaches, eating away at any towns that tried to stay. The map hadn't been redrawn since the virus, but the dark stations told the story of towns abandoned.

"Damn." Nick swore, but didn't feel angry.

"Problem?"

He pointed to a dark station. "This line doesn't go as far as I remembered. We'll have to go west to the next south running line and then catch the lateral here."

Wisp nodded. It was more roundabout but much more swift than walking.

"I don't know when the other lines run. We might get stuck for a day waiting if we miss a connection."

"Then we wait."

Nick felt resigned. He checked a bag that hung from a hook on the wall. A flicker of disappointment. "No mail today."

"Is that new?"

"Just started."

"Perhaps it doesn't come every day."

Nick paced a little, his emotions finally settling down. "Are you looking forward to seeing your brother?"

"Yes."

"When's the last time you saw him?"

"Three years."

"You don't visit?" Nick's question was innocent. He didn't feel at all cruel.

"Khi is owned by the army. I do not have a keeper. Biobots without keepers are considered rogue. To be terminated."

Nick's sadness crept back. "Still?"

"I do not test the law around those that once enforced it."

"Probably a good idea."

The train slid into the station, dust swirling up in the headwind. A chime sounded as the doors opened. Wisp reached out with his senses. There was no one on the train. He and Nick entered and took seats.

"Just us today, huh."

"Do you see many people?"

"Different parts, yeah. Past Clarkeston more people use it."

Wisp hoped that the people who used the train would not notice him.

* * *

They caught all their connections without undue delay arriving at Laurel late in the evening. Wisp suggested that they stay overnight at the station. There were people in the area that he did not like the feel of. The station provided security and relative comfort compared to camping in the open. Nick readily agreed. They settled into cubbies and slept early for an early start.

The next morning Wisp didn't feel the dangerous people around, and so told Nick that it was safe to travel. They left the station and skirted a small settlement that had sprung up in an old strip mall. They passed by on a high ridge and were able to look down on it, while remaining well hidden in the trees. The jumble shapes were hard to identify in the pale light of dawn, but a sense of corruption tainted the area.

"That does not look like a place I'd want to visit." Nick said in a low voice.

Wisp looked at the garbage piled behind the building. Unsanitary and dangerous. Two of the stores had broken windows. A fire was burning unattended in the parking lot. Anger and fear poured off the people hidden inside like toxic smoke. "There is cruelty in there," Wisp warned.

Nick tasted of disgust with tinges of regret."I don't doubt it," he said as he glared at the dilapidated building.

Wisp touched his arm to bring him back to the present. He didn't need to read minds to know that something down there had triggered bad memories for Nick. They crept back through the trees and moved away cautiously. Wisp kept his senses stretched. The countryside immediately around them was empty for the moment. He could feel his brother, Khi, not far to the south of them. This close, he could pick up some of his emotions. Khi was worried. Without context, it could mean anything. Wisp put that thought aside.

"Are you..." Nick made a wide circle with his finger.

"Checking for trouble? Yes."

"How far are we going?"

"It's difficult to translate into miles, but not far." Wisp checked the sky and the terrain. "Perhaps before lunch."

"But you've been here before, right?"

"No. The last time I saw Khi he was in the southwest."

"Then how do you know where he is?"

"I can feel him."

Nick frowned, but there was a grudging acceptance in him. They moved quietly down the slender remains of a neglected road. Saplings crowded the edges, sharply narrowing it in places, so that they were forced to walk single file. The day went from warm to sweltering before the sun was much above the horizon. The still, hot air hung on them like wet laundry adding weight to every step forward. Wisp appreciated Nick's ability to travel easily on different terrains. Alone, he was used to moving very quietly and quickly. It appeared that Nick would not slow him down appreciably.

The road dipped down before going over a heavily forested hill. Wisp could feel that Khi was very close now. Probably on the other side of the hill, probably a military installation. He moved off the road into the trees. Nick followed without question. Wisp slowed his pace to make less noise, forcing his way through the thickets of young trees. Nick followed his example without being told. Wisp began to appreciate Nick in a new light. The man was smart and capable. He didn't seem put off by working with a biobot. Wisp squashed the next thought before it was fully formed. Much too early to be making assessments.

They worked their way quietly to the top of the hill. Wisp found a break in a cluster of saplings to peek through. Down in the valley below them was a massive installation. A compound of blocky buildings surrounded by high walls topped with razor wire. Guard towers perched on either side of the massive front gates. From their position on the ridges, they were high enough to see into a good portion of the compound. Wisp could make out the tops of Jeeps and trucks that appeared to be parked at random between the buildings. For the size of the complex, he was only sensing a handful of people. It was late enough in the morning that more people should be about. Sleeping people gave a slight trace. Wisp reached out searching for hints of more people.

"Wow." Nick's surprise was tinged with a feather's weight of envy and tumbling down to alarm. "That's a huge installation. What's it for?"

Wisp shifted his position so that Nick could hunker down in the weeds next to him. "Khi does research."

"That's more than research."

Wisp had to agree. That degree of security meant something of great importance was inside those walls. But that stood in conflict with the lack of people that he felt.

"The gates are wide open," Nick said in a low murmur. "That doesn't feel right."

"The guard towers feel empty."

"Is it abandoned?"

"No."

"So where is everybody?"

Chapter 26

"It wasn't until I started trying to gather information that I discovered such a dearth. We had been transported backward to a time before statistics. Settlements and med centers were not required to keep track of people at first. Even then, round numbers were all that were required for ordering medicine."

History of a Changed World, Angus T. Moss

Tilly frowned at her husband, then turned her gaze to Martin. "You don't think he's being careless? A biobot? Really."

Martin gave her a one shouldered shrug without meeting her eyes. "It's weird, yeah. But Nick trusts him."

Tilly's eyebrows shot up. "And that's good enough?"

Angus chuckled. "My dear, I think you are overreacting."

"The biobot killed," Tilly stated flatly.

"The biobot helped rescue a settlement under attack," Martin countered.

"And we still don't know why!" Tilly could hear the shrillness in her voice. She took a sip of her coffee, trying to regain her composure. The three of them sat in the empty cafeteria, but she was sure there were eavesdroppers in the hall. She would have preferred to be having this conversation behind closed doors.

"I don't think it's about Wisp," Angus said. "He wasn't involved with the original murder."

"Or so he says," she snapped. There was something about that creature that put her teeth on edge.

Angus took her hand and squeezed it. "It is worrisome, these well-armed men killing indiscriminately. But Nick thinks they got away clean—"

"And he brought us some powerful new weapons," Martin interjected. "I've got extra men watching the roads and the train station."

"But a biobot? Angus, your curiosity cannot come before the safety of the med center."

Now it was his turn to raise eyebrows. "What are you accusing me of?"

"I don't think he should stay," Tilly said firmly.

Martin tapped his pen on the table. "I think I'm going to disagree with you about that."

Tilly felt her blood pressure rise. And when she saw it, wanted to slap the grin off of Angus's face. Sometimes her husband was as thoughtless as a child. "He's a *biobot,*" she said as if that explained it all. And she felt it should. Angus reached for her hand again, but she pulled away. "Am I the only one that considers him a threat?"

Martin leaned back in his chair stretching his shoulders. "I've spoken with Bruno. He says Wisp is a true finder. That could be to our advantage. He'd be a boon to the perimeter defense. According to Nick, he's a dead shot and highly skilled in hand to hand. At the very least, he'd be a big help with the Watch's training. Also, he doesn't like to be around too many people. He might settle in the neighborhood, but I don't think he'll want quarters in the building."

Tilly shook her head. "I don't like it."

"Why?" Angus asked.

"He's not human."

"Of course he's human," Angus said "He's just put together a bit differently."

"Then why all the laws restraining them?" Tilly asked. Images and headlines flashed in her memory. Biobots killing keepers. Biobots spreading contagion. Biobots at the core of every crime committed. It made people look twice even at close friends. A horrible time of fear and suspicion. Not something she cared to remember, but with a biobot in their med center, she had to consider all the repercussions. Angus would want him to stay just so he could talk to him. She did not look forward to that argument. Her husband knew her too well and usually found a way to bring her around. To her surprise, Martin was the one that answered.

"You know, a lot of that was a smear campaign."

Angus leaned across the table toward Martin. His face had that greedy-for-knowledge look that Tilly had seen so many times before. "How do you know?"

Martin gave him a slight head-shake in a tiny denial. "There weren't enough of them around for everything they got blamed for." He stared at his hands, his mouth twitching with unsaid words. "I worked with some. Angus is right, Tilly. They're just like us."

She didn't want to back down, but she knew that Martin would never endanger them. His terse endorsement intrigued her. Over the years, he'd given enough hints that made her assume he'd been part of some sort of special military group. "Then why all the laws?"

"That was mostly for them, I think," Martin said avoiding her eyes.

Angus snorted. "When they declared them not human, people took the kind of liberties that we don't allow to happen to animals. They were slaves, property. And they died in too many horrible ways until someone finally put together some laws. They were treated as a new entity, like an alien from another planet. People blamed them for everything."

"But I saw reports. I saw people who'd been attacked," she countered.

"Like all humans, there are good ones and bad ones."

Tilly was silent as she thought about the possibilities. The men waited. She eyed them both, anxiously. "So how do we find out if he's a bad one?"

Chapter 27

"The ether was equally useless for research. Many docks stopped functioning as staff fled and power sources failed. Those with automated power supplies continued to function for awhile, but the information quickly became outdated."

History of a Changed World, Angus T. Moss

After watching the silent compound for a half hour, Nick got bored. He was hot and itchy lying in the brush. "Let's knock on the front door."

Wisp shot him a startled glance.

"Well, *I* can. I'm just an average citizen looking for some answers. You can wait up here in case I need to be rescued," he said with a grim smile.

Wisp frowned, his eyes wandering back to the gates. Nick could almost tell what he was thinking. That wasn't a place he'd want to have to break out of. The stone walls were too smooth to scale without equipment. From here, it looked like there was only the one gate. They were certainly outnumbered. An installation that large could have a small army of security. The shiny new vehicles parked in the compound told him these people had access to resources that weren't available to people like Nick.

Wisp gave a small grunt of agreement. Pale eyes gave him that sizing up look again. "It might be best if you let them think you're my keeper."

Nick flinched inwardly. Wisp was giving him a little too much trust. "Huh. Not sure I ever wanted that title, but if it makes you feel better."

"It will *not* make me feel better. But it might make me safer." With that curt comment, Wisp worked his way back through the underbrush to the road. Nick followed right behind him. It only made sense to approach from the road. Sneaking out of the woods would surely raise suspicion.

They walked up to the open gates slowly, eyes on the dark windows of the watchtowers. Nick's back prickled with sweat. They were completely exposed. A heartbeat later he knew something was wrong. In the shadow of the wall, a body lay crumpled on the ground. As they moved into the compound more bodies came into sight. Nick automatically ducked into cover behind a large cargo truck that had stopped just inside the wall, possibly the reason why the gates were open. Wisp crouched beside him.

"That's not good," Nick said with a nod toward the bodies. The men on the ground were in the same black uniform that the mercenaries wore. He could see the driver of the vehicle slumped over the steering wheel. He worried that they might be walking into the aftermath of an attack.

"I'm not sensing very many people," Wisp said, his voice barely above a whisper.

"Is your brother in there?"

"Yes."

"Is he scared?"

"Not scared, but he is concerned." Wisp leaned around the edge of the truck, checking the immediate area.

Nick did his own reconnaissance. Just inside the gate was a large grassy area. It looked like a park, but Nick knew anyone passing through there would be visible to the guards in the towers. The entry road ended at a chest high wall that was topped by wrought iron spikes. To the right and left gated driveways headed further into the compound. He could see the roof lines of a couple buildings inside. The gate on the right side was open.

The silence was unnerving. Nick heard a bird twittering in the woods, the soft rumble of an engine, but no voices or footsteps.

"Can you tell if they are under attack?"

Wisp gave him a puzzled look. "Do you see something I don't?"

"I see dead bodies. I want to know how they got there."

"I feel no emotions that would indicate battle or aggression. There is only worry and confusion in there," he said, gesturing into the compound.

"That's the same uniform as the guys that hurt William."

"Yes."

Nick hesitated a minute before he asked the hard question. "Does your brother wear that uniform?"

Wisp shrugged. "It's possible that he's been sold. I haven't visited him here. Last time I saw him, he was wearing civilian clothing and a white lab coat. But even if he is in that uniform, they wouldn't give him a weapon."

Nick had to agree with that. Arming biobots was against the law. And to be honest, against human instincts. "You're sure he's here?"

"I can feel him."

Nick scanned the area. Nothing was moving. He gave Wisp a tight nod, and they moved out. The road went between the walls for awhile before taking a sharp turn inward to run straight as an arrow past several buildings. A large boxy structure on the left looked like a warehouse. The three story brick-faced building on the right looked like a barracks. In the uncanny silence, they passed more bodies and vehicles. At a branch in the road, there was a truck with the back doors open, boxes marked as vaccine scattered on the ground and more bodies. They looked as if they had dropped while loading the truck. All the hair on Nick's body stood up. Everything he was seeing said chemical attack.

Nick moved slowly, from one point of cover to the next, a truck, a jeep, a low wall surrounding a neatly mown lawn. Wisp shadowed him. It was too quiet. Something about the bodies was off. Then it hit him. "Look." He pointed to the nearest body. "He never pulled his weapon."

Wisp slunk over to crouch by the body. "I see no wounds."

A shiver shook Nick, raising goose bumps. "Can you tell how long he's been dead?" He cringed a little when Wisp touched the body.

Wisp turned a puzzled frown on him. "Still warm."

They both jumped at a loud clanking sound in the strange silence of the compound. Down the road was a squat building with no windows and a heavy metal access. The door creaked on its hinges as it opened wider. A tall man, broad shouldered and strong looking, with red hair and light brown eyes frowned into the sunlight. He caught sight of them and looked mildly surprised. "Tau?"

"Is that your brother?" Nick glanced at Wisp. He nodded without looking at Nick. "Why doesn't he have a tattoo?"

"He does, but it isn't on his neck." Wisp stood up,

but Nick shouldered him aside to look like he was leading. The man focused on Nick, his expression becoming uncertain.

"Who are you? Why are you here?"

"I'm Nick from High Meadow Med Center. We came looking for you to see if we could find the Vaccine Center. It's gone off line."

"Khi, he is trustworthy," Wisp added.

His brother frowned. "High Meadow? That's..." He turned to start down the driveway and stopped short at the sight of bodies in the street. His eyebrows shot up. "What has happened?"

Nick stared around the compound. Bodies on the ground. Trucks with doors hanging open. "I was hoping you could tell me."

"Kyle! Kyle, Kyle, Kyle!" A woman's voice screamed the name repeatedly from inside the building.

"Come," Khi beckoned to them as he ran toward the screaming.

Nick and Wisp followed him into the building and found a woman on her knees beside a man on the floor. They both wore lab coats. She was sobbing. She looked up when they arrived. "It's Bobby! He's dead!"

Khi knelt and put an arm around her. "I'm so sorry, Ruth."

"They're all dead! Why are they all dead?" Her voice was high and shrill with fear.

Wisp backed up. Nick could feel the woman's panic, he was sure it was much more intense for Wisp.

"Ruth! Calm yourself. These men are here to help us."

Nick looked sideways at Wisp. Whatever made him think that?

Chapter 28

"We were failed by our own brilliance. Many appliances and gadgets that we used daily had a planned obsolescence built in because we all knew that in a few year's time something faster, easier, better would arrive. And so it was that within a few years after Zero Year that all the things we were accustomed to relying on broke down."

History of a Changed World, Angus T. Moss

"Cannibals?" Tilly checked the bedside monitor to see if Jean's fever had gone up. The story she was relating sounded implausible "That's patently absurd. No, I'm sure he was wrong about that."

"But the children?" Jean's eyes were bloodshot. She was pale against the brightly patterned sheets of the infirmary. Although the flu wasn't taking much of a toll on her, the memories of the past few days were.

"Just hostages," Tilly sputtered, trying to come up with easy answers to an evil situation. "Parents will do anything for their children. They were probably holding the children to ensure that the parents would be compliant."

"The parents...," Jean's voice trailed off. She had a haunted look in her eyes that made Tilly worry.

"Don't think about them. There's nothing to be done now. You all arrived in time to set them free. I'm sure they are very grateful. But it's done and over, and we must move on to the next thing before us."

Jean brightened a bit under Tilly's insistence. "And what's next?"

Tilly forced a smile for her. "I've a chore list as long as your arm. As soon as you are cleared for duty, we will find some work for you."

"What kinds of things do you do here?"

Tilly relaxed. She was in her element now. "All sorts. There's the basics of cooking and laundry and housekeeping. There's the farming and animals. There's the library and entertainment. Oh, and of course Angus's research."

That seemed to get a rise out of Jean. "What kind of research?"

"He's trying to put together a census."

Jean blinked at her for a minute. "Why?"

Tilly's good spirits sank. The reality of the new world was always more grim than she wanted it to be. "Well, I think he's trying to track the illness and see if there have been any changes over the years." It was only a shading of the truth. That was part of what Angus looked for. But he was also trying to count survivors. And he worried, with the population growing so thin and isolated, of inbreeding. Although it was years too early for that to be an issue, Angus wanted to have some data in place to head it off.

"Oh." Jean stared at the wall, lost in thought. "And what would that tell him?"

"You'd have to ask him, my dear. That sort of thing is not my forte. I feed hungry mouths and keep the floors clean. But if that interests you, when you're up and about, you should speak with him. I'm sure he'd be glad of your assistance."

"Really?"

"Sorting through data can be quite time consuming. I'm sure he could use an extra pair of eyes."

Jean smiled for the first time since she'd entered the infirmary. It warmed Tilly to see her looking more cheerful. The poor thing had been through some very trying times. Tilly mourned the loss of her settlement, but didn't bring the issue up. Jean needed time to heal. Reminding her of her losses wouldn't help.

"Thank you," Jean said in a shaky voice. Her eyes filled with tears. "I hope I haven't brought any bad luck with me."

"Nonsense," Tilly chided her, although a chill shivered down her back. "Bad things happen whether we are there to witness them or not. It's just the ones under our noses that hurt the most."

Chapter 29

"I have tried to construct population figures, but as they change dramatically every flu season, I am always trying to catch up. In Year Ten, I believe our numbers to be equal to that of the mid 1800's."

History of a Changed World, Angus T. Moss

Nick looked at the dead man, the sobbing woman and tried to decide if he should leave now. No wounds on the bodies meant they died of sickness. The fact that they'd all dropped in their tracks probably meant it was too late to escape whatever contagion had taken them. He shivered, but it wasn't unexpected. He was surprised every time he survived another round of flu.

Wisp planted himself in front of his brother. "Khi, I don't know how we can help. Neither of us have the kind of skills that deal with the virus," he said calmly. "It might be best if we can go somewhere and assess the situation."

Khi helped Ruth to her feet. She was panting, close

to hysteria. Standing, she barely reached his shoulder. Her dark hair was caught back in a tight bun. She covered her mouth, smothering her sobs.

Nick agreed with Wisp's suggestion. He touched Khi on the shoulder. "We need to go somewhere to talk."

Khi looked confused. The armful of sobbing woman probably didn't help.

"You got a conference room?" Nick asked.

The confusion left Khi's face. "Of course. This way." He led them into a warren of corridors with offices and labs behind glass doors. Three corridors later they entered a mid-sized conference room. Khi put Ruth in a chair and turned to them. "I'm not sure what's happening."

"The men in black uniforms, they work here?" Nick asked.

"Yes."

"They aren't army," Nick said.

"No."

Nick's frustration kicked up a notch at Khi's terse responses. He turned a sharp eye on Wisp, who nodded acknowledgement.

"Khi, we need to know who these men are, and what this compound is. Please proceed as though we are totally ignorant of your mission here," Wisp said.

"Oh." Khi pulled out a chair and sat down next to Ruth, who was crying quietly. "I am rattled. Things are very much out of the ordinary."

Nick's irritation backed off a little. He took stock of the typical-looking conference room: long table with a dozen chairs, smartwall and controllers. In the corner, was a plant with large spade-shaped leaves trained up a stake to the height of a man, probably to help ease the lack of windows. A credenza held a water dispenser and a rack of glasses. He filled glasses for all of them and set them out on the table. Wisp took a seat opposite his brother. Nick sat next to him. "Okay, Khi—"

"No!" Ruth snapped. "His name is Kyle."

Nick nodded calmly at her angry glare. Her heated reaction told him a few things about *Kyle* and his relationship with Ruth. He tucked away those thoughts for later. "All right. I'm Nick. I come from High Meadow Med Center. We got worried when the ether dock for the Vaccine Center went down and came to see what happened." It was close enough to the truth for now.

"The ether dock is down?" Kyle looked shocked. "That's wrong."

"Oh God. Oh my God!" Ruth buried her face in her hands.

The situation was a hair's breadth from spiraling out of control. Nick prepared to wade in, but Wisp beat him to it.

"Report, Khi," Wisp said a crisp tone of authority.

Kyle spun to look at his brother, astonishment clear on his face. "What? Why are you..." He took a puzzled glance at Nick, then shook his head hard, as if trying to clear it. "I'm not being helpful." He took a sip of water then sat a little straighter. "Yes. Let me tell you what we do. Ruth and I head Green Team. We work on the vaccines. This is the new vaccine center. Dr. Rutledge won the contract three years ago. Prior to that, Ruth and I worked in the Vaccine Center in..." He paused, looked at Ruth, then at them. "Well, elsewhere." He gestured toward the door. "This is a private facility. Those men in uniform are the hired guards. Ruth and I were working in the lab late last night on a new...issue that came up. We worked straight through. When we came out for breakfast, we found the bodies."

"Can you tell me how they all died?" Nick asked.

"I don't know," Kyle said.

"It's Gold Team," Ruth spat. Her swollen eyes

narrowed in anger. “They were working on the next layer. It wasn't ready. I knew it wasn't ready, but Bobby lied to Rutledge. He said it worked.” She wiped tears away and smoothed a few loose hairs back into the bun.”They were late. He cut corners.”

Kyle let out a long breath. “It killed them.”

“How?” Nick asked.

Kyle frowned. He looked at Ruth. “I am not familiar with this year’s composition.” He paused waiting to see if she would offer more information.”

“How come it didn’t kill everybody?”

“The guards and staff are vaccinated first.”

“What about you?”

Kyle kept looking to Ruth. She kept her head down, sniffing and sighing. He looked uneasy as he answered Nick. “We are protected here. Only people that go out into the world are required to be vaccinated. They aren’t allowed into this building. We don’t go out. Our dormitories are accessed through restricted tunnels. Therefore, we are never exposed. These protocols were established after an entire research team was lost in Year Five.”

“Well, you’re exposed now. High Meadow has the flu, and we just came from there.”

“This year’s vaccine wouldn’t help,” Ruth snapped. Her voice nearly a growl. “They tried to take it too far.”

Kyle put a restraining hand on her arm. “We shouldn’t discuss this right now.”

She pulled away from him to fetch a box of tissues from the credenza. The room was silent, making Ruth’s uneven breathing sound even louder.

Nick thought about what Kyle had said. The researchers at the Vaccine Center had done something stupid and left the country without a viable vaccine for this year’s flu. Even worse, they’d managed to kill themselves off in the process. He didn’t want to think about how that impacted future research. Nor could he see how this connected to the men who hunted William and Lily. The answer to those questions would have to wait. First, he needed to sort out the problem in front of him.

"Wisp said there are people here that are frightened. I think we should round up all of the survivors right away."

"Wisp?" Kyle asked.

Nick pointed to him.

Kyle smiled. "A curious name."

Wisp shrugged. "It was earned." He glanced to the left, with the far-away look in his eyes that Nick was beginning to recognize as an inward focus for his extrasensory listening. "Do you have prisoners here?"

"No. This is a research facility," Kyle said.

"Subjects for experimentation?"

"No," Ruth said firmly. "What would make you ask such a thing? We aren't barbarians. We use simulations."

"Who are the people locked in the next building?"Wisp pointed at the back wall.

Nick was turned around from the warren of corridors. He wasn't sure which direction Wisp was pointing, but Kyle seemed to know.

"That's the barracks. More guards, I suppose."

"They don't feel like guards."

Nick stood. "Let's go look. We need to find anyone alive, or anyone sick and make a plan."

"The guards might not be the best place to start," Ruth said. "I think we should start upstairs."

Wisp looked at the ceiling. "There is no one alive above us."

"That can't be! You can't possibly know that!" Ruth rushed for the door.

They followed her panicked stumbling down the corridor and up the stairs to the second floor. Nick held back, giving her time to burst into office after office.

They were either empty or had a corpse. Some rooms had bodies slumped at their desks. Men and women, some in business attire, some in lab coats, all dead. The name plates all had Director or Supervisor of something on them. This was the upper echelon, and they were all gone. Nick made a mental note that there were a whole lot of bodies to be disposed of. If they didn't act quickly, this area would become unbearable. Nick saw Wisp ease back, putting a little more room between himself and Ruth's hysteria. He couldn't blame her. If he'd discovered the same thing at High Meadow, he'd have been hard put to be reasonable.

Ruth staggered into the hallway, eyes wide with shock. "They're all dead. Kyle! They're all dead. Bobby's killed them all!" She lurched away from them heading for a fancy double doorway at the end of the hall. She burst through the doors leaving them swinging open in her wake. Nick and Kyle were right behind her.

Nick walked into an elegant waiting room with thick carpeting and original artwork on the walls. It had a high receptionist's desk and banks of chairs along the walls, a small meeting room on one side and a shiny, carved door on the other. Ruth plowed through the ornate door, making a keening sound as she panted in distress. Nick followed as far as the doorway. A brass plate, to one side, said *S. S. Rutledge*. Sounded like a ship to Nick. Unfortunately, this ship had sunk. In the office, a stocky man sprawled on the floor in front of a massive desk.

"No, no, no." Ruth was on her knees, just inside the door, rocking and mumbling.

Kyle went to her, holding her gently. As he steadied her, Nick saw that Kyle's biobot number was tattooed on the inside of his right forearm.

Giving them some time, Nick moved back to where Wisp had remained in the corridor. "Why's his tattoo on his arm?"

"It was a request of his first keeper. I think he had a locator chip also."

"Huh. Didn't know a keeper could ask for something like that."

"He was sold to the army. They can request anything."

Nick winced at the bitterness in Wisp's voice. He gestured to Ruth and Kyle. She leaned against him with a comfort of habit. "Are they a couple?" he asked in a low voice.

"Biobots are not allowed to."

"That's not what I asked."

Pale eyes scrutinized him. "Why do you need to know?"

"This is not the situation I was expecting. We're gonna need a new plan. If it's going to include them, I'll need to know about them."

Wisp dipped his head in acknowledgement. "They have strong feelings for each other."

"That'll do." Nick raised his voice. "Let's head back to the conference room. We need to sort this out."

Kyle held on to Ruth, half-carrying her back down the stairs. By the time they had gathered around the table, Ruth had settled into numb shock.

Nick took the lead. "This is a big place, but it looks like most of the people here...didn't make it. Wisp can help us track down the living."

"How?" Ruth demanded. "He doesn't know this place. Hell, I don't know half of it, and I've been here for years."

"He's a finder," Nick said with a glance at Kyle.

Ruth scoffed.

Kyle put a hand on her arm. "Ruth, this is Tau."

"What?"

"My brother, Tau."

"How did you get here? Who is your keeper?" Her voice rose as she started into another panic. "Kyle, this isn't good. He shouldn't be here."

Nick raised a hand to stop her. "Easy. Let's not worry about that right now. We're hip deep in dead bodies. I think that's a little more important.

Ruth swallowed nervously. "Yes. Perhaps you're right."

Nick gave her a reassuring nod. "Okay. Kyle, you got a map of this place?"

Kyle put a map of the compound up on the smartwall. He marked each space with usage and probable occupancy.

Nick looked at the search area with a sinking feeling. It could take more than a day to go through all the buildings if people decided to hunker down.

"Should we split up?" Kyle asked.

"No. Wisp and I don't belong here. You two do. I think we should all stay together in case someone decides to shoot first and ask questions later."

Kyle raised an eyebrow. "Why would you phrase it that way? This is a research and production facility. Our security is not that aggressive."

Nick gave him a shrug and a tight smile. "Let's just say I'm the paranoid type."

Ruth murmured something to Kyle that Nick couldn't catch. It made Kyle frown at her. Nick worried that she might bolt at the first chance. He wondered if he and Wisp should just walk away from this mess. But that wouldn't answer the questions piling up.

They started a systematic search. Ruth had clearance for all the buildings allowing them full access. There were labs and offices, a few private homes tucked into the back corner, a warehouse and production facility, barracks for the guards and slightly nicer dorms for the staff. After completing each building, they returned to the conference room to mark that building done and drop off the few stunned survivors they found. Nick left notes at exits and stairways as to where they would be gathering. He let Ruth choose the order of the buildings. He knew that if she could feel like she had control over something, it would take some of her fear away. She was barely hanging on as it was.

Chapter 30

"Some industries were totally wiped out, while others were able to manage. Small farms continued as before, sometimes pulling in neighbors to replace the fallen. Religious organizations continued as before. Some factories were able to downsize production and continue output. But the fact that their customer base had diminished drastically was not as great an issue as the disintegration of currency. Money no longer stood for anything of worth."

History of a Changed World, Angus T. Moss

With Wisp leading them, Nick was relieved that they wouldn't spend more than a few hours tramping through buildings. Their search turned up a mix of scientists and support staff. Three had been sleeping and were totally unaware of the situation. The others had been isolated until they were found. All were skeptical at first. Once they crossed a body-strewn street, they had no more doubts. Shocked and panicked, they were willing to remain in the conference room while Nick, Wisp, Kyle and Ruth finished locating those still alive.

Leaving the guards' barracks for last, they returned to the conference room to get a better sense of the situation. Nick paused in the hallway, signaling Wisp to join him as the last few survivors filed into the room. "Is this it? Can you feel anybody else?"

"I need to move away from all these people to be sure."

"This is a lot less than I expected." Nick stared at the lab workers talking among themselves in subdued tones. Wisp had been invaluable in finding them in the labyrinths of corridors and offices. But Nick felt that he needed one more check. "Take a weapon off one of the dead guards. Walk the perimeter. I think we will end up bedding down here for the night. I want to make sure we are secure. We'd better shut the gates. I don't want to advertise the lack of personnel here."

Wisp gave him an odd look. "How long do you intend to stay?"

"I'd like to get out of here first thing tomorrow."

"You think you will find answers by then?"

Nick glanced down the hall, halfway down a limp hand lay across a threshold. "I'm gonna try."

Wisp gave him a nod and walked away.

Nick went into the conference room and found all eyes on him. "Okay folks, here's the situation as we know it. Bad vaccine seems to have killed off a hell of a lot of people. Maybe a couple of cases of flu also. I'm from High Meadow Med Center. We came here to ask some questions. We got any supervisors here?"

Heads swiveled, but no hands went up.

"Let's go round the room real quick, and see what we've got." Nick went over to the smartwall to make notes. Each person stood, gave their full name and position then sat down. The next person then did the same. He was amused by the formal recitation. Very orderly. Despite, or perhaps because of the tragic situation, they all seemed to be remaining calm. There were eight scientists, four guards, four lab techs, a file clerk, groundskeeper and a janitor. As they were speaking, Nick took the time to look them over. A lot of nervous faces in the group, mostly among the scientists. The guards looked surly. He expected trouble there. "How many people do you normally have around here?"

There was a little mumbling, but no one offered him an answer. He needed more information before he could put a plan together. "Okay, let's try it another way." He started a new column on the smartwall, calling out questions. "How many teams are there? How many scientists per team?" Several times people tried to correct him on titles, but eventually he got solid numbers. There were four basic sections: research, production, shipping and administrative. He drew a line and added them all up.

"About two hundred people work here." He pointed to the list of survivors on the other side. "This is all you've got. Can you still run this place?"

One of the guards shifted in his seat for a minute before reluctantly raising his hand. Nick nodded at him to go ahead. "There were a couple of...um, groups sent out awhile back."

Nick kept his face passive. He was sure the guard was talking about the men hunting William and Lily. "Out where?"

The guard turned to look at the others in uniform. He shrugged without meeting Nick's eyes. "Some project of Rutledge's. It's been awhile, so I guess maybe they aren't coming back."

"Found better bennies," the fellow next to him grumbled, to which most of the guards chuckled.

Nick's mouth went dry. He felt a little guilty for hoping that he and Wisp had killed all of them. But he didn't like the thought of a bunch of mercenaries out there on the loose looking for a new source of *benefits*. "Okay, but that was guards, right?" He pointed to the list on the board. "Do you need all these jobs filled?"

Silence answered him, but the question was mostly rhetorical. The people in front of him looked stunned. He needed to get them thinking. "Ruth thinks this is bad vaccine. I saw boxes of it on the trucks. Did any get delivered?"

There was a rustle around the room as people turned to look at one another.

"I don't think that there is anyone here from shipping," Kyle said.

Nick felt a pang of loss for people he'd never met. More human beings lost to stupidity. Angus would have a fit. But he needed some answers. He was going to have to break it down again. "How many delivery trucks are there?"

"Fifteen," one of the guards answered.

"How many on site right now?"

"Twelve," another guard answered. "Ten in the garage and two parked outside."

"That makes three trucks unaccounted for. Are they delivering vaccine? Do we need to contact settlements?"

"No." Kyle stood to speak. "The shipments go to the distribution warehouse."

"Okay. Contact them."

The staff looked back at him uneasily. Kyle cleared his throat. "Who should do that?"

Nick snorted. Geniuses didn't always make good leaders. "Don't you have some kind of contingency plan? What if a tornado had killed these people?" He saw a couple of faces brighten.

"The disaster plan," Kyle said. "Yes. That is exactly

what we should do." He glanced back at his colleagues. "I am not authorized."

One of the scientists lurched to his feet. Red Team, Nick thought he'd said. A tall, lanky fellow with long brown hair."I can look into it, Kyle."

"Thank you, Jonas. Perhaps you should take someone with you?"

Jonas gave him a half-shrug. "The dead don't scare me. I'll go find the procedures and report back." He looked toward Nick, but avoided eye contact. "Okay?"

"Sounds like a plan. If we're not here, I'll leave a note on the board where we've gone."

The scientist squinted at the list of survivors. Nick watched his Adam's apple lurch as he swallowed nervously. "Right." He walked out, shoulders hunched, hands in his pockets.

"Okay. Good." Nick looked at all the blank faces staring at him. "Next is probably food and shelter."

Kyle stood up. "I believe the first thing we should do is to remove the dead to a single location."

Murmuring skipped across the room. Nick heard more than one person complain about physical labor. He let them grumble, aggravation was better than shock. Kyle was right. The dead needed to be dealt with if they were staying, but Nick didn't want to be here a minute longer than he had to. They could clear out a space for the night then leave in the morning. He wasn't sure what should be done here, but he didn't want to be the one in charge of it.

Nick rapped his knuckles on the board until people quieted down. "We now have twenty-one people. Out of about two hundred. That means that there are possibly one hundred and eighty-nine corpses spread out in these buildings."

"That can't be right!" A woman in a lab coat waved her arms in a violent negation. "You must have counted wrong. That's an eighty-seven percent mortality rate.

That's...that's..."

"Inexcusable," Ruth snarled.

"Are you accusing gold team of this...this..." she waved a hand, at a loss for words.

"It wasn't ready, Kim," Ruth snapped back at the woman. "He added—" she pointedly glared at Nick. "It wasn't ready."

"But Rutledge said we all had to have it..." Kim took a shaky breath. "I was scheduled...I, oh God, I was supposed to get it this afternoon."

Nick saw the change in the room. The scientists looked worried, the labs techs looked scared and the guards got angrier. "Food and shelter," he said, in an effort to get them back on track. "A cafeteria would work. We're all going to need to eat before long. And we can easily bed down where we're eating. I would recommend not going out where there are bodies until we are sure that they all died from the bad vaccine."

Silence answered him again, but this time it was one of assent.

* * *

Nick left the group discussing the best place to spend the night. There were already factions forming. A few people wanted to leave. He decided that wasn't his problem. If people came to him for help, he'd gladly supply it. If they wanted to go off on their own, less for him to worry about. He grabbed Kyle and Ruth and headed for the last building that needed to be searched. Wisp caught up with them as they reached the barracks. He was glad to have the biobot back at his side. It surprised him to realize that he trusted Wisp to watch his back.

The main door was propped open. Nick led them in. The ground floor had communal rooms: cafeteria, lounge, gym and a few offices. He assumed the upper floors were sleeping quarters. Any rooms that had been occupied now held only dead bodies. Wisp led them into the main lounge with the insistence that there were living people in the building.

"There's no one here but the dead," Ruth said accusingly to Wisp. She pulled a corner of her collar over her nose. In the heat of the day, the bodies were beginning to stink.

"They are in the lower levels. We need to find a way down."

Ruth looked reluctant, but Kyle's quiet acceptance of Wisp's declaration brought her around. Nick sent them off in different directions to search for stairs or an elevator. All of the staircases they found started at the first floor and went up. Next they searched offices.

The fact that the door to the lower levels was in an odd little foyer behind the head of security's office, set off alarm bells for Nick. He'd opened a door, expecting a closet and found a short passage. Pretty sure he'd found what they needed, he called the others over. At the end of the passage was a small room with two doors, a table and four chairs and a long row of cabinets that took up one entire wall. Three of the chairs held bodies dressed in the ubiquitous black uniform, which inferred to Nick that they were on duty. Nick opened the first door. It led into a large kitchen. A man in whites was sprawled on the floor by a walk-in freezer. He shut the door. They could look around the kitchen later. The second door was heavy steel with a keypad lock.

"Can you open that?" Nick asked Kyle.

"I can try."

While Kyle tried a variety of pass codes on the door, Nick checked the cabinets. He pulled open all the doors. Bottles of pills, towels, stacks of surgical scrubs in pastel colors. He grabbed one of the pill bottles and handed it to Ruth. "What is this stuff?"

She squinted at the label for a second before her eyebrows shot up. “It’s well, sort of...” She handed the bottle back like a hot potato, her mouth turned down in disgust. “Um...chemical restraint.”

The alarm bells in Nick’s head clanged a bit louder as he thought about why they might have large bottles of stuff like that.

“Makes sense,” Wisp said. “The people I feel are very subdued. They are probably drugged.”

The door gave a two-note chime and swung open. Kyle led the way down to the basement. A door at the bottom of the stairs was locked, also. This one was older, having a keyed lock. Ruth located the keys hanging within reach and let them through.

They entered a pristine area of white walls and grey-tiled floor that smelled of refrigerated air and disinfectant. A long corridor stretched out in front of them with doors evenly spaced along the length of it. Nick had only a vague impression of the size of the building above them, but it was obvious that the corridor in front of him was a good deal longer than that. The doors had simple slide locks on them. In the wall, next to each door was a long, narrow hatch also with a slide lock. They stood in a small foyer. To the right was a short hallway that lead to an elevator. Nick figured it must come down from the kitchen. Food carts were parked along the walls. To the left was a desk, several filing cabinets and a wall rack holding charts.

Kyle looked at Wisp. “How many people are being held here?”

Wisp closed his eyes, a frown creased his forehead. “More than ten, less than fifty.”

“It must be like a jail,” Ruth said. “For people who break the rules.”

Nick shook his head. “I don't think so. This is a little too elaborate for the occasional drunk or insubordinate soldier.”

"What if these are criminals?" Ruth asked in a scratchy whisper.

Kyle frowned at her. "This is a research installation. We have no reason to be dealing with criminals."

"Even for experimentation?" Nick asked.

"I would never condone such a thing!" Ruth snapped.

"Perhaps that's why you didn't know about it," Nick said pointedly.

"They are held against their will." Wisp interrupted. "They are confused and hungry. I don't sense the emotions of habitual offenders. There is resignation underneath it all. It's late in the day. Do you think the guards died before or after these people were fed?"

Nick rubbed his eyes and ran both hands back through his hair. More questions, more problems. He'd like to tell Ruth to sort it out and walk away. But that wasn't going to give him any answers. And she didn't look like she had the kind of training needed to deal with a disaster like this.

"Let's go see who these people are."

Chapter 31

"Distribution was an issue also. The extensive highway system of our country could not survive without maintenance. Years of extreme weather, frost heaves, flooding, baking sun and the constant incursion of plant life made many roads entirely impassable. It all came down to the trains."

History of a Changed World, Angus T. Moss

At the door to the infirmary, Tilly stood absolutely still, hugging herself and trying not to react. She took a long breath and spoke calmly. "Four dead?" She didn't want to know their names. She'd feel their absence all too soon. Tears burned in her eyes, but she swallowed them down.

Dr. Jameson nodded without looking at her. "It's the fever. It comes on so fast, we can't cool them down in time. The last one, Joan, she spiked to 108." He looked over his shoulder at a sheet-draped gurney.

"Oh, Joan." Tilly's sigh caught in her throat. Joan was young, only in her thirties, still capable of child bearing. She was a hard worker in the fields. "She will be missed."

Jameson swung his head from side to side, a look of deep sadness on his face. "Still no word on a vaccine. Have you heard from Nick?" He turned hopeful eyes on her.

Tilly gritted her teeth against a sudden premonition. This was going to be a very lethal year. She could feel it in her bones. There would be a lot more losses before they got through the season. "It's still a bit early. He had quite a ways to go."

"Mmm." Jameson stood staring into space. His blue eyes were bloodshot from lack of sleep. His shoulders slumped with fatigue. Tilly thought he was in his late sixties, but he refused to tell her his age.

"You should get some sleep," Tilly said gently, knowing he'd resist. They were lucky to have a real doctor on staff. If they lost him, they would be just a distribution center. *If* they ever got any vaccine.

He gave her an exaggerated shrug. "This thing moves so damn fast I'm useless." He stalked away before she could speak. And for that she was grateful because there wasn't any proper response that would help.

She headed for the kitchens out of habit. Lottie caught up with her before she got halfway there.

"Tilly, I've got a lot of my crew in the infirmary. I'm going to need more hands in the fields today."

"What's coming in?"

"Nothing. The carrots are knee deep in bindweed. There's a flock of crows in the cornfield and half the chickens are missing."

"Ask Martin if he can spare some of the watch."

"That'll work," Lottie said brusquely before rushing off.

She made it all the way to the door of the cafeteria before being accosted again.

"Tilly." Bruno limped down the hallway toward her, leaning heavily on a tall walking stick. He was a big man, but more muscle than fat. She worried that he and Angus would eventually bump heads over the running of the med center. Bruno was used to being in charge, even though Riverbank had been a young settlement. His battered face was healing. The swelling was down and the bruises were fading to greens and yellows. The mercenaries had dislocated nearly every joint in his body torturing him for information he didn't have. Luckily he had survived with no broken bones, and yet survival itself was its own wound. His dark eyes carried the haunted look of someone dealing with great losses.

"How are you feeling today, Bruno? Should you be walking on that leg, yet?"

"I need to be doing something. I can't lie in that bed another minute."

Tilly's heart went out to him. She knew exactly how he felt. Busy hands helped you ignore the burning ache of grief, but he was too weak to work in the fields. "Harley can always use a pair of eyes. Can you get down to the horse field?"

"Wherever I'm needed." He limped past her, resolutely.

The walk there would exhaust him. He'd probably nap for a bit, chat with the men and limp back to his bed. Or so she hoped. When she stepped into the cafeteria, Martin was waiting.

Tilly forced a smile, expecting more bad news.

Martin started in without a greeting. "I've got six men out in the cemetery digging graves. Lottie says she needs at least ten men to help in the fields today. Three more men are in the infirmary, and we lost Old Joe last night."

"That's a big chunk of your staff," Tilly said. She ignored the loss. Old Joe wasn't old, mid-thirties at the most. He was simply the oldest of three Joes at the center. She pushed that thought to the back. If she let herself start to grieve, she'd be useless.

"We need to set some priorities."

Tilly looked at the set of Martin's jaw. He was worried. That made her more worried. "Security, food, grave digging."

"I almost think food should trump security."

"If it comes to it, we can use the train food to hold us over."

Martin's lips flattened in disagreement. "I don't want to touch the reserves. We just got them all stocked up. A couple of people have told me that they feel better knowing we have a plan. They might have griped about doing the drill, but I think everyone was glad to see that we have some forethought."

Tilly agreed with him about that. She had felt the same sentiments rumbling through the center lately. People had voiced skepticism about evacuating down to the storm shelter, but they had all readily participated. The rumors about the attack on Riverbank had everyone on edge. People were less worried when they knew there were procedures in place. Even if those procedures might prove to be horribly inadequate. She pulled her attention back to the issue at hand. "All right. We should probably get in at least a week's worth of train food for the kitchen."

"Any word from Nick?" Martin asked, despite the fact that he would be one of the first people to know.

"No. Do you think they got there already?"

"I looked at the old schedules. Depending on how far outside Laurel it is, they should arrive sometime today."

Tilly sighed. "I suppose it's asking too much for everything to work out fine."

Martin gave her a rueful grin. "If wishes were horses, everyone could ride."

Chapter 32

"Extreme weather hammered our country for decades before we accepted the change and began the massive reconstruction of our infrastructure, which also took decades. There are few left alive that can remember what it was like to pump gas or see skyscrapers. The virus changed the world overnight and ten years out, we are still struggling to adapt."

History of a Changed World, Angus T. Moss

Kyle stepped forward awkwardly to block Nick's way. "Don't you think we should look at the charts first? What if these are isolation units?"

Nick gazed at Kyle, trying to read him. He seemed sincere, if rather baffled. "Where are the suits?" Nick waved vaguely around the foyer. "No protective gear. No showers. No airlocks. Fancy place like this could afford to have stuff like that." Nick let that sink in for a minute.

"But..." Kyle frowned down at the floor.

Nick got the feeling he was thinking through more scenarios and repercussions than Nick would be familiar with. “You can go get some gear if it’ll make you feel better, but I don’t think there’s a filtration system in here.” He pointed to the ceiling, typical of a basement, banks of lights hung on bare wires below water pipes and power conduits. “We’re already exposed.”

“This doesn’t make sense,” Kyle said.

Nick looked over to Ruth, surprised that she hadn’t joined in. She had an armful of charts and was paging through the topmost. “Ruth?”

She startled, looking up with a wide-eyed look. “Some of these people have been here for years.”

“Why?” Kyle asked.

“I can’t figure it out. They don’t have any names, just numbers.” She juggled the charts to reorder them. “And ages. This one is a female. Only seventeen. She’s been here for...” She paged back through the files. “My God, she’s been here five years.”

Kyle frowned. “That’s before Dr. Rutledge won the vaccine contract. These people may have nothing to do with the work we do now.” He took one of the charts from Ruth. “Why paper files? This is so inefficient.”

“Can’t be hacked,” Wisp said. “Easier to keep a secret if only a few people have access.”

“Okay, I’ve heard enough,” Nick said. He snagged a marker off the counter. “Let’s open the doors, and see if we can get some answers.”

Nick walked over to the first door on the right side of the corridor. No one objected, but he got the feeling that everyone froze. He tapped on the door then slid the lock open. The door was surprisingly heavy.

“Hello?”

Inside was a small cell with bed, sink, shower and toilet. It reminded Nick of the shelter cubbies at the train station. A drop ceiling made the room feel even smaller. Beside the door, on the other side of the small hatch was a shelf large enough to hold a food tray with a plastic scoop chair set close by. The room smelled of death. A body lay on the bed, curled on its side. Nick took a step into the room. He couldn't tell if it was male or female.

"Dead." Wisp stood in the doorway. "A couple days by the smell."

Nick got close enough to see a beard and backed out. "Male. I'd say maybe forties."

Ruth held up a chart. "Him most likely. Puts him at forty-three. He's been here for two years." She glanced at Kyle.

Nick took the chart and slid it halfway into the food slot. Then he marked the door—male/43/dead—pocketed the marker, and stepped to the next door. He looked back to see Ruth and Kyle staring at the big black letters on the pristine white door.

"That's how we did it in the cities. Lets everyone know what's in there."

"Efficient," Wisp said. He stood next to Nick. "This one's alive."

Nick knocked, then slid the lock open. A young man was sitting at the shelf. He was dressed in white drawstring pants and a pale green shirt, like those in the cabinet upstairs. His hair looked like it hadn't seen a comb in years. He raised his eyes passively and blinked at them slowly. "The door opened."

Nick beckoned to him. "Come out."

"Out?" The boy looked at the shelf, then slowly pointed to the hatch. "The food comes in here. Where is the food?"

Nick glanced down the hall. If all the people held here were this submissive, he needed a plan before he stacked them all up together. He went back to the dead man's room and took the chair. In the foyer, at the foot of the stairs he started a row. When he turned to get the boy, he found Kyle looking intrigued and Ruth clearly alarmed. Wisp had grasped his idea. He had the boy by the arm, gently guiding him down the hall to the chair Nick had placed.

"Good. Thanks, Wisp. Ruth, got his chart? Male, adolescent?"

She continued staring at him for a half second before shuffling her charts. She handed him one. Nick slid it under the chair.

"Kyle, can you be in charge of food?"

"That is not my forte."

Nick snorted a chuckle. "This isn't my forte either. You got train food here?"

"Train food?" Ruth frowned at him. "What is that?"

"Packaged food that's stored at train stations," Wisp answered. He had taken the chair from the boy's room and set it next in line.

"I believe I know where there are some emergency rations," Kyle said.

"Please get some for these people. They've probably missed a couple meals."

"Yes. I understand, " Kyle said before heading upstairs.

Nick made a mental note that Kyle called train food *emergency rations*. That meant they must have fresh food here. He wanted to check out their supplies before he left. Maybe barter for the hard to find stuff. Susan would be so happy. But first to the problem at hand, Nick headed back down the hall to the next door.

Chapter 33

"I fear the loss of any remaining infrastructure. If we have another bad flu season losing more than 10-20% of our dwindling population, we run the risk of losing more of the individuals that know how to make things run."

History of a Changed World, Angus T. Moss

The little door never opened.

She drank water from the sink to fill her rumbling stomach. The lights stayed on a very long time. So long that she lay down and slept even thought it wasn't dark. When she woke again she wasn't sure if it was morning. But her head wasn't full of cotton. Something had changed. Maybe she was being punished. But for what? She tried to think back over the past few days, but they were a blur of sameness.

She was hungry. The room felt claustrophobic. She paced, counting her steps, passing the time impatiently. What had changed?

She drank more water, but it didn't help the

hunger pains.

The floor was cold. She wished she had some slippers or socks. Her hair itched, and she wondered when was the last time she'd bathed. She looked at the tiny stall shower. No soap. Only one faucet. She shivered then, knowing that the water was cold, but not sure how she knew.

Something was very wrong. She was frightened. What was this place? How long had she been here?

She sat on the bed and wrapped the blanket around herself. The air conditioning was on too high. She felt chilled to the bone. She needed to think. Figure out where she was, and what was going on. Her memory was fuzzy. She couldn't find her most recent memories. They were all a blur of white walls and cotton head.

There was a tap on the door. It sounded unreasonably loud in her silent room. She wasn't sure how to respond. That had never happened before. Then the door opened. She was so surprised, she almost didn't see that a person was there in the doorway. A tall man stood there, green eyes watching her. Amazing. She could smell him, sunshine and sweat. Thoughts and images tumbled in her brain so fast it made her breathless. "My name is Melissa," she blurted it out. Needed to say it aloud to make it real.

"Hello Melissa, I'm Nick." He stepped back and beckoned. "Come out please."

She bolted to her feet. Out! She needed to get out of this tiny stifling room. He led her down the hall to a row of chairs. All sorts of people were sitting there. Some were staring into space, some eating food out of packages. She took her seat, winded by the short walk. Another man, this one with red hair and dark golden eyes, brought her a package of food and a bottle of water. He opened it for her. It had the crunchy food inside.

Crunch. She crumpled the white wrapper. The smell and taste was familiar now. This was train food. Was she in a train station? Had there been a bad storm, and she'd gotten trapped in here? That didn't seem right. But, at the moment, all she wanted was food.

As she ate, she watched the rescuers. There were three men and one woman. The man who gave her food stayed here with the seated people, watching over them. He looked very strong, but there was a gentleness to his face that made her think that he wasn't a threat. The green-eyed man, Nick, seemed nice, also. Her eyes sought out the third man, and a thrill of fear crawled up her spine when she saw the tattoo. A biobot. White hair and pale eyes. When he came close, carrying a chair, she strained to see the numbers. He paused as if feeling her scrutiny.

"You have questions?"

"Who's your keeper?" The words rushed out of her. Fear welled up inside her. She began to shake.

"Nick." The biobot pointed to the green-eyed man.

"Stay away from me."

"You are safe here."

"Not with you here!" She heard her voice rise to a near shriek. The fear crashed over her, and she struggled to her feet, needing to run.

The biobot moved away. The big man with the golden eyes came to her making soft noises. She let him put her back in the seat.

"You are safe. I promise you that no one will hurt you."

"Keep him away."

"Would you like more food?"

She snatched the food from his hands, her mouth filling with saliva.

Chapter 34

"Ten years into a new world and the children we have may not be able to rebuild the world as we remember it."

History of a Changed World, Angus T. Moss

Wisp moved away from the frightened woman. He could feel Nick's curiosity and went to join him down the hall where he stood before the next door.

"Is there a problem?" Nick asked in a low voice.

"She's afraid of me." Wisp watched the woman devour her food. She was obviously starving. Her long brown hair hung in greasy tangles down past her shoulders. Like all of the prisoners, she was slender, extremely pale and weakly muscled. Her large blue eyes narrowed in concentration as she stuffed her mouth. She had elegant long-fingered hands and narrow feet marred by long nails that were chipped and dirty. Clean and healthy, he thought she would be beautiful.

Nick huffed out a sigh of frustration. "She's the first one that reacted. What makes her different?"

"She looks familiar."

"You've seen her before? I checked the chart, she's been here five years."

"I don't think it's my memory." He shrugged at Nick's raised eyebrow. "It'll take me a bit to sort that out. In the mean time..." He gestured to the next door. "No one alive in there."

Nick opened the door to an empty room. Wisp could feel his relief. Despite the fact that Nick had no responsibility for any of the people imprisoned here, he felt guilty. Every dead body gave Nick another small burden of regret. Helping rescue the others seemed to ease that burden a little. All of which seemed very odd. Wisp wondered how long Nick would remain here. Every minute entangled them further into a disaster not of their making. He wanted to leave as soon as possible.

Nick shut the door and marked the room as empty. He tipped his head toward the next door. "How about that one?"

Wisp reached out his senses. He could feel Ruth, standing to one side as a cloud of disapproval laced with fear. Kyle focused on the task before him, calm and resolute. The rows of prisoners were still subdued, foggy, mildly confused when they could form a thought at all. Except for that one woman. She was struggling with her emotions, fear and anger and longing overlapping with top notes of desperation. He blocked those minds out and reached toward the row of rooms yet to search.

"Nothing. Empty or dead."

"Good. I'm going to bet empty." Nick pulled open the next door, glanced inside, then shut it and marked it. Took him only a few minutes to deal with the final ten doors.

"How many do we have?" Nick asked.

"Twenty-three living, four dead," Kyle announced.

Wisp felt that twinge of guilt hit Nick again. "There wasn't anything you could have done to stop those deaths," he offered.

Nick gave him a sad smile. "Thanks." He turned to survey the group of released prisoners. "Let's get these folks upstairs.

"These people can't climb the stairs," Kyle pointed out.

Nick realized he was right as soon as he said it. The prisoners had barely been able to walk down the hall to the stairs. They were weak from their incarceration, and possibly malnutrition. "There's an elevator."

He saw that thoughtful, inward look on Kyle's face again. He gave him a moment to think his plan through. "It makes more sense to remain in this building and bring the others here. They are more mobile."

"Yes." Nick eyed the prisoners. They were mostly staring into space. "You and Ruth stay here with them while Wisp and I find a place to settle them upstairs.

They took the elevator up to the kitchen. Nick and Wisp moved the dead cook into a back hallway. Nick's first choice was the cafeteria. Unfortunately, there were too many bodies to move, and they'd already left a considerable mess. Nick didn't want to spend the afternoon sanitizing the place. They located a large lounge that should accommodate everyone and had a minimum of deceased. Then they moved all the corpses that the prisoners might pass and the few from the lounge. Once they got all the prisoners upstairs and settled, Nick went with Kyle and Ruth to bring the rest of the survivors over. He watched them for reactions when they heard who these people were. Two of the guards exchanged guilty looks. Everyone else was amazed that Rutledge had locked up these people.

In the time that they had been dealing with the prisoners, one guard and the two members of Blue

Team had left. Nick asked, but no one had thought to inquire why or where they might have gone. That made him uneasy.

"We reported in," Jonas said. "They haven't received any shipments. Should any arrive, they are forewarned not to use them. The agencies have been briefed on our situation. They will conference with us tomorrow afternoon with new orders."

"*They* who?" Nick asked.

"Minister Ackerman?"

Nick was stumped. "When did we get ministers?"

Jonas gave him an odd look. "Ah, I'm not sure. He's the Minister of Health and reports to the president."

Nick chuckled. "Wow. We have a president."

Jonas tipped his head like a puzzled dog. "Where are you from? Of course, we have a president."

Nick shook his head, too full of questions to allow himself to start in that direction. "Never mind. What did he say?"

"He wasn't available. We'll conference with him tomorrow morning."

Wisp came out of the kitchen area. "There is food to prepare."

Nick was thankful for the change in subject. He was battling a scope of emotions about this. Where was this government? He'd talked to plenty of people in settlements all up and down the train lines. No one else knew about them. He needed to get more information, but right now, he was hungry. He asked for kitchen volunteers and wasn't surprised that it was the janitor, the file clerk and the groundskeeper that came forward.

He joined Wisp in the kitchen. The supplies were shocking. They had things he didn't think still existed. There were oranges, bananas and boxes of sugar. It made him wonder if the archipelago of Florida had started trading, or perhaps one of few remaining

Caribbean islands. There was a whole cabinet full of packages of coffee. The walk-in refrigerator had cold cuts, fresh vegetables, margarine and fruit. He felt tears sting his eyes as he stood there with the chill sinking into him. It was like stepping back in time to a pre-virus world. Wisp called him away to show him a rack filled with loaves of bread. For a few minutes his swirling emotions coalesced into anger. Apparently, in the new world, he was a member of the have-nots.

"Why does this make you angry?" Wisp asked.

"Do you know where to get supplies like this?" Nick snapped. His anger was getting the better of him. It seemed so unfair that the settlements could be closed out of access to food.

"I try to live off what I find. I don't go looking for things like this. Perhaps it is some sort of compensation for the work they do here."

"Huh," Nick grunted a reply. It made sense. Money didn't exist. Why else would people do work that wouldn't put a roof over their heads or food on the table? Food and shelter had to be a given. Maybe for their families too. Which gave him another idea. "I want to bring some of this back to High Meadow."

"There is more here than the existing survivors would need. Will you ask, or just take?"

Nick stared at the overflowing shelves. They must have just gotten a shipment. The fresh food would spoil soon. He needed to find out who the survivors had put in charge. Once he knew who that was, he'd know whether asking would work.

* * *

Nick went to see what the volunteers had come up with. A couple of the guards had dragged in two long tables from the cafeteria. Quinton, the groundskeeper, had assembled a tray of sliced bread with margarine and was handing it out to the prisoners. Nick was glad to see that people were warming to their tasks. Most of them were shocked and scared. Familiar things helped. In a very short time, they sat down to a meal of sliced turkey in canned gravy with carrots and peas. He would have liked mashed potatoes, but he wasn't about to complain.

After they'd eaten and gotten volunteers for clean up, he waited to see who would take charge. As he was stacking dirty plates in the dish room, Jonas came over to him. "What should we do now?"

Nick handed his stack off to Lester, the janitor, who was doing double duty. "This isn't my gig."

"I'm a chemist," Jonas said simply. "And I've got no place to go now. We can't do the work Rutledge contracted to do with a handful of people. They'll give the contracts to our competitors, and I doubt they're hiring."

"Competitors?"

"There are a couple of labs that do similar work."

Nick nodded, relieved, but a small voice nagged at him that the damage done here was irreparable. Of the men and women he'd seen sprawled across sidewalks, hallways and desks, the youngest was probably in his late thirties. There had been a decade of chaos after Zero Year. Schools closed and people were too worried about survival to think about education. He knew of older children at High Meadow that hadn't learned to read yet. The young men and women now in their twenties had left formal education ten years ago. There were no brilliant science majors competing to fill these positions. A portion of the smartest, most skilled people left in the world were gone. The loss of workers was bad enough, the loss of teachers was crippling. He pushed down hard on the rising fear. "Who trains you people?"

Jonas stared at him for a long minute. Nick could

see the realization crowding in behind his eyes. "We lost a lot of good people here." His voice caught. He cleared his throat, looking at the floor. "I hate to admit it, but Ruth was right. Rutledge was pushing us all the time. The vaccine wasn't ready." He glanced over to the prisoners. "And I haven't a clue who those people are. This all just stinks. I need a new job."

"You're welcome to come to High Meadow Med Center. We can always use another pair of hands."

"Thanks, but I'll wait to hear what my options are when we hear from Ackerman tomorrow."

Nick slipped away to an office to contact Angus. He sat at the console with a groan. He was tired and achy and just wanted to walk away from this mess. He opened a line to High Meadow knowing that Angus was probably still at dinner, but hoping he was working.

"Nicky!" Angus greeted him with a smile. "I am delighted to hear from you. Is all well?"

"All is very complicated. Don't want to go into it right now."

Angus's smile slipped. "Are you all right?"

"I'm fine. Might be delayed a day or two returning. I didn't want you folks to worry." Nick saw Angus look past him for clues to his whereabouts. He'd picked up on Nick's hint that all was not going as planned.

"Have you found what you were looking for?"

"Found what we needed to know. Don't think there will be any vaccine this year."

"Oh." Angus looked like he was struggling to contain the million questions that Nick knew were boiling around in his brain. Normally, Nick contacted him from train stations, as that was about the only place with ether access anymore. Whatever Angus could see of the office must surely have him puzzled.

"I'll give you the long story when we get back. I might be bringing guests."

"Guests are always welcome."

“How are things on your end?” Nick felt sure that anything Angus would say would be generic enough that it wouldn’t get them into trouble. And that thought had him skidding to a halt. He didn’t know what he was trying to hide from whom. But in a situation like this, he decided to follow Wisp’s lead. He did not want to bring himself or High Meadow to the attention of anyone who had access to heavily armed men. It would be best for them to leave first thing in the morning.

Chapter 35

"When a people are migratory they do so in clans and tribes carrying their traditions, their very civilization, along with them. When our people went on the move, it was often solitary and without plan."

History of a Changed World, Angus T. Moss

The breakfast meeting in the lounge was brief. Nick did a head count and saw that more of the guards and another lab tech had left. That made less people for him to worry about. The prisoners trooped in, guided by Kyle. Someone had brewed up an urn of coffee. There was orange juice, toast and hard boiled eggs, brought from the kitchen on the food carts from the basement. Adequate, but he missed Susan's cooking. With all these supplies, she'd have whipped up something really special.

Angus had warned him that the flu was moving quickly through the settlement. It seemed to randomly hit some people harder. So far they couldn't tell when it would be a mild case or lethal. Angus warned him of fatalities but didn't mention any names. That worried Nick most of all. But other news about the Riverbank folks lightened his mood. Jean was back on her feet and Bruno and William were making progress. He made Angus a promise to get home in a few days and signed off. Although he would have loved Angus's advice, he didn't feel comfortable talking about the situation on an open format. For all he knew, the calls from this lab were monitored by the government. Nick got a coffee and joined Kyle and Ruth at a table. "Where's Wisp?" he asked them.

Kyle shrugged. "He's around somewhere."

Ruth gave him a searching look. "Why don't you know where he is? Isn't he your responsibility?"

Nick decided the truth could come later, when it wouldn't interfere with more serious issues. "I give him a long leash."

That didn't seem to satisfy her. She snatched Kyle's empty plate and stacked it with hers, slamming the china hard against a plastic tray. "I'll check on the prisoners."

Nick waited for her to get out of earshot before going into the problem at hand. "I need to find out what kind of drugs the prisoners are on."

"I don't know. I've spoken to some of the others. No one knew they were down there."

"Can you test their blood?" Nick asked.

"I am not a phlebotomist," Kyle said with alarm. "We don't deal directly with people."

"We need to know what's going to happen when this stuff wears off."

A muscle twitched in Kyle's jaw. His eyes scanned the room for Ruth. "I can research the drug, its effects and duration."

"Thank you. I would appreciate that."

Nick figured that Kyle was probably the best

person to ask about the prisoners. As a biobot, he understood the workings of ownership. “Will the government assume authority over the prisoners?”

Kyle looked lost for a moment. “This is Dr. Rutledge's lab. He is dead. He won the contract for the vaccine, but we are no longer in a position to fulfill our obligation. Another one of the consortiums will have to take over the contract. I don't believe that the people he detained would be part of that contract because our research is proprietary information. The lab is not required to share its sources.”

Nick felt almost dizzy with the shift in perspective. There was a whole world he wasn't privy to involving consortiums, contracts and ministers and even a president. But a great rush of relief hit him because there were backups in place. “So there's another lab that will start making vaccines?”

“I believe so. We will know later today when we receive our orders.”

* * *

The prisoners remained at the tables after they’d eaten. Some looked more alert than others. Nick got a second cup of coffee and made the rounds. One by one, he sat down, introduced himself and asked a few questions. Most of them couldn’t even remember their names. They gave one word answers or stared at him blankly. He wrote everything down, even garbled nonsense in the hope that it might make sense later. The woman, Melissa, seemed in better shape. She couldn’t answer his questions either, but in her case, he felt that she was hiding something. When he finished, he saw Wisp had arrived and was filling a tray with food.

“Where were you?”

“Made a circuit. The bodies out in the open are in

bad shape. Looks like we had some small predators in here last night. Crows came in this morning." Wisp took a mug and filled it with coffee. "The people that left took equipment along with vehicles."

"I don't care about that."

Wisp nodded agreement."I didn't know what the equipment was for, so I don't know its value to a place like High Meadow."

"Not on the agenda today," Nick said shortly. He hadn't even thought about that. If he had more time, he might consider looking for things they could use in the infirmary, but he wanted to be out of here as soon as possible. His gut was telling him to move, pronto.

"There are six vans like the one we took from the mercenaries. I think we could fill one with supplies and leave."

Nick refilled his mug with coffee and took an orange, feeling very luxurious about the amount of food available. "I want to wait and hear what this Minister has to say."

Wisp gave him that pale blue assessing look again, but didn't question him. "After I eat, I'll start loading a vehicle."

Nick nodded, absently. He didn't know when he'd gotten to be in charge. It seemed to be happening to him an awful lot lately.

* * *

Nick arrived just minutes before the conference call. It was set up in a small briefing room. The remaining survivors settled in seats facing a smartwall. He stood out of the sightline of the camera. He didn't have a right to be here, but he wanted to hear what was going to happen.

"Gentlemen." The link opened without notice. A stern looking man in a suit greeted them. A wave of nostalgia hit Nick. He hadn't worn a suit since Zero Year. The man looked pressed and starched, and it made him wonder where he got that sort of thing done. Laundries and dry cleaners, department stores and tailors, there were so many things gone out of the world.

Jonas took the lead. "Minister Ackerman." He gave the man a courteous nod. "You have the recommendation of the Health Agency for us?"

"Yes, Dr. Pruitt. We have spoken with the other labs. They are preparing to take on the additional work. They are also willing to take on some of the staff there. I'm sending you the lab locations and which positions they are looking to fill. We all agree that it is best to abandon that installation. We have no use for it at this time. We are sending an army unit to take an inventory of any equipment that might be helpful at the other labs. They will also deal with the deceased."

"And the rest of us?" demanded a man.

"What are your skills?"

"I'm a lab tech."

Ackerman glanced to one side, his eyes moving as if reading. "I believe there are positions available."

"For what kind of pay?"

Nick perked up. Were they using some kind of money?

"The usual. Food, shelter and access to private markets."

The disgruntled man jolted to his feet and stomped out. Nick wondered what he expected from the world as it was. Or maybe these people didn't know about the world the have-nots were living in. There couldn't be many places where he could work. He was curious about the private markets. He'd like to know a little more about that.

"Will we be required to remain here until the army arrives?" Ruth asked.

"Is there any danger to leaving the place empty?"

"There aren't any bandits in the area that we know of," Jonas said.

"The unit has already been dispatched. They should arrive there sometime tomorrow, I believe, and everyone will be expected to depart at that time. If the place is empty when they get there, I suppose that makes their job easier." Ackerman leaned forward, frowning into the camera. "Once the army takes possession of the compound, they *will* be in charge."

It seemed pretty cold to Nick. This was their home, and they were being kicked out with barely twenty-four hour notice.

"Understood Minister," Jonas said smoothly. "Anything else?"

"No, I think that covers it Dr. Pruitt."

Jonas cut the connection and tossed the list of positions on to the side wall. The scientists and lab techs crowded together to get a look. The guards left the room arguing among themselves. Nick was tempted to follow. They posed a greater threat than any of the other people in this room.

Ruth turned from the list with anger in her eyes. "Are they serious with this?"

"What?" Nick asked.

Jonas slumped in his chair. "All low level positions. Cleaning test tubes for some big shot."

"We're being punished," someone grumbled.

Ruth folded her arms tightly, scowling at the blank video screen. "We failed. We go to the bottom of the ranking now." She gave a frustrated huff in Nick's general direction before marching out the door..

Jonas rubbed his face and turned bloodshot eyes on Nick. "We gotta get out of here before they arrive."

"You think there will be trouble?"

"I think that anything I want to take with me might suddenly become government property."

"What are these private markets?" Nick asked.

Jonas gave him that curious look again. "Why do I get the feeling you just arrived on the planet?"

Nick smiled, trying to put him at ease. "You're a have. I'm a have-not. The settlements and med centers don't have access to the private markets."

"Well, yeah, 'cause they're *private*." Jonas scoffed at him. "Wait, you guys didn't even know about them?"

"Nope."

"Huh, that doesn't seem right. I mean, how do they hire people if nobody knows what the rewards are?"

"When's the last time they were hiring?"

Jonas frowned. "I think you're scaring me."

"I think you've got an elite system going here." Nick leaned against the wall. The rest of the people filed out, grumbling to one another. Nick watched them go. They were all well fed. Their clothes were new and varied. "Most of this stuff isn't available anymore."

Jonas cracked his knuckles, one by one, his frown deepening. "I don't understand what that means."

"I travel around looking for settlements to barter with. Very few are self-sufficient. More than a few survive entirely on train food. I haven't seen an orange since I went out to the Nevada coast. And even then it was just a few trees in an mostly destroyed orchard."

"Really? I didn't think things were that bad."

"Out there it feels like nobody's minding the store."

Chapter 36

"Despite the dwindling numbers of human beings on the planet, some members felt it was a time to prey on their brothers and sisters."
History of a Changed World, Angus T. Moss

Nick headed back to the lounge to check on the prisoners with Jonas following close behind. Kyle intercepted them, pulling them both into a small office. Ruth had pill bottles and papers spread out on the desk. Jonas leaned over and picked up one of the bottles. He whistled under his breath.

Ruth took the bottle out of his hand and placed it carefully back on the table. "These are very strong drugs."

"You called them chemical restraint. Do you mean they will keep them passive?" Nick asked.

"And obedient," Jonas said. He rubbed his hands on his pants like he had something nasty on them. "With enough of this in your system, you'd walk off a bridge if someone told you to."

"That sounds about right considering how they behaved yesterday."

"Perhaps that's why they were in cells," Kyle said. "To keep them safe."

"I doubt it," Nick said. He knew the reasons for their incarceration wouldn't be quite that benevolent. "How long till it wears off?"

Ruth shuffled her papers, but Nick got the feeling she was just stalling. "It may depend on how long they have been taking them."

"Can you make a guess as to how long it'll take them to get back to normal?"

Kyle pulled the papers away from Ruth and stacked them neatly. "I can make a guess at body weight and dosage, add in the time spent here. It won't be exact."

"I don't think we need exact right now. Ballpark'll do it. Can you figure out if they will need to be weaned off?"

"Oh, most definitely," Ruth said, avoiding his eyes. "I need to look at the charts." She left the room in a hurry.

"Great," Nick said although she was already gone.

"What do you plan to do with all these people?" Kyle asked. His big brown eyes made him look disarming despite his burly stature.

Nick ran a hand back through his short hair. "If they're drugged, they can't make an informed decision. I don't want to leave them here for the army to deal with." He gestured to the papers. "Not sure how long it's going to take to get them back on their feet. It isn't just the drugs. They're incredibly weak. Vulnerable. I can't walk away and just leave them here."

Jonas moved closer, knotting his fingers and biting his lip. Nick could smell the nervous sweat on him. "Are you going to take them to your, um, your settlement?" Jonas asked. He avoided Nick's eyes speaking very softly. “They may not fare well in that sort of a situation.”

“It’s a med center,” Nick said. “They can recuperate there until they they are able to decide what to do for themselves.”

“You won’t restrict them?” Kyle asked.

“They will be free to go or stay.” Nick looked at Jonas and back to Kyle. “What about you?”

“Rutledge assigned Ruth as my Keeper. I must go where she goes.”

“Come to High Meadow,” Nick said, including Jonas in the invitation.

“You have a lab there?”

“No. But you shouldn't make a decision right away. Come back with us for a couple days to recuperate. Then you can take a better look at your options.”

Kyle dipped his head in thanks. “That is good advice. Ruth is deeply shaken by these events. Her job, as a physician, is to make sure our formulas are always beneficial. She had advised against proceeding in the direction that Gold Team took. Therefore, she feels some responsibility for not being able to stop this calamity. I don’t think she should feel that way. She was quite adamant to Rutledge. It was his decision to proceed. That was a very heated meeting.” Kyle shrugged one large shoulder. “She needs to get away from here to think clearly.”

Nick nodded agreement. “High Meadow is a pleasant place.”

“So Wisp has said.”

Kyle gathered up his papers. “I will get to work on this for you.”

Nick left Jonas reading over Kyle’s shoulder and headed out to inspect the vehicles. He was going to need space for about thirty people if everyone wanted to come. The vans could easily hold ten people each, with a good stack of supplies packed in. He’d drive one,

Wisp could take the second and if Kyle agreed to join him, he'd trust him to drive the third. Somehow he doubted he'd have more than that many who would want to go with him to High Meadow.

He got outside to find that Wisp had parked a van by the front door and had started loading. That was when Nick realized that Wisp's priorities differed from his own. Weapons and ammunition were the first things stowed. A stack of body armor was waiting on the sidewalk. Nick hoped there would be room for the food he was planning to take. When he thought about bringing the boxes of coffee, oil, sugar and other supplies that were hard to find, he had to smile. Susan would be delighted. Tilly would be in seventh heaven. It would help to get them through the winter if any of their crops failed completely. Filling up the larder was a small piece of security that he could offer in a world without any sureties.

He took some time to go through the rest of the buildings looking for anything that High Meadow could use. He found a couple of first aid kits, two tool boxes and hit the stockroom full of office supplies. That would definitely please Angus. After leaving his findings for Wisp to pack, he went on to the kitchen for a final inventory. There were too many supplies for him to take them all. Oil, salt and sugar were at the top of his list. He'd take everything they had. Spices, flour and canned goods came next. A giddy smile kept appearing on his face. It wasn't often that he got to bring home such a treasure trove. Finally, he put all the fresh food aside—meat, fruit, vegetables—anything he didn't think would travel well and planned to serve it for lunch. Once the prisoners were fed, they could get on the road. He wanted to be well gone before any soldiers arrived. There was no way to know if Ackerman had lied about their arrival times.

Ruth came to him as Nick was sorting through the

janitor's room. Cleaners and disinfectants would go, too. Those were extremely difficult to find. He wasn't sure about the paper products. They were awfully bulky, but toilet paper was in short supply. Maybe he needed to add another vehicle to the caravan.

"You plan to *take* all these people to High Meadow?" Her tone was more accusing than curious.

"I *invited* them," Nick corrected. "It's not mandatory."

"Your settlement will be able to handle this many?"

"We're a pretty small community," Nick admitted. "But we've planned for growth. There's plenty of room for everyone."

"Your...leader, won't object?"

"Angus?" Nick chuckled. "He feels the more the merrier." A glance at her frown made him change gears. "Angus is a free-thinker. People come and go as they please, but everyone who remains must contribute to the community as they can. That doesn't mean we'll put you to work digging in the fields. People do what they're best at. You and Kyle are welcome to come test the waters. If it doesn't appeal, you can move on somewhere else."

"I'm not sure about any of this," she said frowning at him.

"That's nice and vague. Care to be more specific?"

Her eyes were still swollen and bloodshot. From the circles under them, he doubted she'd slept. She was a small woman, but she straightened her spine and squared her shoulders. "I can't condone your assumption of the prisoners."

"They are not prisoners anymore."

"But they aren't free either."

Nick put down the box of tissues he was holding. Ruth was scared. He could see it in her eyes and how rigidly she held herself. But she was challenging him because she feared for the prisoners. He gave her his full attention, speaking softly so his words wouldn't sound like a challenge."What do you recommend for all those drugged people? Hand them over to the army? Push them out the door?"

"No. No, that isn't right either."

"We don't have a lot of options here. If you've got any ideas, I'm open to hearing them, but I meant it Ruth. High Meadow is a safe place. And we have a doctor there. They can recuperate and make a decision when they're in a better state of mind."

She looked at him skeptically. "Why are you so altruistic?"

Nick sighed. "Because we are all there is. If we can't treat each other with respect..." He couldn't finish that sentence because he knew how rarely it was true.

Ruth looked down the hall, chewing on her bottom lip, while Nick waited patiently. "Very well. I will go with you."

Nick nodded at her. "We leave after lunch."

* * *

The day's heat was becoming uncomfortable as Nick helped Wisp finish loading the vans. He'd managed to get almost everything he wanted. Wisp had nodded approval at some of the supplies and given him an odd glance or two on the others, but he'd packed it all in with great efficiency. Once the vehicles were ready, Nick got everyone into the lounge to eat.

"We lost some more," Wisp said as he joined him at the head of the room.

"Lost how?"

"Some are missing, three are dead."

"I don't care about missing. People can make up their own minds. If they can walk away from here, that's just less for me to worry about. Dead isn't good. Do we know what caused the deaths?"

"I'm going to assume flu. They didn't get the vaccine."

"Which means that the prisoners aren't special when it comes to flu. I was hoping that might be the reason they were there, some kind of super immunity. I guess we'll have to leave those bodies and let the army sort it out."

"They won't be happy to see the mess we've left them."

"Not my problem," Nick said curtly. "This government needs to take care of stuff. Not just trains and vaccines. People need to know about them. We need better information."

"Be careful what you ask for," Wisp said in an undertone.

Nick grunted an agreement. He needed to find out a lot more information before he went looking for the government. He nodded toward the people sitting at tables eating fresh, hot food."How many have we got left?"

"The guards that left this morning took a couple of smaller vehicles and some equipment. A couple of the lab techs decided to go to the other lab. They all went in one car. We're down to twenty-five people and us." Wisp gave him a rare smile. "Looks like we'll only need the three vehicles, but that frees up some cargo room. I've got them all charging now."

Nick gave him a thumbs up and went to get his own lunch.

* * *

They convoyed out with Wisp and Nick in the lead. Nick hoped that Wisp would be able to sense any trouble, so they could avoid it. In that case, he wanted Wisp close at hand. Kyle and Ruth drove the second van. Jonas had asked to come. He and the file clerk,

Ellen, had the third van, which had less people and more supplies. Nick planned to stop at a train station around dinner time. They'd eat there and bed down the prisoners in the shelter cubbies. If they were able to find good roads, they could be back to High Meadow in two days.

They followed the train line as best they could. Nick estimated that they would pass two stations before hitting the one where he wanted to spend the night. Around mid-afternoon, he told Wisp to pull into the next station, so they could all hit the restrooms and get fresh water. As soon as they pulled into the parking lot, it was obvious that the station was closed. Nick was stunned. What would happen to the people in the area that relied on it for food and shelter? Wisp led them up the driveway, which was in surprisingly good shape, to the front of the building. There were steel shutters down on the entrance to the lobby. Nick hadn't seen that before. The other two vans pulled up behind them, but no one got out.

The radio beeped announcing an incoming call from one of the other vans. "Why is it closed?" Jonas asked.

"This line services the lab. Perhaps they felt it wasn't worth the effort to keep it open," Kyle offered.

Nick didn't like any of the other possibilities he was coming up with. If this entire line was down, they might have to find a lateral line that wouldn't be affected by the shut down. He brought up some maps on the dashboard. There were two immediate options, one being a much longer drive and taking them slightly out of the way. He was debating it when Wisp leaned over and tapped the farther station.

"Avoid the obvious?" Nick asked.

"I'd feel more comfortable with a few more miles behind us."

Wisp's words sent a shiver down Nick's back. He

radioed the other two cars to let them know that dinner would be late.

Chapter 37

"There were the normal roving bands of evil men who felt the easiest way to survive was to take whatever they needed wherever they found it. When their surroundings became depleted, they moved on to a new source."

History of a Changed World, Angus T. Moss

It was full dark and spitting rain when they rolled into Tupelo Station. They had circumvented a small settlement. Nick didn't want any complications right now. They had been forced to go out of the way several times to find acceptable roads. The driveway into the station parking lot was shattered into hard lumps of broken pavement and barely negotiable mud pits. The vans wobbled slowly through the worst of it up to the drop-off area. Nick was achy with tension and glad to finally be done for the day. Still, he had everyone stay put, engines running, while he and Wisp checked out the station.

The building was fairly new with an extremely low

profile. They walked down a short flight of stairs into the main waiting area. The ticket booth was closed up with dusty glass and a door rusted shut. The floors were shiny from a recent buffing, which made Nick relax a little. This station was in use. He checked the supply room and was glad to find it full of the usual stocks of Stew-goo and Crunch. Not the most appetizing dinner but a very convenient one.

"Anybody around?" he asked Wisp.

"There're two people in the cubbies." Wisp turned in a full circle frowning in concentration. "Otherwise, no one closer than that settlement we passed."

Nick huffed out a sigh of relief. "We'll man a watch for tonight."

Wisp nodded as he continued a visual inspection of the area. "Let me catch a few hours sleep. I'll take the midnight to dawn."

Nick started to say he didn't need to, but realized he was the best resource for it. And how quickly he had gotten used to Wisp's talent. He accepted it without a thought now. "Thank you."

Wisp's mouth quirked in a half-smile. "Just makes sense."

Nick went out to give them the all clear. He helped with the unloading of the prisoners, who were exhausted by the trip, the change in routine and surroundings. There were nine people from the lab and eleven prisoners. Nick reminded himself to start learning names. These people weren't prisoners anymore. The sooner he stopped treating them that way, the sooner they would begin to feel normal. On a last trip out to the van, he dug through the supplies until he found some light colored tape and a marker. Then he went back and put a name tag on everyone while they ate.

He should have known it would have an impact on things. The ex-prisoners were delighted to be named.

And all but one was able to remember his name. An older man, confused and frail wasn't sure who he was. Nick couldn't say if it was the drugs or an underlying condition that made him unable to answer. They agreed on a name in the meantime. Apparently he wanted to be called Cyril. It was such an odd choice that Nick was sure it must be his real name.

The people from the lab didn't seem to be as pleased about the nametags. Nick didn't give them a choice. He put one on himself and Wisp also. Then he noticed the looks. Several of the scientists, Kyle and Ruth included, were staring at Cyril.

Nick went over to Kyle. "Is there a problem?"

Kyle turned a thoughtful frown on him. "Is that really his name?"

Nick shrugged. "Does it matter?"

"That was a project name for a..." Kyle paused, his eyes automatically turning to Ruth.

"Classified?" Nick asked.

Kyle made a point of looking around the station at the people gathered there. "It may not matter anymore. It was a research project on blood-borne illnesses."

"Like West Nile?"

"Mm. More like Ebola."

"Don't like the sound of that. Do you think he was involved in it?"

"It was a large project that continued over nearly two decades. Many people were involved."

"Were you?" Nick asked.

Kyle ducked his head, then hesitantly nodded. "It was the first thing I worked on after the army took possession of me."

"I'd appreciate it if you would think it over and see if there is any reason why your lab would want to keep someone from that project imprisoned."

"You mean Dr. Rutledge's lab." Kyle corrected him automatically.

"Right."

"I cannot imagine what it would have to do with the work that was being done there, but I will consider the coincidence and try to form some hypotheses."

Nick bit his lip to keep the smile off his face. Kyle's extremely formal response had struck him as remarkably absurd in the current circumstances. Nick started to leave, but Ruth reached out toward him, which stopped him in his tracks. "What can I do for you?" She seemed a little unsure, so he forced a smile for her.

"Well, I was just wondering...it isn't a criticism, you know, just, I was just wondering..."

"Yes?"

"Are you specifically avoiding towns?"

Nick stared at her, trying to gauge her intent. "How long have you been in research?"

She seemed startled by the change in topic. "Since college. I started working with the army right away." An honest smile graced her face. "It was where I met Kyle."

Nick thought about how to phrase it. She was obviously completely in the dark about the true state of the world. He tried to make his voice gentle. "There aren't any."

"Don't be ridiculous."

Nick licked his lips and the moment stretched a little too long. A worried frown creased her forehead. "I'm sorry, Ruth. There are a few settlements, a couple of med centers within a day's train ride from the lab. We did circumvent a small settlement two-three miles back. I don't like to show up at places I haven't already checked out. But there aren't any towns as you remember them. Largest settlement I've been to is Westridge. They've got about fifteen hundred folks spread out. It's an old summer camp. They'll let folks spend the night, might even let you stay permanent, but it isn't like a town."

Her frown changed from worry to annoyance. "They can't all be gone. Where are all the people?"

"In settlements and med centers. Angus is working on a census. He thinks there's only about thirty-three million in the whole country right now."

Ruth opened her mouth to respond, but nothing came out as Nick's words sank in. "Are you serious?"

"I've been all over. Well, anywhere you can get to by train that is. The population is shrinking every year."

"But that can't be right!" She grabbed Kyle's arm and dragged him away.

Nick went to check on the others. Ruth would find out soon enough what the world looked like. His insistence wouldn't speed that along any. As soon as everyone had finished eating, he herded them all down to the shelter cubbies and tried to escort the ex-prisoners in. Unfortunately, the drugs were wearing off, and they weren't as accommodating any more. A few people balked at being sent into small rooms. He pointed out that these doors locked from the inside, which calmed most of them. One man refused flat out.

"We're a family," he said firmly. His nametag said Mike. He looked to be in his forties, pale and worn out, ragged brown hair with a few streaks of gray framed a square face with sad blue eyes. He had his arm around a woman his age and two teenage girls huddled against them. Nick felt sick. All four of them had been in separate cells at the lab. A whole family, imprisoned.

Nick gestured to the next aisle in the shelter which contained a few multi-user cubbies. "Take a big one. You can all sleep together."

Mike blinked at him, surprised or appreciative, Nick couldn't tell. Then he shuffled off, his family glommed on to him like limpets. It was a small step, but it made Nick feel that he'd given them back some dignity.

Nick took the first watch. He checked all the cubbies. Then he went upstairs to the main waiting area. He collected enough Crunch for everyone's breakfast and stacked it on the benches where they had eaten dinner. Then he went to the big map to check the lines. As he had suspected, the entire line from the lateral to Laurel was dark. Although it was true that the lab was no longer in use, there were probably a number of settlements using those train stations. Now they were without food and emergency shelter. That worried Nick. He couldn't decide if it was vindictive or prophylactic for that line to be shut down. And if it was to prepare for something else, what could that something be?

He walked the perimeter of the station stopping from time to time to listen to the sounds of the night. A rumble underneath his feet told him a train was passing through. Other than that, a few night birds called to one another. The light rain had stopped but heavy clouds moved in, blocking any moonlight. A breeze brought the scent of wet pavement and cooling greenery. The air was heavy with moisture. The lights from the station were all there was in the vicinity. Once he stepped into the deep shadows of the surrounding woods, he could only see what caught the pale glow of the security lights.

He stood listening to the occasional spatter of rain shaken from the trees by an errant breeze. Cicadas started cranking out their deafening call. The night was suffocatingly warm, the humidity making it nearly unbearable. A tropical system must be moving up from the Gulf. There might be rain all day tomorrow. That could make travel difficult. He'd use the ether at the station to check the roads from here to High Meadow. He was just starting a second circuit of the station when he heard the crunch of gravel in the parking lot.

Nick slipped behind a thick tree trunk, into deep

shadow. He stayed very quiet. Voices came to him. A man and a woman arguing. "I said we should go this way!"

"Why?"

"Because that's the way we came. We don't want to go that way."

"But I think this way is quicker."

Nick crept through the undergrowth as quietly as possible. Between the cicadas and the argument, he doubted anyone would hear him. He got close enough to see the two of them, standing in the lights in front of the station. Not intruders, ex-prisoners. They finished their discussion and started walking across the parking lot, after a few feet, they held hands. Nick smiled. They were probably going to get into a whole lot of trouble, but if they wanted to leave, that was their decision.

He finished his circuit of the station and went inside. The sudden change into air conditioning made his clothes feel damp and heavy. He did a quick round of the cubbies, but all was quiet. He went to the ether booths, there was a row of them all along the back wall of the main waiting area. He took one that let him see the room easily. He called up a mapping program. It didn't open. He tried a geography plotter, to no avail. The weather site responded with information that was already three days old. A chill ran down his spine that had nothing to do with the air conditioning. More sites on the ether were failing. He checked a few more that he used regularly. Two produced errors. Nervously, he requested the site for High Meadow.

A sketch of wildflowers opened into the main page for the med center. Nick breathed a sigh of relief as the usual information scrolled across the page. There was a recent note posted that the center had flu cases and that there would be no vaccine this year. Symptoms were listed and suggestions for simple home remedies. The message bar indicating whether the center was still taking patients was green, which meant they were still open for business.

Nick sent Angus a short, vague text message. He knew that Angus might be awake at this hour, but he was nervous about a live call on a public line. It would let Angus know all was well so far, but not let anyone intercepting it know anything more.

"You should rest."

Nick jumped, startled to find Wisp at his side. "You scared me."

Wisp smiled. "Sorry. I move very quietly out of habit."

"Two people left," Nick reported.

"For the best, if they weren't happy with your plans."

Nick shrugged. He gestured to the console. "Sent a note to Angus. Looks like the mapping program is down."

"Odd coincidence?"

"Don't know."

"We are safe here at the moment. Get some rest. I'll wake you if anything comes up."

Nick gave him a salute and headed for the stairs. All of a sudden, he was feeling drained. He stumbled down to his cubby in a fog of exhaustion. The steel shelf felt like a real bed. He was asleep in seconds.

Chapter 38

"Although many people depended on the train food, the ubiquitous Crunch and Stew-goo, no one knew where it was produced. Very few witnessed the arrival of train cars full of packaged food or the stocking of the supply rooms."

History of a Changed World, Angus T. Moss

Tilly went through the motions of her normal routine all the while knowing that they were in serious trouble. Three more deaths. Her heart ached with loss. She'd allowed herself a few tears at the graves, but no more. She had to be strong for the rest of them. Most of the time. Here, in her bedroom, alone, she could let down the wall for a little bit.

The people that had recovered from light cases of flu were now caring for the sick. It seemed logical that they would be inoculated. Angus couldn't find any indicators that would let them know who might be hit harder than another. But in the end, she thought that might be a blessing. Who would want to know that this year's flu was your death sentence?

Eventually it would come down to not enough hands to do all the work. She stifled a sob of frustration and loss. It all seemed so futile some days. Why fight the inevitable? Man had been stupid enough to sow the seeds of his own demise. She should just sit down and wait for death to overcome her.

Letting the grief and pain wash down through her helped ease it. You could only hold it at bay for so long without repercussions. She took a few deep breaths. Her image in the mirror showed her a stranger, a bony old hag with dark-circled eyes and chapped lips. This was the worst season in years.

She had a long list of things to do but couldn't get started today. There were faces missing. Great gaps in the community that she didn't know how to fill. The pain rose again, and she let the tears flow. Somehow she had to get everyone through this.

A knock on the door had her scrambling for a handkerchief. "Come," she said wiping her eyes.

Angus came in with a steaming cup. "I brought you some tea, my dear." He set it on the corner of her dressing table without comment. She loved him a little bit more for that. "Bruno has been foraging again and turned up three kinds of mint. Smells lovely, doesn't it?"

She gave him a hug. He held her for a long time, not speaking. His arms were a familiar weight against her back. This was what made her put up with all his eccentricities. His ability to know when she needed him most. And the uncanny way he had of soothing her by doing nothing, just being present. "I love you."

"And I you." He kissed her forehead.

She slipped out of his warm arms and stood shivering for a moment. She felt so vulnerable all of a sudden. "Is breakfast done?"

"People have eaten, but they're wandering around

asking for you."

"I take one day to sleep in a little and the world falls apart," she chided with a forced smile.

"You are the queen of this small domain." Angus gave her a courtier's bow.

There it was again. He told her that she was needed without demanding she take her place, without accusing her of failing or insisting she work harder. He knew how hard she pushed herself. She didn't need anyone to point out her lacks or failings. She just needed support. And she knew she could always rely on his.

"Is Martin pulling his hair out?"

Angus turned a hand up in a shrug. "Martin is always fussing about something. I don't think we need to worry about some mysterious invasion in the middle of a flu season like this. Just about anyone with a brain will hunker down with family or friends."

Tilly nodded. Like the ancients waiting to war until spring, bandits and bad guys waited for end of flu season to attack. People were more vulnerable then, recovering from illness and loss. Plus the med center had a plan in place now. If they were attacked, everyone would evacuate down to the storm shelters. Martin had rigged them to his own design, claiming they were highly defensible. Whatever that meant. And if the attack came from below, something Tilly hadn't even considered, they should hide in the chapel.

"What would we do without Martin?" Her voice was a bit rough, but she managed to speak without a tremor to her words.

"We would muddle by," Angus said gently. "I love them all too, dearest, but no one can be irreplaceable anymore. Including you and me."

She chuffed out a sigh. "I suppose that means more planning."

Angus paced a few steps in a way that warned her

he wanted to broach a difficult subject. "This is a bad year."

"Yes."

"We need to make a plan for the center beyond our tenure."

She smiled at his choice of words. "Planning retirement?"

He returned her smile. "Abdication at a proper age for the crown prince to come into his own."

She chuckled. "We'll talk tonight?"

"It's a date," he said with a twinkle in his eye. He spun on his heel and left with a jaunty walk.

Tilly smiled at the door. Angus had cheered her up. She was ready to go out and face the day.

Chapter 39

"The country was badly situated to lose its population. When the numbers were this low, in the 1800's, local farms were hauling food into rapidly growing cities. We had no such infrastructure to fall back on."

History of a Changed World, Angus T. Moss

Nick flinched at the sound of a howl, human and deeply discontent. He was in the stock room trying to decide if he should pack food for lunch or bet on hitting the next station. The morning had been proceeding very orderly. As people woke, they came up from the cubbies, and collected train food for breakfast. They settled in small groups, some chatting quietly.

"What do you want from us!" The voice sounded young and female.

Nick followed the sound out to the waiting area. It was one of the teenagers who had slept with her family in the big cubby. She was standing in the middle of the room sobbing. Her long brown hair was knotted and snarled. Her clothes were awry from sleeping in them.

He approached her slowly. She raised her eyes to him, her face twisted in hysteria. "Who are you? What is happening!"

Nick glanced at her nametag, thankful that it had survived an obviously rough night. "Doreen?" He spoke very gently.

Her gaze locked on to his face, as her eyes widened in terror.

"It's okay. You're safe here. I'm Nick. Do you remember me?"

"What are they going to do to us? How did we get here? What did they do to Sara?" Her words ran together, slurred by drugs and fear.

"*They* are gone." He stayed still, not moving any closer to her. "We have left the lab. We are going to a safe place."

Her eyes clouded with confusion. "Lab?" She looked around, only now seeming to comprehend her surroundings. "This is a train station."

"Yes. We spent the night here."

"Doreen!" Mike shuffled into the waiting room, the rest of the family trailing after him.

Nick took a few steps back as Doreen stumbled to her father's arms crying and stammering her confusion. He saw Kyle and Ruth watching from a bench where they were eating breakfast. He went over to check in with them.

"How many times is that going to happen?" Nick asked.

Ruth gave him a tight nod. "You handled that very well."

Nick felt muscles tighten across his back at the way she sidestepped his question. "Do we need to have a meeting before we put everyone back in the vans? I don't want any breakdowns like that while we're in transit."

Wisp jogged across the room toward them, a look of urgency about him.

"Nick." Wisp waited until he was close enough to speak in a low voice. "There are three dead in the cubbies."

"Damn. Flu?"

Wisp glanced at Ruth for a bare second before looking back at Nick. "I can't tell. There's no blood. No obvious wounds or violence. The doors were locked from the inside. Might be a reaction from the drug withdrawal?"

Ruth stood up, but spoke with her eyes on the floor. "It shouldn't kill them."

"Let's take a look." Nick ushered them all downstairs to the cubbies. Wisp had jimmied the doors open. The three cubbies were from different areas of the shelter, so it wasn't location. The first one they checked was Cyril's.

"He was very frail," Nick said.

"I agree," Ruth said. She pointed to his face, sunken and pallid. "Indications of cardiovascular complications." She studied his hands for a moment. "I would say not flu. Natural causes, though. Heart attack or stroke."

"Thank you," Nick said.

He let Ruth enter the next cubby, first. She did a quicker examination. "This one is most likely flu."

The third looked like flu also. Nick stood in the hallway staring at the doors as Kyle, Ruth and Wisp waited by the stairs. "Should we leave the bodies?"

Kyle tipped his head in thought. "I believe the stations are prepared to handle deaths like this. It must happen every flu season."

"No." Wisp's voice was low but firm. "It's a trail."

Nick caught his eye. Wisp gave him a microscopic shrug. "He's right," Nick said.

"What kind of trail?" Ruth asked nervously.

"To us," Nick said. He walked past her up the stairs. "I'll find a shovel."

* * *

Kyle, Jonas and Lester, the janitor, helped Nick dig graves to bury the three bodies. They got on the road a lot later than Nick wanted. He headed the convoy north toward High Meadow. They spent the day driving in and out of showers. A couple of times, they had to stop until a cloudburst moved on past them. The dirt roads were mud pits. The paved roads were pocked and shattered. By lunch time, they were battered from the rough ride.

"Any idea where we are?" Nick asked Wisp under his breath. They sat on worn benches at a derelict rest stop on the remains of an old highway. He had handed out train food, relieved that he'd chosen to pack it, in case.

Wisp glanced at the sun, then across the road to the woods. "Closer than we were."

"I'd hoped to be there by tomorrow."

"We might still make it."

Nick slumped in his seat. The tension was knotting up his shoulders. His gut was so tight he could barely eat.

"We are safe for now," Wisp said.

"For now," Nick repeated sourly. He forced down the rest of his Crunch. He couldn't face the Stew-goo today. He walked around the vehicles checking the tires. Then he checked all the chargers. They'd parked in the sun, to top off the batteries.

"Nick?"

He turned to find one of the ex-prisoners approaching him. His nametag said *Tonka*. He was a middle-aged man who looked like he'd be burly once he put a little more weight on. Right now he was starvation thin with the thick knobs of bone showing at wrist and knuckle. “Everything okay?”

“Any seconds?” he asked with a shy smile.

Nick chuckled. “I think there’s a couple left.” He led Tonka over to the van with the food.

“I, um, wanted to, you know, thank you.”

“No problem,” Nick said automatically.

“No, I mean it.” Tonka grabbed Nick’s arm. “I know what was going on. I know that if you guys hadn’t found us, we would have all starved to death in that place.”

“Why were you there?” Nick asked as he handed him another packet of Stew-goo.

“I didn’t do anything wrong.” He avoided Nick’s eyes as he eagerly took the food. “Thanks.” His hands shook as he stood there, holding the food, not looking at Nick. “Why do you want to know.”

“Rutledge’s men killed a girl. I’m trying to figure out why.”

Tonka’s mouth tightened for a minute before he nodded. “He was ruthless. A bastard. An evil bastard.”

Nick waited, wondering if the drugs would keep Tonka just babbling without any clear point. “What do you remember?”

“Not a lot. I know I hate him.”

“He’s dead.”

“Good.” Tonka’s gaze flickered from the ground to Nick. “Okay to go eat?”

Nick sent him on his way with a mental note to check back in with him in a day or two. He started packing up when Kyle approached him.

“You want seconds, too?” Nick asked.

Kyle looked uneasy. “If there is extra food, I would like some.”

His passive response reminded Nick that Kyle lived as property. Just as Wisp preferred to be unseen and disregarded, Kyle had no expectations of equal treatment. Nick handed him an extra packet each of Crunch and Stew-goo.

"Thank you. But I came to tell you that I was thinking about your question concerning the Cyril Project. I believe there were a number of researchers that worked on that project who then went on to work on the first team that researched the virus."

"And why would that get them locked up in Rutledge's basement?"

Kyle's unease increased, as did his careful phrasing. "In the early days of research there were many different approaches put forward. Some were more, um, aggressive than others."

"Let me guess, Rutledge was aggressive."

"He was very vocal concerning his thoughts on the proper direction of the the research. I wasn't present, but I heard from others that he was very angry not be put in charge of the federally funded lab."

"And the old man was?"

"No. It was a woman, if I remember correctly. At least at the beginning. I think they lost a few directors in the first year."

"So the old guy could have been involved in that and Rutledge locked him up out of spite?"

"Dr. Rutledge had a very...um, volatile personality." Kyle looked away, clutching his packet of food.

"Go eat," Nick said, waiving him away. "Thanks for letting me know."

"It's simply conjecture, without any further information..."

"All the same, thanks."

* * *

They got back on the road and continued heading in a general north-westerly direction. Nick was getting more tense. Without the mapping site, he had no way of knowing where he was. Wisp seemed to know from the lay of the land, or the angle of the sun or some other arcane method. Nick wasn't sure if he should trust Wisp that blindly, when he had no way to corroborate the biobot's assertions.

About an hour after lunch, the road they were following dead-ended into a massive chasm with white water at the bottom. Nick called a halt. They all got out to look at the water.

"That looks like it's new," Jonas said.

"I don't know this river," Nick grumbled. He was worried about how much backtracking they were going to have to do. Somewhere in the past hour, he'd gotten the feeling they were being followed. He looked around to find Wisp.

"He's up a tree," Jonas said with amusement.

Wisp came back down with a plan. To Nick's relief he'd found an alternate route that took them past the new river and back to a highway that was in reasonable shape. They traveled due east for another hour until they saw the remains of an old sign that told them they'd driven twenty-six miles past their turn off. Instead of turning around, Wisp found a new road with a more north-westerly route.

As the sun sank behind the trees, Nick's stress kicked into a higher gear. Since he didn't know where he was, it stood to reason no one else knew where they were. So maybe they weren't being followed, or tracked, or watched. His nerves were so raw that everything seemed a problem. They might have to sleep in the vans. He wasn't sure if they had enough supplies to cobble together some kind of dinner. Should they build a fire? Would it attract attention? He'd gotten himself pretty worked up by the time they hit the barrier.

"Shit!" In the dim light of the late afternoon, the barrier looked imposing. It reminded Nick of the cannibals. He didn't want to have to try to protect three vehicles in a situation like that. He had no idea how Kyle or Jonas would react. Did any of them even know how to use a firearm? Which made him realize that he should have distributed weapons before they left. He only had the handgun he'd tucked into the driver's side pocket. He started to reach for it when Wisp put a hand out to stop him.

"There is no one here," Wisp said.

Nick almost grabbed for him as Wisp jumped out of the car. He followed a second later after taking a big breath. His hands were shaking. He wasn't sure if that was his nerves, lack of food or something else. He loosened his collar which was damp with sweat despite the air conditioning in the van, and wondered if he was running a fever.

Wisp was already hauling timber out of the road when Nick got to him. Now that he was up close, Nick could tell it was just flotsam. Thin streams of sand across the road showed where a flood had traveled, pushing and pulling branches and mud with it. In a minute Jonas, Lester and Tonka joined them. Using his muscles, stretching, lifting and dragging the debris helped loosen some of the tension. By the time the road was clear, Nick was feeling much better.

Unfortunately, the flood had done serious damage to the roadbed for over a mile. They limped through the remains of the pavement, around more piles of debris and over mounds of mud. Nick was thinking about where they should stop for the night when Wisp made a pleased sound.

"There it is."

Wisp pointed to a side road, clear and in excellent condition. Nick turned up it hopeful that they were getting closer to a train station. If they could find one in the next hour or so, they'd be set for the night. But an hour later, they were deep into the woods with very little sightline ahead and the last vestiges of light failing. Nick's nerves kicked up again. Why was this road in good shape? Who used it? Wisp seemed to know it, did he know where they were going? He was about to start barking questions when a light appeared up the road.

It was a handmade sign with a solar powered light on it. "Creamery 3 miles."

"That's a good place, too." Wisp said.

Nick nodded.

"We can stay there tonight."

"Okay."

Wisp frowned at him. "You don't believe me."

"Things change. We'll see when we get there."

Wisp gave him a half nod, half shrug. Nick forced his fingers to loosen on the steering wheel. They approached the turnoff. Nick slowed and turned onto a well maintained gravel road. He slowed again as it wandered around a big oak and over a short bridge. In the gloaming, he could see open land to either side. Split rail fences lined the road. Ahead there was a stockade wall that stood close to ten feet tall with spotlights mounted to shine on the road. The wood was raw, probably just taken from the fields on either side. The gate was closed. Five men with shotguns stood facing them.

Nick pulled the car to the side of the driveway and the other two vans followed.

"They fear the vehicles," Wisp said.

Nick radioed to the other cars for everyone to get out. He got out with his hands in the air. "I'm unarmed," he shouted. "I'm Nick from High Meadow. We're just looking for a safe place for the night. Maybe barter for some dinner?"

A soft murmur called his attention to a group of men at the top of the stockade wall. More guns. There was a bit of a discussion before someone answered.

"What's High Meadow doing with vans like that?"

Nick looked back at the slick black vehicles. "Well, that's kind of a long story. But we're not looking for any trouble. We're willing to put in some work for food if you've got it to spare."

There was a little more discussion. "What kind of work?"

Nick raised his shoulders in an exaggerated shrug. "A couple of us can do anything, dig ditches, chop wood. I've got some scientists..." Nick paused, not sure what they could possibly offer a dairy.

"What kind?" The voice sounded very eager. "You got any chemists?"

"I am," Jonas raised his hand and stepped forward.

A smaller door in the gate opened and a broad shouldered man stepped through. Nick realized the men must be related. All of them had thick builds, cornflower blue eyes and shaggy blond hair. The man hesitated by the door, giving them all a thorough look. His eyes lingered on Wisp, then wandered to Mike's family and on to Jonas. He gave determined nod. "I'm Bert. Welcome to the Creamery. Sorry about this, but we've had a bit of a rough time lately."

Nick waited for Bert to approach, then met him halfway to shake hands. "I understand. Had some rough times myself." He gestured back at the vans. "They're sort of borrowed. I didn't think about what we might look like driving up in them. Are you the folks that put out the flyer about cheese?"

Bert grimaced. "Yeah. Turns out it's not such a good idea to advertise." He glanced back at the stockade.

Nick looked a little closer at the men with guns. None of them held the weapons with confidence. One man, a youngster really, had both hands on the stock, neither near the trigger and Nick was going to bet that the gun was unloaded. These folks had recently been forced to mount defense. "I'm sorry to hear that. Your flyer really cheered me up. I was looking forward to working out some trade with you."

Bert brightened. "What have you got in mind?"

"I do the trading for High Meadow. We've got some crops in the ground that we might be able to trade. What sorts of things are you looking for?"

Bert got a thoughtful look on his face. "Sounds like we should have a talk. You're welcome to come spend the night. But I'm sorry to say we don't have much more than cheese to share right now."

Nick laughed. "I've got the perfect thing!" He sprinted back to the second van to break out the box of bread, and looked up to see men with guns, a lot closer. He grabbed a loaf and held it out. "Bread!"

Their looks changed from animosity to pleasant curiosity.

Bert grinned. "That'd be mighty welcome." He waved to the men atop the wall and the large gate wobbled open.

Nick noted that the wall wasn't all that well constructed. Definitely a rush job. He thought about asking Martin to come down and sort this place out. Once inside, it was even more obvious that they were scrambling to shore up defenses. The wall was only half finished and petered out a few yards in. They were living in what was probably an old hunting lodge. It looked ancient, constructed entirely out of logs, but carefully tucked into a shallow hillside. Thick beams supported a deep porch where women and children watched their approach.

There were a few introductions as they filed into a high ceilinged lobby where trestle tables were set up. Nick had thrown a few things into a box to share: two loaves of bread, a box of coffee, a small sack of sugar and a larger one of flour. He handed the box to an older woman who thanked him without even looking at the contents. She had only gone a few feet when she realized the bounty he'd gifted them with. She gasped, soon surrounded by two other older women. Nick smiled. It felt good to share.

Dinner was cheese and tomato sandwiches with a thin vegetable soup that had probably been watered down to stretch. Nick smiled at everyone as he sorted them out. The spouses that had married in were obvious in contrast to the clan's strong genes. There were a couple of dark-haired women, a redheaded man whose genes held strong producing three children with strawberry blonde hair, and a wife with white-blonde hair like wet silk. She looked willowy and frail next to the solid, curly-blond women of the house.

Talk at the table stuck to generic topics of weather and wildfires. What condition the roads were in. Where was the closest train station. Mostly folks just ate. There was dried apples and coffee for desert. The Creamery families seemed cautiously pleased.

Nick sat down with the elders of the clan. They had been living here since the area got depopulated. They had been building up the herd since the hoofed-flu took about ninety percent of their stock. They had just reached a point where they could market some wares. Their flyer had brought in bandits and troublemakers. They hadn't had any troubles before.

"We've got a Watch at High Meadow," Nick said. "We don't get much in the way of bandits either, but a couple armed guards gets them moving on their way."

"We can hardly spare a man," grumbled an older man who looked enough like Bert to be his brother. "Cows're a lotta work."

"It isn't easy," Nick agreed. "You need to bring in a guy who has the experience."

Bert's brother frowned at him, his blue eyes suddenly cold. "Like you?"

"Me?" Nick forced a chuckle. "I don't do that stuff.

I can talk to Martin, the head of our Watch, if you like. He might be able to give you some suggestions."

The icy blue eyes warmed a bit. "We don't have much to offer."

"A warm place to sleep, food and company is all most people are asking for," Nick said.

"Well we've got the space and the company," Bert said bitterly. "Damn bandits cleaned out our larders."

"I'll do it."

Nick looked up to see the last guard standing nearby. He still had his nametag on. "Stan," Nick said. He gestured him over. "Why don't you folks talk a bit, see if it might work for both sides." He slipped away from the discussion to check on the rest of his charges. Wisp had stayed with the vans preferring a meal of train food to the gathering of so many busy minds. Jonas was deep in conversation with an younger man and woman. Nick looked around to see how people had fallen out into groups. Mike's family was sitting with a family with children of the same age. He wouldn't be surprised to find a few more people staying behind.

* * *

Melissa sat quietly at the table chewing the dried apples. She gave the room furtive glances trying to judge the various knots of people. No one looked familiar to her. She was relieved and a little concerned. How long had she been held in that white room? The memories had no anchor, all the days of captivity had been the same. She didn't know how she fit into this group of pale, shaggy victims. Noticing the beards and unkempt hair on the others made her very aware of her own grubbiness. Her hair was disgusting. She tried to wash up in the cubby the night before, but she needed a whole lot more than a sink-bath. Maybe that was what gave her anonymity. Cleaned up, people might know who she was. That thought gave her a new set of worries. Since she didn't know why she'd been imprisoned, she didn't know if being recognized was a liability.

The thin woman with long blonde hair brought her a cup of coffee. "Hello." She spoke loudly and slowly.

"Hello. Thank you," she said taking the coffee. She wanted her voice to sound normal, but it creaked like an old wheel.

"You are safe here."

"Really?" That came out a little sharper than she'd meant.

The blonde sighed. "As safe as we can be in times like this."

Melissa felt bad for bringing up the obvious. She didn't know what more to say and was glad when the woman moved on to hand out more cups of coffee. Memories and thoughts were still circling her head like gulls over a trawler. She couldn't reel any of them in long enough for more than a glimpse. There was something wrong. Something so very terribly important that she was forgetting about, and it scared her to death.

Chapter 40

"Without leadership, people scramble for mere survival. Without foresight, communities work for the wrong goals."

History of a Changed World, Angus T. Moss

In the morning, Jonas and Stan were waiting in the hall outside Nick's bedroom. The guests had been put up in the hotel portion of the lodge. The rooms were small and a little dusty, but welcomed. A hot shower and real bed had Nick feeling more like himself.

He opened the door to find the two men leaning against the opposite wall. "Problem?" Nick asked.

Jonas and Stan exchanged guilty glances. "We're staying," Jonas said.

"Okay."

"You're good with that?" Stan asked. "Cause I know we probably owe you."

Nick waved his concerns away. "Nope. You guys hitched a ride. This is where you want to get off. That's fine with me."

"They want to look into some different kinds of culturing," Jonas said. "This really is more interesting to me than the work we were doing." He shuffled his feet and ducked his head shyly. "Cheesemaking was a hobby of mine."

"Perfect match then," Nick gave him a congratulatory slap on the shoulder. "I'll be looking forward to seeing what you come up with. Haven't had a good blue cheese in a decade."

Jonas's grin widened. "Thanks Nick."

"You don't know," Stan said quietly, "but I was in the army. The real army. The gig at Rutledge's was boring most of the time. And the people he hired," Stan's mouth tightened as he shook his head. "Some of them were nuts. They'd do anything he told them. And Rutledge was nuts too, you know."

"You knew about the prisoners?"

"Rumors. There were a couple of us guys trying to keep things above board. We knew there was something weird going on. But nobody that knew would talk to us. Rutledge was always sending guys out on searches. Didn't know then, but I'm guessing it was for people."

Nick forced his face to remain placid as thoughts of Lily and William got his blood pressure up. "Any idea why he wanted them?"

Stan twitched a shoulder in a shrug. "I hate shit like that. Here, things are nice and clean. Good folks farming. There aren't any secret agendas."

Nick nodded, meeting his eyes. "They seem like good people."

"They are. I want to help keep them safe."

Nick shook hands with Stan. "Do that."

Jonas and Stan hurried down the hallway ahead of Nick. He was glad that they were staying in a place that suited them. And he had to think that the Creamery clan would be glad of a couple more single males.

He headed down to the lobby following the smell of fresh brewed coffee. There were biscuits with cream cheese and apple butter set out for them. Nick saw that most of his people were at the table. The Creamery clan was probably already at work.

"Good morning!" He was greeted by the willowy blonde.

"Thanks for putting us up," Nick said.

She held out a cup of coffee to him. "I think you more than paid for it."

"I know where you can trade for coffee and tea. Cheese is a pretty rare commodity. You should be able to barter for almost anything. Have you got someone in the family to travel for trading?"

She shook her head, her long blonde hair sliding over her shoulders. "We need all hands on the farm. Cows can't wait to be milked."

"Maybe I can help," Mike said. Nick noticed that he had a little more color to his face today. His voice was stronger and his family didn't need to constantly reach for one another. "I'm Mike." He offered his hand.

"Deidre," she responded with a hearty handshake that nearly took him off his feet.

Nick left them to work out the particulars. Creamery seemed to have plenty of space. Another couple with two girls could be a good addition. He slathered some biscuits with cream cheese and apple butter then carried them out to the vans. The stockade gate stood open. In the bright light of morning, he could see the fields, with their stubble of tree stumps, dotted with brown cows. Wisp was leaning against the fence watching them. Nick offered him a biscuit.

"Nice," Wisp said as he accepted the food.

"Are they contented cows?" Nick asked. He popped the last bit of breakfast into his mouth and licked the apple butter off his fingers.

"Very," Wisp said with a mouth full.

"You been here before?"

"I've stayed in the woods above here. The people seemed pretty nice from a distance. They take very good care of their animals."

"Well I'm glad we found this place last night. I needed a good night's sleep."

"We should make it to High Meadow by tonight if we push through," Wisp said.

"Mm." Nick stared at the cows, the sun warming his shoulders. He almost wanted to stay another day. "I think we should barter off some of this stuff. They seem like they're in pretty bad shape."

Wisp looked up the hill to the treeline above the lodge. "The woods here are full of food."

"Maybe they don't know that," Nick said. He dusted the last crumbs off his shirt and headed for the van.

"Do you want me to forage for them?"

Nick stopped and turned back looked at Wisp. "You don't feel the need to help them?"

"Life right now is a barter. What do I get for feeding them?"

"Their good will? A place where you will be remembered as a friend?"

"I try not to be remembered at all."

Although he said it without undue emotion, Nick felt a deep sadness at Wisp's aloneness. He lived a silent solitary life in a very dangerous world. "I would appreciate it if you would gather some food for them." He handed Wisp an empty box.

"As you wish. When will we be leaving?"

Nick glanced toward the sun where it was sending beams through the tree branches." Say about an hour?"

Wisp took the box and melted into the woods. Even though Nick was watching him, even though he knew where he would enter the woods, as soon as Wisp stepped into the shadows at the edge of the trees, he vanished.

Nick took a quick inventory through his precious supplies. Some things they needed more than others. He had wondered why the Creamery folks weren't using train food to get by until Bert told him the closest train station was about five miles away. That was a long walk with a sack of food. He wondered if this might be a better place for Harley's horses. But he was getting ahead of himself. He put together three boxes of supplies including the largest first aid kit, industrial sized cans of vegetables, some spices, a canned ham and three small salamis. With only seventeen of them left, he decided to leave one of the vans, too. Aside from a tractor, the Creamery didn't have any vehicles, and could surely use one. So he shifted the supplies he was keeping to the other two vehicles. Almost as an afterthought, he added a couple guns and some boxes of ammunition for Stan. By the time he was done, Ruth and Kyle had come out to check on him.

"You plan to give all of this to them?" Ruth asked with suspicion in her voice.

"No way," he snapped back. "I'm bartering for cheese. That stuff's like gold. I want some for us, and I can barter the extra away for things we need."

Ruth cocked her head at him. "Where do you normally get things like this?"

Nick gave her a a smirk. "We don't."

He drove the third van up to the lodge with the supplies he'd chosen for barter. After announcing his intention to Deirdre, she sent the youngest child, a girl around ten, running off to find the grandfather, Abel. The old man came limping out of the barn with a tight look on his face.

"I'm told you want to trade?"

Nick beckoned him to the back of the van to show his goods. Abel shook his head. "I heard Bert tell you, all we got is cheese."

"Abel, that's gold. You may only have cheese, but you are probably the only dairy in the country with it!"

Abel gave him a look of disbelief. "Anybody can make cheese. Ain't hard."

"*If* they had cows," Nick said. "Believe me, they are very rare right now."

"I can't give you my whole lot for this. Gotta save some back for the family. Bandits did a job on us, all right."

Nick lowered his expectations. "What have you got?"

Abel led him to the side of the lodge where an entrance to the cellar had been enlarged to accommodate a ramp and a wide door. He took Nick down a flight of steps into a clean bright room. It was a working room with tables and vats and an industrial stove in the corner. Jonas was already set up with a computer and stacks of cups around him. He gave Nick a distracted wave before diving back into his alchemy. The room had a pleasant smell that he couldn't quite place.

"This is where we age 'em," Abel said pulling open a heavy door. "We were lucky, the bandits took all the food outta the kitchen larders. Didn't check down here." Inside tall racks held wheels of cheese. Nick's jaw dropped. Rack after rack retreated into the huge room.

"Wow."

"Well, you might think it's a lot, but this bunch here, it ain't ready yet." Abel led him past the first few rows. "This is the year old. It'll do, but I prefer at least two years. Now back here we got the really good stuff."

Nick grinned. This was more than he had hoped for.

They ended up lugging a dozen small wheels and three massive ones up to the van. He got a crock of cream cheese, three blocks of butter and a small urn of fresh milk. He hoped the air conditioning in the car would keep it all fresh until they could store it at High Meadow. By then Wisp had arrived with a box full of mushrooms, last year's walnuts, enough greens for one dinner, a double handful of asparagus stalks each thick as a thumb, and a kerchief full of blueberries. The women thanked Nick for the canned food and grilled Wisp on the locations for the fresh food.

Bert was grinning from ear to ear. "I sure am glad I didn't turn you away last night."

"Me, too, " Nick said, admiring his cheeses before closing up the van.

"You folks must have a pretty big settlement."

"Nope. I'm going to barter some of this for stuff we don't have. There's a settlement with sheep that's got spun wool to trade. They've got some weavers starting up too. Another place out toward the coast does tea and coffee. I know they'll really like this stuff."

Mike sidled up to him. "Can I take notes?"

"I'll let you know next time I'm going out. You can join me."

Mike blinked at him. "Really? But isn't that your route?"

Nick chuffed out a denial. "I'm not a travelling salesman. I barter for what we need with what I've got. It's not a competition, Mike."

"I'm grateful," Mike said offering a handshake. "The last few years have been a nightmare."

"Why were you...locked up?"

Mike shrugged. "I'm not sure. Competition? I ran a small manufacturing plant. We made fine gauge needles. The kind they use for the vaccine."

"You think Rutledge kidnapped you for your plant?"

"For my equipment more likely. He tried to buy me out, but I said no. It's our family's business. We've been making needles since they were invented."

"So he kidnapped you and took what he wanted," Nick said, frowning at the thoughts forming in his head.

"Who would stop him?" Mike asked sadly. He looked up the driveway to the big house. "I hope we'll be safe here."

"You will be," Nick said with more force than he intended. He had to believe that this settlement would survive.

They left the Creamery folks in good spirits. Nick and Wisp driving one van, Ruth and Kyle driving the other. The rich smell of cheese permeating both vehicles. Bert had given them directions to the nearest highway with warning about a bridge that had collapsed. They would need to go out of their way one more time before crossing the river and working their way back to the road that lead to High Meadow.

Chapter 41

"The history of the United States shows us leaders convincing the populace to back their goals. This country was stitched together by people who wanted the same things."

History of a Changed World, Angus T. Moss

Tilly looked out across the fields hoping to see Nick coming up the road. He said he'd be back today. She wanted to hold him to his word. Right now, she needed to keep eyes on all her people. Her gaze wandered toward the back meadow where they were digging another grave. She bit her lip as her eyes prickled with tears.

"Any sign?" Martin stood beside her, sweaty and muddy from his turn in the cemetery.

"Not yet."

"He'll be here." Martin squinted at the deep blue bowl of a sky overhead. "Hopefully it's going to stay clear. Has Angus found out anything more about the weather site?"

Tilly shook her head, not trusting her voice to stay calm.

"Strange. Maybe Nick can go check that one out next."

Tilly took a deep breath that caught in her throat. "I don't know how he would find that one." Talking about stupid things like Nick's next trip, if there even was one, helped her move a few steps away from grief. "Wisp knew about the vaccine center didn't he?"

"Actually I think it was a brother. Maybe he has another one working for the weather forecasters."

Tilly tried to force a smile on her trembling lips but failed. She hoped her mouth wasn't stuck in a grimace. Her people were being whittled away. One by one, they fell before her eyes. They'd lost two more during the night. Angus said he thought they might be on the backside of it now. That everyone in the center had surely been exposed and should have gotten sick by now. But he'd said that in other years and been wrong when the virus mutated and came back to take the ones that had survived.

She realized she was gripping Martin's hand and didn't remember taking it.

"It'll be all right, Tilly," he said in soft voice. "We'll get through this."

"I'm fine," she lied. Martin didn't know her like Angus, but he was trying to comfort her, so she shouldn't be short with him. "Thank you."

"We found the missing chickens."

"Do I want to know?"

"They'd holed up in an old pump house. Not sure what attracted 'em. Bugs maybe."

"Yes. Maybe."

"Bruno found a grape arbor that he said will bear a heavy harvest this year. We could try our hand at some wine."

"Yes. That would be good."

"Lottie transplanted some more of those herbs Bruno found for her. She's got a nice variety going now."

"That's good." She knew Martin deserved more than her terse answers, but she could barely speak for the ache in her throat.

"Miss Tilly?"

She turned at Harley's call, glad for any distraction. "Yes, I'm here," she called to the nearly-blind man.

Harley stood on the grass patting the neck of a tall bay horse. "Jelly here is getting a bit jittery. I think there's gonna be some bad weather. Just thought I'd let you folks know so you can cover the crops. I'm gonna take em all in now." Harley hustled off toward the stable.

Tilly felt a smile tug at her lips. "Martin, would you sound the alarm. Seems we have a weather-horse now."

Chapter 42

"In the viral years, people suffered from a lack of faith. No one could be trusted. No one could be expected to live beyond the next year. Therefore, communities were rare."

History of a Changed World, Angus T. Moss

"Wind's kicking up," Wisp observed. They were passing through thick forest, climbing at a steep rate. The trees bent and shivered across the road.

Nick looked at the peaceful blue sky. "Have you tried the forecast dock today?"

Wisp obediently tried to open the dock on the dashboard screen. "Still that old forecast."

Nick cursed under his breath. "Keep an eye out for some shelter in case we need to go to ground."

"We might be better off down by the river."

"Maybe. If you see a side road, let me know."

A gust of wind hit the van making Nick correct slightly. The road was fairly decent with minimal potholes. "I think we're going to need that shelter sooner rather than later."

"We're almost to the top. Maybe we'll have a better view from there."

Nick heaved a sigh of relief when Wisp was right. They crested the hill and found a breathtaking view before them. Storm-tossed trees littered the hillside giving them a partial view of the basin below. The river had crested its banks and was creeping across the floor of the valley. Someone had cut a path through the fallen timber. It was a tight squeeze, but Nick got the van through with only a few scratches. Kyle followed carefully behind him.

Long fingers of ink-black clouds were reaching across the sky as they started the downward trek.

"There," Wisp said pointing to the switchback visible below them. "See that jut of stone?"

Nick slowed to focus on where Wisp was pointing. Rugged stands of rock sheltered the road from the drop off on several of the hairpin turns. Down on the left was a pull-out tucked in between the sheer wall of the mountain and the outer ring of stone. It was as good as they were going to find. The light was fading and fat drops of rain spattered on the windshield. "Let Kyle know," he instructed Wisp.

They crept down the mountain on a slick road in pounding rain. Nick backed into the shelter to keep an eye on what might come down the road towards them. He put his right side as close to the rock as possible, giving him just enough room to squeeze out of the door in an emergency. Kyle did the same, pulling in close to them. One more vehicle could have fit if carefully maneuvered. Nick was just about to say how lucky they were when the rain turned to hail. The racket was deafening. Nick worried about the windshield, then remembered it was bullet proof. The vehicle was probably safe.

A big branch landed in the road in front of them.

Nick's hands tightened on the steering wheel. He had a nasty feeling this was going to be a bad one. Hail covered the road with a blanket of white, pounding down and bouncing off rocks. Another branch sailed past, blown by fierce winds, tumbling along the ground. The temperature dropped. Nick turned off the air conditioner, but left the van running. He wanted a quick getaway if needed. The battering from the hail slowed, but rain quickly made up for it. Water began running down the road toward them, pushing flotillas of ice. The shelter was graded at a slight pitch toward the road. Both streams joined to plummet down the switchbacks gathering strength at each of the sharp curves buttressed in stone. A few small branches rushed past in a heap of leaves.

Nick was glad they were out of the main road. The water looked about ankle deep and running fast enough to knock a man off his feet. The sky was still dark, but the rain was slacking off. He took a breath hoping they'd gotten through unscathed.

"Not yet," Wisp said softly. He was watching the sky.

Nick forced himself to relax in his seat. There was nothing to do while they were stuck here, so he might as well take a minute to stretch. Maybe get a snack.

"Get down!" Wisp yelled as he hunched over.

Something hit the van hard sending a deep shudder through it and blocking the windshield. Nick had ducked, arms covering his head. He looked up, but the van was too dark to see. Wisp flipped on the interior lights.

Nick looked around. "Everyone okay?"

Everyone was seated, looking a bit surprised. There was no apparent damage to the interior of the vehicle. Nick looked closer at the windshield, it was covered with branches, apparently a tree had come down on them. He grabbed the radio. "Kyle? You guys okay over there?"

"We are fine," Kyle answered. "There is a dent in the roof."

Nick listened, but didn't hear any rain. He tried the door, pushing against another branch, but couldn't get it open more than a few inches. "Damn. Wisp, try your door."

Wisp's door was also blocked. Nick released the side door which slid back about a foot before snagging on something. He squeezed out of it into a faceful of pine needles. He could feel that the branches were fewer lower and got down on his hands and knees to crawl out. Twigs grabbed at his clothes and hair as he burrowed his way toward the front of the van. He stumbled out into the road, finally clear of the tree, into a light rain. Only to find he was surrounded by the debris of a massive tree that had fallen from high above on to the road to shatter into pieces. The trunk was blocking the road, the canopy was on the vans.

Wisp wiggled out from under the branches. Kyle came out a few feet further up the tree. He looked around at the mess. "This presents a problem."

Nick burst out laughing. "Yes it does."

Chapter 43

"Whenever someone, or a group of people, managed to create more than they needed for survival and started looking for communities to trade with, they opened themselves up to attack."

History of a Changed World, Angus T. Moss

Nick laughed till tears ran down his face. One by one people crawled out of the vans to stand nervously watching him. He knew it was worrying them. He could feel the hysteria building inside himself and the safest release right now was laughter. They wanted him to be a leader when all he wanted was to be on his own. All the tension and anger flowed out in great guffaws. His stomach hurt, and it was getting hard to catch his breath by the time the giggles petered out. Wisp hadn't said a word. The biobot walked away from the group toward the rock wall on the side of the road. Nick caught his breath, brushed the pine needles out of his hair and checked the sky. The storm was moving, wind pushing the darkest clouds towards the east.

"Nick!" Wisp was standing on the wall looking out over the road.

Nick walked over to him. "Is the storm coming back?"

"People in trouble." Wisp pointed.

He climbed up the pile of stone next to Wisp. Below he could see the final four switchbacks down to the wide river valley. He could just make out where the road should be under the river which lay muddy and bloated across the valley. To the south of the road, a horse cart was struggling toward higher ground. It was piled with crates. A man and a woman were in the bed and two men were walking. The water wasn't dangerously deep, maybe knee high, but from the way the horses moved, the cart was stuck. The woman was screaming. He could barely hear her. She stood on the back of the cart, struggling against the man, trying to get off. Behind them, small figures floundered in the water. Children?

Kyle joined them. "If we can get the horses up here, they could help us move the tree."

Nick looked back at the chunk of tree laying on the vehicles. There was no way that they would be able to move it without help.

"They're stuck," Wisp said. "And I think they can't swim."

"Okay, Kyle, let our folks know what's happening, and get some guys to help. Wisp come with me."

They hiked down the road. The rain petered out to a heavy mist. As they rounded the second switchback, they could hear the woman screaming. She was calling out to the youngsters floundering in the water behind the cart. He couldn't imagine why the man on the cart wouldn't let her help them. The two men were at the front were trying to calm the horses who were fighting against the dead weight of the mired wagon.

The last section of road was ankle deep in cold

water. Nick and Wisp splashed down the road toward the horses. The people hadn't noticed them, being so caught up in the horses and children. Nick called out, "Hello the cart!"

Heads snapped towards him. "We're stuck up the road," Nick yelled as they approached them. "Thought maybe we could help each other out."

One of the men at the head of the horses slogged toward them. He was a little younger than Nick and looked very strong. He wore a worn leather vest over a thick cotton shirt that looked handmade. He raised his hands as if pushing them away. "Nothing for you here friend."

Nick swung wide of the man and made for the children with Wisp silently following. No one could move quickly in the muddy water. The footing was uneven and slippery, sloping down toward the river. As he splashed past the cart the water rose above his knees, slowing him even more. The people on the cart saw him

"Help them!" she cried.

Nick saw now why the man was holding on to her. The woman was heavily pregnant. As he got closer, he saw that he'd been wrong about the children, too. For a minute, he wasn't sure what they were, until he saw the tattoo. They were biobots, but small. A tiny man and woman barely up to Nick's waist, which put them nearly chest deep in the water. The man was struggling to hold up the little woman, who looked barely conscious. Nick slogged forward and scooped her up in his arms.

"No!" the small man yelled reaching after her.

"It's okay," Nick yelled over his shoulder. "We're just here to help."

"What do you want with us? Leave us alone!"

Wisp grabbed the man by his jacket, half dragging him out of the deep water.

Nick turned so the small man could see his companion. "I promise I'm a good guy," he said, hoping humor would help.

"There aren't any," the man replied bitterly.

Kyle had arrived by then with Tonka, Lester, Quinton and Richard. They took on the stuck wagon rocking it out of its mud pit and pushing it across the rough terrain back on to the solid roadbed. Wisp and Nick brought the biobots across the road and up some rocks to dryer ground. The other men staggered up to join them. The pregnant woman was carefully helped down by her man. Muddy and exhausted everyone sat on the wet boulders catching their breath. It took a few minutes before the strangers pulled back into ranks. Nick wondered if weapons were about to come out when Ruth, Ellen and Lara came down the road with clean water and cheese sandwiches.

"Who are you people?" asked the man who had tried to stop Nick.

"Just people," Nick said around a mouthful of sandwich. "We're stuck up the road. Figured if we gave you a hand, maybe you'd return the favor." He put out a hand, "Nick of High Meadow."

"Everett," the man responded shaking Nick's hand. "We've had some tough times."

Nick took that as an apology. They finished introductions between bits of sandwich. With Everett was his brother Joshua, Mary, Joshua's wife and Harold, Mary's brother. The biobots were Dieter and Elsa. Nick noticed that they didn't even blink at Wisp. Although Dieter's eyes did linger a bit.

"Cheese," Mary said with such longing in her voice. "You have cows?"

"No, just traded for it. Creamery has cows." Nick gestured behind them. "Other side of the mountain."

"You're a trader," Everett said the word as if it were new to him.

"Yup. I usually travel by train, but this trip was a little different."

Ruth snickered, a touch of scorn in her voice. "You can say that again."

Harold had been walking around the horses checking them and the harness. Now that they were closer, Nick could see that they were some sort of big workhorse with massive shoulders and feathered fetlocks. Harold came back and accepted a sandwich from Ellen with a nod of thanks. "They look OK, but I think they're going to need to rest." He took a bite and his eyes got large. "Cheese?"

"They don't have cows," Mary said quickly.

She and Harold exchanged a look. He shrugged. She looked away. Nick felt that he'd missed a whole story in those few gestures. He looked at the wooden wagon. It had seen better days. There were a few crates tied down and a place for Mary to rest. Otherwise it looked like the men walked. Everyone was wet and the wind was whipping up again. He looked at the sky.

"I think we've seen the worst of it," Elsa said. She had a soft voice with a slight accent that Nick couldn't immediately place. "Thank you for helping us."

"You're welcome."

"What do you ask of us?" Dieter asked sharply.

"Actually it would be the horses," Nick said. "If they're okay."

"They are not for sale," Everett said firmly.

"There's a tree down on our vehicle," Nick said gently. "We just need some extra muscle to pull it away."

It took a little more discussion and an offer of payment in cheese to get the newcomers to agree to bring the horses up the road. The farmers had axes and a couple lengths of rope with them. To Nick's relief they also seemed to have to experience hauling big things with the horses. With all the men and the strength of the two horses, the tree was shifted quickly. Everett and Harold looked a little alarmed when they saw the vans underneath, but Nick kept smiling and Wisp handed out packaged cookies from the lab.

Harold walked the big horses over to the rock wall where a thin strip of weeds was eating away at the edges of the asphalt. He unharnessed them and left them to graze. Joshua settled Mary on a log to rest before the long walk back down to the wagon where the biobots were waiting. Everett lingered to repeat his thanks for the aid and to collect their payment in cheese. His eyes widened when he saw Nick's bounty.

"The least I can do is offer you the hospitality of High Meadow," Nick said. "We have a doctor. You can rest there for a little while before going on." He didn't ask where they were going to, that was too personal a question these days.

"A doctor?" Mary frowned. "Really?"

"And horses," Wisp added.

"You have horses? How many?" Harold asked.

"Four?" Nick looked to Wisp for confirmation. "They just arrived a few days ago. Got lost in a storm. We found their owner, and he's decided to join us."

"Mares?"

Nick looked to Wisp again.

"Molly's female I assume," Wisp said with a shrug. "I'm not sure how old she is."

"What do you use them for?" Everett asked.

"Right now they're recovering. Not sure that we have a plan for them," Nick said. "Although our Watch captain might be using them for messages. But the manure's a plus for the crops."

"Crops?" Everett moved closer. "What do you grow?"

"Well, we're not very good at it," Nick confessed. "We do some grain and vegetables."

"Are the fields safe?" Mary asked. There was a deep

sadness in her eyes.

"Safe?" Nick asked trying to draw her out.

"Bandits burned us out. We fled..." Tears filled her eyes as she turned to Joshua who put his arm around her.

"We lost good people," Everett said flatly.

"Sorry to hear that," Nick said. "Ran into trouble a while back at a small settlement. Riverbank lost almost everyone to some well-armed men "

Everett gave him a tight nod. "We didn't have a chance against that."

"High Meadow has a Watch run by a soldier. He keeps us safe," Nick said. He needed to tell Martin to beef up security. He didn't like to hear of another settlement that had been attacked.

"We'll have to discuss it," Everett said, avoiding his eyes.

Wisp shifted his position. "It is a good place. Your biobots will be safe there."

"They're not mine," Everett said, then backtracked. "I mean, Mary's their keeper."

Nick waved a hand in denial. "Not a problem. Wisp doesn't really have a keeper."

"Huh." Everett looked over at the horses. "Well we're looking for some farmland. Couldn't hurt to have a strong neighbor."

Nick smiled despite the sudden sinking feeling. Things had changed. He could feel it in his gut that the world had just made one more loop in its death spiral.

* * *

Melissa sat on a high rock by the side of the road and listened to the farmers natter on with Nick. She wasn't interested. Something about this trip had jarred some memories loose and she was trying her hardest to pull them out into the light and get a good look at them.

The tall farmer laughed and moved away, so she could see the young woman in profile. She was very pregnant. Had to be close to her ninth month or with twins. And the memories burst open.

Melissa froze, overwhelmed by the knowledge that crashed into her. She was a mother. She'd borne three children. Her husband was dead. It was only her taking care of the children, keeping them safe. They had run from the city after the riots. They had run from the small town when the people in charge tried to wall them in. Those were her last memories of them. They left in the darkest part of the night with only what they could carry. She remembered walking all night with the littlest one so exhausted. Her mouth went dry and her hands started to shake.

Where were her children?

* * *

Nick set about sorting everyone out and planning the route. Wisp assured him that they were only a few hours from High Meadow. They made a caravan with the horse cart bringing up the rear. He didn't want to box them in with the two vans, it might make them feel trapped. He drove slowly enough that they could keep up. The road out of the valley climbed a low hill and flattened for a long straight line north. The flooding had wiped out the road completely in some places. It was better on the rise, but turned into a potholed mosaic on the straight-away. After an hour of jostling along the rough road, Joshua accepted the invitation for Mary to ride in one of the vans. She was joined by Elsa, although Nick couldn't imagine how the small woman could protect her if things went sideways.

They crossed a river on a high stone bridge then on to a dirt road that was thick with mud. It slowed the horses even more. Nick was beginning to worry that they would have to stop to rest them. He kept waiting for Everett to signal for a break. None came, and they inched along the road making painstaking progress. The sun was low behind the trees when the High Meadow train finally station came into view.

Chapter 44

"Some foods are gone. Pigs have all died off, that I am aware of. Chickens are making a comeback, and I have heard that a few wild turkeys have been sighted. Sausages, cold cuts, hot dogs, all sorts of manufactured meat produces are no longer being made because no one has the knowledge or the machinery."

History of a Changed World, Angus T. Moss

Tilly checked the stove. The people who had volunteered to help cook had done a decent job. They were transferring all the food into serving trays and loading up the steam tables. The warmth of the kitchen and the familiar aromas of cooking eased her emotions. She checked the dish room, made sure the flatware was set out. The multicolored pile of napkins caught her eye. Old Agnes, who was truly old, had spent weeks hemming scraps of old sheets so that they could have a steady supply of napkins. Tilly looked over the crowd of people wandering into the cafeteria for Agnes. The old woman was seated with a few other old-timers at a table in the corner. Tilly relaxed a little. They hadn't had a case of flu today. She was cautiously optimistic.

She stood at the back of the steam tables watching people fill plates, chatting among themselves. They settled at tables in their customary clumps and bunches.

"Everything all right, Miss Tilly?" Harley held a tray in one hand, but he'd stepped behind the steam tables to check on her.

"Yes, just keeping an eye out that folks don't waste food."

He nodded gravely and rejoined the line.

Angus wandered in, his eyes on a notebook. Tilly felt a smile tug at her mouth as she watched people work their way around her husband. Angus moved erratically as he read more than walked. Tall Joe came in and guided Angus out of the way seating him at a table. She gave Joe an appreciative nod as he collected a tray. People were good to her husband.

Martin arrived looking flushed. His eyes skipped over the room till he located Angus. Tilly left her station to join her husband.

"What?" she asked nearly breathless with anxiety.

"A couple vehicles just passed the train station."

"Nick?" Angus asked.

"Maybe. Probably."

Tilly's heart sank. "But you don't know."

"They'll be here soon. Where's Harley? They've got a horse cart with them."

Angus let out a sharp laugh. "Then it is most definitely Nick!"

* * *

Tears threatened when Tilly saw Nick get out of the van. She ran over and gave him a hug. She could tell he was surprised, but she didn't care. She even hugged Wisp, who surprised her by hugging back. "We were so worried!"

And then she met all the people that had been prisoners, and scientists, which had Angus nearly tap dancing with excitement and a pregnant woman and more biobots, tiny ones. She launched into her role as lady of the manor ushering them all in for dinner. She had rooms made ready. Harley came out to comment on the horses and show the young man where to bring his. Nick called her over to see the loaded cart he was bringing in.

She was thrilled with his discoveries. Poking through the boxes, she praised him.

"Where's Susan?" he asked with a smile. "I knew she'd be over the moon with this lot."

And there it was. She had to huff out a few breaths before she could speak. "We lost her, Nick."

He went very still for a moment. "I'll miss her," he said. Simple and heart-felt.

Tilly fought the tears that threatened. Her plans for putting Nick and Susan together were over. She didn't even know if it would have worked. "It was a bad season. They went so fast."

"It is a bad one. Took a lot of people at the lab."

Tilly nodded not trusting her voice.

"I'll get someone to help me with this," he said, pushing his cart down the hall toward the supply room.

He deserved more praise for what he'd pulled off. From what she saw, they would get through the winter more comfortably. She determined to make sure she talked to him later. Now she needed to check with all the new people and all their new needs. She hurried back to the cafeteria to find that Lily had taken the small biobots in hand showing them to the children's table, which was more appropriate for their size. Tilly worried that they might have been designed for entertainment, or worse. She couldn't imagine why someone would want people the size of children.

"How are we doing here?" Tilly asked with her best welcoming smile forced upon her lips.

Lily gave her a real smile. "They're all grown up, but they're still little," she said.

"I'm Tilly. Is there anything you need? Any dietary restrictions? Or, um otherwise?" She stumbled over her concerns. "I know that Wisp can't be around large groups of people, so we found him some space in the field house."

"I am Elsa." The little woman said, putting out a slender hand. Tilly shook her hand gently, noticing how fragile her bones felt. "It is kind of you to accommodate him. I was unaware of his sensitivity."

Tilly got the feeling that Elsa was fishing. The man sat watching. He hadn't said a word, nor touched the food in front of him. She decided to take the first step. "They tell me he's an EE." Elsa's eyes widened, so Tilly figured she must know what that means. "He's been very helpful around here. Nick says he's a finder. I believe that's how he makes his living."

"He found my brother!" Lily piped up gleefully.

Elsa glanced at the child. "How did you lose him?"

"We had to run away from some bad men with guns. He went back..." Lily looked away, her lip trembling. Someone caught her eye and she sucked in a gasp. She grabbed Tilly's arm. "Tilly, Tilly, who is that lady?"

Tilly looked where she was pointing. "That's one of the people that were being held prisoner, sweetie."

"By the men with guns?" she squeaked.

"I haven't heard the whole story yet. I don't know if there were bad men there. Do you know her?"

"I have to find William," Lily said and she dashed out the back door of the room.

Tilly looked back to Elsa. "Kids," she said with a

sad smile. "To finish Lily's story...the children got separated. William was taken prisoner and badly beaten. Lily went to Wisp for help. He found the boy for her."

"No one here would help?" The man asked in a tone that immediately put Tilly's back up.

"Oh, I've jumbled the story haven't I. It's a good deal longer actually." Tilly took a breath trying to consolidate the convoluted story of Nick, the notebooks, Lily and the massacre at Riverbank. "Lily isn't from here, she just ended up here. Nick was in the right place at the right time to run into her and William and Wisp." She shrugged, suddenly uneasy with the turn the conversation had taken. "But I wanted to find out if you needed anything."

"We are quite fine, thank you," Elsa said, a bit formally.

"I'll have rooms ready for you by the time you're done eating. Do you want..." she hesitated, unsure of their relationship, "um, to share the same room?"

"Yes, please. Dieter is my husband."

"Good," Tilly said then flinched at her tone. "You must excuse me, I have to check on the others." She came away feeling that she'd made a mess of things. She went over to see how the pregnant woman was doing. Some of the young mothers had already gravitated that way. She'd be up past midnight sorting out this lot, but part of her was deeply grateful for the distractions.

Chapter 45

"After years of train food, we had a great celebration, in Year Seven, for the harvest of our first potato crop."

History of a Changed World, Angus T. Moss

Wisp snagged a tray of food and headed for the field house. Too many emotions in an uproar back there. The farmer folk were excited and worried in equal measure. The small biobots had a feel unlike any other he'd encountered. That worried him a little. He had no idea what their skill was. The fact that they had been with the farmers said that they were probably innocuous, but he needed to have a quiet word with Nick about that. He hadn't been alone for more than the time to pee in days, and he could feel the tension in his shoulders and neck. His head ached from holding on to his mental barriers so tightly. It was a relief to be more than a few feet away from people. Walking across the campus to the field house helped the ache in his head. The press of human emotions receded, and he could reach out beyond himself again. He could feel the horses' contentment. Harley and Harold were down there brushing them. The chickens were already in their coop, tiny flickers of sleepy thought. Further out, the Watch was doing the rounds, a few more than before. He approved of that. Beyond the watch, were the families up in the woods—no more nor less than the last time he'd been here.

The food wasn't as good as the previous time he'd eaten here. He'd heard that the cook died. Nick's happiness at being home had dimmed suddenly. Wisp supposed he was hearing about the people they had lost. There were less people here now than when they'd left for the lab. He didn't know if it was deaths, or if people had left. He ate slowly, relaxing in the quiet, as cramped mental muscles eased.

Angus would want to talk to him. With all the scientists arriving, Wisp was sure that Angus would be busy with them for awhile. He needed to think about the events at the lab. It would be great to spend some time with Kyle, but he wasn't sure what Ruth wanted. It was clear from some of her comments that she hadn't experienced the reality of the new world. She loved Kyle. That was quite obvious, even to a unskilled mind like Nick. How far she was willing to allow that to go was a different question.

The destruction of the lab and the shut-down of the train stations were important in and of themselves. There was a bigger concern here. One he needed to think about, and he knew Nick and Angus would be chewing on it for weeks. How did the accident at the lab impact the lives of the people at High Meadow? There wouldn't be any vaccine this year, but he knew plenty of settlements that survived without it. More important to Wisp, was whether the government would want Ruth and Kyle back. They were skilled assets. Someone somewhere would realize that eventually. Whether enough of the government was left standing to demand the return of two scientists was another issue that needed to be parsed. That was something he needed to discuss with Kyle. But for now, he wanted to enjoy being alone.

A sudden spike of joy shimmered out like fireworks. Three people. Wisp feathered it, unraveled it and felt the distinct pattern that was William, and one that felt like Lily. And the image that he'd remembered as someone else's memory came clear. The ex-prisoner that he'd recognized—Melissa was William and Lily's mother. The memory was of Melissa braiding Lily's hair. He found himself smiling, coasting along on their happiness. Another distraction for the High Meadow folks. Another complication to take up a few hours of the day before anyone got back to working on the more serious issues at hand.

He finished his dinner and went for a walk out towards the stream. Martin had declared it unstable and off limits. That meant it should be a quiet place for Wisp. He sat on a fallen tree breathing the night air and enjoying the low murmur of people far in the background.

Chapter 46

"It's a death spiral of ignorance. If you don't know what you don't know, how can you learn? If you don't know what you could know, how do you seek it?"

History of a Changed World, Angus T. Moss

Nick was in Angus's office first thing after breakfast, which had been a fabulous cheese omelet. Tilly was doing the cooking, and it looked like there were a few new faces in the kitchen. It had been hard to not see Susan there. Every year, he tried to not get attached to people, and every year he found himself mourning the loss of another friend. It snuck up on him, friendship. A smile here, a joke there and before he knew it, he was looking for certain faces in the room.

He settled in the old armchair to the left of Angus's habitual seat. Someone had brought in a tray of coffee for the meeting. Nick proudly noticed the addition of the milk and sugar. Angus was at his desk gathering up way too many papers, which made Nick worry that the meeting might take all day. He helped himself to a cup and sank back into the comfort of the old chair. It felt good to be home and to not be in charge for once. If he was lucky, the only decisions he'd have to make today would be plain and simple, like whether to have seconds at lunch.

Ruth and Kyle arrived, hand in hand. Nick wasn't sure how he felt about that. Kyle really wasn't human, despite what Angus insisted. Biobots were printed, not born. He didn't know if they could reproduce, but even he could see that the possible complications were staggering. They hadn't been around long enough for anyone to sort these things out. And now there were so many questions that needed to be answered, and so few people capable of figuring them out that whether biobots could reproduce seemed pretty inconsequential. Unless of course, you were dating one.

Ruth was of childbearing age. She must reproduce. It was imperative. For the race to survive, every woman had to have at least two children. More was better. But if Kyle was sterile, which might be an urban legend, then Ruth's children couldn't be Kyle's, and that was a nasty path he really didn't want to go down. He knew Angus wouldn't force a woman to get pregnant, but he had heard of settlements that did.

They took seats opposite him. Nick offered them coffee. Angus came over, but he was still putting his papers in order, which was probably the only reason Ruth got a chance to speak first.

"This is a very interesting set-up you have here."

Nick heard the condescension in her tone and bristled a little. "From what I've seen, it's one of the best."

"Your doctor is in his seventies, at the least." She avoided his eyes by sipping her coffee.

"He's a good doctor," Angus said defensively.

"But surely he doesn't do surgery. His vision and

hand strength couldn't be up to it. Where do you send people?"

Angus stared at her, his thumb softly tapping against his pile of papers, then looked to Nick, who shrugged, then back to Ruth. "There is nowhere else. People come here from all over for medical treatment."

She stared back, a frown forming on her brow. "Where's the nearest hospital?"

"Wow, what planet have you been living on?" Nick asked harshly. "There are no hospitals." He knew she'd been sheltered, but this was more than annoying.

She gave him the same look she had when he'd told her there weren't any towns. "But..."

Angus started shaking a pen at her. "Yes, you see, I knew it. The country has become quite stratified. There are those like you who have been protected, coddled even. You don't know about us, out here in the trenches and for the most part, we don't know about you in the mansions."

"We weren't in mansions," she snapped. "I was working eighty hour weeks in the lab for a vaccine for you people."

Angus giggled. "Eighty hours." He leaned over and slapped Nick on the knee. "When's the last time you heard someone talk like that?" He turned back to Ruth and gave her a gentle smile. "I don't mean to make fun of you, my dear. But you have to realize that we, out here, have been roughing it for the past decade. And for you, I imagine, life has gone on with little disruption. You still do the work you trained for—"

"I have an MD, and two PhDs—" she burst in.

"Of course. I don't mean to make little of it. But none of us can do that. None of us here do the work we went to school for, trained our whole lives for. Look at Nick. He was an FBI agent. My wife, Tilly, ran a hospital. We have accountants and architects and insurance salesman and even a stock broker. None of those people can do their jobs anymore. Now they work in the fields or bake bread or mop the floors. The only professions out here deal with survival."

"I can't do that!" she snapped. She slammed her cup down on the table. "Do *not* expect me to mop floors."

"Ruth is a doctor," Kyle said in an even, calm voice. "You have need for one."

"Yes, doctors are rare and very welcome," Angus agreed in an equally calm voice.

"I am a biochemist. But I am strong. I can work in the fields."

Nick flinched at the resignation in his voice. This conversation had gotten off on the wrong foot.

"Only if you wish to, Kyle," Angus said. "We don't force people to do anything here. Find something that interests you. Do something different every week if you like. We keep a jobs list going on the message boards of things that need to be done. And that's supposing you folks choose to stay." He said it calmly, but the look he gave Ruth was firm.

"What do *you* do?" Ruth demanded.

"I run this place. I chart the course we take. My research is a sideline. Also, I keep an eye on the power plant and pretty much anything mechanical. If it breaks, they come to me to fix it."

"What did you do before?" Ruth demanded.

Angus smoothed his papers with a sigh. Nick saw a rare moment of sadness and loss that drained the vibrancy from his face. Angus never talked about what he did before. If asked, he usually said that it didn't matter.

"I designed vehicles for exploration on other planets, orbiters, landers, that sort of thing."

"Huh." Nick was impressed. He would never have guessed. He grinned at Angus. "So you're a rocket scientist."

A bit of life trickled back into Angus's eyes. He gave Nick a small smile. "Yes. Now, as I was saying, if you choose to stay, we will have a meeting to discuss having you join the community. Everyone here helps to keep this place going. Whether you want to make soap or bread or muck out the stable, we need every hand here to make it work. We are a community, and all that entails. We share the chores and the harvest. We have rules. All of that will be made clear to you before you make your decision. My wife and I run this settlement. If you don't feel able to accept our rules and our vision, then it's best if you go."

Nick felt a rush of pride. Angus was seen as a day dreamer, a whimsical pied piper that many people loved at first sight, but it was this man, the nuts and bolts sincerity of him that had won Nick's heart. And every time he saw that in Angus, he was glad he'd found his home here.

"What kind of research are you doing?" Kyle asked.

"A bit of everything. I'm trying to compile a census of the established settlements and med centers. I also keep an eye on weather patterns to see if the lack of human intervention has caused any shifts. I've been trying to make an estimate of the mortality rate of each year's flu."

"How do you collect your data?" Kyle asked.

"Nick mostly."

Ruth scoffed. "You're working with hearsay," her voice was dismissive.

"That's pretty much all there is," Angus said, peering at her over his glasses. "Unless you know of a government entity that is doing that."

"Well, they must be. How else would we know how much vaccine to prepare?"

"We put in orders," Angus said.

Ruth blinked at him. She turned a stricken face to Kyle. "This is insane."

"May I look at your data?" Kyle asked.

Angus puffed up with a touch of pride. "It's a bit rough, still. Jean has been helping me sort through it." He led Kyle over to a monitor and brought up his research.

Nick followed them over. He didn't care about Angus's research, but he wanted to see how they would react to it. Kyle scanned through page after page, too fast for Nick to read, but slow enough that he wondered if the biobot was actually absorbing the data. He started mumbling to Ruth, words that didn't make sense to Nick. He glanced over to see Angus nodding.

Ruth stepped away looking pale. "This information must be incomplete."

"Of course. As I said, I get most of my information from Nick. There are a few med centers on the ether that I get numbers from, but there isn't any dock with official numbers that I could find."

Kyle looked up at Angus from where he sat at the monitor. "May I?"

"Please do."

Kyle started a number of searches. Nick couldn't see what he was typing, but dock after dock came up "unavailable."

"No, that isn't right!" Ruth barked at yet another broken dock. "That can't be. Did you use my password?" She leaned against Kyle to watch his fingers as he typed. A few more unavailable pages came up. "Why are they all down?" Her voice had a tremor of panic to it.

Kyle leaned back, a thoughtful look on his face. "I don't know."

"Perhaps we in the trenches are not allowed access," Angus said quietly.

"I don't believe that is the difficulty. It seems that they are not operating at this time."

"Like the Vaccine Center's dock or the weather

dock or the mapping dock," Nick said tiredly. "Those are the ones we really need. We're in trouble if the weather dock is permanently down."

Angus gave Kyle a thoughtful look. "Do you know where the weather center is?"

"The physical location? No, I'm sorry."

Angus turned to Nick. "I was thinking that might be the next place you need to go."

Nick slumped a little. "I'd like a couple of days..."

"Of course, Nicky. You've been away quite a bit. I only meant that this is our new mystery."

"I don't think we ever finished with the old one," Nick said irritably. "Why did the security guards for Rutledge's lab kill Lily's sister?"

Ruth spun around. "What?"

Angus shooed everyone back to their chairs. "Do we have anyone from the lab's security here?"

"No. We left the last guy at the Creamery. But he told me that not everyone was briefed on the prisoners. Now that we know Rutledge was locking people up, I guess that they were trying to take the kids into custody, too. Iris fought back, and they killed her."

Angus turned to Ruth. "Have you any ideas why they were there?" Nick heard a faint note of appeasement in Angus's voice. He was trying to be nice to her.

"I don't," she said tersely.

"Nicky, did you interview the prisoners?"

Nick poured himself a second cup of coffee. "I talked to a couple of them, but they were still pretty loopy from the drugs. Mike said he thought that Rutledge wanted his factory. That he'd tried to buy it at one point, but his memory was still fuzzy. Maybe in a couple days people will be more lucid."

"I do not think any of them are criminals," Kyle said tentatively. "Wisp said that none of them felt, um, like criminals."

Angus grinned. “Your brother is amazing! I am so delighted to have him here.”

“And now you have two biobots,” Ruth said, some bitterness in her voice.

“Four actually, with the little folk. I haven’t had a chance to talk to them yet. Kyle, you said that your skill is biochemistry?”

“Yes.”

“Excellent, excellent.” Angus got that distracted look about him. Nick knew he’d be gone for a bit, wandering off after a stray thought.

“You two get settled in okay?” Nick asked.

“The room is adequate,” Kyle said.

“Do you all live in here together?” Ruth asked.

“Mostly. I hear Bruno, one of the survivors of Riverbank, is working on some housing down the street in the old neighborhood.”

“Wisp told me about Riverbank,” Kyle said in a near whisper. He hunched his shoulders looking dismayed, which suggested to Nick that Wisp told him everything about Riverbank.

Angus lurched to his feet with a grunt. “Kyle, I would like to show you something.” He went over to his desk and poked through a few precarious piles of paper. He returned with a small blue notebook. He stood before Kyle clenching the notebook for a moment. “Please let me know what you think of this.” He handed the book over slowly.

Kyle took it reverently. “This is more of your research?”

“No!” Angus responded sharply. “Absolutely not. I, we, well let’s just say we stumbled upon it.”

Kyle nodded, a look of mild consternation on his face. He opened the notebook and started reading.

Nick finished his coffee and contemplated a third cup. He trusted Kyle a bit more than Ruth because he had come to trust Wisp, but he was concerned that the information in that little notebook was a game changer. What Ruth would want to do with it was up in the air. She trusted Kyle, so if they could rely on him to convince her... His thoughts stumbled there, because he wasn't sure what they needed to do with it.

Kyle shot Angus a startled look. "This is..."

Angus jumped on it. "Is it?"

Ruth saw the look on Kyle's face and leaned forward. "What is it?"

They all waited for Kyle to answer. Nick felt a collective breath held.

"I think it is," Kyle said in a hushed voice, as if afraid of being overheard.

Ruth inched closer and asked again, in a whisper, "What is it?"

Kyle closed the notebook and held it firmly closed. "The BEHHM Virus."

"Is that what you folks call it?" Angus asked eagerly. "What does it stand for?"

Ruth sat a little straighter. She put out her hand to take the book, but Kyle would not relinquish it. "Let me see it please."

Kyle looked at her with indecision on his face.

"More minds at work on a problem solve it quicker," Angus said.

Kyle handed over the notebook without a word. Ruth leafed through it skipping over the journal pages to the ones with formulae.

"BEHHM," Angus repeated, "What does it stand for?"

"Biobot Eradication High Human Mortality," Kyle said.

"Did it really kill off biobots?" Nick asked.

"That was what we were told it was intended for, but I have not been privy to the statistics of its efficacy."

"Anecdotally?" Angus ask carefully.

Kyle shrugged. "It did not affect me or Wisp."

"Or your other brothers?"

Kyle gave Angus a look of surprise. "No. None of my brothers who were alive at the time were affected by the virus."

Angus nodded, tapping a finger to his lips. "So it was genius that created the virus, but all based on the wrong assumption."

Kyle frowned at Angus. "What do you plan to do with this?"

"I don't know *what* to do with it," Angus said plaintively. "I don't know if it's real, or the ravings of a madman."

"Or a little of both," Nick added.

Angus gave him an agreeing nod before continuing, "And if it is real, is it useful?"

"My God," Ruth said in an awestricken voice. She looked up from the notebook at Kyle. "If this is..." She leaned toward him pointing to a line. "This."

"Yes." He gave her a tight nod, pressing his lips tightly together.

"This *could* be it," Ruth raised frightened eyes to Angus. "Where did you get it?"

"Doesn't matter," Angus said waving away the question. "Is it useful?"

"I can't say," Ruth said, her eyes wandering back to the notebook. Like Kyle she shut the notebook and held it closed. Angus looked to Kyle.

"The virus has mutated regularly," he said. "It is interesting to see how it began, but at this point, it is a completely different organism."

There was a bland vagueness to Kyle's statement that made Nick think he was lying. "So if this is useless, a young woman was killed for no reason."

"Well, at least not for this reason," Angus said gesturing at the notebook.

As if she knew the course of the discussion, Lily

skipped into the room. "Oh, sorry, I forgot to knock."

Angus gave her a warm smile. "That's OK sweetheart, is my wife looking for me?"

"Um, no, I don't think so. But my mom said that she thinks you should talk to her."

"Where did your mom come from?" Nick asked. He was glad to see that the shadows and sharp angles were gone from Lily's face. She was safe and well-fed, and it did his heart good to see that small success.

Lily giggled, looking younger than her age. "You brought her, silly."

Nick felt a tingle of danger work its way up his spine. "What does she want to talk to us about?" he asked in as casual manner as he could muster. Both Kyle and Angus sat a little straighter letting him know his concern came through.

"Grown up stuff, I guess?"

"How old are you?" Ruth blurted out.

Lily smiled, despite Ruth's abrupt tone. "I was just twelve, and we had a party and Harley let me ride Socks!" She gave a little hop of joy. "He said I can ride him again."

Angus's eyes twinkled at the sight of her. Nick felt his spirits rise a little more.

"Tell your mother that we would be glad to speak to her. She should come by whenever she's free."

Ruth's eyes followed Lily to the door. She whipped back around and skewered Angus with a penetrating look. "Her eyes are red."

Angus tipped his head to the side. "I think it's more like burgundy."

"Her eyes are not normal."

Angus nodded. "It's a side effect of the flu I think. Children have very strange eye color these days."

Ruth sputtered. "What?"

Nick settled back into his chair, letting Angus weigh in on this.

"I noticed it about three years ago. We had a child born here with orange eyes. Very unusual. And then purple. Somehow the flu must be affecting our DNA."

Ruth's mouth dropped open. "But, but, no..." She turned to Kyle. "Have we done this?"

Kyle licked his lips, blinking a few times. "Possibly. Probably."

Nick felt a deep anger building. "You? You people making the vaccines did something to change the kids?"

Ruth's hands fluttered as if she was trying to physically shape her thoughts. "No. Well, yes. But not for that. We were improving, strengthening..." She grabbed Kyle's hand.

"The work we did was to combat the disease. The change in eye color is incidental," Kyle said bluntly.

"Like killing off eighty percent of the lab was incidental?" Nick snapped. Angus frowned. Nick hadn't had a chance to tell him the whole story.

"No." Kyle raised a hand as if to stop him. "That was fool hardiness on Rutledge's part. But Lily is *twelve*," he said to Ruth.

Her eyes widened. "She's too old for our work to have had an effect on her. Someone else must have done that."

"That would be my husband's handiwork."

All heads turned at the sound of a new voice. Melissa stood in the doorway watching them. Angus jumped to his feet again. "Please come join us." He offered her a chair. "I think there might be some coffee left," he said giving Nick a stern look.

"No, thank you, I'm fine. I'd like to have my say and get it over with."

Angus took the notebook from Ruth and offered it to Melissa. "I believe this might be yours."

Melissa leaned away from it. "No. I want nothing to do with it. The man was sick, insane. But he didn't start out that way."

Chapter 47

"Biobots were highly trained, and the few remaining were of inestimable worth."
History of a Changed World, Angus T. Moss

Wisp could feel the high spirits of the farmers. It was contagious enough that he found himself smiling as he finished his breakfast in the solitude of the field house. He walked out to the fields to find them. Mary and Joshua were walking hand in hand around the football field. Something green and grass-like was growing about knee high. He approached slowly, so that they would see him coming.

Mary swirled around, a wide smile on her face. "This is marvelous."

Wisp had to smile back. "They try hard."

"They have chickens!"

"This is an excellent set up," Joshua said. "The field covers are ingenious. We lost a lot of crops to weather. How long have they been breeding this flock of chickens?"

Wisp shrugged. "I am new here, too."

"Really?" Joshua frowned at him. "I thought you and Nick were old friends."

"We met during an attack."

"That makes fast friend," Joshua agreed with a grimace. "Nick said they have guards here?" He looked around the field.

"They call it the Watch. They have men out on the roads." Wisp reached out to find the outlying men. "A few in the woods. They are well trained by Martin."

"Will I have to join?"

Wisp could sense the oscillating emotions in Joshua. Fear and relief, excitement and dread. He was afraid to accept that they were in a good place. "I don't think so. Angus says that people should work to their strengths. If you know about working the land, they will want you to do that. They aren't too sure about things."

Joshua nodded enthusiastically, gesturing to the field. "This is pretty small for a field of wheat. And I'm not sure what else they have growing here. The round field over there has hardly enough potatoes for a family much less a settlement. And they have a couple of places that they could use better in rotation."

"They will be very pleased if you choose to stay."

Mary's smile wilted a bit. "Do we have to live in there with everyone else?"

"No. Have you met Bruno?"

They both shook their heads. "I heard he had a vineyard," Joshua said.

Wisp sifted through the thoughts and emotions for the taste of Bruno's mind. He was away from the med center. "I can take you to him."

Mary looked a question at Joshua. He smiled. "Why not? As long as it's not too far," he added with a pointed look at Mary's swollen belly.

Wisp led them at a comfortable amble across the

campus, past the incipient orchard, which also caught Joshua's attention. "What are they growing here? Apples?"

"I'm not sure."

Joshua inspected each tree. Wisp realized there were some subtle differences in them. "Fruits and nuts?" he asked.

Joshua grinned pointing at a sapling. "I swear that's an olive tree."

"Olive?" Mary's emotions hopped up into joy, and Wisp felt a slight echo in the child. "We could get olive oil." She laughed. "No more cooking with old bear fat!"

Wisp winced at the thought of it. He was fine with toasted over a campfire if it came down to it. They had butter from the Creamery now. Nick brought back oil occasionally. Without animal fat, there were very few options.

They walked two blocks past storm-damaged houses to a short cul de sac. Five low profile houses crouched on the street, two to either side and a slightly larger one at the end. The first one on the right showed signs of habitation with curtains in the windows and a tidy front yard. Wisp couldn't feel anyone, but he wondered who had chosen to leave the main building. Reclaimed lumber, pipe and other construction materials were stacked outside the big house on the end with a handcart and a few tools. Wisp could feel Bruno concentrating deeply inside the house.

He walked up to the front door and knocked. After a moment Bruno limped out. "Wisp, my friend. You are back safe and sound!" Bruno slapped him on the shoulder.

"I've brought some new people that might be interested in a house."

Bruno stared at Joshua and Mary where they waited on the front path. "A young couple." His voice was tight with grief. Wisp felt them flinch misinterpreting his grief for something darker.

"Their farm was attacked," Wisp said.

"Bastards!" Bruno swore. He approached with a hand out to Joshua. "I'm sorry to hear that. Everyone okay?"

Joshua shook his hand. "Um, no. That's why we're here."

"Lost my whole settlement," Bruno grumbled. "Still don't know why."

"Oh!" Mary took his hand in both of hers. "I'm so sorry."

Bruno melted a little. "Look at you with a babe on the way. Of course, you need a good place. A big place with room for a family." His voice broke a little. He stomped past them, gesturing them to follow. "Come!"

Bruno led them around the corner to a long low house on a large piece of property. The yard was overgrown, but a path had been cut through to the front door. "This is a good one. Has a greenhouse in the back. And a nice lawn for the kids to play on." His kind words were in contrast to the gruff tone he'd taken. Wisp could sense a growing compassion in the couple. They could see beneath Bruno's bluster to the sorrow he was drowning in.

The entry way was full of light showing a dusty, empty home. Bruno gave them a tour. There were two wings with a total of six bedrooms, three in each. A big country kitchen, with a table that would seat twelve, had a wall of glass looking out on an overgrown yard that sloped down to a stream. Mary looked around the kitchen and started to cry.

"What's wrong?" Joshua was alarmed. He grabbed a chair for her.

"It's a-maz-ing," Mary hiccupped through her tears. She sat in the chair and sobbed.

Bruno grinned at Joshua. "Women get a bit emotional when they're that far along." He took

Joshua's arm. Look here at these walls. Good solid construction. The appliances are electric, so everything can be left as is."

Wisp slipped back out the front door, unnoticed. He was sure that the farmer folk would stay. Another asset for this settlement. He headed back across the campus to his room, surprised at his feeling of ownership. It was a good space, safe and somewhat isolated. He could always take a place further out in the neighborhood. He wondered if Kyle and Ruth would stay. She was the sticking point. Kyle would go wherever she wanted to go. He wasn't sure what he could find that would make her want to stay.

Wisp stopped at the edge of the campus, where he could see the young fruit trees, the green fields. Someone in a big hat was crouched in the vegetable garden, probably weeding. A horse called, and all six of them ran across the back meadow kicking up their heels. It was a happy day, but something was off. This was a good place, for now, even a safe place. But there was something in the wind that abruptly put him on edge. Something was coming, and he had a feeling that it might be a good time for him to stay put. He checked the sky, brilliant blue and without a cloud. Sometimes he felt this way before a big storm. There wasn't a breeze, the day was hot and still. Could be a storm.

Chapter 48

"Consistency was the difficulty. The communities that thrived could only do so with great redundancy built in. That required that sustainability be tied to larger numbers."

History of a Changed World, Angus T. Moss

The room was silent after Melissa's announcement. Nick couldn't believe that he was going to hear the story of the creation of the virus. It was a mystery everyone living would want explained.

"I'd love to hear about this if you're willing to tell us," Angus said gently.

"There's not a lot to say," Melissa said, bitterness lacing her words. "About the time I got pregnant with Lily, he started to change. Now when I look back, I think it must have been a small stroke or a tumor. But the change was gradual. I didn't realize how bad he'd gotten until he locked me out of his study. He was doing some kind of secret research, but that wasn't anything new. He'd done work for the government before that he couldn't talk about." She stared at her hands, knotted in her lap.

"I knew he'd done something to me when Lily was born. Her eyes. It scared me. I asked him if he did something to her, but he just kept saying it was all for the good." She took a deep breath before continuing. "Then one day he disappeared, and so did our savings. He'd booked himself an around the world trip."

"He was patient zero," Kyle said in a stunned voice.

"I guess so. He started in New York, Miami, Houston, Chicago, Los Angeles, Hong Kong, Beijing, Delhi, Bagdad, Paris, Amsterdam. He died on the flight into London."

"But how can you be sure?" Ruth asked.

"He left me a note saying that he had created a virus to kill off the biobots."

"Why?" Nick asked.

"Who knows? He was so secretive he wouldn't even share that with me."

"Did you work with him?" Angus asked.

"No. I'm a kindergarten teacher. I never had anything to do with his work."

"How did you end up at Rutledge's lab?" Nick asked.

"He kidnapped me," she said with a shrug. "I don't know why. Maybe he didn't realize Ben was already dead. Maybe he thought Ben did something to me. I'm pretty sure Rutledge took my blood." She showed them the faded bruise on the inside of her elbow. "So he must have thought there was something in my blood. I don't know, maybe Ben did change me." She rubbed her face wearily. "I want to thank you for taking care of Lily and William."

Angus went to his desk, and after poking through a drawer returned with Iris's scarf. He offered it to Melissa. Her eyes glistened with tears when she saw it. "My sweet Iris. Were you there? Do you know what happened to her?"

Angus looked to Nick.

Nick hesitated, not sure how to soften the blow, but considering her recent past, he decided to be blunt. "She was shot by Rutledge's guards."

Melissa's eyes went wide. "What? Why?"

Nick bowed his head. "I'm sorry, I'm not sure. I think Rutledge sent the guards to kidnap your kids. She fought back. Gave William and Lily time to escape. She killed one of the guards."

Melissa jerked back from Nick's words. "She...my little girl killed a man?"

"I'm guessing by the positioning of the bodies. I wasn't there for the confrontation. She had a shotgun. The man down had an automatic weapon."

"Why?" she moaned. "Why would he kill my daughter?"

"Was she different, too?" Kyle asked.

"No. I had Iris when he was teaching. He hadn't gone into research, yet."

Nick felt let down. There was no great reveal. No grand conspiracy, just two petty men doing weird things. Silence settled over the room. Nick had a lot more questions, but he wanted to let Melissa recover some more.

"Well, that's all I wanted to say. Let you know who we are. I'll get the children. We'll go."

Angus scooted to the edge of his seat. "You have a place to go?"

"We'll find something," she said, eyes on her hands.

"You are welcome to stay. We have grown very fond of William and Lily. And Lily has her heart set on learning to ride Socks. And William is still quite traumatized by his capture. It would be best to let him stay here where he feels safe."

Melissa shrugged. "Are you sure people will want

us?"

"Absolutely," Angus said firmly. "To most of the people here, you are simply Lily and William's mother. We are delighted to reunite the family. That doesn't happen too often. Rest and let your past lie undisturbed. But I thank you for letting us know." Angus stood up.

Melissa let him help her to her feet. He escorted her to the door. "My door is always open," he said in parting.

Chapter 49

"Children born during this time have an entirely different understanding of family. Mother, father, sister, brother changes to whoever survives to care for them. In their lifetime they will lose, on average, fifty percent of their relatives and friends."

History of a Changed World, Angus T. Moss

Wisp changed course toward the main building. He wanted to talk to Nick about this odd feeling and to get a sense of what kinds of things he should be doing for the settlement if he decided to stay. He saw a man walking up the street that led to the train station. As he got closer, Wisp realized he was wearing a uniform. The man saw him, waved and headed for him. Wisp could feel his general uneasiness, even before he saw Wisp's tattoo.

"Hello there."

Wisp nodded a greeting. "Can I help you?"

"I was looking for Nick. Do you know where I

could find him?"

Wisp escorted the man into the building. It was then that he noticed the lack of security. People knew him, and he looked different from most people with his long white hair, so he was easily identifiable. But anyone that managed to elude the Watch could enter the med center uncontested. Another thing he should tell Nick.

Wisp took the man to Angus's office, where he sensed Nick. The door was open, but he knocked on the doorjamb, and entered before the stranger when Angus beckoned.

Nick, Angus, Kyle and Ruth were gathered in a meeting in the circle of comfortable chairs that Wisp had been in once before. He thought it said something about the man that his meetings took place in comfort with refreshments. Despite the thoughtful accommodations, Wisp could sense it wasn't going well. There was a heaviness to the room, frustration and concern were the top notes.

"Frank?" Nick said as he stood to shake hands with the stranger. "What brings you here?"

"Well, I, um..." he hesitated, looking around at all the people. Wisp felt the uneasiness tumble into distress. "I don't mean to interrupt anything important."

Nick seemed to catch the same feeling. He introduced Frank as the manager of High Meadow train station.

"Of course, we know Frank," Angus said with a welcoming smile. "You come over every year for your flu shot. Sorry to say there isn't one this year. Is that what brings you?" Angus waved Frank into a seat.

Wisp stayed because he thought this might have something to do with that sense of wrongness he'd felt earlier.

"I thought you folks should know that the station is

going to close for a bit."

"Shit," Nick snapped.

"Nicholas!" Angus scolded.

"Sorry." Nick shot Angus an apologetic look. "What happened Frank?"

"I'm not sure. We got the notice that the Continental Line is being shut down for about two weeks. No explanation. Just get out and maybe we'll tell you when to come back," Frank said, his voice sounded sullen, but there was great apprehension underneath.

Wisp felt Nick's emotions flicker between fear and anger. Nick looked over to Angus. "He can stay here, can't he?"

"Of course, of course," Angus said. "You're welcome to stay as long as you need to Frank."

"Um, my wife Etta..."

"Is welcome also."

Frank's deep sigh of relief, stuttered with raw emotion. "Thanks. I've been with the trains since I was a kid. Started with them polishing floors. I don't know what I'll do if they don't reopen the station. And Etta, well she's beside herself. We've been living in those quarters since before Zero Year. It's our home."

"Do you need help moving some things?" Nick asked. "We've got a van and plenty of space here. We can store some stuff for you, if you want."

Wisp moved back as Frank's emotions overflowed. He was fighting tears. "I always knew you were a good guy, Nick." Frank swallowed hard. "I wasn't sure what to do. But I thought I would check with you. You're a smart guy. And you, you..."

Nick patted Frank on the shoulder. "We need to help each other."

"Exactly" Angus was on his feet in a flash. "I need to let Tilly know we will have a few more guests. Come join us for lunch." He checked his watch. "It's about that time. Then we can take you back in one of the vans with a few strong hands to get your things." He glanced at Kyle. "Why don't you and Ruth set up in the lab. Nick and I will work on the other things."

Angus effectively broke up the meeting. Frank left mumbling his thanks, headed for the cafeteria. Ruth made excuses about needing the lavatory and left the room. Nick joined Angus at the ether console. Kyle stood staring at a key in his hand.

"Lab?" Wisp asked him.

"Angus gave me the key to the chemistry lab."

"Makes sense."

"I don't know where it is."

Wisp led Kyle through the school to the science labs. He pointed out the four rooms labeled *Chemistry*. "I guess you can take your pick."

Kyle peered into each room, finally choosing the first and largest one. They stepped into a dusty classroom that smelled faintly of chemicals. Wisp could feel Kyle's contentment.

"You are pleased."

"Angus asked me to do some research that coincides with my personal interests."

"Will you and Ruth be staying?"

Kyle tipped his head in thought. "I think she will find this to be a comfortable place. Things are more degraded than we realized."

"She didn't know."

"No." Kyle shook his head. "And I think she doesn't fully believe Nick. We have been very isolated in our work."

Wisp felt Kyle's unspoken question. "Nick's right. I've been cross-country from coast to coast. I've been down to the gulf and up towards Canada. There have been days, weeks that I traveled without feeling another human mind. Whole cities abandoned to squatters and looters, but there are so few that they can take what they want without ever seeing each other. Restaurants, department stores, factories, supermarkets all abandoned, torn open and emptied of useful things."

"How can that be?"

"I think there is a tipping point that makes people move. A town can lose half its population, and people remain. Other times a smaller loss makes them scatter. Perhaps it is who is lost or a certain percentage that is too much and people move away. I don't know the statistics. I bet Ep could tell you."

Kyle smiled. "I bet Epsilon is working on that sort of thing right now." Kyle looked around the lab. "Where do people move to?"

"Another question for Ep, but I imagine to a larger population center."

Kyle's thoughts went fuzzy. Wisp recognized the feel as his brother concentrated on a problem. He left without Kyle noticing. Ruth was wandering down the hall checking doors. Wisp pointed out the lab for her, then headed back towards Angus's office. He passed some of the rooms that were private quarters now. At a cross corridor, he noticed Elsa and Dieter standing in the doorway to their room.

"Is there a problem?"

"We'd like to go outside," Elsa said.

"We don't know the rules," Dieter snapped.

Wisp understood that completely. "I will show you the rules," he said. "Come with me." He led the small biobots back toward the entrance. As they approached the front doors, he turned and pointed behind them. The entry way was a two-story box with doors leading off to stairwells and hallways. Across from the front doors was a large display case holding a colorful poster clearly painted by children. It said: Be nice to everyone. Do your fair share. Be generous. Dance when you hear the music.

"As far as I know, those are the rules here."

Dieter spun with an angry glint in his eye. "Is this a joke?"

"No." Wisp couldn't sense his emotions. That struck him as very odd. "This settlement is a good place. Safe. You have full access to any common areas. The private rooms should be treated as people's homes—knock to gain entry. If you have questions, you can ask anyone. Meals are served in the cafeteria." He led them down the hall to the cafeteria pointing out the menu board and hours of operation.

Elsa smiled. "Thank you for letting us know."

"What will be required of us?" Dieter asked.

"What is your skill?"A long minute passed while Dieter stared at Wisp. He waited, curious about not feeling the little man's emotions. Sensing the need for a bit more give, Wisp took the first step. "I am an EE. Mostly I work as a finder," Wisp offered.

Dieter seemed to come to some decision. "We are Fonts. I am sciences and Elsa is arts."

Wisp wondered if the Fonts were so packed with knowledge that there wasn't any room for emotions. He'd never met anyone with an eidetic memory. Perhaps that was why they felt so different. "Angus will be very excited about that. Would you be willing to set up a school for the children?"

Elsa clasped her hands and went up on her toes. "Really? They'd let us teach?"

"They are concerned that the children are getting a patchwork education. That there will be no one to replace skilled workers in a generation."

"My fear as well," Dieter grumbled.

"Do you wish to speak to Angus yourselves or would you like me to broach the subject with him?"

"Could you?" Elsa asked. "We don't know the people here. You could judge it better, I think."

Wisp nodded. A group of people came down the

hall heading for the cafeteria. They smiled and waved to the biobots. Wisp nodded back. Yes, this was a good place. He started to ask the Fonts if they were ready for lunch when a wave of anxiety stopped him.

"What's wrong?" Elsa asked. "You have a strange look on your face."

Before he could answer, the storm alarm went off. Dieter grabbed Elsa, and they backed to the wall.

"Storm coming," Wisp shouted over the klaxon. He stood by the small people to make sure they didn't get knocked over.

The storm shutters started to close with a rumble throwing the hall into darkness. A few men ran out the doors to the fields.

"Where are they going?" Elsa asked.

"Bring in the horses and chickens, or make sure the shielding is up on the crops."

The klaxon stopped replaced by an announcement. "Wisp please come to my office."

"May we come?" Elsa asked.

Wisp nodded and led them to Angus's office. Nick and Martin were already there. Angus had storm tracking up on the forward wall.

"It's working?"

"Apparently," Angus said shortly. "This is going to be a bad one. I would appreciate it if you would check for stragglers. We need everyone inside now."

Chapter 50

"The changes in architecture and power distribution demanded by the extreme changes in weather, decades earlier, became instrumental in the establishment of settlements. The hub system made it simpler to find and maintain suitable edifices."

History of a Changed World, Angus T. Moss

Wisp headed outside at a jog. Harley and Everett were bringing the horses in. Joshua and Mary were helping to move the chickens indoors. All the animals were nervous and acting up. That was a bad sign. Long streamers of dark cloud stretched across the sky as the temperature dropped. A few fat drops of cold rain spattered on the sidewalk.

Wisp reached out around the center. He could feel the Watch moving in from their positions. Bruno and a few other people were heading back from the neighborhood. Three children were racing from the brook. He expanded his search. Worried minds in the outliers. They heard the storm alarm. He hoped they had good shelters. He reached farther. No one by the train station. No one on the road in the opposite direction. And yet, there was a tingle over there. An animal? He trotted out to the road to clear the clutter of the minds in the center. With more space around him he could feel it. A child?

"Wisp?"

He turned to see Nick and Martin approaching.

"What is it?" Martin asked.

"I'm not sure. Something, maybe a couple people. Up this road."

Martin radioed for someone to bring a van. Wisp started walking. The sooner he could identify what he was feeling the better they could help. Nick kept pace with him. Wisp had noticed that Nick tried to quiet his mind when Wisp was searching. It was admirable of him to try. And it was helpful.

"I think it's children."

"Plural. Our kids? Angus was doing a head count."

Wisp heard Martin behind them on the radio checking on that head count. He jogged to catch up. "All of ours are accounted for."

The wind picked up, tossing leaves and debris at them. Rain pattered down as the light faded. "How far?" Nick asked nervously.

Thunder rumbled far away. Martin looked up at the clouds. "It's moving fast."

One of the new vans arrived with three of the Watch, and they jumped inside. "Up ahead," Wisp said. "More than I thought. They might be drugged or sick."

"Or just exhausted," Martin said as the headlights showed them a bedraggled crowd on the road. "What are we seeing Wisp? Ambush or victims?"

Wisp reached out around the numbed group searching for snipers, bandits, concentrated minds up in the trees. "Victims."

The van approached within a few feet of the group. Martin and Nick jumped out of the vehicle just as a bolt of lightning lit the sky. Wisp and the other men joined them. There were wheelbarrows and handcarts, a bicycle and two wagons filled with small children, pushed, pulled and carried by older children. Wisp took a quick count of twenty-six, with no one older than William's age.

A skinny boy, tall and gangly stepped forward brandishing a walking stick that was taller than he was. "Are you from High Meadow?"

"I'm Nick, you're safe now."

Wisp felt the boy's uncertainty. He moved closer. The boy's eyes found him. "You're the finder?"

"I am."

"We need you to find our parents."

Chapter 51

"The sheer numbers of dead overwhelmed all infrastructure. For people living outside of large cities, it may have seemed a calamity. However, in the cities, it was horrific. It is hard to conceive of for those who did not witness the dead lying in the streets, or the house to house search for children and elderly left with no caretakers."

History of a Changed World, Angus T. Moss

Thunder cracked right overhead and rain pounded down. Nick saw Martin pull out the radio, probably for a second vehicle. "We don't have time, squeeze em in," he yelled over the rumble of the storm. Nick grabbed a toddler and carried him to the van. Martin ushered the rest of them closer.

Reaching for the next child, Nick looked around for Wisp. He was standing back, away from the children. He met Nick's eyes, as if waiting for the question. "Any stragglers?"

Wisp squinted against the rain, back the way the

children had come, his long white hair plastered to his skull. He stepped a few more feet away. Nick hoped there weren't any kids lying in the road back there. The storm was getting worse. They needed to get into shelter now.

"No one alive back that way," Wisp said. He took one look at the crowded van and shook his head. "I'll run." He took off before Nick could argue and as he watched, Wisp settled into a ground-eating lope that looked effortless.

Nick went back for another child. He rearranged bodies putting kids on laps, some on the floor. They were exhausted and shivering from the cold rain. Too many youngsters on their own.

"All in!" Martin yelled and squeezed into the back. They drove as fast as they could back to the school. Water sprayed up from puddles on the road making the van hydroplane. Nick tightened his grip on the armrest and grumbled a warning to the driver.

"Where are you kids from?" Martin asked

The skinny boy, who had two crying babies on his lap, looked over to Nick with weary, bloodshot eyes. "Barberry Cove."

Nick didn't know it. The inside of the van was steamy from the press of bodies. Babies were crying, and some of the younger kids were sniffling. They were scared and tired. And it became apparent that some of the babies needed a diaper change. It broke his heart to think of these little ones travelling any distance without help.

Martin radioed ahead for them to open the garage. They drove straight in. A crowd of people were waiting at the entrance to the school. As soon as the van doors opened, there were many open arms for the children.

Nick moved away from the crush. He saw Jean, Melissa and Mary each carrying a dripping wet child. Angus was at the door directing traffic. "Get them to the cafeteria. Hot food first. There are blankets and towels in the cafeteria."

Martin was on the other side of the van talking to two of his men.

"Has Wisp arrived?" Nick asked.

"Just came in the front door," Martin said gesturing to his radio.

Nick looked for the skinny boy. Bruno had an arm around him, and they were limping away. He followed them into the building and up a flight to the cafeteria. Tilly was trying to be everywhere at once. Hot food was being brought out table by table. The children were wrapped up in blankets, all but the oldest on laps.

Angus came over. "Where did they come from?"

"The boy said Barberry Cove, but I've never heard of it," Nick said.

"Where were they going?" Angus snagged a towel off the pile Tilly carried past them and handed it to Nick.

"Here." Nick rubbed his hair and face with the towel. His wet clothes were heavy and cold against his skin. "They were looking for Wisp. Said they wanted him to find their parents."

Angus's eyebrows shot up. "They're missing?"

Nick shrugged. "They're exhausted. I don't know where they came from, but they can't have come very far. Angus, they had babies in wheelbarrows." He knew the sight would haunt him, as many others still did. If they hadn't gotten to them in time...he didn't want to finish that thought.

Angus squeezed his elbow. "They are safe now. We will take care of them. Good job."

Ruth, Kyle and Dr. Jameson, each carrying a baby hurried out of the cafeteria. Tilly stomped over. "They haven't eaten all day!" Nick could see the bluster was holding stronger emotions at bay. "Where the hell did they come from?"

"I think, my dear, we will need to give them a day to recover before we get all our answers," Angus said quietly.

Tilly took a deep breath. "Yes. Of course. I think I will bed them all down in the toddlers' play room. Probably not a good idea to separate them yet." She nodded to herself and sailed off.

"Nick I don't think it's a coincidence that these things are happening," Angus said very quietly. "The trains shut down, people disappear. The weather center comes back online just in time to warn us of a monster of a storm. I don't like the possibilities here."

"I'll deal with what's in front of me right now," Nick said tiredly. "How long is the storm supposed to last?"

"As I said, a monster. It'll go through to tomorrow morning."

"Then there's nothing to be done right now. The kids are taken care of, the animals are safe. I'm going to get some food and hit the sack."

Angus smiled. "Extremely practical."

Chapter 52

"It took years for us to establish the settlements and more time before they were organized beyond mere refugee camps. By the time many were ready to think about self sufficiency, the tools were hard to find. Racks of seeds in stores were years out of date. Seed companies were nonexistent. If you were lucky you might find a vegetable garden that had scattered its own seeds in an old neighborhood."

History of a Changed World, Angus T. Moss

Tilly handed off another stack of blankets and closed the cupboard. The children were fed and settled in the toddlers' playroom. They seemed to quiet down as soon as they got back together. They were so exhausted from the travel and fear that a few had fallen asleep with food in their mouths. Her heart pounded a little harder at the thought that they wouldn't have know all those children were in danger without Wisp. If they had arrived after the storm shutters were closed, they would have been shut out with no way to signal those inside. Tilly decided then and there that some sort of doorbell had to be devised for such events.

That got her wondering if Wisp was all right. She hadn't seen him since just after the children arrived. She headed for the kitchen to make sure he'd eaten. And maybe she'd ask for a few volunteers to keep the kitchen open all night. Storms made people restless, and there were a lot of new people stuck inside together.

She wasn't surprised to find a number of people sitting at tables sipping tea and talking. There was a game room, but it was rarely used. Angus would probably have a fire in the new firepit later. That always helped calm people down. She found her volunteers easily. Restless people like tasks to keep them busy. She set up some things for snacking, made another urn of mint tea and started prep for breakfast. With all those babies, she wished Nick had gotten more milk.

Just as she was finishing up, she saw a long white braid in the hall behind the kitchen and called out to Wisp. He came in and gave her a formal nod.

"Do you need me?"

"No, I wanted to thank you. I can't even think about what might have happened to the children."

"I've had some flashes from them. I think they are from the settlement that is harvesting the wood from the big blow-down north of here."

"Oh." Tilly wasn't sure what he was talking about. "Did you have dinner?" Wisp smiled at her. She was surprised at how warm a smile he had. His pale eyes and white hair made him look so unusual, but when he smiled, he looked almost normal.

"Yes, I am fed and dry and will probably sleep on one of the lower levels if you don't mind."

She was about to tell him where to get a cot and blankets when he held up a hand.

"Angus is looking for you."

"Oh." Startled, she left immediately. Then wondered if it was a ploy to get her to stop fussing over him. Some men are just better on their own, and it seemed to Tilly that Wisp was probably one of those men. All the same, she checked in with Angus.

His office was crowded. Martin, Nick, the new fellow Kyle, the small people and Frank were all there. She paused in the doorway wondering if she should bring some tea and snacks down. But Angus beckoned her in.

"Tilly, love, I think I want you here."

That disturbed her. They always divided the work. She didn't mess with his, and he steered clear of hers. She had more than enough on her hands without going to his meetings too. "If you really need me," she said, hoping he'd get the hint.

He gave her a look of sadness that scared her. "Yes, I'm afraid so."

She took a chair to his right without another word. For a moment, everyone sat quietly while Angus sorted things out in his head. He sat forward in his chair, hands on his knees, head bent as if listening to things far away. "Hmph." He sat back and looked around the circle of people, a look of speculation in his eyes. "Kyle, please, I would like you to repeat what you told me earlier.

Kyle glanced around the room nervously. He licked his lips and spoke hesitantly. "This is...difficult...information."

Tilly watched the emotions cross her husband's face, distraction, annoyance and finally compassion. It was that last shift that worried her the most.

"Kyle, I understand that you have worked for the government all your life. In that capacity, you have been required to keep confidential information secret. At this point, I don't think there is much need for it.

Secrets kept now could be lost. Too many people are dying and taking their knowledge out of the world. From this point on, I want as many people as possible to know...everything." He flung a hand wide to encompass the world. "If I can't act on the information you share, I can remember it and tell it to someone else."

Kyle nodded without looking up from the floor. "The notebook you gave me. Ruth and I took a closer look at the notations. She wished to continue to work on them." He clasped his hands together tightly, breathing out a sigh. "The virus wasn't meant to kill. It was a carrier."

"For what?" Martin asked.

"An upgrade."

Martin scowled at him. "What does that mean?"

Angus patted the air in a motion to quiet Martin. "I read the journal. The man, Benjamin, was afraid of biobots. They were being engineered to be geniuses in various fields. He feared that they would eventually be running the world. In his mind, he imagined the tables being turned, and we becoming the slaves to this new brilliant elite. So he tried to even the odds by re-engineering the entire human race."

There was a stunned silence following Angus's explanation. Tilly tried to understand what that meant, but her mind skidded over the facts. *The whole human race,* the words repeated in her brain. Someone had tried to change her, against her will, to compete with the biobots. "That's absurd," she snapped.

"To a sane man, perhaps," Angus said calmly. It was the voice he used when he had to tell her someone had died. Hairs stood up on her arms as goosebumps shivered over her. "But it appears he was equally brilliant because he succeeded."

Nick lurched to his feet. Tilly worried that he might hit someone. His face was beet red with anger. "We are changed," he snarled.

Angus nodded.

"And the ones that couldn't, died," Nick snapped. "He released that *thing* because he thought we were too stupid to survive?"

Angus tipped his head in thought. "He feared enslavement as we had enslaved the biobots. Sit, Nicky, don't let your anger take over. There is more we need to hear." He gestured to Kyle. "The rest of it please."

"The vaccines we have been working on are useless...because we have been trying to do the same thing."

Tilly bit her lip to stop the angry words from pouring out. Angus beckoned to Kyle as if to encourage him to continue speaking.

"The original virus should have infected people, implanted the engineered DNA and run its course. But it didn't. Looking at the model and at his notes, I can only assume that the virus mutated in him, Patient Zero. What he spread was not what he expected because he had done some previous experimentation on himself and his children. I don't think he took into consideration the fact that he might have already changed himself."

"But you've studied the virus," Tilly said. She could hear the pleading in her voice, the longing for an answer that didn't doom them all. "The vaccines should have worked."

Kyle rubbed his hands on his pants. She imagined his palms were sweaty with all eyes on him. "They're not true vaccines. The virus mutates too quickly. It changes from one settlement to the other. Which might be why they shut down the trains. Spreading it now could make it worse. Or not." He twitched a shoulder in a half shrug. "We were working along similar lines as, as, him. Trying to make people immune."

"And Rutledge pushed it a step too far and ended

up killing over two hundred people," Nick said in a deadly cold voice that scared Tilly even more.

"Don't kill the messenger, Nicky," Angus said softly. "Especially an indentured one."

"If we are already changed, then we are not working from the correct standpoint." Kyle spoke softly, his eyes still on the floor.

"Which is something the labs need to know," Angus said. "And we will be sure to make certain that information gets through. However, Kyle has a bit more bad news for us. Please tell us your conclusions concerning the recent flu."

"The information is anecdotal," Kyle murmured as he shifted nervously in his seat. Tilly thought his posture looked very defensive, his arms folded tight against his body, head tucked. She felt sorry for him.

"All research right now is anecdotal," Angus said calmly.

Kyle shuffled his feet. "I don't want to cause a panic because it is a very small sample."

"We will take it as incomplete data," Angus offered.

"All of the flu victims here at High Meadow had brown eyes."

"No," Tilly found herself on her feet without realizing she'd stood. "Bruno has brown eyes, and he recovered."

"I am still conducting my research, but it appears from the DNA samples on file here that all of the victims were brown-eye and had a non-brown-eyed mother. Both Bruno's parents had brown eyes."

Angus tapped his finger against his chin. "Can you give us a percentage of the population that will be affected by this?"

Kyle shuffled and shifted again. "No."

Tilly heard something in her husband's voice that she hadn't heard in a very long time. He cleared his throat and folded his arms. She knew him too well. He was scared. “It appears that this flu may be a great deal more lethal than I had anticipated. Here at High Meadow we only lost twenty-three people, which is less than twenty-five percent. I fear that the death rate will be much higher in the general populace if Kyle’s supposition is correct.”

The formal way that Angus spoke frightened her to her core. His spark was diminished. He spoke staring at his papers as if looking for answers, or avoiding the eyes of his audience. The next time he spoke, it was barely above a whisper.

“If this is true, the country is losing a significant portion of its population this year. The kidnapping could be a conscription of some kind.”

“Leaving the children behind?” Tilly demanded. “That’s insane, it’s cruel, it’s...” she sputtered to a stop unable to verbalize her contempt for the perpetrators.

“They were taken for a reason,” Martin said calmly, but she saw a coldness in his eyes that for once, reassured her. “That reason didn’t want, or need the kids.”

“Wisp said he thought the kids were from a blow-down?” She offered hoping it made sense to someone else.

Nick took the cue. “The folks harvesting the wood. That makes sense. They’re not too far north of here.” He turned to Martin. The look they exchanged spoke volumes.

“I’ll get guards on the doors,” Martin said.

“Wisp will help,” Nick said. “He can give us warning.”

Martin nodded and left the room. Angus watched him go, then turned to Nick with a puzzled look.

“We could be next,” Nick said.

“Why?” Frank asked.

Nick shrugged, lips tight with anger. “Can’t answer that without knowing why the parents are missing. But the fact that they were taken, leaving the kids abandoned, says it isn't a good thing."

"What if they come here?" Elsa asked.

Tilly was amazed at how calmly the little woman spoke. Her own heart was pounding so hard, she could feel it in her ears.

"We're well armed," Nick said calmly. "The Watch is well trained."

"We have a plan," Tilly added. "The new people need to do a drill."

Angus gave her a small smile. "That's a good point, dear. We have a lot of new people here. And the children. We need to pair them off, so they have someone making sure they get to the shelters if needed."

"I'll put up a notice on the message boards. We'll do a drill right after breakfast." As always, now that she had tasks lined up, she felt better.

"Thank you," Angus said with a fond nod. "However, I think this year's flu may be a tipping point." He looked at Dieter. "What are your thoughts?"

He waited, inspecting his audience before speaking. "A loss of even twenty-five percent may be more than some communities can absorb. Higher losses will most likely cause the collapse of many settlements."

"People will be moving," Angus said.

"In bandit season," Nick added. "We need to warn people."

"How would you do that without warning the bandits?" Elsa asked.

Nick rubbed his face. He looked tired. "The folks at Creamery were already attacked. They're setting up some defenses, but I don't think they're ready."

"Priorities," Tilly said firmly. "You have to look to yourself before you can help others. It isn't any good falling in the quicksand alongside them. Once we are sure we can defend ourselves, we can reach out to others."

"Well said!" Angus clapped his hands. There was just a hint of sparkle in his eyes, again. "Excellent. Let's start planning how we should—" Angus was interrupted by an alarm.

"Fire?" Nick asked.

Angus hurried to his desk to get the radio. "No, that is the lower level access alarm."

Chapter 53

"Every year the flu takes more people than are born. The population numbers have decreased dramatically every year since Zero Year."

History of a Changed World, Angus T. Moss

Nick jolted to his feet unsure of where to go. He hadn't been here for any of the drills, so he didn't know what his assignment would be.

"Oh dear, Wisp said he was going to sleep down there. Did he set it off?" Tilly said. But Nick knew that the trigger would be someone coming in, not just wandering the halls.

"How could anyone get into the lower levels?" Elsa asked.

"This is the local storm shelter. There are tunnels coming in from the neighborhoods, right?" Frank asked.

Nick nodded at him. "Five of them that dump into a staging area.

Angus went over to his desk and checked in with

Martin on the radio.

"Southwest tunnel," Martin responded. "Taking a look now."

"Wisp may be down there," Angus said.

"Got 'em," Martin said. "Let's do this right. Evac to the chapel."

"Will do," Angus replied.

Nick turned to Kyle. "Can you or Ruth handle a weapon?"

Kyle shook his head. "I was never trained. Ruth is a doctor. She will refuse."

"In that case, I'd like you to herd the children to the chapel," Angus said. "Tilly will you make sure the doors are open? Dieter, Elsa, I think you should join her. Frank?"

"Give me a gun."

Angus gave him an appreciative nod. "Go with Nick to the armory, please." Angus handed Nick another radio. "Keep us apprised."

Nick felt the urge to salute. As he led Frank to the lower levels, he was so proud of the orderly evacuation of the residents. People in night clothes, half asleep stumbling down the hallway to the chapel. Nick hoped everyone would fit. It was a medium size gathering room at the deepest point of the hill. It only had one entrance, so it was easily defensible. Nick figured Martin had set up some barricades and fall back points in the long hallway leading to it. Otherwise it could just as easily become a bloodbath. The hallway notice boards were flashing just the word *chapel*. Nick noticed that all of the signs indicating how to get there were gone.

He and Frank arrived at the new armory. Their recent acquisitions had required a larger space. Martin had taken over a teachers' lounge and added a Dutch door. The top door was open and Nick could see two long tables covered with guns. Harley was there handing out weapons and ammunition. And so was William.

"Too young," Harley said firmly,

"But I can fight," William insisted.

"You're not on the list." Harley tapped a clipboard he was holding.

Nick stepped up and put his hand on William's shoulder. "Here's the deal, William, Martin has a plan. If he didn't assign you a weapon, he doesn't know to deploy you. I'll let him know that he needs to add you in next time." He tightened his grip as William started a denial. "This time, you'll have to settle for being a runner. Harley, we got a spare radio?"

Harley gave him a tight nod and handed one over.

Nick called Martin on the radio. "William's going to be a runner for you. Where do you want him?"

"Bottom of the south stairwell with Jim and Toby."

Nick turned to William. "You know where that is?"

"Course."

"William, it's really important that you do what you're told, okay?"

William gave him a surly nod and stomped off to the stairs.

"He's itching for some action," Harley said as he handed guns to Nick and Frank.

"If you'd been through what he has, you'd want to get a little back, too," Nick said.

Frank looked over the automatic weapon. "Where'd you get this?"

"Bandits," Nick said. It was close enough.

Frank looked amazed. "Barter?"

Nick gave him a serious look. "Nope."

"Oh."

Nick collected his ammunition and headed for the lower levels. They met Wisp on the stairs. He saw that Wisp was armed and waited for Frank's reaction, but the station manager didn't even blink.

"Feels like only about ten men," Wisp told Nick.

"You're sure they're bandits?"

"No doubt."

"Martin say where he wants us?" Nick tried to summon up a memory of the warren of tunnels around here. He'd only been down a handful of times. Five tunnels came into the school from streets in the surrounding neighborhoods. Each tunnel led to its own staging area, the size of a small auditorium, that had been planned as a reception hall to sort and assign space to people seeking shelter. Each staging area then fed into a central chamber that had the access stairs for the massive shelter, one level lower. If the tunnels were secure, no one from outside could reach the storm shelter. Only certain stairways in the school had access to all areas.

Wisp took a doorway off the stairs to a short hallway that led to one of the staging areas. They passed Dr. Jamison setting up triage in an alcove. Wisp took them to the end of the corridor and indicated the steel, double doors. "Martin wants you here in the first fallback zone," Wisp said. "They haven't come out of the tunnel yet. They're waiting for something."

Nick felt his adrenaline kicking in. "For what? Do they have an inside man?"

"No." Wisp's tone was solid enough that Nick felt better. He cocked his head to one side and frowned. "Someone just joined them."

"Waiting on the boss?"

Frank glanced from Wisp to Nick. "He got an earpiece?"

Nick chuckled. "No, he's psychic." Frank laughed, but his uneasy look said he wasn't sure if Nick was kidding.

The sound of automatic gunfire brought them all alert. A scream punctuated another round of firing. Wisp winced.

"Ours or theirs?" Nick asked.

"Ours."

Bruno burst through the doors with a body slung over one shoulder. Nick reached to help, but he bulled past them. "Prepare to cover, Martin's drawing them back," Bruno said as he headed back the way they'd come.

Nick slipped through the door to find a stack of barrels set up for cover. The Watch were shooting from similar positions. The staging area was a labyrinth of barrels and tree trunks laid out to give the defenders the most advantage. Nick gave Martin credit, he must have spent days lugging all this stuff down through the tunnels. The sides of the room had been closed off funneling anyone coming in from the tunnels into a narrow corridor of about five feet. The few overhead lights working deepened shadows and added confusion. Martin was sending men back one by one towards Nick's door, pulling the bandits deeper into the maze. Wisp took a stance to one side and started firing. That drew fire back towards them. Over the radio, Martin called for cover. Nick crouched behind a barrel and laid down gunfire for the retreating men. There were two bodies on the floor in front of the storm door from the tunnel.

Another bandit went down, and Nick felt that twinge of regret that another human being was dead. But if they were going to come in shooting, they certainly couldn't have good intentions.

Bruno came back, his clothes stained with blood. He crouched next to Nick. "Anyone hurt?"

"No one on our side," Nick grunted as he reloaded. The gunfire was deafening.

The radio crackled, Martin called for Bruno.

"Where?" Bruno responded. An arm came up over a barrel just long enough to spot. Bruno crouched along the line of a tree trunk then disappeared into the maze.

Nick peeked around his barrel. The bandits were attacking blindly. They couldn't see the High Meadow men, so they were firing indiscriminately. A waste of ammunition, in Nick's opinion, and considering the tight, intermittent response from the Watch, Martin's also.

Another bandit went down with a scream. Bruno reappeared half-carrying Tall Joe who was holding his bloody ribs. Wisp lay down cover fire, taking out two more men, backing along in Bruno's wake. Then Bruno was away through the doors.

"Martin's down to eight men in the maze," Wisp said.

"Against how many?"

"I can only use visual right now." Wisp said, his eyes never leaving the bandits. "About the same?"

The bandits attacked with more fervor, automatic weapon fire rattled across the drums. Wisp stood up and took out three of them. Two of the Watch scooted into cover beside Nick and Frank. Wisp stumbled and went down. Nick pulled him deeper into cover.

"How bad?" he asked, looking for the blood. Wisp was unconscious, the left side of his face covered in blood.

The men of the Watch returned fire more enthusiastically. Bruno came back through the door, saw Wisp and dragged him away without a word.

Nick was worried. Head wounds were bad. And Wisp was one of their best shots. *One* of...he had a few marksman awards of his own. He crawled over to where Wisp had been standing and took a peek over the barrel. Without a thought, he stood and took out two bandits that were reloading. He ducked before anyone could return fire.

And then it went quiet. There was a scuffle and one final gunshot. When he looked over his barrel, Martin was standing on the trunk of a tree, scanning the area in front of him.

"All clear!" Martin yelled. He was answered from the left and right. Then he turned to check the men behind him.

Nick stood up. "All clear."

Chapter 54

"After several fairly mild years we had grown complacent. In Year Ten, a lethal strain took approximately 40% of the country's population. I cannot say how it affected other countries because we have lost communication beyond our borders."

History of a Changed World, Angus T. Moss

Tall Joe was in surgery when Nick got to the infirmary. Martin and the rest of the Watch were sweeping the other tunnels. Nick heard Martin on the radio tell Angus he wanted everyone to stay in the chapel until they searched the entire building. Thunder rumbled faintly. Nick knew the storm had to be really bad to hear it this deep inside.

He checked for Wisp and the other man that Bruno had carried out. It made a certain sense that Bruno would want to be the one to rescue the wounded, a recompense of sorts for all the lives lost at Riverbank. And he was a big powerful man, so he could easily carry anyone.

Wisp was in bed, his head bandaged, still apparently unconscious. Kyle was standing by the bedside watching him.

"He okay?" Nick asked.

"A deep graze. Concussion. He'll have a scar." Kyle spoke in clipped tones.

"He was amazing."

"He was well trained."

"But not you?" Nick asked, not expecting an answer.

"My skill was obvious. I went into the sciences when I was only a few days from awakening." Kyle shifted uneasily, reaching toward Wisp, but not touching him. "We knew what his skill was, but none of us told, so it appeared that he had no skill. He was trained in many things as Hendricks sought to discover what he was good for."

"But Hendricks didn't want any double Es." Nick said softly, trying to encourage him to speak.

"No. He made that clear when he shot Gamma in front of us. Which I suppose is the real reason that Sigma killed himself."

Nick responded automatically. "I'm sorry."

Kyle turned quizzical eyes on him. "For what?"

"For your loss. They were your brothers, weren't they?"

Kyle looked around the room, a puzzled frown on his face. "Yes. And we loved each other. Although we learned quickly not to let that show. We had a pact. We..." He shot a worried glance at Nick. "Forgive me. Seeing him like this makes me emotional."

Nick clapped him on the shoulder. "He'll be okay."

Kyle nodded. "Thank you."

Nick was just starting to feel awkward when William burst in. "Martin wants you in the south tunnel."

"Both of us?" Nick asked.

William pointed to Nick as he panted to catch his breath.

"Problem?" Nick asked.

"Dunno," William said with an eyeroll. "He just said to get you down there."

Nick returned to the staging area to find it looking very different. All the overhead lights were on making the maze less daunting. A few key obstacles had been shifted creating a path straight through the center. Nick was half way through when he met up with Martin headed in the other direction.

"Oh good, he found you."

Nick looked at the men working on the maze, tightening some areas, dragging branches and rocks to make the path uneven in others. "Doesn't look too urgent?" Nick said as more of a question.

"Not sure. I wanted you to take a look at these guys." Martin led him through the other half of the maze and out the storm doors to the access tunnel. Nine bodies were laid out, their weapons at their feet.

"Wisp said he thought there were ten," Nick commented.

Martin gestured toward the mouth of the tunnel. "There's one vehicle out there. Big black van like the ones you brought back. The rain's made a mess of any tracks, but the underbrush looks like a second vehicle was parked there."

"So you think someone got away."

"He was wounded, I think. I hope. Blood trail on the floor and on the outer door."

"I don't think he's going far in this storm. Those vans are sturdy, but he's going to have to shelter somewhere."

Martin nodded, his eyes narrowed against the harsh overhead lights. He pointed to the bodies. "Anybody look familiar?"

Nick checked each one. There were three in the black gear of Rutledge's guards. The other six wore mismatched gear or none at all. One man was in only jeans and a t-shirt. Nick noted the headshots, probably Wisp's work. "These two were at the lab." He folded his arms against a sinking feeling in his gut. "I invited them here."

"You think there'll be another attack?"

"These two were bully boys. They're probably looking for an easy mark. Figured any place that would take a bunch of drugged prisoners and scientists couldn't have good defense."

"They figured wrong," Martin said smugly.

"Yup."

Martin frowned down the tunnel again. "You think this has anything to do with the missing parents?"

"No. Kids would have said if there were guns involved. And this lot wouldn't have left witnesses."

Martin grunted his agreement.

"By the way, nice maze," Nick said with a smile.

Martin chuckled. "You should see the one in the west tunnel."

"You need me for anything else?"

"No. Just wanted you to see these guys before we buried them."

Nick went back up to check in with Angus.

Chapter 55

"The hope of survival dwindles with every flu season, and still we fight and kill our brethren."
History of a Changed World, Angus T. Moss

Tilly watched the storm shutters retract with a unreasonable fear that fluttered in her stomach and clutched around her heart. The pale light of dawn shone in through the main doors. She forced herself to walk to the doors and look out. There were no bodies on the steps. Somehow during the night she had convinced herself that they had shut out some stragglers or children. She put her hand on the cold glass and let out a sigh of relief.

Lottie marched past her and right out the door followed by Everett and Harold. A burst of cold wet air rushed down the hallway raising goosebumps along Tilly's arms. She watched them head for the controls for the storm sheeting that covered the crops. There didn't appear to be any damage, but Lottie would want to make a careful inspection.

Tilly looked out over her small kingdom once more but found nothing amiss. She went to the kitchen to see if breakfast had been started. All of her new helpers were there, Mary, Jean and some of the ex-prisoners. Coffee was ready and hot food was being put into serving trays for the warming tables.

"Crazy night," Jean said as she handed Tilly a cup of coffee.

"Yes," Tilly said. She wrapped her hands around the warm mug. "A little too crazy."

"But we're all here," Jean said sharply. "All of us."

Tilly shared a relieved look with her. Jean would carry the scars of surviving Riverbank's massacre for a long time. It was that much more important for her to see a successful defense. They'd had no casualties. All of the men who'd been shot would survive. "Our plan worked."

Mary startled her with a hug. Tilly hurriedly handed her mug back to Jean as the young woman squeezed her tight.

"You saved us," Mary said tearfully. "This is why we had to leave our beautiful farm. Bandits. They were heartless. When it started happening last night, I thought I would just die."

Tilly patted her back. "You're safe here dear."

Mary let her go and stepped back to look at her. "I don't know if that will always be true, but at least it is for now. And you can't know how much that means to us. We lost..." She shook her head breathing hard against the tears.

"We lost damn near everyone at Riverbank," Jean said bitterly. "Didn't have a chance against automatic weapons."

Tilly saw the look that went between Mary and Jean. She knew the two of them would bond through their losses. "It's become a very cruel world," Tilly said softly. "We need to keep civilization alive as best we can."

"Well said, my dear," Angus said as he entered the kitchen. "We will be having a meeting in the small auditorium after breakfast. Please spread the word. It's posted on the hall boards, but let's all make sure the children attend."

Tilly poured a coffee for him. "I've assigned minders for all the new children."

"Excellent." Angus gave her a kiss as he accepted the coffee. "I must speak to Martin and Nick now, I'll see you in a bit." He twirled on his heel and strolled out of the kitchen.

"How long have you been married?" Mary asked.

"Nine years," Tilly said with a smile at the dead silence that followed. People thought she and Angus had been married forever. And usually it felt that way to her, too. But the truth was a little stranger, as real life often was.

Chapter 56

"We are stuck in a backward progression of civilization. As we lose the numbers needed for manufacturing, we are forced to return to cottage industries. Unfortunately, we must learn those skills from old books and manuals as extremely few living know how to build a loom or kiln or butter churn."

History of a Changed World, Angus T. Moss

Wisp took the bandage off his head to look at the wound. A bloody line as thick as his finger went from his temple to above his ear. It ached, but already the pain had begun to fade. He healed very quickly. There were men in pain, and people worried nearby. It made his head hurt worse. He waited for an opening in the people visiting and slipped out of the infirmary unnoticed. He took a side corridor to the north stairs and down to the back of the cafeteria. He felt Tilly in the hallway even before he'd come around the corner.

She smiled at him and held out a tray. "I knew

you'd be sneaking out."

He gave her a smile back. There was a lot of fear underneath her grin and he respected her for keeping such a tight grip on it. "Thank you, that's very kind."

"Angus said you took down half the bandits yourself."

"Possibly."

"Let me know if you need anything."

"Thank you."

He took the food and headed for the field house. It would feel good to have some distance between him and so many worried people. He ate quickly knowing it would be a busy day. The horses were out in the meadow, so he had the building to himself. A few people were working in the field, but their thoughts were clean and simple about dirt and weeds and sunshine. He rested the intangible muscles of his brain, relaxing in the comparative mental silence around him.

After breakfast, he walked the perimeter listening for any minds that didn't belong. He passed the men on Watch. Some caught a glimpse of him and waved. Nothing felt out of place. He went back to the field house and ran though some martial exercises to stretch his body and warm up his blood. He was thinking about getting some more food when Nick arrived with a second breakfast for him.

"Tilly said she already fed you, but that was at the crack of dawn," Nick said. He put the tray on the desk Wisp used as a table.

Wisp noticed that there were two coffees on the tray. Nick helped himself to one and sat heavily into an armchair. Wisp gladly sat down to more food.

"You are uneasy," Wisp said between bites.

"I want to know where those kids' parents went."

Wisp nodded. "We can leave as soon as you like."

"I promised Martin that we would just take a look around and not engage with anyone."

"An approach I prefer myself," Wisp said. He could sense that Nick was armed. He wanted more than the belt knife he was carrying, but wondered if Martin would allow it. He cleared the plate and swallowed the last bit of coffee before rising to show Nick his readiness.

* * *

Nick drove one of the black vans up the road where they'd found the children the day before. Branches and greenery were scattered across the pavement. A large tree had come down but was far enough away that just the top of the canopy brushed the edges of the road. Nick drove over the shoulder on the far side and cleared it easily.

Wisp spread out his senses as they left the Med Center. He could feel the horses in the pasture. The chickens meandering through the fields. Further up the hill, he could feel the outliers, and then they were behind him. As they climbed into the forest, he felt a scattering of small wild animals deep in the trees, possibly foxes or raccoons, rabbits probably. There were no bright minds of higher intelligence nearby.

Nick stopped the van at the blow-down. They got out and followed the trail of sawdust back through the tumbled tree trunks to a river. Wisp thought the stream behind High Meadow must come off this larger waterway. Further down the bank, along a well worn trail was a saw mill with a working water wheel.

"Well look at that," Nick said, excitement rising in him.

"You know this place?"

Nick chuckled and Wisp could feel the mist of memories rising in him. "It's a museum. I was here as a kid on a school trip. Looks like they've got it working."

They inspected the mill. Tools lay scattered across

the floor as if suddenly dropped. Lunchboxes and jackets were in the cloakroom. Wisp carefully touched a few objects to sense the owners, but he didn't delve into any of them. "Alive," he said brushing his hand over a jacket. "Alive, alive." A lunchbox, a hat, a work glove.

"Can you tell where?" Nick asked.

Wisp picked up the work glove and concentrated. The owner was a short man with a hot temper. He was furious at the moment, but the heat of his anger was faded by distance. "Far away," Wisp said. "West, south-west of here."

"How far away?"

Wisp tried to tie the feeling to geography. "Further than the lab. Maybe twice as far."

"Are they together?"

Wisp went back to the hat and the jacket. "Yes. They feel like they are in the same area."

"Any clues?"

"They are angry," he pointed in turn at the glove, hat and jacket, "frightened and resigned."

"Don't like the sound of that," Nick said with a scowl.

"I can't say more without delving." At Nick's raised eyebrow, he explained. "I'd need some quiet and an article of constant use. I might be able to pick up a bit more than just surface emotions."

Nick nodded. "Not today." He turned back toward the entrance. "I promised Martin we'd just look around."

They were walking down the front steps when Wisp felt it. He missed a step and stumbled. Nick grabbed his arm, flooding Wisp with Nick's thoughts—concern, curiosity and anger. "What?"

Wisp pulled free to clear out Nick's thoughts. "Pain." He turned feeling out around himself carefully.

"Yours?" Nick asked with some skepticism.

"No." Wisp replied, feeling uncharacteristically

proud of Nick for figuring it out. He leaned into the pain. "It's fading. That usually means they're fainting. He. It's a man." He followed the strongest sense of pain around behind the stairs. There was a low door.

"Wait," Nick stepped in front of him, gun in hand. "Let me go first." He pushed the door open carefully.

Wisp hung back. Nick went into a dirt-floored storage room. Light from the door showed stacks of boxes, a pile of pallets and a few fifty-gallon drums on the left. A foot was showing from behind the drums. Wisp stayed at the door while Nick checked the man. He reached out one more time to double check the area. A group of deer was drinking from the river on the other side. A flock of starlings flew overhead. Nothing human was nearby.

"He's been shot," Nick said. "Give me a hand."

They carried the man to the van and raced back to High Meadow.

Chapter 57

"With constant uncertainty dogging our steps, we struggle in the day to day. This rarely gives us the luxury of time to plan for the future."
History of a Changed World, Angus T. Moss

Nick stood with Angus and Martin in the hallway outside the infirmary. The man from the mill was in bad shape, gut shot, blood loss, dehydration.

"As soon as he is out of surgery, we will have the youngster...do we know his name?"

"Micah," Martin answered.

"Micah, yes. We'll have him take a look at this fellow and see if he can identify him. Martin, have you spoken to the children?"

"Just Micah. The others are too young to be much help. I can't believe he got them all together and on the road." Martin shook his head in admiration.

"What could he tell you?"

"Not a lot. Nine families. Most of them work at the mill. They have a small settlement on the other side of the river in an old neighborhood. There were four mothers who watched all the kids. Men showed up in black vans and took the women. Micah ran up to the mill, and there was no one there either. All the kids are told to come down here to High Meadow in times of trouble."

"And yet we don't know them," Angus said curiously.

"Micah said they weren't supposed to talk to people."

Nick's internal alarm went off. "Why not?"

"Don't know, but he was wearing new jeans."

"Who is the lumber for?" Nick wondered. "Most folks are in settlements like this. No one is building."

"And they don't advertise," Martin added.

"Black vans, armed men, new jeans," Nick grumbled. "Sounds like something government related again."

"Why would they abandon the children?" Angus said shaken and angry.

"If they're hired muscle like Rutledge's men, they aren't too smart," Nick snarled. "We need to go back and take a look at their settlement. Maybe we can find something that would help make sense out of this."

"Yes," Angus said slowly, thoughtfully. "Also if there is clothing for the children and diapers. Tilly is beside herself over that."

Martin nodded. "I'll send a group over. I want them armed and with plenty of back up."

Nick relaxed a little, glad to not have to be the one going out again. And yet, a little annoyed at not being asked. "And keep an eye out for anyone that managed to elude the kidnappers. You might want to bring Micah to coax out anyone hiding."

"Right," Martin said as he turned to leave.

"Be careful," Nick added.

Martin shot him a look.

"Now you know what it feels like," Nick mumbled.

"Problem, Nicky?" Angus asked.

"No," Nick said with a smug smile.

"Come," Angus said beckoning him along. "I want to pick your brain."

They headed back to Angus's office. When they arrived there were already a few people waiting. Nick stayed in the hall as Angus dealt with the others.

"Nick?" Leo, one of the ex-prisoners, approached with a look of conciliation.

"Hey. Settling in all right?"

"Yes. Fine. This is all that you advertized." Leo rubbed hands together in a nervous gesture.

"But you doubted," Nick said gently.

"I've got good reasons."

Nick squeezed his shoulder. "I'm sure you do, and I'm glad you know now that I didn't lie to you."

"Yeah, well, I'd like to clear some things up."

"Should we wait for Angus?"

Leo shook his head. "No, you can tell him. It isn't earth shaking, I just thought you should know...I, um, I used to work for Rutledge."

Nick frowned. This was a new twist. "Okay."

"But I saw where he was going with the...um, vaccine, and I fought with him. Next thing I know you're breaking me out."

"How long were you in there?"

"Best I can tell, three years."

"But no one recognized you."

Leo chuckled, bitter sounding. "I was pushing three hundred pounds back then." He scratched at his beard. "When I shave this off a few people might recognize me. I'm sure Rutledge told them I left. They might have forgotten me."

"Did you recognize anyone else in there?"

"Just Melissa."

Nick got a sinking feeling. "Did she work for

Rutledge, too?"

"Nah. She's not a scientist. Her husband, Ben, worked for him."

Nick blinked at Leo for a minute. That linked a few things in a way he hadn't considered. "So the prisoners might be people that didn't agree with him?"

"Well that's my story. Can't tell you what got Melissa put away. Thought you should know."

Nick nodded distractedly as Leo walked away. Rutledge was sounding more crazy than ever. And he was the man in charge of creating the so-called vaccine for the country. When in reality, he was trying to change the entire human race. Nick shivered. If he was the best they could get, his hopes for the country's survival were shrinking.

It looked like Angus was going to be tied up for awhile so Nick headed to the cafeteria for some lunch. He saw Jean making herself a cup of coffee and went over.

"How are you doing?"

"Nick. Wow, do you get to stay put for an hour?"

He laughed. "It does seem like that sometimes."

She gestured to the tables. "I'm taking a break, care to join me?"

He gave her a smile, grabbed some food and sat down at her table. "What are you taking a break from?"

"I'm writing up Angus's notes for the history."

"Really? I didn't think he was anywhere close to that point."

"I've been sorting and organizing," she said with a proud smile that crinkled her almond-shaped eyes in very attractive way.

"What do you think?"

Her smile faltered. "It's scary. You know here it's comfortable and well managed, and I can almost forget what life was like a decade ago. But then I read through the notes, and I'm hit by this devastation." She stared into her cup for a long moment.

"It's hard," he offered, knowing there was no solace for what they had all lost.

"Yes. And this year looks really bad. Some of the notes he's making really worry me."

Nick put his fork down. He wasn't sure he wanted to know. "Why is that?"

She licked her lips and wrapped her hands around her mug. "It's possible that there won't be enough people left to run things."

"Things?"

"Like the trains." She took a shaky breath. "Or the factories where they package train food."

"We don't know that." Nick meant for the comment to be reassuring, but it sounded a little panicked to his ears.

"No. Maybe not."

Their discussion was interrupted by an announcement to attend a meeting in the large auditorium. That startled Nick. When Angus wanted meetings, he usually planned them a couple days out and posted a message on the hall boards. They had never been compulsory before. Jean gave him a nervous look. He shrugged and forced a smile for her. They left together, without a word.

Nick stayed at the door watching people filing into the big room. Everyone had a similar look on their faces. It ran a short gamut from apprehension to flat out fear. When it looked like most of the residents were in attendance, he took a seat in the back row.

Angus stood on stage waiting for everyone to settle down. After a long moment of silence, he spoke. "Thank you for coming. I know everyone has worries and questions. Half of you have been in my office asking those questions all morning. I think it's best if we discuss this as a community, and let everyone hear the same words.

"First of all I need to tell you that this is an extremely lethal flu season. We've been lucky here in our few losses. They will all be deeply missed, but our numbers were very low. I believe that it is going to hit other communities much harder, which means we probably will be taking in people again. If the settlements get hit too hard, they will not be able to sustain themselves, and people will scatter. I'd like to put together a plan to gather refugees. I'll post a sign-up sheet, and we'll have a meeting tomorrow to discuss our options.

"The next issue is a bit harder." Angus paused. He walked over to a table that held a pitcher of water and glasses. Taking his time, he poured and drank some water, letting people brace themselves.

"We need to plan for a worst case scenario. That means no trains, no medicines, no train food." He sipped his water and let the words sink in. The auditorium remained silent.

"We have some new people who can help us learn some old skills. But we need to prepare now for a winter without any outside help."

"Are they shutting us out?" someone asked.

Angus gave the speaker a sad smile. "I don't know. Maybe. We don't even know who *they* are. Have they survived? Will they continue to send us food and supplies? I just don't know any of those answers. And that is the problem. We cannot plan if we cannot rely on those things. Therefore, I think it best to plan without them. We will work on building up our self sufficiency. We will grow, barter or gather food. Distill our own medicines. We have this good sturdy building to shelter us. And Martin will be expanding the Watch to keep us safe. Food, medicine, shelter, security, I think those will be our priorities.

"We will form committees for planning and execution. Tilly will be helping with that." He looked around the auditorium with a sad fondness. "This is a dark time for humankind. We must be smart. We must cooperate with one another. Our very survival depends on it. And as my brilliant wife pointed out, we need to plant our feet firmly before pulling anyone else out of the quicksand. Our community must have a viable plan for survival, and be acting on it, before we can assist anyone else." He bowed. "Thank you."

Nick didn't move out of his seat. For a time, no one did. The tension in the room felt like a held breath. Then Tilly was on her feet yelling about committees and sorting people into groups. She had a clipboard in her hand and was directing a group of people as they moved tables on stage. Nick felt a deep love for her and Angus. He knew that this community would survive because of their foresight.

Martin scooted down the row and sat next to Nick. "Think we should still check out the mill town?"

"Since we don't know why they were taken, or who took them, I think it's still important to pursue."

Martin leaned his arms on the back of the chair in front of him, staring down to where Tilly was reorganizing people. "I've never seen Angus like that."

"It's stuff like that that makes him a fantastic leader."

Martin grunted an agreement. "Gotta check in with the Watch," he said then squeezed past Nick to leave.

Angus wandered down the aisle looking distracted. He stopped when he got to Nick's row.

"What do you want me to do?" Nick asked.

"If you would head the committee to search for refugees?"

Nick nodded. He'd already started planning in his head as soon as Angus had mentioned it. "Anything else?"

Angus gave him a tired wink. "Father some children."

End of Book One
A Changed World Series

Thank you for choosing this book!

I hope you enjoyed it. The best advertising for authors is word of mouth. Tell your friends, and please take a minute to review this where you purchased it.

About the Author

Alice grew up in suburban New Jersey with a brother and three sisters, sidewalks to play hopscotch on and friends to walk to school with. She developed a bad case of wanderlust, which might be blamed on nomadic ancestors or all that speculative fiction she devoured. After attending college in New Jersey and Massachusetts, she finished her Bachelors in Fine Arts at the University of New Mexico. Since that time she has worked a variety of jobs on both coasts and in the middle, Boston, Los Angeles, Grand Junction, Long Beach Island. Now she lives in Asheville, NC, where she gardens and writes.

For more information on her upcoming mystery books and **Book 2 of A Changed World Series** see her website:

All There Is...And The Rest of It.
http://allthereisandtherestofit.blogspot.com/

Or on Facebook:
https://www.facebook.com/AliceSaboBooks

Asher Blaine was an actor with significant star power before destroying his career with drugs. After years of cycling through rehab and relapse, he finally had his epiphany and chose sobriety. While carefully piecing together the ravaged scraps of his life in a quiet suburb of LA, he is arrested for murder. The victim, his ex-business manager, was shot with a re-fitted prop gun from one of his movies. A coincidence proves his innocence, but subsequent violence casts doubts. Asher realizes he must mend all his burnt bridges a lot soon than he'd planned When he turns to the people he trusted most, he discovers he must convince them not only of his sobriety, but of his innocence.

A series of calamities raises the stakes, and he uncovers a stunning lie from his past. He must track down a man that he thought long dead: a man who's been planning Asher's death for years.

UNINTENDED
CONSEQUENCES
ALICE SABO
By the author of *White Lies*

A gruesome crime scene shocks a small town. When faced with a bloody room and a missing body, Detective Ethan Anderson is forced to look at the dark truths of his childhood and the secrets he keeps. Evidence in the investigation could implicate his cousin—something he won't believe to be true. His loyalties are tested, but when another person goes missing, he knows what has to be done. He has to find the killer and face the consequences of exposing those long held secrets.

Ethan knows too well that bad parents make broken children. He's about to find out how one broken child grew up to be a killer.

18729578R00204

Printed in Great Britain
by Amazon